## *About the Author*

Mark Hayden is the nom de guerre of Adrian Attwood. He lives in Westmorland with his wife, Anne.

He has had a varied career working for a brewery, teaching English and being the Town Clerk in Carnforth, Lancs. He is now a part-time writer and part-time assistant in Anne's craft projects.

He is also proud to be the Mad Unky to his Great Nieces & Great Nephew.

# Six Furlongs

The Eighth Book of the King's Watch

MARK HAYDEN

www.pawpress.co.uk

First Published Worldwide in 2020 by Paw Press
Paperback Edition Published
October 01 2020

Cover Design – Rachel Lawston
Design Copyright © 2020 Lawston Design
www.lawstondesign.com
Cover images © Shutterstock

Paw Press – Independent publishing in Westmorland, UK.
www.pawpress.co.uk

ISBN: 1-91-414500-3
ISBN-13: 978-1-914145-00-1

## For Chris

*For Creating a virtual pub.*

*It made Lockdown Monday nights*

*Something to look forward to.*

# SIX FURLONGS

## A Note from Conrad

The last couple of books have had separate lists of characters. Mr Hayden has decided not to include them this time, because there aren't too many new ones.

There is, of course, a full list of everyone and a glossary of magickal terms on the Paw Press website:

www.pawpress.co.uk

That means we can get straight on with the story.

Thanks,
Conrad.

# *Prologue*

## Scene by the Lake
## Thursday 29th October

He heard them before he saw them, their heels crunching on the path from the School House to the lake, their voices raised in anticipation and carrying through the still night air.

He looked over his shoulder at the moonlit water. With no wind to shift it, mist was already rising at the edges. It was a good job that they weren't going far.

The girls came into the pool of light by the jetty, holding each other for support and laughing. They were wearing what they thought girls should wear to the casino – some choosing long and slinky, some opting for short and glittery, and none of them wearing a coat. All of them were carrying greetings cards that were too large to fit into their tiny purses and bags.

He'd been leaning on the wooden post and stood up straight when they got nearer, adjusting his tuxedo jacket and smiling. When he saw the girl on her own, behind the others and the only one not wearing heels, he nearly frowned. What was Perci doing here? He didn't have her down as a gambler. Not like this, anyway.

When the girls were sure of their footing on the concrete dock, they separated and sorted themselves. Perci stepped forward to join in, both part of the group and one of a kind at the same time.

He cleared his throat and checked who else was present. When he saw Io, he pursed his lips and hoped that the coming confrontation wouldn't spoil the evening.

He smiled to the girls and said, 'Good evening, ladies. Have you got your homework?'

They passed the white envelopes along the line, and it was Perci who handed them over. She was shorter than the others, the only who hadn't grown out of her Junior Prom dress. She could afford a new one, but when you don't go out, why bother?

'There you go, sir.'

The cards were all unsealed, and he checked each one to see if the six twenty pound notes were present and correct. While they waited, a couple of the girls shivered, casting envious glances at the infra-red heaters already glowing on the boat.

'Thank you,' he concluded. 'Sorry about this, but I do need your Exeats as well. You don't want me to get in trouble with the Housemaster, do you?'

Some had them ready, some had to fumble them out of their purses. He soon had eight passes, all correctly signed and none of them enchanted. 'Io?' he said. 'Exeat?'

'Sorry sir,' said the girl with a drawl. 'I left it in the dorm.'

'Shall we wait while she gets it?' he asked throwing it back on the others.

Io's closest associates examined their party shoes. Perci rolled her eyes, and it was left to Willow, the Head Girl, to speak out.

'Give it up, Io. He's not budging, and he knows you're gated. And, yes, we will go without you, won't we Jo?'

'Don't spoil it for everyone,' said Jocasta, Io's regular partner in crime. 'You can come next time. Can't she, sir?'

'Of course,' he said with a smile. 'Careful getting aboard, everyone.'

He handed them up the short gangway and on to his mid-week home, the motor yacht *Thunderer*. As soon as they'd turned their backs to board the boat, Io sniffed and flounced off into the dark.

While the girls headed to the stairway, he took a circuit of the boat deck, bringing up the magickal Silence that would stop the good citizens of Lakeland complaining. He started the engines and disconnected the power supply leaving the network cable in place for now, and then he joined the girls up top.

They had gathered near the heaters at the bow, where there was room to circulate; under the awning, the green baize table took up most of the space. He took a bottle of fizz from the fridge and started pouring. 'Welcome to Harry's floating poker bar,' he announced. 'And that's what you call me tonight. Harry.'

He finished pouring the wine and proposed a toast. 'To Lady Fortune.' They clinked glasses and he took a small sip. 'Last chance for selfies while I finish checking your homework.'

They amused themselves at the bow, some lighting cigarettes, while he sat down and powered up his laptop. He spread out the greetings cards containing their homework and the cash payments, including Io's. She could afford to lose it. Some of the girls had picked up whatever card was to hand (*Happy Silver Wedding, Mum and Dad*), while many had opted for fortieth birthday cards. Ha ha. It was nine years away, in fact.

One by one, he dipped his fingers in a dish of water and rubbed them over the handwritten messages. The ink smudged and re-flowed with the Lux from his fingers, rearranging itself into messages and cash amounts — £400, £300, £400 … £1,250! Who was Iolanthe kidding?

'It's time,' he said. The eight girls came in, taking random seats and placing their phones in front of them. 'Okay. I've marked your assignments. Willow, you have very neat writing, but the Charm was sticky. More Lux, please. Jo, that was sloppy – far too many blotches. And Perci, please check your spellings first. One "L" in "Grateful", OK? As you know, this is a cash game, not tournament, and the buy-in is the lowest bid over £250, and tonight's it's £300. Make the transfer, and we'll begin.'

They picked up their phones and started tapping. While he waited for the money to appear in his online bank account, he shuffled an old deck of cards thoroughly. When the money was all present and correct, he placed a metal box on a cloth to protect the table. 'Phones in here, please. Willow, can I trust you to hand out the chips?'

'Of course, Harry,' she said. Willow knew the score: she was a veteran of last year's floating poker school. She rose to fetch the chips, and Harry offered the deck to Perci to cut before dealing one card to each player. 'Lowest card sits to my left and gets the dealer button on the first hand.'

They looked at their card and started to work out who sat where. Harry took the box of phones, locked it and put the Seal in place, isolating the devices from all electronic signals. He stood up, put the box in a cupboard and announced, 'Help yourselves to more fizz and be at your places in ten minutes. The bathroom is down the forward stairway. Can't miss it.'

The girls ogled the chips as Willow started dishing them out, and the volume of high-pitched chatter rose. Another reason for the Silence. He circled the table, and Perci caught his arm.

'Don't forget the Wards. And did you get the message?' she whispered.

'I got it. I'll sort it over half-term,' he replied. He slipped down the stairs and pulled the gangway on to the boat, before jumping on to the jetty and unfastening the bow first, then the data cable, and finally the stern. He jumped back on the boat and reached into a drawer. Damn. His Little Book of Wards must be in the classroom. Ah well, who would be on the lake at eight o'clock on a Thursday night? He gunned the engine and moved away from the jetty.

He didn't go far, sticking to the western shoreline and choosing a spot where a small headland would conceal the boat from the town, not that they needed much concealment with the mist getting thicker. He throttled back the engine and threw the anchor over the side.

The girls were all in position when he got back, chips neatly stacked and glasses charged. Harry opened the lacquered black box with Japanese scenes in which he kept the cards and tokens. Before he flipped the lid, he ran his fingers delicately around the drift of cherry blossom, the tips barely skimming the surface. He took out two new decks and the game buttons before returning the box to the locker behind him.

'Limit Hold'em is the game,' he said, unwrapping the decks. 'One pound small blind, two on the big for the first session. You may cash in your chips at any time.'

Jocasta had ended up on his left. He placed the button in front of her and activated the Charm inside it that brought alive the magick in the green baize that would stop the players doing anything stupid like trying to see each other's cards.

He made eye contact with each of the players in turn, his fingers now still and resting on the first of the new decks. He nodded and said, 'Good luck,' and then his fingers were a blur.

The Silence around *Thunderer* kept out the sound of screeching owls and foxes barking in the woods. All eyes were on Harry's hands as he riffled the cards, and no one looked beyond the awning into the mist.

Around a hundred yards away, a small light glowed silver. It came not from a lantern or a Lightstick, but from the two silver figures standing in the shallow silver punt. The man was holding the punt pole loosely in his hands, not that he really needed it: the punt floated just above the water with the occasional wave lapping through the spectral boat.

'It's her, isn't it?' he said.

'Yes, it's her,' replied the woman.

Years of pent up yearning quivered over her face, and she stretched out her hand. A gossamer ray of light, finer than silk, span out of her hand, over the water and on to the boat.

Willow shivered suddenly. 'Can we turn up the heating?'

'I'll fold,' said Perci. 'No heating for me. I've got a glow on.'

Willow blinked. 'Must have been the breeze. I'll fold, too.'

'I've got a good feeling all of a sudden,' said Jocasta. 'I'm in.'

# 1 — *Strange Meetings*

How do you celebrate Halloween if you're a Mage?
    You don't.

If you're part of the Circles of magick – the Daughters of the Goddess, the Arden Foresters, the Sisters of the Water and so on – you celebrate *Samhain* on the last day of October, and that's a religious affair, so not for me or most of my crew.

If you're a Chymist, a graduate of Salomon's House, you have a party: grown up and civilised or drunk and debauched, according to your age and inclination. We'd opted for grown up, and Mina had said, 'I hope it's less eventful than the last two. I mean that, Conrad.'

'What? It wasn't my fault.'

'Sofía????'

'You can't blame me for my father's indiscretions.'

'And Princess Birkdale?'

'I didn't invite her!'

'But she wouldn't have turned up if you weren't here, would she?'

'You could say that about most of the guests.'

'Ha!' she pointed the finger at me like a barrister who'd scored a big point in court. 'See what I mean?'

Even if I'd understood, there'd been no point replying, because she was already on her way to the next job. Welcome to pre-party nerves, Elvenham style.

In case you've forgotten, I'd gained a nineteen year old half-sister at our summer do, and at the Bollywood party my other sister had become Entangled in the world of magick. Meeting Sofía for the first time like that had been very awkward, but I wouldn't wish her away for anything. Poor kid.

The jury in Mina's imaginary court case is still undecided on the question of Rachael's Entanglement. And if that hadn't been enough, I'd been catapulted into my new job as Deputy Constable and Guardian of the North following the appearance of a Fae Princess.

And so, we're having a civilised meal and bridge night tomorrow, with no pumpkins, fancy dress or trick and treaters. Or that was the plan. I've learnt not to count my chickens.

Halloween is tomorrow, and tomorrow is a Saturday, so that makes today Friday, and Shabbos begins at half past four tonight. Yes, you've guessed it, the Boss is in the house.

The full-time members of the Watch (Hannah, Vicky, Saffron, Scout and me) gathered in the library at three o'clock for a meeting to discuss, "The Recent Events in France," as the Boss insists on calling them.

Vicky, Alain and I had taken a spot of French Leave to sort out some unfinished business, and at the end of it, the last fugitive of the Dragon Brotherhood had taken her own life: *suicide by cop* they call it, and the *coup de grace* had been dealt by Vicky. The fugitive was Adaryn ap Owain, once a fellow Druid of Myfanwy's, and Hannah had had a restorative talk to both Myfanwy and Vicky.

Because Myfanwy was involved, their talk overran quite a bit, and Hannah looked almost flustered when she and Vicky dashed into the library. Saffron and I had already established the secure video link to France, and we were making small talk with my associate, Alain Dupont. He had stayed behind in Brittany when we left, partly to deal with the Sûreté de Magie and partly to spend time with his new girlfriend. I'll come back to her later.

Alain sat up straight. '*Bonjour Madame Préfet*,' he said to Hannah, adding, "Allo, Vicky.'

'Good afternoon, Monsieur Dupont,' said the Boss with a smile. She knows full well that Alain is petrified of her and likes to rub it in occasionally. 'How are things over there?'

He nodded enthusiastically. 'Good. Mostly good. I think. Keira Faulkner is out of 'ospital and back with the Ménards. The Sûreté de Magie are 'appy. Or they will be soon. I 'ope.'

Hannah groaned. 'What's the problem?'

Alain's eyes moved to where Vicky was on his screen. 'I have a message from Mademoiselle Tangi.'

'What?' said Hannah before Vicky could respond.

'The message is very long, very formal and very 'ard to translate – the *bottom line*, as you say, is that her mother has retired as Chief Druid of their gathering, and Maëlys wants the Tangi Mace back. She says that the Tangi Sword and Flail are much weaker without it.'

'I'm sure they are,' said Hannah dryly. 'She must know that Vicky would be mad to hand it over, and that they'd be even madder to come looking for it.'

'Oui. As a gesture of reconciliation, they offer ...' He checked his notes. 'They offer a Mirror of Captromancy. Is that right?'

'Ooh, yes please,' said Vicky quickly. 'I'm not a bash-them-with-a-mace kind of girl. Not really.'

Hannah is very much that kind of girl. Woman. 'Are you sure, Vicky?'

'Hell, aye. So long as the mirror works.'

Alain coughed politely. 'They have thought of that. I am to bring the mirror. If you like it, I shall return the mace. So long as your sister will allow me time off, Conrad.'

Alain's employment status is both complicated and irrelevant for now. 'You leave Rachael to me, Alain,' I said. 'You can have another weekend with Morane. Has she invited you to Samhain tomorrow?'

During our French Leave, Alain had gone undercover for ten minutes – *ten minutes* – and managed to hook up with a Breton Druid called Morane Guivarc'h. Love at first sight, apparently.

He looked excited and nervous at the same time. 'She has had me practising their dances. She says it will be a night that I never forget.' He treated us to his most eloquent shrug – a mixture of sadness and resignation. 'After this weekend, 'oo knows, eh?'

'Enough already,' said Hannah. 'Drop all the paperwork off with Vicky when you're in London next week. And thank you, Monsieur Dupont. The King's Watch is very grateful for your service.'

Alain bowed, and Saffron disconnected the video link. Hannah sat back and folded her hands in her lap. 'I need to speak to Erin before Shabbos starts. Are you leaving straight away, Vicky?'

'Aye, if Saffron's ready.'

I know the Boss well enough to sense that she was holding something back. It wouldn't be good news, and I firmly believe that bad news can *always* wait. 'Yeah. I'm all packed,' said Saffron. 'I'll go and get Erin and see you outside, Vicky. Have a great weekend, ma'am, and you Conrad.'

'Aye,' said Vicky.

'You too,' said Hannah.

The girls left and Hannah fixed her gaze on me. 'A good weekend? We'll see about that. I still haven't forgiven Mina for blindsiding me like this. If I'd wanted to meet Chris Kelly's wife, I could have picked up the phone in London instead of schlepping out into the mud zone. It's not just the potential for embarrassment, I still think that she should have been prosecuted for what she did. You're not really going to have him as your best man, are you?'

'No. I've asked Ben, but Chris will be one of my supporters, as will Lloyd.'

She shook her head. 'Some wedding this will be with the most boring man in Clerkswell, the consort of a Bodysnatcher and a Gnome standing up for the groom. And to think that I agreed to be Matron of Honour.'

I kept a straight face. 'And they're all taken, I know. Sorry about that. Try not to be disappointed, ma'am.'

'What's so funny, Hannah?' said Erin from the doorway.

Hannah stopped laughing and pointed to me. 'Him. He makes me want to cry so often, I have to laugh. Come on, Miss Slater, take me to your room and show me your Parchment.'

15

On the way out, Hannah got a text and paused to read it. She turned back to me. 'I've got a surprise for you, Conrad. You won't like it, and that brings me great comfort.'

I stood up, and so did Scout. The unofficial mascot of the Watch had spent the meeting curled up on the rug.

'What do you think she's plotting, boy?' I said to him. 'Shall we go for a walk and chew on some scenarios to see if they squeak?'

'Arff.'


Elvenham House has become something of a regional base for the Watch, with Myfanwy as the Base Commander (on account of the fact that she can't leave).

Now that I've been posted Up North, and Mina's giving evidence in London, and Vicky wants to be in her new flat as much as possible, there's a constant stream of comings and goings in Clerkswell, much to the amusement of the village.

Friday night saw Vicky and Saffron leave early for Saff to drop Vicky at Oxford station. Vicky had been very evasive about her plans for Halloween, and I suspect that drunkenness and debauchery are on her agenda, unlike the aristocratic soirée that Lady Hawkins will be holding at the Cherwell Roost. Saffron is not looking forward to it.

'She really is trying to marry me off,' she'd complained. 'I'm only twenty-three!'

Mina had given her a dark look and muttered something about *arranged marriages* and *Hindu matchmakers*.

Erin left after Shabbos supper: she's an Arden Forester, and Samhain is as big to them as it is to Morane Guivarc'h's Druids. As well as the religious obligation in the Forest of Arden, a decorous evening at Elvenham was never going to be high on Erin's social calendar.

The arrivals began on Saturday morning once the Boss had been safely delivered to the Cheltenham Synagogue. I was outside when a big limousine glided into the drive at the funeral pace favoured by the Mowbrays' driver, Maggie Pearce.

First out was Rachael, full of life and mischief. She was put on three months of gardening leave by her employers last week – she's starting her own business, and they don't want her stealing clients. That's the business that Alain is now working for, and technically he's the only employee until Rachael is free to take the reins. This means that Rachael has far too much time on her hands, and you know what the Devil does with idle hands.

Actually, I have no idea whether there is a capital "D" Devil and whether he has an Idle Hands Work Programme. I must find out soon.

Rachael bowed to the family dragon and bent down to say hello to Scout. By this point, Eseld and Sofía had got out, as had a rather bewildered Kenver Mowbray.

I went to shake his hand and welcome him to Elvenham House. 'Good trip?'

'Erm...'

Maggie had got out, too, and said, 'I had to raise the privacy screen. What a racket from the back. Poor Mr Kenver.'

I showed Kenver the dragon, and he made a very formal bow. The lad is only nineteen and the weight of Cornish magick had been dumped on his young shoulders when his father was murdered. If that wasn't enough, he's also stupefyingly rich, and that makes him a target for Rachael's wealth management business. It's a good job his no-nonsense uncle is also his guardian.

Kenver Mowbray also enjoys the support of his siblings, and his older sister is of course Eseld. When Rachael became Entangled, I had asked Eseld to be Rachael's friend just at the time that Eseld had moved to London to teach at Salomon's House. It's a friendship that seems to be working.

Maggie was getting the luggage, but Sofía had taken one item with her in the back of the car: a travel cage for Pedro the rabbit. Pedro? Peter Rabbit? Get it?

I confess that I didn't at first, much to my embarrassment. Pedro was part of the props for Sofía's side hustle, which she'd be rehearsing on Sunday.

I kissed both of my sisters and went to do the same to Eseld, but Scout beat me to it, and not in a good way. He jumped up and gave Eseld's leg a good dry humping.

She had the grace to laugh. 'I think he's pleased to see me.' She detached him from her jeans and gave him a chaste scratch behind the ears. 'You're growing up, aren't you, boy? We'll have to watch you round the ladies, you randy dog.'

'Arff.'

Rachael looked aghast. 'That's just what we need – a rampant dog. Can't you give him a cold shower or take him for a walk or something, Conrad? Better still, get him neutered.'

'Cover your ears, Scout,' said Eseld. 'You're a champion, you are. No operation for you! Any chance of coffee? It's been a long drive. As usual with Maggie.'

Rachael led them off, leaving me to start humping the luggage. As it were. I offered hospitality to Maggie, but she declined.

'I'm off to my sister's in Worcester. We're going to see a new exhibition at the contemporary art gallery this afternoon then get steaming drunk tonight. It's what we do. See you tomorrow, Mr Clarke.'

Scout helped me get the luggage inside by carefully smelling each case first. Well, he thought he was being useful. I did wonder about some of the boxes myself – I could feel the magick tingling inside them. I hope that Sofía knows what she's doing.

I put Kenver's small case next to his sister's whopper and reflected that Kenver Mowbray was the richest guest we've had here, the Fae Princess Birkdale notwithstanding. I'd been surprised when Eseld said that he was coming and I'd said, 'Shouldn't he be lording it over the manor of Pellacombe?'

'In theory, yes. I told Ethan to fill in this year because Kenver's just not ready. Losing Dad hit him hardest, and I'd rather he didn't fail spectacularly. Don't worry, Conrad, he only gets one free pass. Besides, I'd have had to support him, and I'm not up to it either.'

That's a measure of how much Eseld has changed lately: the old Eseld would have done exactly what she wanted and damned the consequences.

Being *The* Mowbray isn't just about lording it. You also have to be a Mage, and Kenver is an apprentice Geomancer, apprenticed to our next guest, Chris Kelly, Earthmaster of Salomon's House. Those who know about these things say that Kenver might be as talented as his father. One day. Another weight on his shoulders. Well, I can't think of a better person to help Kenver adjust than Chris, and talk of the devil…

'C'mon Scout, more people to bark at and get frisky with.'

Chris Kelly has two nicknames at Salomon's House. The staff call him *the Pillar* because he's even taller than me; the students call him *Baldy Kelly* for equally obvious reasons. How his wife came to be known as the Bodysnatcher is a bit more controversial.

Myfanwy and I had saved Vicky's life after magick was used to stop her heart. During that eight and a half minutes, Vicky's essence – her spirit, her soul – was also magickally suppressed in an enchanted coma. She remembers nothing, and if we'd failed, her essence would have drained away as her body started to decay.

When Kenver's father was murdered, his essence was trapped into an Artefact and later released, allowing him to become a Spirit, leaving the material world behind. This is not uncommon with powerful Mages.

There are other ways. Some poisons and Works of magick (strictly illegal) will dissolve the victim's essence as if it were water soluble packaging, leaving the contents unharmed. At that moment of dissolution, it's possible for another Mage to merge their essence into the dying body, and that's what forty-two year old Tamsin Kelly had done when fourteen year old Melody Richardson took an overdose. You can see why Hannah isn't happy.

The King's Watch hierarchy of the day had decided that there was no case to answer, on the basis that Melody had tried to take her own life and that there was no evidence that Tamsin had conspired with her. The Watch may have decided that there was no case to answer, but the wider world of magick had thought otherwise.

They'd treated Chris with professional distance, and it was only my total ignorance of the situation that had led me to accept an invitation to dinner. If I'd known about Tamsin/Melody, I'd still have gone, because Chris had saved my life, asking nothing in return. Dinner at their mansion on the Thames seemed the least we could do.

And when we'd got there and learnt the truth, Mina had taken to Tammy. My love thought that Tammy deserved the same second chance that she'd been given, and Mina had arranged tonight's party as a way to squeeze the Kellys into our little corner of the magickal world.

I took up my station on the steps and watched Chris dash round the car to open Tammy's door. When we first met, Tammy was dressing for her inner age, not her biological one, and she's toned it down since then. If you saw Tamsin and Sofía together in a selfie, you'd think they were just two students. Chris looks his age, which makes him look old enough to be his wife's father, so displays of affection in the mundane world are pretty limited, too.

'Welcome to Elvenham House. May I introduce our dragon? Scout you've already met. Down!'

After bowing, Tammy flicked her eyes all over the house and grounds. 'Where is everyone? Where's Mina?'

See? She'd assumed that she was being snubbed because it's happened to her every day for over five years. Hard to blame her.

'The others have just this minute arrived. Everyone's in the kitchen saying hello and drinking coffee. There's a cup waiting for you, Tamsin. Put your cases in the hall and I'll get Mina.'

Tammy had been practising her *namaste* and showed it off to full effect in the hall. She even added something in Hindi, which is more than I can do.

'Don't be daft,' replied Mina, taking her into her arms. 'You do know that this is a house of madness, don't you? You'll fit right in.'

And she did.

A few minutes later, I was giving Chris and Kenver a tour of the house, leaving the women in the kitchen. You can draw your own conclusions about that or you can accept my version: by the time Chris and I had arrived, there was no room left, and Kenver looked even more like a frightened rabbit than the actual rabbit, who'd gone to sleep.

'How was it last night?' I asked Chris.

He and Tammy have three girls under five, and tonight they are staying with Chris's mother, Bridget. She is *Oma*, the leader of the Arden Foresters, and until yesterday had refused to welcome Tamsin/Melody to their grove or even meet her. It didn't help that they hadn't got on brilliantly before Tamsin's transmigration (to use the technical term that sounds less invasive than *bodysnatching*).

19

'It could have gone a lot worse, put it that way,' said Chris.

Kenver pretended not to be listening. He has to live with Chris when they're doing field work, so he knows the score.

Chris continued, 'So long as the girls were there, it was fine.'

'They are rather cute.'

'And when they were in bed, Mother suddenly found that she needed to oversee the Samhain rehearsal. Erin made a point of looking after us, though. She really made an effort.'

'She can be a great friend. I'm glad she was there.'

Eseld sauntered out of the kitchen. 'Do you want to do that Ley line before or after lunch, Conrad?'

I swallowed hard. I was not looking forward to this. 'Before. That way if I make an arse of myself I'll have the afternoon to recover my dignity. I'll let you unpack and we'll meet in half an hour, if that's okay.'

She patted my arm. 'You'll be fine. You've got two of the best teachers at Salomon's House to help you.'

'I've got Chris. Who's the other one?'

'Ha ha. If I'm good enough for Sofía, I'm more than good enough for you.'

'We'll see about that. Smoker's corner at noon.'

After the guests dispersed, Mina, Myfanwy and I gathered in the kitchen. 'How did it go?' I asked.

Mina looked at Myfanwy, who said, 'We're not the problem are we? We all do what Rani here tells us.'

Mina wasn't sure whether to be flattered or insulted. Like the true Brahmin she is, she decided to be flattered and nodded to show that this was the correct attitude, then added, 'If only that were true.'

Myfanwy tilted her head and closed one eye, like a blonde pirate. 'If you don't look at Tammy, it's just like having Jules Bloxham in the room, you know. You hear the voice of a confident, funny working mother. Then you open both eyes and wonder what this kid is doing here.'

'What about Rachael?' I asked. 'She never does what anyone tells her.'

Mina snorted. 'Your sister did what she always does. When she found out that the Kellys' mansion comes with Chris's job, and that he's on a salary, she said, "Will you be working in a private capacity, Tamsin?" I'm surprised she didn't ask to see her online bank balance.'

Myfanwy elbowed Mina in the side. 'Lay off it, Mina. She was trying to help, wasn't she?' She stood up. 'Right, I'm off to Ben's for some peace and quiet. See you later.'

'And that means I'd better start lunch,' said Mina. 'Try not to die horribly in the garden, Conrad.'

We stopped for a long kiss. It's not often we get the kitchen to ourselves.

'I'll try.'

## 2 — *Family Affairs*

You've been to Elvenham plenty of times now. You know all about the Clerk's Well at the bottom of the garden. What you might have forgotten is the Gift of the Eldest, just down the slope: my own personal magickal oak tree. Or it will be when it's grown.

To really flourish, the tree needs more Lux, and even more important are the Wards which Eseld had installed before the Bollywood party. They are sophisticated things, and currently running off a sort of battery. The whole thing needs a Ley line to be drawn from the well, which as the former door to a Fae realm has plenty of Lux. And that's why Chris, Tammy, Eseld, Kenver, Scout and I set off with a purpose through the cold October air. It was time for me to take my next step in performing actual magick.

But first we headed for the stable to see Evenstar, my equine gift from the Mowbray Estate. Eseld went into the mare's stall to give her a good checking over. Her brother is more into boats than horses, and started checking his phone. Chris and Tammy stood back admiringly, their arms round each other and Tammy's hand on his chest.

'She's so beautiful,' said Tammy. 'Makes me wish I'd been a pony girl at school, not a bookworm. It's not too late, is it Chris?'

'I think Evenstar might be a bit of a handful,' he replied. 'There's a few stables upriver. You should check them out.'

Tammy relinquished her hold on Chris and walked closer to the stall. 'Feel the magick!'

'That'll be Erin's Scriptorium,' I said, pointing to the converted unit in the other half of the building.

'No,' said Tammy. 'It's the saddle. Can I?'

'It came with the horse, but Eseld won't tell me what it does, so I haven't dared use it. All suggestions gratefully received.'

Eseld stuck her tongue out at me and put her hand on her hip to watch Tammy caress the soft, intricately tooled leather. Their eyes locked, and Tammy said, 'It's from the other worlds. Why?'

'Conrad should know,' said Eseld.

Jargon alert: *other worlds* is Circle-Mage speak for the different planes of existence. The first version of Tamsin had no talent for plane-shifting, but Melody did, and some things are innate. Tammy is now studying with the Fae; they are the masters of plane-shifting, the most skilled creatures below the gods.

I racked my brains and clutched at the only straw I had. 'The chases. Like the Waterhead Chase. Do they really take place on different levels?'

'Some of them, yes,' said Eseld. 'Dad won the Swaledale twice when he was young. He was going to start one in Cornwall, you know.'

'I'm sorry. Did you try?'

She smiled. 'Believe it or not, when it came to riding, I used to be very timid. You should get some lessons, Conrad. They have a few Seniors races.'

'Seniors!'

She grinned. 'Over thirty-fives. It really is a young person's sport. You should ask Tamsin to look at the well.'

Tammy made a slight frown which she quickly turned into a smile. 'I was going to ask.'

'Of course. Lead the way, Eseld.'

This is what I know about the well: there used to be a sídhe in the hill behind it, and it was abandoned when my ancestor chucked himself in the water and drowned. A sídhe is the underground home of the Fae, and yes, for generations, my ancestors really did have fairies at the bottom of the garden. Just don't let the Fae hear you use the word *fairy*.

Tamsin walked twice around the well, running her fingers over the stone. She smiled at Chris, vaulted over the lip of the well and vanished into thin air. Just like that. Scout went bananas, and we all felt a shiver of magick.

'Wow, did you see that?' said Kenver. 'Sorry.'

'You just said what I felt, Kenver. Will she be okay, Chris?'

'Yeah. Fine. Let's set up while we wait.'

Lux runs in straight lines unless you're a very, very good Geomancer like Chris. Sometimes it behaves like water, sometimes like electricity, and sometimes like molten glass. And that's how I feel it: sticky, ductile and very, very hot.

Kenver walked back to the house and planted a charged wand at the point where Eseld had anchored her Wards. It would be my job to draw a flow of Lux from the well, take it through the gardens and join it to that anchor point.

I got out my dowsing rod and laid her on a cloth – I use the female pronoun advisedly, because the Spirit of Madeleine lives in the willow wand, and I need her help. Just to make life really difficult, she senses Lux as water, and as you know, fire and water rarely mix well.

Chris was going to supervise, and Eseld was there in case I got in trouble, then she could use our bond to help me out. We both wanted to avoid that because I'd fail the test if she helped and because our bond is rather more intimate than either of us is comfortable with.

'Arff!' said Scout suddenly.

'The Clarkes really are blessed,' said a newly visible Tamsin. She'd been here all the time, of course, but on a different energy level, with us as invisible to her as she was to us. The gods can see our world, dimly, but only if they concentrate really hard – or join us by manifesting on our plane.

Tammy continued, 'There's a small grove of Fae wood still alive and flourishing, and that's why there's Lux in the well.' She looked at Eseld. 'If word gets around, there are Mages who would kill for a spot like this. Shall we keep it our secret?'

Eseld flushed a little. 'There's enough Mages after Conrad without me adding to the list, Tamsin. He keeps our secrets, so I'm keeping his.'

Tammy looked down. 'Sorry. I'm always on edge after shifting back on my own. I'm still new to all this.'

'You're a natural,' said Chris smoothly.

Ouch. That was not the right thing to say: Melody was the natural plane shifter.

'Let's get it over with,' I said before anyone could feel awkward.

'I'm going to get warm,' said Tamsin. 'Good luck, Conrad.'

She headed for the house, and I was surprised to see Rachael coming towards us. 'What are you doing here?' I asked.

'Sofía's cleaning out the rabbit, so I thought I'd watch my brother perform magick. It's one thing to work with Sofía, another entirely to see you do it.'

'What have you been doing with Sofía?'

Rachael came over all mock-innocent. It's an annoying hangover from childhood. She used to hide my RAF uniform the night before a posting and deny all knowledge. 'Didn't she tell you? I'm her assistant. I can't do anything else while I'm on gardening leave, so I thought I'd pitch in.'

I looked at Eseld. 'You could have told me.'

'I told her it would be a nice surprise,' said Rachael.

Eseld looked guilty. I sighed. My fault for asking her to be Rachael's friend. Rachael turned her attention to the well and the Gift of the Eldest, secure behind its dog and deer proof fence.

'You're telling me that stick is a magickal Artefact?' said Rachael. 'What happens if I touch it?'

'Try it and see.'

She walked over to the fence and looked at the staff. 'Never mind,' she said. 'I don't want to look daft.'

Eseld went up to her and put an arm round her shoulders. 'And that's how the world of magick stays hidden. I've put a Ward on the fence. It makes people think better of touching it.'

Rachael looked embarrassed. 'Oh. Is it so easy to control minds?'

'If only. It's a minor Discouragement. My dad used to call them *Pound Spells*, because if I offered you a pound, you'd touch the staff. They're still very useful, though, and take very little Lux to work.'

'Lux. That's magickal energy, right?'

'Right. Also the force of life and free will, but we won't go there today.'

Rachael smiled. 'Good. So this stick is worth protecting?'

'It is. It was a gift from the last leader of the Daughters in Glastonbury. It was taken from their sacred oak.'

'And you're going to make a power supply, Conrad?'

'Under supervision, yes.'

Chris had been standing back politely. He's only known Rachael for a couple of hours. Eseld knows better.

'Raitch, for Conrad's sake, can you sit here and keep quiet?'

Rachael looked at me. 'This has the potential to go horribly wrong and be embarrassing, doesn't it?'

'Yes.'

'Then I shall be as still as...' she cast around for a simile, '...as that tasteless statue of a nymph shagging a tree. Why did Myfanwy think that was a useful addition to the garden again?'

'Dryad,' I said. 'It's a Dryad, not a Nymph. And it's magickal.'

'Oh. Right. It's not going to come to life, then?'

'No. It's a scarecrow. Keeps the birds away from her herbs.'

'Then I shall be as still as a scarecrow, until you make a mess of things, and then I shall laugh.'

Eseld looked at me. 'Has she always been like this?'

'Always. You don't know how lucky you are having Kenver as a younger brother.'

'Let's not go there. Right. Ready?'

I took hold of my dowsing rod and gave Rachael a warning. 'Try not to freak out if you see the image of an Edwardian lady.'

Rachael nodded, but Eseld was nonplussed. 'Come again?'

'Ah. Didn't I tell you? My dowsing rod is possessed by the Memorial Spirit of a woman called Madeleine.'

'No you did not fucking tell me, Conrad. How the hell did you come by that, and do you know what you're doing?'

'Most of the time.'

She looked worried, and that made me even more worried. Even Rachael had picked up that this wasn't a laughing matter.

'Have you used it much?'

'Enough. It's how I got out of Niði's Labyrinth.'

'And you're sure it's a Memorial Spirit, not a full one?'

'The wand was cut from Maddy's Memorial tree at Lunar Hall.'

Eseld shrugged. 'Then let's go for it.' She turned to Chris.

I laid my jacket on a chair and stood in front of the well. I closed my eyes, letting my focus settle on the dowsing rod. It became warm in my hand, and the familiar presence of Maddy manifested itself at my side, just like someone standing next to me.

Maddy shifted, and I felt something bump my hip, as if the two of us were in a very dark, very cramped lift. Not at all creepy. I've sensed the well many times, with and without Maddy's help. When I started to feel the heat of Lux, I knew that I had to take it further.

I focused on the heat source, driving my attention closer and laying an image of a glass furnace over the top. It worked. I was so shocked that I nearly opened my eyes. Perhaps I was getting better at this.

I kept my focus on the red hot glass in the furnace and moved my hand towards it. In the imaginary light, my dowsing rod had become a long pole. I dipped it into the glass and rolled the end to gather the molten magick into a ball.

'You're doing well,' said Chris. 'That's spot on, Conrad. Now try backing up and drawing it out.'

I moved away from the well, back two steps, and a string of glass followed, dropping onto the floor but still connected at both ends. That was good.

Less good was the heat building in my hand: the rod had gone from warm to very warm, and I was breaking out in a sweat. Even my titanium tibia was throbbing. Steadily, step by step, I moved back from the well. Kenver called out occasionally to help me avoid mundane obstacles, and things were going well until my leg went into spasm.

The titanium rod had got hotter and hotter, even hotter than the dowsing rod, and then when my weight was on that leg, the muscles seized, pitching me over. The line of glass/Lux crashed towards me, and I thought my day had come. Maddy had other ideas.

Her presence had grown more solid as more Lux floated around. When I fell over, she became visible, diving in front of me and letting the stream of Lux hit her full in the chest. I hit my head on something and Rachael screamed.

I still had my eyes closed to the mundane world, and what I saw in the magickal one was like a scene from hell: black as midnight and illuminated by a river of fire.

The Lux from the well was overflowing, out of control. Maddy was keeping it away from me, and then two other shapes stepped in. One was a giant, and that had to be Chris. The other was a waif, barely visible. It danced behind Chris and moved to support him, like a spun sugar buttress. My friend raised his arms and brought them together, as if he were doing a slow-motion hand-clap.

The Lux flowed into a contained channel, and then he walked forwards, pushing it back into the well and calming it down.

Suddenly, there was no magickal light, and I opened my eyes. Chris was standing in front of the well, with Eseld wrapped round him like a cloak. He was going to say something, but all our eyes turned to Maddy, fully visible in her garden party finery. And she wasn't alone.

A man in riding breeches and a hunting coat had appeared from nowhere. He was dirty and looked like he'd been in a fight. As I started to scramble up, he reached out to Maddy, and Eseld shouted, 'Lucas! No! Leave her!'

*Lucas? Lucas of Innerdale?* How in the name of Odin had he got here?

Maddy glowed with health. The massive influx of Lux had brought her more to life than ever before. She took a step back from the man and her hand flew up to her mouth. 'Father? It's not you! It can't be.'

'Yes, Maddy, it's me. Don't worry, child, I'm here.' His voice was clipped and from another age. Even so, I could hear the faint echo of the Lake District.

She was distraught. 'You're dead. The Fae took you. You can't be here.'

I had regained my feet and moved towards them. I had never seen his human form before, but Eseld had. She had been there when the Familiar Bond between me and Scout had been severed. She had seen the Spirit who'd merged with the dog, and she'd said that it was Lucas of Innerdale, last seen disappearing into the ground in Cornwall. And now he was here.

Scout looked terrified, and came over to protect me. Poor thing. He knew that something was wrong, but not what. Dogs can smell their own scent. Perhaps Lucas smelled of Scout in some way.

I opened my mouth to speak, but there was someone else with far more skin in the game than me: Eseld. She untangled herself from Chris and said, 'Where's my father? What have you done with him?'

According to Saffron, who was there, the Spirit of Lord Mowbray had wrestled the Spirit of Lucas into the ground, and they'd both disappeared.

'Peace,' said Lucas. 'Your father and I came to an understanding. He's gone, Lady Eseld. He won't be seen in this world again.'

'Did ... Did he say anything?'

'I was there, remember? On Mark's Barrow. I was there. His last words were that you were his favourite, and you promised to look after Kenver. There's nothing he could add to that, and he's gone where you can't follow in this life.'

Eseld started blinking back tears, and I spoke up. 'How come you're on the loose, Lucas?'

'Lord Mowbray and I had this in common: we love our daughters.'

You could see the likeness between Lucas and Madeleine. She had her father's wide eyes and dimpled chin, and it couldn't have been an accident that the Spirit of Lucas started hanging around me after I'd been presented with Maddy in wand form. By some fluke, I hadn't used my dowsing rod once after Lucas had bonded with Scout.

Lucas took his daughter's hands. 'I'm sorry I couldn't save you, but it's not too late to save the next one.'

'Really father? I have been asleep so long, and this new world is so far from ours.'

Yes, Maddy does talk like that, with the sharpest cut-glass accent you can imagine.

'Let's go, Madeleine. There's someone else I want you to meet.' He gave a low whistle, and Scout walked uncertainly towards him. He lowered his hand, and it turned silver. 'Remember that smell, boy. Understand?'

'Arff.'

Maddy had turned to look at me. 'Thank you, Mr Clarke. You have been a perfect gentleman, and I have done my best to leave you with something suitable. Goodbye, and good luck. May the Goddess guide you.'

The pair looked into each other's eyes and vanished.

'She's lying,' said Rachael. I saw the shock on her face and guessed what was coming. 'You've never been a perfect gentleman, Conrad.'

With that, Rachael collapsed on to the swing seat, and I heard a mutter from behind me. 'And I don't need looking after, neither,' said Kenver.

In the next second, we were overrun. Everyone in the house had sensed the outflow of Lux and come running. I found out from Mina that Kenver had stopped them getting any closer, just in case, even to the point of grabbing Mina and using magick to deter Sofía and Tamsin.

I found myself leaning on Mina and shaking as if I had hypothermia. She used all her strength to push me to the seat and stared into my eyes like a paramedic checking for concussion.

'I'll take that,' said Chris, relieving me of the willow wand.

'Lunch, I think,' said Mina.

## 3 — Back in the Saddle

It was Chris who insisted that I have another go after lunch. He and Tammy came to smokers' corner with the willow wand and said, 'I've checked it out, and it's a perfectly good dowsing rod. Very good, in fact. If you're ever going to do this, Conrad, you'll do it today.'

'Are you sure?' said Eseld. 'What about his leg?'

'It's got an Artefact in it,' said Tammy.

'Hang on,' I said. 'The surgeons at Queen Elizabeth were good, but they're not magicians. As it were.'

Tammy looked at the sky, as if checking for ravens. 'I think it may have something to do with the Allfather. You know that Lux is partly stored in bone marrow?'

'No.'

'It is.' She swept back her hair, putting on a serious face. 'When Odin enhanced you, he must have modified your skeleton. Slightly. The gods aren't infallible. Maybe he'd never come across a titanium insert before. It's like a super battery, but you need to control it properly – stop it discharging when it's full.'

'How in Odin's name am I going to do that?'

She flinched, unhappy at me invoking my sometime patron. 'You need help.'

Chris took over. 'You can forge Ley lines, Conrad. You've got it. You were so nearly there this morning, and you just need practice. You need help from someone who knows nothing of Geomancy so that you can focus on the line and they can help isolate your leg without interfering.'

'You have a bond with Eseld,' said Tammy earnestly. 'You should strengthen it.'

Tammy was between Eseld and me. I looked over her head and saw Eseld's eyes widen, just a fraction, as she inhaled smoke. I felt exactly the same.

I smiled at Tamsin. 'I have bonds with Mina, Vicky and Myfanwy, too. Only one of those am I keen to strengthen.'

'Don't be so mundane,' said Tammy with the same voice that Grandma Clarke used to say *don't be so bourgeois.*

'Sofía,' said Eseld, crushing out her cigarette vigorously. 'They may have got 95% of their magick from different mothers, but they're both Clarkes.'

The third smoker, Sofía herself, looked alarmed. Eseld turned to her student and said, 'It's a module in your second year course, Sofía. If you help Conrad today, I'll write you a pass certificate. Not that you should need an incentive.'

'If you think I am ready, Doctora Mowbray.'

'It's easier than what you're doing tomorrow.'

'Good,' said Tamsin. 'I'll tell Kenver, and leave you to it. It's bloody freezing out here, and I promised to help Mina sort out tonight's food.'

'It's a takeaway, no?' said Sofía, worried that she'd missed something. She would be mortified if she thought that there was a domestic duty she'd shirked.

'Home delivery from the Inkwell, to be accurate,' I said. 'And two gallons of Inkwell Bitter, freshly pulled. If you're happy, Sofía, I'd be honoured.'

She frowned and nodded at the same time. 'Good.'

After the morning's drama, this afternoon's Geomancy was straightforward. Hard, but straightforward, and I passed my test, as did Sofía.

She really wants her degree from the Invisible College, and I want it known that I'm learning. I have a sort of honorary degree – Master of the Art of Alchemy – which means little more than that I am a Mage. I'll never get the Fellowship that Sofía's studying for because it's a general qualification in all (legal) areas of magick, but in theory I could become a Doctor of Chymic. In the same way that I could theoretically run a marathon in two and a half hours.

When we set up by the well, Eseld showed Sofía what to do, and suddenly I could hear things differently when Sofía bonded with me. The rooks were a lot louder, for example. And cars roared along the bypass that I hadn't heard for years. I really do think that Adaryn damaged my hearing with that bloody harp of hers. Another reason I'm glad she's dead.

I also felt, not younger exactly, but sort of warmer inside. It was a lovely feeling. I think. Also slightly disturbing when you're sharing it with your little sister, and Sofía definitely got the shitty end of the stick.

She hissed with pain and swore in Spanish when she understood how my leg can feel to me. Most of the time, I block it out. When she'd gritted her teeth and got a grip, I felt Lux flow down my leg and into the metal. Metal. I was actually feeling the rod for the first time, as if it had nerve endings. Before I could digest that, Sofía kept her right hand on my shoulder and bent to grab my knee.

'Do this with your mind,' she said. She pulled slightly on my knee, and it was like turning the top of a flask a quarter turn. She opened it again. 'Like that.' It took a few goes until I got the hang of it, and a very relieved Sofía relinquished my shoulder. 'What was so funny?' she asked.

'Sorry?'

'I heard laughter. From far away. And a really boring Spanish guitar. You were playing a trick.'

'I wish.'

She shook her head. 'Probably echoes of ghosts.' Impulsively, she leaned up and kissed me. 'Good luck.'

I clutched the now lifeless but well-behaved willow wand and started the mini Ley line again. I finished (to applause) with a rather disturbing sensation as I linked line and anchor.

'I've just had a message from my house,' I said to Chris. 'Either that or a ghost who lives there.'

Chris looked at Eseld. 'Did you slip a naughty Work in the Wards?'

'Me! No! I'm a professional now. And I didn't sense anything. You've lived here, Sofía, and you're a Clarke.'

She gave a Spanish shrug. 'It is a very nice house, but it is not haunted. Not that I have seen.'

We were interrupted then as Ben and Myfanwy returned.

'Do I really have to fetch Hannah from Shul?' said Ben. 'She scares me.'

'And she scares me, too. This is the problem: she hates the countryside and doesn't understand cricket.'

'Poor woman.'

'I know. Ask her to tell you about what happened to Myfanwy in the Undercroft.'

He frowned. 'She's never talked about that.'

'I'm not surprised. Hannah will tell you. See you later, Ben. Here are the last of the guests, and I need refreshment.' I gave him an encouraging pat on the shoulder and went round the front.

Mina was on welcome duty, giving Lucia Berardi a big hug, and her greeting of Lucy's partner, Tom Morton, was warmer than it would have been a few weeks ago. After all, Tom had once arrested Mina for murder and money laundering. Since then, Tom and Lucy have joined the world of magick, and he and Mina were both kidnapped by Gnomes.

I shook hands and went for the cases; Mina and Lucy had already disappeared inside. 'How's Elaine?' I asked.

Tom's sidekick, Elaine Fraser, had been shot in the leg with an arrow by my ex-sidekick, Karina Kent. I'd like to tell you that it had been an accident. It wasn't.

'Recovering,' said Tom. 'She's on office duties from next week. I've had an idea about that. I'll tell you later.'

'After tea and briefings.'

We got into the hall and I bolted the front doors. From now on, all comings and goings would be through the back entrance.

Tom took a good look around. 'I love the carvings, Conrad. This is a beautiful house. What briefings?'

'We're playing bridge tonight, and Mina takes bridge very seriously. You'll also discover that Mages can be very competitive. I did warn you that tonight's entertainment could be full-on, didn't I?'

'Nothing can be madder than watching a naked girl turn into a wolf before your eyes.'

'Fair point. Mina is going to have a seminar for beginners after tea. You already play, don't you?'

'I do. Are any of your wolfpack here? And if not, why aren't you with them, given that you're their patron?'

There was a twinkle in his eye when he said that. When he saw me become their patron, the queen had offered herself to me, in the fullest sense of the term. 'No, Tom. They're safely hidden away. Tonight they will be hunting in wolf form and feasting. They'd have to behave if I went up there. The Witch who's looking after them will keep an eye on things. Next year might be different.'

He nodded. 'Did you say something about afternoon tea?'

'Follow me.'

Mina set up her card school in the dining room after tea, which had only been fraught at the beginning, when Mina introduced Hannah to Tamsin. Perhaps Hannah had spoken to the rabbi earlier, because she chose to sit next to Tammy and Chris during afternoon tea, and Hannah had even offered to muck in and help clear up the mess afterwards. Goodness knows what they talked about.

Mina has been indoctrinating Myfanwy, Ben and Sofía in the dark arts of bridge for weeks now, and as you know, no one argues with Mina when she's in Rani mode. The least enthusiastic pupil had been Sofía, mainly because bridge is the driving passion of my mother, and my mother is not Sofía's mother.

Mina gathered her class of six and settled down. Tom and I had stuck our heads in to make sure that all was well. Lucy looked a little intimidated to be left on her own in that company, and delayed our departure by saying, 'Tom had a question.'

It looked like that was news to him. 'Did I?'

'Yes. He wanted to know why we were having a bridge tournament tonight instead of a party like normal people, or a séance or something magickal.'

Mina deferred to Hannah, who said, 'Thank your Victorian ancestors. When women were admitted to the Invisible College, the Warden's wife wanted entertainments suitable for young ladies of magick that didn't involve nakedness and fornication, so the tradition of parlour games was started. Tonight it's bridge.'

Tom Morton used to be a lawyer and is now a senior detective. His father is a judge. He leaned forward and said, 'Lucy has a question, too. She wants to know if there's naked fornication in the Arden Foresters, and can we go there instead next year, please?'

Lucy went red. 'Tom! I said no such thing. Go away! Hang on, where are you going?

31

'We're taking Scout for a walk,' I said hastily.

'You've got an hour,' said Mina. 'Be in the kitchen at six o'clock.'

'Have fun.'

Tom and I grabbed our coats; Scout was already waiting at the back door. When I let him out, he snuffled round a bit, cocked his leg and then did something I haven't seen since he stopped being my Familiar: he picked up the scent of the Ley line and started following it back towards the well.

'I'll be blowed.'

'What?' said Tom.

'Scout. Looks like he's got the scent of Lux again. I don't know whether to be thrilled for him or groan that I've got yet more training to do.'

We sauntered after the mad mutt and gave him a treat when he barked at the well. I slipped the lead on him and we headed for the road. Now that he's getting frisky, I'll have to ration his freedoms.

'What do you think of the madhouse?' I asked.

He blew out his cheeks. 'I keep having to recalibrate. It's hard to work out what's going on when there are so many new rules to learn. Can you answer me a question honestly?'

'If I give you an answer, it'll be an honest one. So long as you don't ask about Four Ashes Farm.'

It was the elephant in the room of my relationship with DCI Tom Morton. On the day that Mina's husband was murdered, the final showdown had been at a farm in Essex, and Mina had left the scene in handcuffs. Tom has come to terms with what happened after that day, but still struggles with what happened before.

It troubled him enough to stop him in his tracks, and I had to rein in Scout. 'I've given that up,' he said. 'Not because I think you're innocent, you understand. I've given it up because it would drive me mad to pursue it. Literally mad, as in discharge on health grounds mad. I tell myself that justice won't be served by pursuing it, and most of the time I believe it. I wasn't going to bring it up, actually, but now you have, I'll just say that I wouldn't be here if Hannah Rothman hadn't vouched for you, and I wouldn't have got involved in that business last month either.'

He started walking again, as if he knew where he were going. 'Now that we are here, I'm treating this as a fresh start.'

'Turn right here, Tom. So what was your question?'

'Do you believe in an all-powerful God, with a capital "G"?'

That came from left field. I had been expecting something much more difficult. 'No. I never have.'

'Does anyone?'

'I honestly don't know. Hannah's PA is a devout Christian, but I have no idea if she believes that he's omnipotent. There are a couple of Muslims in the

Invisible College, I think. It's not a topic that comes up, to be honest. Why do you ask?'

'Curious. If you were wondering, I don't either. It doesn't matter. To change the subject, I've had an idea about the *Codex Defanatus*. What did you call that project again?'

That book, the Codex, is behind most of the big problems I've faced in magick.

'The search for the book is called *Project Talpa*. After Moley. I knew there was a good reason I sought you out, Tom. I'm all ears.'

'It might be nothing. I've been reading those files you gave me, and it struck me that there are now a few witnesses.'

'The only one we knew had been part of it was Adaryn. I think one of the reasons she took her own life was to avoid being put in the Undercroft. I think she would have cracked under pressure, and she was afraid that she'd be intercepted first. You read my secret report on what happened to Isaac Fisher, didn't you?'

He shivered. 'I did. It gave me nightmares. Why do you think the Fae dealt with him like that?'

'Because of Irina. She was pregnant. He would have done a deal to protect her, and the Fae knew that.'

'But she's still alive, so is Myfanwy, so is Keira. And others.'

'Who are all ignorant, even if they're not innocent. I'm pretty sure of that.'

'I agree, but in a big enquiry, it's the little things. If you and Hannah weren't up to your armpits in Dragons and suchlike, I'm sure you'd crack it.'

'You're being polite now. Just say that we're blundering around.'

He stared at me. 'Hannah is a good copper. She doesn't blunder. Nor do you, to be fair, Conrad. It's just that you'd admit that you're more of a hunter, and you've got no scent of the quarry, have you?'

It's a metaphor I've used myself. 'You're right, Tom.'

'What if Hannah lets me interview them, systematically, and then I use police resources to track back forensically? I could get Elaine to do a lot of the screen work while she's recuperating.'

This time it was me who stopped. 'You're a genius. Why didn't we think of that before?'

'Honestly? I suspect Hannah has thought of it but didn't want to get her twin sister involved.'

I pulled my lip. 'Tell her tonight. She'll go for it. In fact ... hang on.' I got out my phone and called Alain. 'Has the party started yet?'

'Non. Soon, though. What's the problem, mon ami?'

'Take an extra day in France. I'll probably need you to get Keira in front of a video link on Monday. I'll square it with her mother. Have fun.'

'Her mother?' said Tom.

33

'Long story. You can talk to Myfanwy tomorrow, if the Boss gives you the green light. And I'd invite Ben to be there. The others may take a little more organisation.'

Scout was taking an inordinate interest in a hedge and wouldn't be budged. Tom pointed to my faithful hound and said, 'What was all that I heard over tea? Something about Scout's Familiar being on the loose.'

'Lucas of Innerdale chose to bind himself to a puppy, and that combination was my Familiar. When the binding was broken, Lucas escaped and became more powerful. Tell me, Tom, have you ever worked with a copper who got in trouble but who you thought simply couldn't be guilty?'

'Not closely. Not as closely as you must have worked with Lucas. Why? What did he do?'

'He set up a group of vigilantes, or that's what people say. His reputation is about as savoury as the Ku Klux Klan, and everyone thought he was gone forever until recently.'

'And you think he's innocent?'

'I've learnt two things about the world of magick, Tom. I've learnt that people often play very long games and I've learnt that it can be brutal. Very, very brutal. He bonded with Scout to get close to Madeleine. Perhaps it was just a father being a father or perhaps they have another agenda.' My ears were starting to tingle with cold, and the fire in the drawing room would be roaring. 'I think it's about time we headed back.'

## 4 — *Devotions*

Myfanwy was a complete bundle of nerves when we gathered in the kitchen. Not surprising, really: for once, it was one hundred per cent her show, and she was wearing her Druid's robes, a lighter patch showing where she'd removed the MADOC badge. She'd been kicked out of that order when she was arrested.

She patted the covering of a wicker basket on the table and looked around. 'Has everyone wrapped up warm?' she said. 'It's turning proper cold out there. Shall I put my woolly hat on, Ben?'

He kissed his fiancée. 'We're all here. We're all ready. You do not need a hat.'

'Good. Right. Where's the candle?'

'On the Aga. Behind you.'

'Oh. Right.'

Mina gave her a metaphorical nudge. 'Shall we all move to the other side to give you some room?' Mina shepherded us away from the window side of the kitchen, and Ben stepped right back.

Myfanwy turned to face the Aga and intoned something in Welsh, then translated for our benefit. 'That means *lit from the hearth, blessed by the heart of the home*. I promise no more Welsh. Not much anyway. Here goes.' She repeated the Welsh blessing and placed her hands round the fat candle. The wick burst into flame and blazed brightly. Moving slowly, with the candle down by her stomach, she turned and walked out of the kitchen. Ben fell in just behind her, picking up the basket, and everyone followed the couple out of the house into the gardens. I stood back until last, and Hannah waited to go with me. As I left the kitchen, I turned out the lights.

Hannah was wrapped in more layers than a pass-the-parcel, including the controversial woolly hat over the headscarf protecting her scars. The hat was pink, the headscarf green; even I thought they clashed.

'Have you read the six hundred and thirteen Mitzvot of the Torah, Conrad?'

As conversational openers go, it was unexpected. 'I've glanced at them. I spent more time on the kosher bit, so that we could feed you.'

'There's a lot about not having anything, and I mean *anything* to do with other gods. And about giving witches a wide berth, yet Hashem gave me power over the world. And your household kept kosher with me last night. I do not believe that the Lord wants me to sit by the fire while Myfanwy celebrates *Nos Galan Gaeaf.*'

'Thank you for coming, Hannah.'

'I've enjoyed myself. So far. I couldn't go to Selena's bash in London, could I? Not when it's a political event this year. The alternative would be trick or treat with my nieces. And we have business in Manchester. Still not sure about your bloody helicopter, though.'

I said nothing. Hannah does like to vent. We were getting near the well, and she lowered her voice. 'Tom told me his idea. I've given him carte blanche. It'll probably come to nothing, but it needs doing.'

We formed a circle around the well, all thirteen of us. Or fourteen if you counted Scout. We'd ended up with this number by accident, and Myfanwy had taken it as a sign that we should hold the Welsh celebration *Nos Galan Gaeaf*, their equivalent of Samhain. In a cut-down version, for obvious reasons.

Myfanwy placed the candle on the lip of the well and stepped back. She took the wicker basket from Ben and removed the cover. Inside was a fresh batch of Welsh Cakes and Bara Brith, the same as we'd enjoyed at afternoon tea. She took a slice of Bara Brith and a cake and placed them to the right of the candle. 'People of the Night, accept our offering.'

She passed the basket to Ben, and he repeated her deeds and words. It was a ritual offering to the Fae, to keep them sweet and to keep them from coming into the house. Up the road in the Forest of Arden, they would take their offerings into the sídhe and there would be a party, thrown by the Prince of Arden.

Everyone, including Hannah, made the trip to the well. Tamsin was last, and Myfanwy had been thrilled when Tammy had offered to add a bonus. There was now a ring of cakes around the well, and Tamsin had placed hers next to the candle. She spread her arms and tipped back her head. 'People of the Night, I deliver this to you.'

She drew on the Lux in the well, and shifted the offerings on to the same plane as the old sídhe. There were no Fae to take them, but if a phantom stag, or boar or raven happened to be in the area, the offering would not go unnoticed.

Tamsin rejoined the circle and we looked at the candle, burning brightly with magick. Myfanwy has been trying to teach Ben some Welsh, with little success (or so he tells me). One thing he has mastered, because he has a good singing voice, is the lullaby *Suo Gân*. They sang it as a duet, with Myfanwy's hands placed over where her bump would soon be showing.

Mina had tears in her eyes when she gave me a smile from across the circle, and they echoed my own. I don't think she wants to wait very long after our wedding next year before she stops taking the pill. I don't want her to wait, either.

She looked to my left, and flinched. I tried to glance without turning my head. Hannah was distraught, with not just tears in her eyes but rivers of them. They finished the song, and Myfanwy took the candle from the now empty rim of the well. We processed back to the house, and this time Mina walked with Hannah, her short arm wrapped round Hannah's well insulated waist.

Myfanwy placed the candle on the kitchen windowsill and we gathered behind her. 'On this night, the doors are open. All visitors are welcome, and a place is laid for our kin.' She repeated herself in Welsh and concluded in English. 'Let us remember those who walked this earth before us and who live in our hearts.'

A human silence descended on the room as we remembered in the light of the candle. Thomas Clarke had appeared here, my 11xGreat Grandfather. I doubted he'd come back – he was with Alice now. I thought of the grandfather I'd never met, of Granny Clarke and of Grandpa and Grandma Enderby.

Myfanwy cleared her throat. 'Lord and Lady, Sun and Moon, bless this house and all who make it home tonight. Bless those who have lived in it before us and those who will live here in times to come.' She paused. 'That's me done. Can I put my feet up now?'

Rachael turned on the lights and we turned our thoughts to dinner. Hannah slipped out before anyone but Mina and I realised she'd gone.

'Want a hand, Conrad?' said Chris Kelly.

'Please.'

'No drinking while you wait for the food!' said Mina. 'Come straight back.'

'Yes, Rani.'

It was a motley crew who got off the bus. The 555 service from Lancaster to Keswick is reputedly one of the longest and most scenic bus routes in England, not that anyone had enjoyed the view since it left Cairndale an hour ago. The Lake District is not at its best in the dark.

A few walkers, a couple of families and a bunch of commuters disembarked at the end of the journey and lingered in the bus station or hurried on their way home. Harry was the last off, and he was one of the lingerers, stretching out the muscles in his back and hoping that the twinge he'd felt earlier didn't turn into a full-blown spasm. When he put his hands behind him to rub his lumbar area, his coat was drawn open and showed off his outfit for the evening.

The female half of an older couple in walking gear cast her eye over him and raised an eyebrow. He smiled at her and walked out of the glorified turning circle that did duty as the bus station, drawing his coat closed to hide the dinner jacket and cummerbund; he was easily the most overdressed person the 555 had seen in weeks.

He was early, of course. When you're told what time your lift will be there, and you're reliant on public transport, you take what you can get. He had at least a quarter of an hour to kill, so he headed for Main Street, lengthening his stride slowly to get as much movement as he could in his back. He got to the top of Main Street and felt the knot easing: he should be fine for a boogie when the dancing started. It was a much happier Harry who took up his position by the supermarket and waited for his lift.

Instead of something small and nippy, the car that pulled up belonged to his Principal: five metres of Bavarian engineering and enough power to pull the 555 bus if it broke down. The driver's window lowered, and the young woman looked down at him with a professional smile. 'In the back. Other side.'

He walked round the front of the car with as much dignity as he could and approached the rear of the X7. He held the door open and bowed. 'My Lord.'

'Well met, Harry. In you get.' As soon as he'd fastened his seat belt they were on their way, roaring down the Lake Road and out into the countryside.

'Thank you for coming in person. I'm honoured,' said Harry.

His Principal was dressed for the outdoors, not for tonight's celebration. He'd taken off his boots, but mud and other things were spreading all over the leather seats. Harry was sure he could smell blood. And probably guts. Yes, definitely guts.

'A pleasure,' said his Principal. 'It means we can get the boring business out of the way. Please don't tell me you're having second thoughts about tomorrow.'

'No, my Lord. I just want to maximise our chances. All I want is a lift to the lake.'

'A lift? What on earth for?'

'My Lord knows that I don't drive, and I don't want anyone to know where I'm going or asking questions. It will be the early hours, after all.'

'Easily done.' He touched the shimmering line of light that ran through the driver's seat belt. It turned from silver to red, and the acoustic in the car changed as the Silence dissolved. 'Harry needs a lift tomorrow night.'

'Where and when, sir?' said the driver.

Harry answered her. 'Bridge House at one am. If everything goes to plan, can you be ready to pick me up about six or seven?'

'Certainly, sir. Do you need anything special?'

'No. Just a lift. And it's an invisible journey, obviously.'

'Of course.'

The Principal touched the Charm and it flashed back to silver. 'Good. Bring it straight to me when you've got it.' He shifted in the seat and more organic matter dropped off his coat.

Harry forced himself not to edge away. 'Has my Lord had a good day in the field?'

'Excellent. Set me up perfectly for Samhain. Now, Harry, there's a gorgeous young filly I want to introduce you to tonight. From out of town. She should be right up your street.'

Harry doubted that, but he had no choice in the matter. Not anymore.

'Thank you, my Lord.'

'A pleasure. Excuse me a moment. I need to check a few things. This new car has Wi-Fi – amazing what they can do these days.'

The Principal took out his phone and started to look something up. Harry turned and tried to look out of the window. They'd left the town, and the lake was on the other side. He couldn't see a bloody thing.

## 5 — *Sleight of Hand*

We left an empty place at the end nearest the door, and as we helped ourselves to food, everyone put a little something on the plate in memory and invitation. Some people spoke a name, some didn't. A more composed Hannah placed bread and spoke in Yiddish, saying *Mikhail* at the end. Eseld dropped a handful of walnuts. 'I'll see you again, Dad. One day.'

For half a second, I wondered if Myfanwy would honour Adaryn, but she chose her great aunt instead. Mina completed the round in Gujarati and invited us to tuck in. There was plenty of food, plenty of drink for the others (I was on a strict limit), and it was a relaxed and happy bunch who enjoyed the meal together.

Before Mina went to get changed, she joined me outside with Scout. 'It doesn't feel right for you to be out here on your own,' she said, shivering. 'It does feel very different tonight. Even when the Morrigan came to visit, I didn't feel uneasy. Tonight is different.'

I knew what she meant. Without knowing why, I got the feeling that there was something lurking outside the pools of light from the windows. 'I had a message today. From the house.'

'The House? Is that a code for something.'

I shook my head. 'When I finished making the Ley line, the house had a message for me. It wants me to change the name back to *Elvenham Grange*. I have no idea why.'

She looked at me as if I'd gone mad. Madder than usual. 'And did your house give you a reason for this?'

'It didn't use words. I just got the impression that it wasn't happy. Not in an end-of-the-world kind of unhappy. Just that it wants the old name back.'

'It? Not he or she?'

I shrugged. 'Let's go in. We can ask Myfanwy later – she spends more time here than we do.'

We walked back inside, and Mina said, 'Myvvy says that she can't leave the village at all. Not for a scan, not for ante-natal appointments, not even for the birth, and there is no emergency clause. That is very harsh.'

That was news to me. 'It is very harsh. I'm due to meet the Occult Council in December. I shall make a point of asking.'

We kissed at the bottom of the stairs, and Mina scampered up them to get changed. She'd made sure all the guests knew that the dress code for tonight was smart, not glamorous, and she was back in minutes wearing a red bodycon dress. 'You look gorgeous, love.'

She swung her hair round to her right shoulder and tilted her head. 'When you were under a magickal obligation not to lie to me, I should have taken more advantage. I'd really like to know whether my arse looks too skinny in jeans.'

I snorted. 'Just because I couldn't lie, it doesn't mean that my opinion is worth anything. And you're forgetting that I think you always look good.'

'Hah! How convenient for you. I shall wear a sack tomorrow, just to spite you.'

'So long as it's not a brown sack. Brown really isn't your colour.'

A voice came from upstairs. 'I'll say, Mina. Red is absolutely your colour.'

It was Tamsin, coming down the stairs a few paces ahead of Chris. 'And blue is yours,' said Mina. 'Where did you get that top?'

'How much of that Inkwell Bitter is left?' asked Chris. 'I could get used to that.'

'Don't worry. We can always send out for more.'

Everyone was prompt. The girls had all gone for bright colours except Hannah. She may have been in black and white, but she'd bought a long silk shirt especially for tonight, and I knew that because Mina had told me.

When it came to the bridge tournament, Mina sat out the actual games because she's too good and because that left us twelve players, perfect for three tables. Only the mundane competitors were allowed to shuffle the cards, and partners were to be drawn by lot. Mina took a place in front of the fire and gathered us round her for the draw. Chris had been talking to Kenver in the corner, and I'd presumed that it was some business connected with Geomancy, because they don't have a lot in common otherwise. Mina had a bag with all the female names in it, and we men were to draw one each; the two women left would form the last pair.

Chris normally stands at the back of everything. Not only is he taller than everyone, he's usually quite unassuming. Tonight he was lurking on Mina's left, and she instinctively turned to him to make the first draw. He fished in the bag and gave it a good swish. The only rule was that if we drew our wives, girlfriends or sisters, we had to put them back.

Chris drew out a Scrabble tile and made a great fuss of presenting it to the room: E for Eseld. Because of the angle I stood at, and my enhanced eyesight, I saw him palm a letter to Kenver while he showed off his own selection. Kenver drew S for Sofía.

We paired up and started playing, and I forgot about Chris. I'd drawn Lucy and had to be on my top game. I've only met her briefly before tonight, and I am very conscious that Tom is devoted to her. Lucy has had a lot to deal with this year, and being thrust into the world of magick hasn't helped. Being a total beginner at bridge is only the latest in a long line of challenges for her.

The alcohol helped, as did her instinct for risk. She is an entrepreneur, after all, and tomorrow she and Mina are going to be looking at the accounts of a coffee shop in Cairndale. We had fun, she took the mickey out of my bald patch (and my shirt, and my shoes at one point), and we didn't disgrace ourselves. We didn't reach the final, either, and everyone gathered round to watch Tom and Myfanwy play against Rachael and Hannah.

The only pairing that hadn't really hit it off was Ben and Tamsin. Not only did they have nothing in common, most of Tamsin's stories revolved around her studies with the Fae, and Ben was too polite to tell her that his introduction to magick was watching a Fae noble pull a man's heart out through his chest and snacking on it afterwards.

Rachael was force-fed bridge from an early age. Mother thought it would teach her all sorts of abstract skills, and who's to say she was wrong? Naturally, Rachael rebelled against that and took up tennis instead, but she knows her way around the bidding systems. Tom and Myfanwy were soon in trouble, but that didn't seem to bother them. Myfanwy was simply enjoying having someone new to talk to, and Tom is interested in learning about magick from as many angles as possible. He's also a very good listener, a vital quality if you spend much time with Myfanwy.

While Rachael was shuffling, the audience carried on their conversations. Eseld was making some joke about Chris having trouble letting his hair down – metaphorically as well as literally. He is *Baldy Kelly*, after all.

'It's a question of degree,' said Chris. 'Not everyone needs to drink like a Mowbray to enjoy themselves.'

'What are you trying to say?' said Eseld. 'Kenver is a model of sobriety.'

'Not tonight,' said Sofía from the other side. 'He keeps giving me the wine.'

Chris went to tick off his fingers. 'Cador has told me he's been drunk in court on at least three occasions. Your father had hollow legs and could drink for England, never mind Cornwall, and as for you, remember what happened the night before Boston?'

There was a sharp intake of breath from my left. Tamsin was not a happy bunny, and Chris hadn't noticed. I think he'll find out later, judging by the pursed lips and daggers that his wife was giving him.

Mina leaned in to cut the cards. 'And now Hannah will deal. One more win and you're champions.'

Hannah dealt. Tom and Myfanwy lost, and Mina came forward with a small trophy. 'Congratulations! You are the first winners of the Elvenham bridge cup. You may also be the last. Conrad, get the Champagne.'

When I handed Hannah her glass of celebration fizz, I kept hold of the stem and said, 'So, ma'am, if not Saffron, then who's drawn the short straw of babysitting me?' I released the glass and tried to keep a straight face while she gave me a smile of evil pleasure.

'I had a very strange phone call on Friday from an unexpected quarter. You'll find out next week. Cheers, Conrad.'

There was no point pushing it. Even Mina tried on my behalf, because she understands how important it is that I get a trustworthy partner who knows magick better than I do. The only hint Mina got was that she should pack something glamorous for Monday.

'Why? Where are we going?'

'Hannah likes Tom Morton,' said Mina, 'and she likes Lucy. They discovered they have something in common. And no, Conrad, I have no idea what she is talking about.'

There was a lot of drinking and relaxed conversation after the formalities of the bridge tournament. Ben and Myfanwy were the first to leave, because they had to be at Ben's parents tomorrow. Shortly afterwards, Tamsin led Chris upstairs. I'm not sure whether she wanted to get him into bed or to have a row. Both probably, and this was a point I put to Eseld when I found her outside.

'Tell me about Boston,' I said.

'Shit. I hoped no one would hear that, or that they'd forget about it.'

'Tammy certainly heard it. I don't think she's going to forget.'

'You and your bloody helicopter. If you weren't flying tomorrow, you'd be drunk like everyone else.'

'Technically, it's the Mowbray helicopter, and don't change the subject. Boston.'

She looked around to see if anyone was coming and looked up to check whether Chris and Tammy's room was on this side. It isn't.

'You didn't know her before she transmigrated. I did. Chris and Dad worked together a lot, and I worked with Dad and Ethan.' She shook her head. 'As you know, I was pining for Ethan, and I didn't always behave responsibly.'

'So I've heard.'

'Yeah, well. Tamsin used to look down her nose at me for some reason. Fair enough – she'd worked hard to get her place at Salomon's House, but she thought I was just a spoilt rich kid who flew around on daddy's coattails.'

I thought there was a degree of truth in that. I also thought that it wasn't what she needed to hear. 'Mmm,' I said instead.

'Then she transmigrated and dropped out of the picture. You know she was in care, right?'

The fourteen year old "Melody Richardson" had been taken into care by mundane social services after Melody's mother attacked her, and the Cloister Court had washed its hands of the whole thing, leaving Tammy/Melody to obey the mundane law or face serious consequences. The same went for

Chris: while Tammy/Melody was under sixteen, he had to stay well away from her.

'Chris told me.'

'So, one night before a job in Boston, we were staying at this hotel in the country, and I got a bit more wasted than normal. When Ethan knocked me back for the umpteenth time, I gave Chris a full-on game of tonsil hockey. And someone filmed it and posted it on Facebook. It was a Mage-friendly hotel, and there were a few too many people there with an axe to grind.' She shrugged. 'From what I remember – which is not a lot – Chris didn't join in very much. The video didn't show that, though, and he had to take me to bed. He's tried to make a joke of it, but Tamsin thought he was playing away.'

'And she still does?'

'I don't know. I think things are worse now that I'm teaching at the Invisible College. I've got my freedom and my feet under the table at Salomon's House. It must be hard on her. Lucy Berardi's jaw nearly fell off when Tamsin made a reference to the size of Chris's manhood during the bridge lesson this afternoon.'

'Ouch. That must have been excruciating.'

'Mina made a joke about it and we moved on to underbidding. Or something.' She yawned. 'Thanks for a great night, Conrad. See you tomorrow.'

When Mina and I finally got into bed, I told her what Eseld had said and what I'd overheard.

She curled up into my arms and made herself comfortable. 'I saw the look on Eseld's face. She wasn't surprised at what Tammy said, only that she'd said it. Eseld was well aware of Chris Kelly's capacity before Tammy opened her mouth. Night night.'

'There you go, Harry,' said the server, putting his drink on the polished wood at the side of the blackjack table.

'Cheers. I'm ready for that.' He was also ready to loosen his bow tie, but that wasn't going to happen while he was playing the dealer.

No. Not *playing* the dealer. He really was the dealer, and he'd already made a lot of money for his Principal. He took a long drink and paused with the glass still on his lips. Someone had joined the table, taking the place of a

Witch who'd have some explaining to do in the morning after blowing the holiday fund.

He didn't want to turn round because he was scared it might be her and scared that it might not. He put down the glass of apple and elderflower cider and took a deep breath. He pressed his hands to the table to steady himself and turned round.

'Hello Harry.'

It was her, and it was a very good version of her, the untidy brown hair piled up on her head, with strands already escaping and curling down. She brushed some away from her eyes, and blinked at him with those thick lashes. The left side of her mouth twitched up and she ran her tongue over her lips. 'I'm ready to play. Are you?'

She looked down at the small pile of chips in front of her, and Harry saw the thin chain of gold that disappeared into her cleavage. She felt him looking and lifted it out, patting the golden horseshoe charm. 'It's been a while,' she said.

It had been a lifetime to Harry. A lifetime of devotion and desire punctuated by deep bouts of mourning and despair for what he'd lost and what he'd become. And now she was back again. How long for this time? He didn't care. She was here tonight.

'Come on,' said the man to his left. 'Are you dealing or flirting?'

There was no point bantering with the man – his urge for repartee was in direct proportion to his stack of chips, and round about now the man's sense of humour was at roughly Stasi levels.

'Everyone in,' said Harry. 'Here they come.'

When it came to her cards, they locked eyes again, just for a second. She lifted the horseshoe to her mouth and she kissed it before he dealt her hand. Memories shuddered through him and the rest of the cards came out of the shoe on autopilot.

# 6 — Home and Away

I do understand that there are people who say, 'I am not a morning person.' I accept that these people exist. I just don't know why.

'Is the coffee on, Conrad?' said Eseld. She is the only other morning person currently in residence at Elvenham. 'And why are you staring at that plate?'

'My offering has gone. Just mine.'

The place we'd set for those departed looked exactly as it had when I locked up last night, except for the gap between Mina's pair of khandvi rolls and Myfanwy's Welsh cake. Hang on. There were two Welsh cakes. And three khandvi. 'Someone's eaten the Single Gloucester cheese and a bit of the dry snacks. And I was the last to bed.'

'Give me coffee. Now.'

I gave her coffee and we adjourned outside.

Eseld put on a grave expression. 'I can think of three explanations, Conrad. First, you were visited by Spirits. Second, you have very sophisticated mice at Elvenham, as befits the chic and sophisticated mistress of the house.'

'No need to lay it on with a trowel, Eseld.'

'Hey! I just want to be loved by everyone. It's because my mother betrayed me and I need to fit in, so I overcompensate.'

'Is your mum still Persona Non Grata?'

Eseld gave me the Mowbray death stare. 'I didn't tell you the third reason, did I?'

She hasn't spoken to her mother for nearly twenty years, not even when Isolde came to Pellacombe. A lot of people thought Eseld would extend an olive branch when her father died, but no. 'Is there anything she could do to make you open the door?' I asked.

The sun peeked round the end of the outhouse and made her shield her eyes. When she turned to avoid it and lowered her hand, there were tears. Biological defence mechanism or a display of emotion? I've never been able to tell with Eseld.

'If she left the Daughters and admitted she was wrong, I might agree to accept her apology. We both know that's not gonna happen.' She paused to see if I was done with the subject. I was. 'So if it's not Spirits or mice, my money is on Kenver. He often gets up in the night and snacks. Do you want me to show you that saddle before breakfast?'

'Please.'

We left our mugs on the upturned barrel and wandered to the stables. 'Talking of Kenver, he texted me in the night. Wants to sit in on the Fire Games rehearsals today and see if he has anything to offer. That's unusually helpful of him.'

Eseld was helping Sofía to develop a sort of magickal entertainment known as a *Fête du Feu* – Fire Games in English. Rachael had somehow managed to infiltrate the project, and now Kenver wanted to get on board. Hmm. Likely story.

'He wants to help because he finds my sister unusually attractive. Has he had many girlfriends?'

She stopped. 'Are you sure?'

I decided not to mention Chris's cheat with the bridge draw. Too complicated. 'I saw him looking at her. I know smitten when I see it.'

She shook her head. 'No. He hasn't many relationships. When you're the heir to Pellacombe, it's a bit like being minor royalty. I think he's been too shy to ask them out, and Dad kept a close eye on him. Shall I keep him away?'

'I've been told not to be over-protective. Sofía can handle herself.'

'That means you'll be on your own today.'

'That means I'll be everyone's butler.'

The Fire Games crew were rehearsing, taking advantage of the time together and access to a proper house of magick. Myfanwy and Ben were at his parents; Chris and Tamsin were going to a couple's spa session in Cheltenham, while Mina and Lucy were crunching numbers, as were Hannah and Tom in a way. Hannah had decided to give Tom a personal briefing on Project Talpa, including her brush with the Revenant, something she still wasn't willing to share with me.

'I'll get Evenstar out,' I said. 'You get the saddle.'

'No need to get her out yet,' said Eseld, going into the tack room. 'I can show you the basics with it on the rack.'

I followed her and helped her clear some of the other gear out of the way. Although a thing of beauty, the saddle is distinctly odd to look at if you know your pommel from your cantle, and the oddest thing is the horn – the bit sticking up at the front. It's where you tie the rope when you've just lassoed a steer. Not a lot of that goes on in England, and that's why it's a feature of Western saddles.

'Have you had a proper look at the stirrups?' she asked.

I hadn't, so I bent down to examine them. They were steel, like an English saddle not a Western one, and was that engraving in them? Yes. I ran my fingers along the arch of the left hand stirrup and felt the magick. For the first time in my experience of Artefacts, the sensation was cold, not hot. I touched the right hand one and it was the opposite, nicely warm with Lux. 'Is there a circuit in here?' I suggested. 'From left to right.'

'Pretty much, except that it goes up through the pommel, into the front cinch, round the horse and out through the right. The horn is a circuit breaker, and when you want to see or move into Asgard, you complete the circuit.'

'Asgard?'

She had that half-amused smile on her lips again. 'You've met the Allfather. You should know what Asgard is.'

I didn't respond. If you're not aware, Asgard is the home of the gods. You get there by climbing up the rainbow. She knew I knew that.

She patted the seat of the saddle. 'This little piece of magick is called *Sleipnir's Hooves*, and it's supposed to have been the Allfather's gift to a particularly attractive Swedish Witch so that she could pop up to Asgard and see him. Or that he could pop down to Uppsala to see her. Accounts vary. Some say she stole it off him, some say she was an evil spirit in disguise.' She looked up. 'You could ask him.'

'If I wanted to get up his nose, I can think of better things to ask.'

'That's gross. Divine nostrils. Ugh. You've been very lucky living here, Conrad, in that no one's tried to rob you. I don't know, but this saddle could be the most valuable Artefact you own. In money terms.'

Eseld had pretended that giving me Evenstar was the gift, and that the saddle was a bonus. It was clearly the other way round. She must have her reasons, I suppose.

She fiddled with some of the straps. 'You may not be able to use this. If it was so easy to plane-shift, all Mages would do it. And of course, it's dangerous.'

'Differential stabilisation?'

'You could say that. Or you could say *Getting lost between worlds*. Either way, the medical impact is like being hit by an express train.'

'I won't tell Mina what I'm doing then.'

She moved towards the door. 'Best not. And don't tell me either.' She said that with her back to me, so I'm not sure if she was being serious. 'I need more coffee,' she added, and that made two of us.

On the way back, I ran my mind over our guests. None of the magickal guests would dream of taking someone else's offering from the plate, nor would Rachael or Tom Morton. I suppose Lucy might be a secret midnight snacker, but I didn't think so. It was so *deliberate* – cheese and something to go with it. I made a mental note to warn Myfanwy.

I didn't get to ride Evenstar properly that day. I did manage to try the saddle and take her for a trot round the paddock, but Eseld had warned me against trying to shift anywhere but near the well. Apart from that, I was busy fetching, carrying and tidying up. And packing. Lots of packing.

Tom and Lucy were staying on until the evening so that Tom could question Myfanwy, but everyone else was clearing out in the afternoon. Chris and Tamsin returned from their spa with the expected healthy glow and were shoving cases in their car when an unmarked minibus turned up. Chris saw who was in it and dashed to open the door. First out was his mother.

Oma Bridget is a force in magick, and I went to welcome her properly. She kissed her son, ignored her daughter-in-law and spoke to me. 'You might want to help Erin get out of the back. She's rather the worse for wear.'

I clambered into the bus and found three sleeping children and a comatose Enscriber clutching a bucket. Oh dear.

Erin's complexion was about the same colour as her top – spring green. 'Come on, Erin. We've got a helicopter to catch.'

'Eurrgh. No. No way. Can't.'

'In that case, I'll get the Constable and you can tell her why you're not coming.'

'Go away, Conrad. I'm comfy here.'

I unfastened her seatbelt and dragged her out of the bus. She's used to it. When she was out, I called to Myfanwy. 'Sort her out and get her packed, will you? We've got half an hour.'

Myfanwy shook her head and propelled her friend round to the kitchen. Chris got into the bus and started to unfasten the child seats, and Oma Bridget forced herself to talk to Tamsin.

'Erin was very good with them,' she said. 'Right up to the moment she started drinking. I decided I'd better come back with them myself. Just in case.'

'Thank you, Oma,' said Tamsin. 'I hope the celebration went well.'

'It did. And you?'

'Lovely, thank you. Conrad and Mina have made us most welcome.'

Ouch. Could this get any more awkward? Oma Bridget decided not to push it any further and turned to me, walking a step away from Tamsin.

'Karina Kent appeared yesterday.'

'Oh? How's her leg?'

The reason I need a new partner is that the last one pretty much self-destructed and ended up with a badly broken leg. And when she's recovered, she's going to be on a charge.

'Humbled is the word, I think,' said Oma. 'She says she has a new understanding of the world. We shall see. She also had a message for you.'

'One she couldn't deliver herself? She still has my number.'

'She wants you to listen and believes that you'll listen to me. She hopes that one day you will allow her to visit, to talk about what happened to her mother. She respects you, Conrad.'

If you don't speak diplomatic code, I'll translate for you: "Give the girl a chance." Karina's mother was murdered when she was very young. Who knows, maybe cold case work would be less dangerous. Ha. Who am I kidding?

'Of course, Oma.'

Mina had appeared and made namaste. 'Would you and your driver like some tea?'

Oma studied Mina for a moment. It's not personal or racist, it's just that powerful Mages find it hard to accept that a mundane person can walk around with a throbbing magickal tattoo. 'You're most kind, Ms Desai, but we have to get straight back. Another time, I hope, and you are always welcome at the Foresters' Hall.'

There was bowing and goodbyes, then a manoeuvre to get the minibus out and Maggie Pearce's limousine in. Eseld had kindly offered Maggie's services to get us to Cheltenham airport, and Ben was going to follow with the extra luggage.

'Good weekend?' I asked Maggie. She was as smart as ever in her uniform, but there were definitely rings around the eyes.

'Oh yes, Mr Clarke, and don't worry – I breathalysed myself before I set off.'

I started humping the cases. 'Did you get to the exhibition?'

She gave Eseld a sly grin and raised her voice. 'We did. It was a retrospective called *Re-imaging the Phallus*. Miss Mowbray would have loved it.'

Eseld can take it and give it back. She peered into the boot and said, 'I'm glad you enjoyed it. It's such a shame that you were so busy. It meant you didn't have time to do any baking.'

Maggie frowned. 'Strange girl. Whatever can she mean?'

She meant that Maggie's baked goods have the texture and durability of Stonehenge, yet for some reason Maggie thinks she should be on the Great British Bake-Off.

When we got everything sorted, the last one out was Hannah, dressed more for a polar expedition than a short chopper ride to Chester. She looked enviously at the Mowbray limousine. 'It's a shame they can't give me a lift all the way to Manchester,' she said. 'I am only going on this flight to prove that I'm not scared, Conrad.'

'Yes, Boss. When we get to the airfield, you can have a choice of seats. You can sit next to Scout or you can sit next to Erin and her bucket.'

I must start learning Yiddish. It would help me know just how deeply into her bad books I've got, and hence how far I need to crawl to get out.

The drive to Cheltenham airstrip, the flight to Chester and the transfer to Middlebarrow Haven were all incident free (unless you count Scout getting out of his travel cage and climbing into the Boss's lap as an incident). It was when we dumped the cases that I nearly blew a fuse.

We were going straight out again, to Manchester, for dinner with the Manchester Alchemical Society, staying at a hotel in the city centre.

'What have you put in here?' I asked Mina when I hefted her overnight bag.

'Hannah said to pack for two nights, remember? And to go elegant tonight and glamorous tomorrow. Not that you know what either of those really means.'

I dropped the bag back on the bed and limped out of the Deputy's Suite to the principal guest room. Knock knock.

'Boss?'

'What?'

'Where are we going tomorrow and why?'

She opened the door a crack. 'I suppose I can tell you now that you've flown me here safely. We're going to Barton Park.'

I frowned. 'The football ground? What on earth for?'

She grinned. 'For Trafford Rangers versus Tottenham Hotspur. My second cousin twice removed has an executive box.'

I don't hate football, it's just that it doesn't interest me. If there's no cricket on TV I'll watch rugby, but that's about it. The only conceivable reason for going was Princess Birkdale, whose husband is a football superstar. 'Is this about Conan Doyle?'

'Don't be silly. He plays for Merseyside. He wouldn't be seen dead at Barton Park.'

She was having so much fun that it was obvious I wouldn't get a straight answer.

'Scout will pine for me if I'm not back tomorrow.'

'Rubbish. Evie dotes on him. You're going, and that's that.'

'I will get you back for this. Ma'am.'

'Back? Back? This is me getting you back for making me have dinner with Tamsin Kelly. Now leave me in peace, we have to go again soon.'

The dinner at the sumptuous building of the Manchester Alchemical Society (Malchs) was purely business, though still very enjoyable. I have two gigs coming up at their place, and we had plans to make. Tomorrow is a dress rehearsal for the Warden election hustings, and later in the month I'm due to open the Occult Commission into the status of Dual Natured Creatures, also known as the W*r*w*lf Committee. See? My new job as Deputy Constable is a lot less exciting than it sounds.

The only thing of any interest at the dinner was a sly dig at Hannah from one of the Manchester Mages. I raised my eyebrows and she put her cutlery down to explain.

'When you became Deputy Constable, Conrad, you were also proclaimed Lord Guardian of the North. I wasn't.'

'Sorry? I know you only did the job for a few months, and I thought they were the same thing.'

'They're not. You are both my deputy and the anointed Guardian. They are separate jobs, and it's up to Nimue to appoint a Guardian. I was the first Deputy not to be Guardian for a long time. I thought it was because I'm a woman. Apparently not, because she was happy enough to make me the Bearer of Caledfwlch as well as the Crown making me Peculier Constable. So there you go, Conrad. Pass those roast potatoes, they're delicious and flying always makes me hungry.'

## *Ms Cordelia Kennedy*

The house looked the same, even in the dark.

Even with no lights shining from inside and only the dim bulb over the front door providing illumination, she could feel the house's presence from the back of the taxi. Hedda shifted next to her and said, 'This is it, dear. If you get out now, there's no going back.'

Cordelia gave a bitter smile, invisible in the dark. 'I think I burnt my bridges this afternoon.'

The old Witch put her hand on Cordelia's. 'Why do you think I came with you? They won't dare accept your renunciation without me. We can turn round and go back. It's not too late.'

Cordelia's voice was barely a whisper. 'Yes it is. It's been too late for a while now.'

Hedda gave her hand a squeeze. 'Then may the Goddess always walk by your side and guide you.' She released her hand. 'You can cancel the Silence now.'

Hedda had lost her magick when a stroke had burnt through her brain, and now she needed others to do even the simplest magickal tasks. When

Cordelia had cancelled the Silence, Hedda spoke up to the driver. 'She's staying. You can get the bags.'

Their driver was an overweight man at the end of middle age. He looked like he hadn't got out of the car once since he'd got in it hours ago.

'I'll get them,' said Cordelia.

'Nonsense,' said Hedda. 'You're going back to a world where you have to get men to do as much for you as possible. And if he wants a tip, he'll jump to it.'

'I am still here,' said the driver.

'What for?'

With a sigh, he got out and got the bags and put them near the door. 'Nice place. Family?'

'Sort of,' said Cordelia. 'Thank you.'

The driver wheezed as he got back in the taxi and started the engine. Cordelia wanted desperately to give Hedda a hug, but she'd been forbidden, *because I can't bear to think of you leaving*. She stood waiting and watching until the silence of a Somerset night had descended, then she turned to get the key.

Rick's final message of yesterday had been sent with the best of intentions:

*Of course you can stay in the Old Rectory tomorrow. The guest room's made up, and I'll leave some food. Key's in the old place. Facetime me when you're there. Kids will love it. Happy Samhain. Rick. X.*

It had still cut her like a knife: she was going to be a guest in the home they'd made together, and she had been invited to video call her children on holiday because she couldn't face being with them for a week. She shivered, found the key and let herself in. She grabbed her bags and headed straight for the guest room.

Rick had left out a fan heater, in case she didn't want to heat the whole building. Of course he had. Rick had always been at his most thoughtful when she wasn't there. And when there wasn't a pretty young woman in front of him. When she saw what was on the dressing table, she burst into tears.

There were two envelopes with her name on. One was stuffed with twenty pound notes – at least a thousand pounds worth. The other had a card with a picture of a spectacular dawn breaking over countryside and the words *New Horizons* above it. The message inside that had finished her off. *I'm always here for you. Whatever you need.*

And he really believed that. He really believed that what they'd had together could be recreated and improved. He really believed that he understood her. Wrong, wrong, wrong. Only Raven understood her.

A bath. She needed a bath, and for that she needed hot water. She slipped out of the guest room like a ghost in her own home and turned on the boiler (water only). When it roared into life, she flitted from room to room, looking to see what had changed.

Not much. A lick of paint here or there. She winced when she realised that two of the pieces she'd bought had disappeared. Had Rick chosen the new look? One of his flings? A professional? It was too tasteful to have been Rick's idea, and he wouldn't have let another woman get her feet so far under the table. A professional, then. She looked behind the jars in the kitchen: he still had the same cleaner, and he still hadn't twigged to the woman's shortcomings.

She made herself a cup of tea and took it back to the now much warmer guest room. Would the Daughters have met yet? Probably. In that case, she was no longer Cordelia, 11th of Ash; she was just Ms Cordelia Kennedy, a private citizen in the world of magick. Time to move on. She wouldn't achieve anything by sitting on the bed staring at Rick's card.

She opened one case and took the black silk scarf out of a box. She arranged the scarf in a spiral in front of Rick's card and got out her phone. She turned off the fan heater to get some quiet and made the first call.

'Hello?' said a cultured but very young voice.

'Is that Saffron Hawkins? This is Cordelia Kennedy.'

There was a hesitation while Saffron put two and two together. 'Oh. Sorry. Daughter of Ash, greetings. Is that right?'

'No and no. Mostly because I quit the Daughters today.'

'Oh. Right.'

'Don't worry, Saffron, I only want to pick your brains. I'm seeing the Boss tomorrow. About a commission.'

'OMG, Cordelia. Seriously?'

'I'm afraid so. There are always vacancies in the King's Watch.'

Saffron laughed. 'Some of us chose to join, you know. And had to go through an assault course to get there. Well, welcome aboard. How can I help?'

'Hannah is assigning me to work with Conrad from Tuesday, but he doesn't know yet. Could you keep it under your hat. Please.'

'Of course, though I'd love to see his face. You must have done something to upset the Boss for that to happen. What did you do? Confess to being an Arsenal supporter?'

Cordelia had in fact approached the Constable and had asked to work with Conrad Clarke, but she wasn't going to tell anyone else that. It was one of her many secrets. 'He can't be that bad, can he?'

'Yes.'

'Go on then, what do I need to know? Confidentially, of course. If I'm not disturbing you.'

'No problem.' Saffron blew out air and paused. 'You know his word is binding, right?'

'I got that when we were all in Cornwall.'

'Two things, I think. First, if he gives you an order – and you'll know when he's giving you an order – just do it. Your life could depend on it. Otherwise, he really is open to suggestions.'

'Good.'

'And when it comes to magick, he has more power than he thinks he does. He just has no idea about how to use it, or about the magickal life in general. He's getting better, but slowly.'

'Right.'

'As for everything else, and you can tell him I said this: you get used to it. Except the weird shit. No one gets used to that.'

*'You get used to it?* That's all?'

'That's all.'

'What about Elvenham House? It sounds like a cross between an army barracks and a girls' boarding school.'

Saffron laughed again. 'You'll get used to that, too. Seriously, everyone is mostly lovely, except Myfanwy, who is totally lovely. And you'll fit in much better if you join the cricket team.'

'I don't think that's going to happen. You said they're *mostly* lovely.'

'And they are. I'll let you make your own mind up.'

That was one of the few things she'd picked up in Cornwall: the women of Elvenham loved to gossip, but only to each other. To outsiders, they closed ranks. For the moment, Cordelia was an outsider.

'Thanks, Saffron. That's been a great help.'

'Any time. I'll no doubt see you soon. Oh, one more thing: practise your saluting. He likes that.'

Cordelia disconnected and stared at her phone. If she left it any longer, either the kids would be tucked up in their sleeping bags, or worse still, they'd be sitting waiting for mummy to call them, getting more and more upset and getting on Rick's nerves. Not that he'd say anything.

She pressed the Facetime button and her eldest answered straight away.

'Hi Mum. What have you done to your hair?'

She fingered the loose tresses and forced a smile. 'Needs a wash, babe. I'm going for a bath in a bit. Now, how's the tent? Have you got soaked yet? Have you pushed your brother in the lake?'

Her daughter turned her head to the side. 'Why are you in our spare room?'

She heard Rick's voice from off screen. 'I'll tell you after, okay? Why don't you tell Mummy about the otters, yeah?'

Harry stepped out from the shadows next to the Bridge House and climbed into the little Suzuki that would take him over the hills and far away. If only. There was no CCTV in this part of town, and he trusted the driver to do her stuff and keep all trace of his journey off the official record.

'You know where we're going, right?' he asked, just to be sure.

'West side of the Wolf's Lake. I presume you know exactly where.'

She'd used the old name for Ullswater: *the Wolf's Lake*. He didn't know if that meant she was relaxed in his company or whether she couldn't be bothered to mind her language: she wasn't supposed to use the old names with people like Harry.

'There's a couple of options. Please tell me you're not taking the Struggle to get there.'

She put the car in gear and gave him a huge grin. 'Of course I am. Too good a chance to miss, and besides, the other road is a good twenty minutes longer. Fasten your seatbelt and don't be a wuss.'

He didn't just fasten his seat belt, he closed his eyes. She took it slowly out of the town, and all too soon they'd left the last house behind and he heard the engine roar as she changed down for the ascent.

The Struggle is a road that leads out of the Windermere valley and is about wide enough for one and a half cars. If you're lucky. It's also steep and full of blind corners. Yes, it was one o'clock on Monday morning, but all it would take is an offcomer of a van driver with a dodgy Satnav...

She started throwing the car into bends, and he had to open his eyes. The stone walls made a corridor of death, and he started scanning the horizon for oncoming headlights. This was not how he wanted to die.

They escaped death somehow, and she slowed down as they approached the Kirkstone Pass Inn. Then she put a Silence on the car, and may the Goddess preserve us, *she killed the lights.*

'Stop squealing,' she said. 'You wanted an invisible journey, didn't you?'

He didn't dare to speak until the Inn was behind them and the lights were back on. At least the road down to Glenridding was wider. 'Yes, but not like that. I expected a blackout Glamour, not blacked out headlights!'

'I'm saving my Lux for the lake road. We'll be there soon, so make your mind up.'

'It's at least one mile beyond Glenridding. Go slower and I'll tell you when to stop.'

They approached the village of Glenridding and he saw the first streetlight since leaving the town.

'An Audi, I think,' she said. She took one hand off the wheel and made a circle round her head. For a couple of minutes, any insomniac tourist or local resident would distinctly remember an Audi passing slowly and carefully through the village.

And then they were out of the light and pushing through the darkness with the flat sheet of Ullswater occasionally visible on the right. 'Slow down. Just round this bend. There should be room to pull in by the gate.'

She did as he asked and stopped by a private boat dock. This time she killed the engine as well as the lights. He peered through her window at the vessels tied up along the jetty. 'This will do. There's no houseboats in tonight. Wait five minutes in case there's a wild camper.'

'Right. You reckon about four or five hours?'

'Yeah. Are you going back?'

'Home? No. I'm going to try and beat my own record for getting back to Borrowdale. Just for fun. If I don't answer when you're finished, it's because I'm dead in a ditch. Try ringing twice, just in case.'

Her voice combined excitement with matter of fact fatality. It was the creepiest thing about her, and there were lots of creepy things to pick.

He opened the door. 'Thanks for the lift. See you later.'

'Good luck. May the Goddess go with you.'

'And with you. I don't know which of us needs her more.'

He climbed out of the car and climbed slowly over the gate. A few years ago, he would have leapt it like a stunt man. Not anymore. His back muscles had survived last night's workout, and he'd taken anti-inflammatories, just in case. He crept down the path and along the jetty, checking every boat for a light or a sleeping bag. He would have had a bigger choice of boats at the hire dock in Glenridding, and he'd chosen this place for two reasons. First it was totally deserted. Second, and more importantly, it was a hell of a lot closer to his target.

He selected a nice, flat-bottomed dinghy and quickly had it in the water. It would have been a lot easier if the sky had been as clear as it had been for poker night, but you can't have everything. He placed his rucksack in the bottom and prepared to work his shoulders. He could have used magick to assist, if he'd been willing to run the risk. Not tonight. He braced his feet and dug the oars into the water.

He didn't miss the target by much – just a hundred metres or so, and it was easy to find a bit of shingle to beach the boat. He wasn't worried about the crunch of stones: the trees would absorb the sound. He pulled the boat well on to land and set off through the trees, following his nose at first. When he came to cross the well-used footpath, he stopped and considered.

The target was up there somewhere, on the lower shoulder of Birk Fell. That was the primary target. If he was too late, if the family had unearthed the treasure already, he'd have to try the Lodge, and that would be another night's work. He got out a torch and started to thread his way through the trees. He kept the torch off for now and tried to move as quietly as he could.

Harry didn't have a huge amount of magick, and that made it safer in so many ways. When he was a good half a mile from the lake, he stopped and opened his Sight. There was a flicker of Lux to the left and something more to the right. He unzipped his fleece and put his hand in his shirt to find the little pebble that he used to connect to the earth. He squatted down and put his left hand into the moss, digging for the soil with his fingers. When he emptied his mind, the little flashes of Lux had gone, and the more substantial pulse to the right was clearer. If you're going to dig a hole on an exposed hillside, you need a fair amount of Occulting to keep the tourists and the Park Rangers off your back. Another quarter of a mile and he'd be there.

He wiped his hands on his trousers and zipped up his fleece. The trees thinned out, and that meant the brambles got thicker. He could smell the overripe blackberries as he tried to navigate the thorns. Damn. He'd have to use his torch to find a clear route. He took it as slowly as he dared, checking the ground in bursts with his fingers over the torch beam. By the time he felt the press of Wards and Glamours, he was sweating badly. At least the ground was clear here. He unzipped his fleece again to let in the air and focused on the Wards.

The dig site was a long way from anywhere, so he wasn't worried about alarms. This time he'd remembered the Little Book of Wards, and he used the torch again, flicking to the page on Lattices. *Find the loose end* advised the book. Easier said than done when you've little Sorcery, and he knew he'd have to try it a different way. He sighed and opened his rucksack.

He smoothed out some grass and laid out Parchment, ink and two quills. How crude was this? If only some bright spark in Salomon's House could invent a proper App to do the job. Until then, it was back to basics. He felt out again for the Lattice until he'd got its measure, then quickly drew it on the first sheet of Parchment. It was the roughest sketch of the magick, but it would do. Taking more time, he drew it again, this time stretching the strands of Lux to leave a gap at the bottom. He waved the Parchment in the air to dry it and packed away his tools. A stray gust of wind blew away his draft copy of the Lattice and sent it down into a patch of brambles. Damn. He'd have to pick it up later.

Time was flying now – it had already been over two hours since he left the house, and sunrise was at seven. There would be a lot of people out and about in the pre-dawn light, especially with it being a holiday week. He had to get that boat back across the lake well before then. He shoved the Parchment in his mouth and crawled forwards. He bumped into the Lattice and breathed out heavily when the Charm in the Parchment bent the Ward into a new shape. He pushed through the hole and a few feet beyond before he stood up and shoved the Parchment in a pocket of his trousers.

The dig was crude by the standards of mundane archaeology, but when you're only interested in the loot, why bother preserving the other stuff? He opened his rucksack again and took out a long, thin strip of leather with brass rings sewn into the ends. He used steel skewers to fasten the leather to the ground, and then took out the Charm that his Principal had given him. He unfolded the Parchment and used his torch to work out the shape. Finally, he touched one of the brass rings and worked his fingers along the leather, unfolding the Charm and sending it down into the ground.

He was half way along the strip when it pinged in his head. Two metres away and one metre underground. He put down the Parchment and froze when he heard a bark in the distance, away to the north. The bark was echoed, and the bark became a howl. A blood-curdling howl that echoed through the trees. Shit.

Shit, damn and double shit. There was a pack of Mannwolves out there, and they'd exchanged to wolf form. Coincidence? No chance. A second howl chilled his blood. They were coming his way.

He grabbed his torch and left everything else behind. The gap in the Lattice was shrinking, but still there. He rolled through it and started running downhill, jumping the brambles and not really caring which direction he was headed, so long as it was towards the lake.

He made it to the thicker wood and put on a spurt now that he was free of obstructions. He thought he needed to go right, and changed his course a little. He was only a hundred yards from the lake path when they came at him from the front. He put his back to a tree and got ready to fight. If there were only a couple of them, he might stand a chance.

The wolves skidded to a halt and howled in unison. When they didn't attack him, he knew he was doomed. They were waiting for the rest of the pack, and the number of answering voices told Harry that his only hope was to surrender and pray that they were on guard duty and not on a hunt. He placed the torch on the ground and lifted his arms.

The larger of the wolves opened its mouth. From the jaws, a great pink tongue emerged and ran round the muzzle. It looked way too hungry, and Harry couldn't stop staring at the muzzle until something glinted magickally at the wolf's neck. An Artefact? The wolf stepped closer and Harry's heart missed several beats.

Great Goddess, was that a collar? How in the name had the wolf been collared, and by whom? A shiver ran deep into his soul as he looked into a very dark place indeed. There was an old Lakeland saying: *Only the Devil collars the wolf.*

59

## 7 — *The Games People Play*

Monday morning at Malchs began with a trial run for the election hustings. In case you've forgotten, there is a vacancy for Warden of Salomon's House, and not only will the real election have a polling station in Manchester, they're running a hustings up here to decide which of the local luminaries will stand for the big job. It was this election that pushed Hannah into making me an offer to take the Deputy's job that I couldn't refuse. Because the electorate are all Mages, we need magick for the ballot, and most of the heavy lifting for that is being done by Erin.

A very sober Erin, I might add. She was on elderflower cordial all night last night.

'This paper's not good enough,' she said when the Malchs secretary gave her some enchanted Parchment. 'Sorry, but the fibres won't bind to the burnt iron pigment.'

I nodded sagely because I had no idea what she was on about. I can't be an expert on everything, can I?

'Sorry,' said the secretary. 'That's all we've got.'

Erin turned to look at me, and I immediately felt uneasy. 'We need to source something better,' she said. 'We'll have to go to the Sextons.'

'We? Are you forgetting what happened the last time I went to Linbeck Hall?'

She waved a hand. 'Yeah, I know. You arrested two of them. That's why I'm not going on my own.'

'I'll drop you at the gate and wait for you.'

Hannah butted in. 'Things have changed. You should go, Conrad.'

'Perhaps I should go,' said Mina. She is here in her capacity as an officer of the Cloister Court, and it would mean we had more time together.

'Good idea,' I enthused.

'No,' said Hannah. 'Marcia has told me – me, the Peculier Constable – that I will be in contempt of court if I don't make sure that the star witness is in London on Wednesday.'

Mina grinned. 'Then as we are done here, Hannah-ji, I think we should go shopping. It would be a shame not to. We can't leave Erin at the hotel tonight, can we? She will need something to wear. And you should re-think those trousers.'

I tuned out at that point and went to see the society's steward about a room for the W\*r\*w\*lf Committee. Okay, I know, you're not supposed to use the W\*r\*w\*lf word. Can we keep it between us? Good.

When we'd had a look round for a room, I checked my phone and saw a missed call and text from Cador Mowbray, Eseld's slightly younger and very mundane brother. *Call me*, said the text. I called.

'I've been served papers,' he said, without preamble. 'From Keswick.'

I'd had to pull strings and beg Hannah, but I got her to let me appoint Cador as Counsel to the Commission. There aren't many occult lawyers, and he's one of the best. The personal connection helps, too. This commission is likely to get nasty at some point, and I want as many allies as I can get.

'The Fae Queen?'

'Who else? Where are you? Have you got a minute?'

'I've just been looking at rooms in Malchs, actually. I think I've found one.'

'Don't make any bookings just yet. The commission isn't going anywhere until we've dealt with this.'

I headed for the little courtyard at the back where we could talk privately (and I could light up). 'Tell me the worst.'

'Her Grace has applied for an injunction saying that the Occult Council has no jurisdiction over Lakeland and that even if it did, it has no authority over the Fae unless it's to do with humans, and the Dual Natured are not human. And that you're biased and have too many interests to be impartial.'

'Don't argue the last point. I might get taken off, which would be a great relief.'

'Ha ha, Conrad. 'Fraid not – the President has told me to fight on all fronts. The Council chose you and they're not going to have the Court say otherwise.'

'I thought you answered to me.'

'I answer to the Enquiry, technically. But more importantly, the Council are paying my fee. If you're willing to double it...?'

'I know how much you charge. Will there be a full hearing?'

'Mmm. Not if I can help it. I'll let you know.'

Mark Hayden

### *Watch Officer*
### *Lieutenant C. Kennedy*

Cordelia smoothed out the piece of paper again and wondered how Hannah had managed to find a fax machine in this day and age. Probably a service offered by the posh hotel where the senior officers were staying. Senior officers. Hah.

Of course, Cordelia was herself now a junior officer. Very junior: a second lieutenant. It said so on the commission document staring back at her from the top of the dressing table. If you could call it a dressing table when a piece of A4 paper took up all the spare space. If she had any money, she'd use some of it betting that Hannah and Mina and Erin Slater all had proper dressing tables.

'You've got to start somewhere,' she said out loud. And it was a start: the piece of paper informed her that Queen Elizabeth was delighted to have her on board. Whoop de do. Nevertheless, she placed it carefully in the new suitcase on the bed and took stock.

All her worldly goods were in this room. Literally everything in the world she owned was either in the cases already or spread around the room in shopping bags, ready to be packed for tomorrow. Hair or packing? She wished she could call her children instead, but they'd moved on, and Rick said that there was no signal at the new campsite.

Hair, she decided. It would take too long in the morning, and she had to be on parade for breakfast with her new partner. Hannah had been quite clear about that – 'Conrad is your partner, Cordy, and you're his. Not equal partners, but partners nonetheless. And a lot of the time, you'll be the senior partner, so take good care of him, eh?'

She started the braid, and forced her fingers into new routines. People like Conrad and Hannah thought that there was one Goddess braid. There wasn't. There were a lot of them, and for years she'd worn the one she'd been entitled to wear as Raven's page. Not any more.

Her eyes automatically went to Raven's scarf in the wardrobe, where it had one of the six clothes hangers all to itself. It hadn't got any easier. Not yet. Perhaps having a new job would make it easier to cope on a day to day basis until she'd settled the score. The fact that the job put her in pole position to extract vengeance only made it sweeter.

She finished the braid and looked at herself in the mirror. Right side? Left side? Hanging down the back? Down the back. She squared her shoulders and smiled at herself. Bigger smile this time. 'Come on, Cordelia. You're looking forward to this. New people. Good people. Even Erin Slater.'

Her inner monologue added the codicil: So long as they take me where I need to go.

She stood to attention and brought up her right hand.

'Lieutenant Kennedy reporting for duty, sir.'

Oh, the disgrace of it all.

'Do you want me to order you to get in there?' said a shivering but very glamorous Hannah Rothman. Relatively glamorous for her, that is.

Somehow, some way, Mina and Erin had convinced the Boss to wear a dress in shiny black fabric and buy some new boots that didn't look like they were designed for dog-walking. I know it sounds curmudgeonly to object to getting into a car with three hot babes (their words, not mine), but male pride is a strange thing.

'Yes, ma'am. The only way I'm getting into a stretch limo is if I'm ordered to. By you or Mina.'

She turned to my fiancée. 'Do you understand this?'

'No, Hannah-ji, I do not, but I will save you the embarrassment. Conrad, get in the car. Now. And don't, under any circumstances say, "Yes, dear." Are we clear?'

I opened the door and stood back. 'After you.'

I mean, a stretch limo. Why? Just because we had to pick up Tom and Lucy from the station, and just because we only had one security pass to get close to the football ground, so what? There must be a better way to seat six. A minibus, for example. I shrugged and got inside.

As soon as we picked up Lucy and Tom, she was bombarded with questions about who was likely to be there, given her connections to the world of elite sport. Both teams have a large number of A List fans, and the executive suite we were heading for was a neutral venue. I suppose I should have been honoured.

'What do you think of the transport?' I asked Tom.

He looked at me suspiciously. 'That sounds like a loaded question. I'll pass.'

'Open the Champagne,' said Erin, 'and don't be boring, or if you must be boring, do it quietly.'

It's one measure of just how far I've come in magick that I put up a Silence around our seats without really thinking about it. 'How did it go with Myfanwy and Keira?' I asked Tom. 'Did Keira even turn up?'

'Oh yes, she did. Don't take this the wrong way, Conrad, but do you think she's bonkers?'

'Totally. I'd say that she's away with the fairies, but that has a special meaning round here. Whether she's got a condition you could label or whether she's just very selfish and very driven, I don't know. She's not daft, though.'

'No, she isn't. Our talk was very illuminating. I got the aliases of both Adaryn and Deborah Sayer.'

I was stunned. I'd questioned Keira and Myfanwy myself and thought I'd done a good job. How wrong can you be?

'Aliases,' I said, still stunned.

'Yes.' A lesser man would have rubbed it in by crowing; Tom Morton rubbed it in by being kind. 'I have never faced down a Dragon, nor do I want to, Conrad. We play to our strengths. Have some Champagne and cheer up. You don't have to fly a helicopter tomorrow.'

'True.'

I cancelled the Silence and sat back as we were turning off the main road, miles short of Barton Park. I sat up straight again.

'Where are we going?' I said to the driver.

'Lowry Hotel, sir.'

'Oh, are we there already?' said Hannah, shushing Erin with an impatient gesture. 'Good news, Conrad. For you and Mina. You're not going to the game. You're having a free dinner at the Riverside Restaurant.'

Mina obviously had no idea about this. I could tell that by the big O her mouth made.

'With my new partner?'

'Your new partner can't afford the prices, and I'm not paying.'

The Boss does like to keep me on my toes, and tonight certainly did that. Who I met and what they said was deeply personal, and it may have a bearing on what happens in the future, but if you don't mind, I'll respect their privacy for now. The food was good, and I enjoyed stretching my bad leg on the walk back to our hotel.

When Mina got back, she and Hannah were clearly in a very good mood. The Boss waved goodnight and headed for the lift, and Mina came over to join me in the lounge.

'Where's Erin?' I asked. 'Throwing up in the bushes outside?'

'Hah! No. She got lucky with some man.' She sat down. 'Hannah wouldn't say who you were meeting. I don't think she wanted Erin to know, but I think she expected me to find out. Was it business or personal?'

'I'll tell you upstairs. I just want to send Erin a text.'

'Saying what?'

'Telling her to find her own way to Middlebarrow Haven.' I got my phone out. 'Who won in the end?'

'It was a draw. Spurs equalised in injury time.'

'And did you have a good time? Really?'

'Yes I did, Conrad. Yes I did.'

We smiled at each other, and I took her hand. I am a very lucky man. I know that because she told me so later.

# 8 — *Partners*

If you look out to sea from the Furness Peninsula, you can see the Isle of Man. When it's not raining.

So not very often, then.

Police Constable Barnabas Smith had been known as "Barney" since before he could remember. When he was about nine, a teacher had added "Rubble", and that's what he'd been ever since. All hand-written notes at the police station said "B. Rubble" and only the computers had "B. Smith". New staff could go for weeks until they realised that they were one and the same person.

The man himself was enjoying the dregs of his flask of tea and waiting patiently for the sun to rise over the fells behind him. He'd never been to the Isle of Man, nor did he want to go in the future. It was like some Camelot to him, a magical place out of reach. He still felt that way after they built Britain's largest offshore wind farm to spoil the view, and his favourite thing of all on night shift was to have time to drive up the hill out of Ulverston and take a moment to enjoy the view.

Cuts to police numbers had been so deep that he was on his own across a huge swathe of south Westmorland and Lancashire over the Sands, all around the top of Morecambe Bay. He didn't solve any crimes, and his real function was to be called on when there was a road traffic incident or a fire. Or the occasional suspicious death.

He was supposed to be making a decision this week: apply for CID or stay in uniform and start studying for his sergeant's exams. The detective section of Morecambe Bay Division was permanently understaffed and over-stretched, and he wasn't sure he wanted to leave the familiar streets of Barrow behind him. Then again, when you've arrested the same drug addict for petty crime forty-seven times, you wonder if this was why you joined the police in the first place. *Forty-seven times.* There was talk on his Relief that Barney would get a medal if he made it fifty arrests.

The outside of Barney's stab vest was festooned with equipment – Taser, body camera, digital radio, flashlight, handcuffs and police phone, and it was the phone that rang. The contract for digital radios had left many, many not-spots for coverage out here. The fact that it reached 98% of the population nationally meant nothing in Lakeland, and this was unlikely to change soon, so first contact usually came via his phone. Not only that, there were a lot of people who could listen in to the radio.

Barney often fantasised what the call handler might look like, and he took the call with a smile.

'Hiya Barney,' said Sasha. She had a lovely voice.

Even though the call would be recorded, they didn't have to follow strict protocol. 'We've had a 999 call reporting a suspicious death out your way.'

He discarded the dregs of his tea and started to walk back to the car. 'Right, Sasha. I'm on it. What you got?'

'The caller said it was murder, but it sounds to me like it might be a suicide or even a hoax. She sounded a bit shaken up.'

He slid into his seat and put the key in the ignition. 'Where is it?'

There was a pause. 'She says she's in a forest off a road out of Broughton Beck. I think I've pinned it down. I'll put the co-ordinates on the system.'

'It'll take me about fifteen minutes. Tell her I'm on my way.'

'Will do. She said to look out for her car, a silver Fiesta, and follow the track into the woods. Caller's name is Rosamund Gardner.'

'Rosy Garden! It can't be. Surely not.'

Sasha laughed. 'Another of your exes, Barney? I thought she was a bit old for you.'

'Mrs Gardner was my English teacher. It must be her.' He checked the hi-tech display of the comms unit and saw that the co-ordinates had come in. 'Right. I'm on my way.'

He made it to the location in ten minutes, not fifteen, because he took a risk and cut through some of the tiny lanes that criss-cross the hinterland between Morecambe Bay and the start of the Lakeland Fells. He slowed down as he climbed the little lane towards the start of a big wood, and a sign made him stop the car completely.

*Friar's Plantation*
*A Peninsular Water Development*
*Private Property*

This was Union territory. Under the agreement with the Lakeland Unions, crime here was supposed to be notified to the Insurance Union assessors, and many times it would be handed over to them for investigation. Another reason for police being thin on the ground. He drove through the open gate and found himself in a small car park that serviced a timber cutting operation. At the far end, next to the tree line, was the silver Ford Fiesta.

He used the vehicle's comms unit to log his arrival on site and grabbed his cap. Had to look the part if he was going to see Rosy Garden properly after – what? Fifteen years? She'd been close to retirement when he left Furness High School and already a widow. He'd seen her a few times in the supermarket or walking around Ulverston. She'd waved and smiled, but they hadn't stopped to talk.

He set off up the track and hadn't got far when he heard a trembling voice call out from the right. 'In here.' This was followed by the bark of a small dog, and Barney soon saw the lady herself, sitting on a tree stump and shivering despite her well-padded jacket. At her feet, on a short lead, was a very protective Jack Russell terrier.

'Is that you, Barney?' she said.

'Yes miss, it's me. PC Smith of Lancashire and Westmorland Constabulary.' She gave him a smile of infinite pain and didn't move off the tree stump. He bent down and let the dog sniff his fingers from a distance. He had absolutely no doubt that there was something bad in the woods now. Very bad.

She didn't wait for him to ask, she pointed over his head and behind him. 'I've been sitting here to keep watch,' she said. 'I couldn't leave him alone.'

He did as he was told and looked round. The plantation was mostly conifers, with a few native slow-growth trees at the outside. One of the largest was a horse chestnut, still mostly in leaf and full of conkers. On the side away from the path, one branch stuck out from the main canopy.

The thing was hanging half way along the limb. Him. It was definitely a him.

Barney didn't realise that he'd taken his cap off until he got closer to the dead man. To the victim. Because this was definitely not a suicide. The rope had been thrown over the branch and then hauled up before being tied off round the trunk. That was a physical impossibility for a suicide unless they had a big ladder. That's what Barney thought to himself as he contemplated the victim, because it made it easier to ignore the other stuff.

There was no smell of death from the victim. Not yet. That didn't mean that the whole thing didn't stink, though. Barney turned round and went back to Mrs Gardner. He squatted down again and he could see that she was teetering on the edge now that he was here. 'Did you see anyone or anything this morning? I take it you'd come to walk your dog.'

She took a deep breath and started to speak. She must have been rehearsing this in her head ever since she sat down. 'I don't sleep well anymore, so I got up early to give Jack a proper walk. The timber people don't arrive until eight thirty, you know, and they don't mind me being here. Anyone can use the footpath, it leads up to the reservoir. I was completely alone, so I let him off the lead. He ran straight in here and I followed him. I found him barking and then I looked up. I haven't touched a thing. Can I go, Barney?'

'Will you be all right to drive, Mrs Gardner?'

'I live in the village. It's only five minutes.'

He held out a hand and helped her up. He kept hold of her arm and walked her back to her car. By the time they got there, she was breathing a little easier and he had come to a decision. It was against all the rules and procedures to let her go, but he was about to break them anyway.

'Mrs Gardner, is there a neighbour you trust?'

'Trust? You mean someone who won't phone the press, don't you? Of course there is. I'll be fine. You do your job and make sure you catch whoever did that.'

'It won't be me, but I'll do my bit. Someone will be with you later for a statement.'

'Thank you.'

He stepped back and watched her reverse and drive out. She did it perfectly, so he turned and went back to the scene, stopping short of the horse chestnut. The sun was about to rise and all around the world was waking. Or already awake. Deep in his personal phone contacts was a number he'd never called before. He dug it out and found it, listed under *Haggis*. He forced himself to look at the victim again and he knew that he was right. He pressed *Call* and waited.

'PC Smith,' said the Commander. 'There had better be a bloody good reason why you're making me swear in front of Mrs Ross.'

Barney was already standing to attention. 'Yes sir. Suspicious death in woods above Ulverston.' He gripped his phone even harder. 'It's a nasty one, sir. Very nasty. And it's on Union property.'

He heard a hiss of breath. 'Who knows?'

'Preston Control Room, sir, but they notified me on the phone, not the radio. The lady who called 999 won't be telling tales, either.'

'Straight up, Barney lad, is it murder?' The Commander, being a true Scot, rolled the *r*s in *murder* with something approaching relish.

'He's dangling from a tree branch, sir. His hands have been tied, there's a big slash on his chest and signs of a beating. Oh, and he's naked from the waist up. Definitely a murder. There's something like a pouch round his neck, too. I can't see from the ground. Could be one of those map cases that orienteerers use.'

'Scene?'

'Woods, sir. A timber company are working them. Starting at eight-thirty, according to the witness. Very limited access.'

There was a long pause. 'Are you on nights, laddie?'

'Sir.'

'I've got someone in mind for this, but they won't be with you for an hour at least, and the Crime Scene people might take a lot longer. I've been waiting for this ever since they changed the boundaries and gave the north side back to me. If I leave you on your own until the cavalry get there, can you cope?'

Barney was about to utter another *yes sir* until he thought about what might happen. 'I'll try, sir. I'll do my best.'

69

'I know you will, laddie. I know you will. I'll get straight on to the control room and allocate the case to my command. Do not move from that site until I or Detective Chief Inspector Tom Morton order you to do so. And well done for calling me.'

The first one to get on his case was the day-shift sergeant. 'Where are you, and more to the point, where is my brand new BMW enhanced incident car?'

'I'm on a job, Sarge. Could be a while. Sorry.'

'I didn't think you were getting your leg over, Barney. Not at this time in the morning. I asked you where you were.'

'On a case for the Commander. You can check with him.'

There was a pause. 'I'll tell Janine she's on foot patrol, shall I?'

'Tell her she's welcome to the car if she can convince the Haggis to send me home.'

'Hunh. Have a nice day, Barney, and don't forget to put your overtime down as a cost to Division.'

Once the sergeant had sorted out his Relief, the message would percolate to the duty inspector. The sergeant would make a few jokes, and that would be it, but the inspector could make his life a misery if she chose to. She called twenty minutes later.

'Could you give me your location and advise me of your status?' she said.

Barney screwed his eyes shut and leapt into the dark. 'I'm on site for a Division operation, ma'am. Assisting an enquiry for Commander Ross.'

'So I've heard. And what would that location be? Precisely?'

The inspector was linked to one of the Unions, somehow. She'd definitely been thick as thieves with the late Petra Leigh. Should he stonewall or lie? The Commander's antipathy to the Lakeland Unions was well known to the inspector, he was sure. What was the one thing that every copper really worried about? Aah. He'd vaguely heard of this Tom Morton bloke, so he lowered his voice and said, 'This is a professional standards job, ma'am. Don't worry, nothing to do with you.'

'I see. Will you be back for night shift tonight?'

'Sorry, ma'am. I'm not being told very much at all.'

'So long as you let us know if you're not coming back tonight. We'll need to put someone in your place. And we do want that car back.'

'Ma'am.'

She disconnected and he wiped the sweat off his forehead. She'd fallen for it. Barney moved rather stiffly down to his car and moved it to block the gate. Right on time, a black pickup roared up the lane and pulled up next to him. He got out, and so did the pickup driver, a man in his forties.

'What's up, officer?'

'Sorry, sir, there's been an incident. The woods are closed off until further notice.'

'What's happened? The rest of my crew will be here in a minute.'

This called for an even bigger lie. 'Some poor sod from London decided to end it all up here. Most of them choose the real Lakes, not this bit. Perhaps it meant something to him.'

'Oh. I see. Look, is there any chance I could collect my wood chipping machine? We can get on and work somewhere else today.'

If he were here, Commander Ross would say no. Barney said yes. 'Where is it?'

The man pointed to an empty bit of cleared ground. 'We've hidden it in there. If you let me pick it up, I'll be out of your way in two minutes. Is the ... you know ... in the woods? If it is, you can guard the path.'

Barney's copper's nose was twitching. He was sure that *something* was going on. Did he want the forester alerting the Peninsular Water Company? No. 'Right. I'll back up.'

'Here,' said the man, offering him a creased flier for his forestry company. 'Text us when you're done, yeah? Or text us if you're gonna be longer.'

'Thanks.' Barney reversed up the car park and the pickup disappeared round a bend. Barney got out and walked up the path, just in case the forester tried to head round through the trees, so he didn't see where the truck went. He could hear it though, and he heard the driver's door slam twice. In less than the promised two minutes, the pickup was heading out of the gate with a huge green chipping machine bouncing along behind it. The driver blew his horn on the way out and waved his thanks, and then Barney was alone again.

Or almost alone.

He made his way back to the small clearing where the victim was hanging and nearly jumped out of his stab vest when he saw the huge bird sitting on a branch. What was that thing? Mutant crow? Something escaped from the Animal Park? And then the freaking thing tilted its head to stare at him.

It's a raven, was his conclusion. Don't they eat bits of dead things? He was about to look for a rock to throw at it when a bona fide crow flew over and landed on the victim's head.

With an almighty cry, the raven unfurled its wings and hopped along its branch. Barney's mouth gaped and he dropped the rock. The crow flung itself off the grisly perch and dived to the ground before opening its wings and gliding up to land with a *caw* of pain in a holly bush. Shortly after, it flew away completely.

The raven made no move to close with the victim and made itself comfortable again. 'Are you gonna keep watch?' he asked, feeling stupid as the words rushed out of his mouth.

'Awrrk,' said the raven.

'Right. Make sure you do.'

It was only when he got back to his car that he realised he'd understood the bird. It had said *yes*. He drove the fifty yards back to the gate and muttered, 'Hurry up, Morton.'

71

The DCI called first, and said he was only ten minutes away. Barney felt a surge of relief.

'You're lucky,' said Morton. He had a smooth, public school voice but not posh. You could definitely hear a Yorkshire twang in there somewhere. 'We were in Manchester last night, and we only decided to come back to Cairndale when we saw that there was a direct train. Don't tell me anything over the phone, but are you still alone on site?'

'Yes sir. Just me and the raven.'

The line went quiet, and Barney thought Morton must be in the dead spot by Greenodd. He cringed when he thought of what he'd said. Why did he have to tell a DCI that?

'A raven?' said Morton. There was a quiet intensity in his voice, and Barney thought he must be in trouble.

'Sorry, sir, I didn't mean to mention it, but it's been a long night.'

'No, you did the right thing.'

What? He'd heard that Morton could be a bit unpredictable. Whatever.

Morton was brisker when he spoke again. 'Access for Scene of Crimes?'

'Good. Only a hundred metres into the wood and most of it's path. I'm afraid that there's been a bit of contamination.'

'That's going to be the least of our problems. I'll see you soon.'

Barney felt reassured that someone would be here to take over. He also felt that he'd somehow changed sides, but had no idea whose side he was now on. He slurped his emergency water bottle and got ready to receive his new boss.

When you look at the trains from Manchester to London, you wonder why they want to spend billions of pounds on HS2. The fastest train takes only 2hrs 10mins, and the one that Mina and Hannah caught was barely twenty minutes slower. I carried their bags on to the platform, and the Boss left us with a cryptic comment.

'I'll find the seats, Mina. Bye Conrad – and enjoy breakfast.'

'What was that about?' I asked Mina.

'How should I know? She's your boss.'

'And your matron of honour.'

'Which is why we're talking weddings all the way to London, now shut up and kiss me goodbye. It may have to last until next week.'

I left the platform with mixed emotions of pleasure and pain, all overlaid on a bed of hunger. Breakfast was well overdue.

'You've a guest, Mr Clarke,' said the waitress who ticked me off the list. 'I've put her round the corner. Someone will be over with a pot of tea in a moment.'

I went round the corner half expecting to see one of the election candidates, come to butter me up. What I saw instead was very much unexpected, and that was just her outfit.

I've only ever seen Cordelia in the robes of the Daughters of the Goddess where she is 11th of Ash, and today she was in a black top and jeans. Cordy is small, barely taller than Mina, and has an infectious, impish grin that she displayed to good effect when she stood up to embrace me.

'Surprise, Conrad!'

'You could say that. You haven't come up from Glastonbury this morning, have you?'

She shook her head. 'I stayed round the corner. Nowhere near as grand as this. Do you always live like this on taxpayers' money?'

'Since when have the Daughters paid mundane taxes? Is this an official visit or have you brought the kids up to Lancashire for half term?'

She looked away and sat down. My tea arrived, and we ordered breakfast. Cordy went for Eggs Benedict, and you can guess what I had: the Full English.

Cordy looked me in the eye again. 'I forgot you're polite. I should have known you'd ask about the kids first.'

'Are they okay?'

'Yeah. They're fine. I'd hoped to say something like, "Meet your new partner – me!" but it didn't quite come out.'

'Erm … Right. Do you want to start from the beginning?'

'The beginning was Raven.'

'Oh.'

Cordy had been Page to Raven, a massively tall woman who'd been created by someone trying to breed a Valkyrie. Raven had died a violent but accidental death in Cornwall, and the last time I'd seen Cordelia was when Raven had been committed to the flames and the water.

She fiddled with her long Goddess braid. 'I'll have to get this chopped shorter. It gets in the way when you're not wearing robes.'

'That top isn't a Glamour?'

'No robes for me now unless it's a festival. I've quit the Daughters. You know what they're like. With Raven gone, everyone jumped to form new alliances, and when the music stopped, I didn't have a chair. They couldn't fire me, but they could give me a job I'd hate. I jumped before they made my life a misery.'

73

That still didn't explain why she was here talking to me and not in Eurodisney with her children for instance. 'What else?' I said, as gently as I could.

'The kids said they wanted to go to camping with their dad.' She shrugged. 'I didn't know it had come to that.'

Cordelia's ex is Rick James, the Senior Watch Captain, and he has something of a reputation. She left him to join the Daughters full-time when they offered her a position and when Rick was caught playing away. He could have had my job – Deputy Constable in Chester. Instead, he chose to live near his children and co-parent. Expressing sympathy didn't seem like the right thing, so I asked, 'Why the Watch? I thought it was completely incompatible?'

'Not since Hannah created the post of Watch Officer. So long as I don't become a Watch Captain, there's a route back. If I want it. And I can still attend the ceremonies. If it works out, I might ask for a posting in Wessex.'

That's Rick's patch. 'He did say you two were getting on okay. You're not hoping for a reconciliation, are you?'

'Now that I'm not with Raven, anything's possible. All that's in the future, though. Right now, I'm focused on being the best partner you've had.'

She said the last bit with her sense of humour restored, so I went right back at her. 'Vicky and Saffron are a tough act to follow.'

'They're only kids. You might find a real woman a different matter.'

Breakfast arrived, and before we tucked in, I said, 'Will Hannah have told Mina by now?'

'Mmm. Probably. Hannah had it all worked out, you know. She was even going to tell Erin not to come down to breakfast, and then Erin goes and gets lucky. It must be fate.'

I attacked my breakfast with enthusiasm. 'Have you got an Ancile?'

'Yes.'

'Badge of Office?'

'Not yet. This weekend, probably. I only took the oath yesterday – Hannah left the shopping trip early to see me in my hotel, so I've got nothing except a letter from her. No formal ID. Nothing.'

'What's your thing, magickally speaking?'

'I'm a Necromancer … What? Don't look like that! It's rude!'

'Sorry. You do know that Hannah keeps giving me dangerous cases, don't you?'

'She said you specialised in *challenging* cases. I can do challenging.'

'What else did she say about me?'

She put a finger to her chin. 'Ooh. Let me see … Nothing.' She flashed a smile. 'I did have a word with Saffron Hawkins before I approached the Constable. It was Saffron who said that I might end up with you.'

I looked at her darkly. 'And what did Saff say?'

'Do you really want to know? It might dent your male ego.'

'If you'd been talking to Mina, my male ego might be worried. Tell me. You know you're dying to.'

'Saff said, "You get used to it," but she wouldn't tell me *what* I'd have to get used to. She also told me your magickal strengths and weaknesses.'

I put my knife and fork down. 'I still can't get my head round the fact that you've become a Witchfinder.'

'Not all the Circles are completely antagonistic. Don't forget, Rick was a Watch Captain when I married him. I've burnt so many bridges just by leaving Glastonbury that a few more won't hurt. So what's on the agenda for today? Assault courses? Sword practice?'

I folded my napkin carefully. 'Have you done any combat training? Martial arts?'

'I ... no. Not really. I learnt the basics of offensive and defensive magick, and I've been practising. I won't let you down.'

I stood up. 'Good. Right, Lieutenant ... what's your last name?'

She stood as well. 'Kennedy.'

I held out my hand. 'Welcome to the North, Lieutenant Kennedy.'

She shook. 'Thank you, sir. I think the whole military thing might have been one of the things Saffron said I'd get used to.'

'And me nipping outside for a smoke. We're heading to Middlebarrow Haven, so we can talk more on the drive. Shall I meet you at your hotel in half an hour? I presume you've got plenty of luggage?'

'What? Just because I'm a woman, I have to have lots of luggage?'

I pointed at her chest. 'You're not Karina Kent. She had an armoury, not a wardrobe. You've just left your home, I'll bet you've got the kitchen sink with you. And we'll need to get you sorted for a combat uniform.'

She groaned. 'If you insist. I'll see you at ten.'

I convinced the waitress to fill my reusable mug with coffee and headed outside. The first thing I did was check my phone. There were two messages, and I went straight for Mina's.

*Cordelia??? Isn't she a bit old for you? Ha ha. Look after her or you'll have Rick on your case. I am going to miss you so much. I love Sofia, but she is not the same. XXXXXXX.'*

I texted a suitable reply on autopilot. The way you do. I suppose Cordelia must be at least thirty-two. No older than thirty-five, certainly. It would be change. And how would it be next week, when her children were back at school? I didn't doubt her sincerity in signing up for the Watch, but I couldn't help feeling that someone – Hannah, Rick or Cordy herself – wasn't telling me the whole story.

I idly checked the other message and dropped my lighter. 'Bloody hell,' I said out loud. It's been a long time since I've had a text from Odin rather than a personal manifestation. What now?

*You need a flag. Preferably with your own coat of arms. Have a look at Gyronny.*

75

Great. Marvellous. What the hell was I supposed to make of that? I scratched my head and stared at the phone. The Allfather had once advised me to always carry curried worms underground, and that piece of nonsense had then saved my life. I put my phone away and headed up to my room.

Tom Morton was already missing Elaine. He was missing Lucy, too, but unless he resigned and went into business with her, he wasn't going to be spending every day at her side. Elaine was a different matter, especially now. When Commander Ross had called this morning, he didn't say a word about *Unions* and *Assessors*. He didn't need to. They both knew the subtext here, even if Ross wasn't aware of the magickal dimension.

Because there was so much magick in the forests and fells, the magickal and mundane worlds collided far more often than elsewhere. Tom had read Clarke's report on the Sexton business, and had a good idea what to expect if he was not careful. On the other hand, he wasn't keen to alert Conrad and drag him all the way up here for no reason.

Fate had already given Tom two helping hands by locating him in Cairndale not Manchester and by having Tracey Kenyon's Scene of Crime team free for a major incident. He knew that the longer he kept the local force out of the loop, the more chance he had of keeping the case. And of keeping the body, but that was another story.

PC Smith looked tired and stressed when Tom arrived at the car park. Tom shook hands and said, 'Thanks for holding the fort, constable. What's your name?'

'Barnabas Smith, sir. Also known as Barney Rubble. Even Commander Ross calls me Barney.'

'Good. Take me up there.'

When Barney headed off the path, Tom tried to keep himself alert to any form of tingle, ESP or other signal that magick might be in play. He'd only felt it once, at that service by Clarke's well, and that could easily have been his heart swelling with emotion. They came to a clearing and ice water ran down Tom's back, followed by a hammering in his ribs as a huge raven took flight from the tree.

'Jesus Christ,' said Smith, and Tom was ridiculously glad that the solid, experienced constable was as scared as he was.

'I don't think Jesus has been here,' said Tom.

'Sorry, sir, I was startled. I won't blaspheme again.'

'Doesn't bother me. Let me have a look.'

As Tom walked round the crime scene, he was conscious of Barney observing him. Probably wondering how he'd got to be a DCI at such a young age. Clarke had said good things about Barney Smith after they'd worked together on the Sexton case, and Tom could see why. Barney's instincts had been spot-on: this was no suicide.

'Talk me through it,' said Tom.

Barney did so, and only got flustered when he said that he'd dismissed the witness. Tom interrupted him to say, 'Good job you did. If you hadn't, she might have gone into shock. Or worse. Then you'd have had to call an ambulance. Carry on.'

When he'd finished, Tom asked him to wait while he took a look further afield. 'The Crime Scene team won't be here for half an hour at the least, and there's literally nothing else to do. I won't be long.'

He went up the path first, until he realised that it had nothing to offer except a route to the reservoir. Tom's instinct – and Barney's – was that this was a dump site, and that the primary crime scene was elsewhere. The path would have to be checked, but with the car park so handy, that would be favourite. He went back down and off to the right, away from the gate. There were plenty of tyre tracks here, because it was grass, not gravel. Most were large tyres from pickups and lorries, again they were unlikely to be significant.

Tracey Kenyon called him at that point. 'We're getting there, sir. The lads want to know if we can stop to get refreshments. Most of them left home without breakfast.'

'Yes. I'd rather that than have to break off. There's a couple of roadside chuckwagons before you get to Ulverston. Use one of those rather than stop in the town. And bring something for the local officer. He's been here since before dawn.'

'Right. Half an hour, sir.'

Barney cheered up enormously when Tom told him about the forthcoming breakfast. 'Where's your own car?' asked Tom.

'Barrow, sir.'

'Drive your squad car into Ulverston and drop it at your local supermarket. Give them the keys, too. Once you've dropped the car, call your sergeant and tell him you won't be back on relief for a few days. Then hide until the Crime Scene team pick you up. I'll call them, and you can guide them here. Clear?'

'Yes sir.' He hesitated. 'Will you be alright on your own?'

'Perfectly. I can start writing my reports. And brief Commander Ross.'

'Good luck, sir. See you soon.'

Tracey Kenyon had done her usual swearing and moaning about contamination before setting up the perimeter, and her team had swept the ground under the horse chestnut. Because Tom had known about the location of the body, Tracey had brought access equipment.

'I want someone up the ladders straight away,' said Tom from the edge of the inner perimeter.

'What?' said Tracey. 'We're nowhere near ready for that yet.'

'I need a swab. There's an open wound in the chest. I need two DNA swabs for special purposes, and I need them now.'

'That's going to hold us up, sir.'

'He's not going anywhere for a while, and neither are we.'

'You're the boss, Tom.'

'For now.'

When the swabs had been taken and sealed in evidence bags, Tom took one of them to a much happier Barney, who'd been fed and watered and was guarding the gate.

'Excuse me,' said Tom. He slid the bag inside Barney's stab vest. 'In a minute, I'm going to drive you to Ulverston Station. There's a train to Preston at 11:40. You're going to catch it, then take that sample to a special lab. Then you're going to go home to Barrow and go to sleep. Tomorrow, you will go to Cairndale via Broughton Beck and get Mrs Gardner's statement. I'll call her later to explain. And you'll be in plain clothes. Is that okay with you?'

'Yes, sir. Is that where the incident room is going to be?'

'Possibly. It is where the paperwork is going to be. Do you know DS Gartside?'

'Yeah. He's been to Barrow a few times.'

'Good. Ask for him, and he'll give you a desk and computer.'

'Right. I've done the Disclosure course.'

'I know you have. Tracey! Put one of your lads on the gate until I get back. Won't be long.'

He didn't wait for the abuse to come back and set off for his car with Barney in his wake.

## 9 — Orders

After Barney Smith had left for Preston, Tom's role at the crime scene had been limited to observing and being told that they had found no evidence. As each section of the scene was checked, the shout of "Nothing" would echo round the trees.

There had been a brief flurry when a doctor turned up to pronounce the victim deceased. They'd had to wait for Ross to organise a medic he trusted with police clearance, because Ross had made it very clear that they were going to do everything by the book. His book.

Tom spent the afternoon squirrelled away in the depths of Cairndale nick, entering statements into the system, checking and re-checking for missing persons (none) and talking to Mrs Gardner on the phone. The one useful thing she added to her original statement was that the forestry company had only started working on that section of the woods on Monday of this week.

He told her that Barney would be along in the morning, and added, 'Don't be too hard on his spellings, Mrs Gardner.'

'I won't, Inspector Morton. I know a lost cause when I see one. Good luck with your enquiries.'

When he got back to the Red Rose Hotel, he asked Lucy what she'd been up to. The weekend at Clarke's place had left her with more questions than answers regarding the independent coffee shop in Cairndale's Market Square.

'I spent most of the day going round estate agents and staring at the building. Mina is adamant that the lease is overpriced and that I should walk away or put an offer in for the freehold. Including the accommodation. It's vacant at the moment, and we won't get a better chance.'

'I'm not sure I fancy living over the business,' said Tom.

She shook her head. 'Don't worry. It's for Bridget.' She paused. 'Do you think you're likely to be here long? I don't mind this hotel, and it's pretty cheap, but…'

'I wish I knew love. Were you looking at houses to rent? For us?'

'A bit. Yeah. I'll have a proper look tomorrow and make an appointment with the landlord of the coffee shop building.'

And so the next morning Lucy headed for Preston, and Tom had carried on past her to travel further down the M6 and then across country.

They don't mention it much on the TV news, but there are very few licensed Home Office pathologists. Regardless of cause, any suspicious death in Westmorland has to go all the way down to North Liverpool.

He sighed as he made his way to the security door at the back of the mortuary and pressed the buzzer. 'DCI Morton, Lancashire and Westmorland police. For Doctor Jepson.'

The door buzzed open and he made his way down the corridor. Michael Jepson was leaning against the wall outside his office as Tom approached. 'You do know that my scalpels are very sharp, don't you, Tom? And I'm not afraid to use them.'

The last time that Tom had sent a body here, it had turned into a pig when Jepson came to do the PM. To be precise, a bunch of Gnomes had used magick to distract the staff and swapped the body in the early hours of the morning. Tom knew that. He'd also been forced to apologise to Jepson and say that he couldn't explain why for reasons of "National Security". The pathologist, normally friendly and helpful, was still not amused.

'We should be alright today, Mike. No one knows we're here. Has Tracey arrived?'

'Yes, and we've already checked. As of eight thirty, the corpus in the chiller was still Homo sapiens, not *Sus scrofa domesticus*. She's finishing the final evidence gathering. Shall we? Or do you want a brew first.'

'Let's get on with it.'

Because the rope had been so embedded in the victim's neck, along with the map pouch, the whole lot had been piled into the body bag before it was sealed, and only now would Tracey separate them. They found her trying to cut the rope without cutting the flesh. Tom donned a protective apron and went to see. Tracey held up her hand to stop them, then fired up one of Jepson's electric saws. In seconds, she cut through the rope without making so much as a scratch on the body.

'Good,' she said. She carefully peeled the rope away from the neck and put it to one side. 'Shouldn't have the same problem with this map case.'

It was a transparent polythene wallet on a cord, designed to allow walkers and runners to inspect the map inside without it getting wet. However, this one didn't contain a map. It contained a blank piece of thick paper with rough edges. Tom had seen paper like that before – it was hand-made, finest quality cotton/linen stock, and another reason he suspected magick. No one leaves a blank piece of paper with a corpse.

'Turn off the lights. It might have been too bright at the scene yesterday,' said Tracey. She had a UV lamp ready, and the technician turned off the electric lights, plunging the room into darkness. 'Nope. Nothing. You can turn the lights back on, thanks.' She stood back. 'We'll have to get creative with this.'

They had checked the victim's trousers yesterday, vainly searching for an ID. What they had found was something like paper in one of the cargo pockets, but it had been scrunched down, and Tracey hadn't wanted to remove it at the scene. She snipped open the pocket and found a smaller, folded piece of similar parchment. 'It's too wet to open in here.' She started bagging the evidence. 'I'm done, now. I'm not going to hang around for the clothes. Good news on the DNA.'

Tom's attention snapped to Tracey's face. 'What news? How do you know about it?'

She put down the evidence bags, now sealed and marked. 'It came in on the regular emails overnight. Familial match to a half-sibling.'

All of yesterday's good luck had evaporated with one stupid, lazy mistake by the lab in Preston. Instead of contacting him personally and exclusively, it was all over the police service, where anyone could read it. And anyone could notify the Union. 'Can you remember the details?' he said.

Tracey was stung by his sharp tone and flinched back. 'I think so. He has a half-brother who's on the elimination database.'

Criminals are on one database. Law enforcement, military and medical personnel are on a different one, for elimination and identification purposes. 'Can you remember the brother's name?'

'Umm. Matthew Eldridge. I was about to leave to come here, so I didn't look him up. I thought you'd have actioned that.'

Matthew Eldridge. According to Clarke's report, he was the assessor for Langdale-Leven. Tom was in deep trouble and he needed help. Quickly. 'Tracey, do you remember Wing Commander Clarke from the case in Bolton?'

'I'm not likely to forget him, am I? Bloody great lamppost of a man with a limp. Nice smile though, when he wants to turn on the charm. Up to his neck in funny business.'

Mike Jepson recognised the case: it was the one with the pig in the chiller. He looked like a pressure cooker about to explode, so Tom cut in. 'Take those evidence bags and go straight to the White Horse Inn at Great Barrow in Cheshire. Do not pass Go, do not collect any speeding tickets. Don't hand them over to anyone but Clarke, and only in the pub.'

Her mouth was hanging open, and it was Jepson who filled the shocked silence. 'If you don't explain what's going on, Tom, I'm going to walk out of here and notify my colleagues and the Home Office. I gave you the benefit of the doubt last time.'

'What he said,' added Tracey. 'I'm not dropping evidence off with the funny brigade.'

'We're on a knife-edge,' said Tom, trying to stay calm. 'I'm trying to stop this going pear-shaped. I want this done properly just as much as you do, and Clarke is one of the good guys. He's a warranted special constable with the L&W. Ring Commander Ross if you want, but for God's sake do it from the car. Please. I'm staying here to ensure the chain of evidence, and I take full responsibility for this.'

Tracey looked at the evidence bags. The contents had been photographed numerous times, and so had the body in the Gnome case. As well as the disappearing body, all the digital and physical trace evidence had been had been wiped or taken from the evidence room. Tracey gave a small shrug of her beefy shoulders. 'Fine. When you say straight away, you mean straight away?'

'As in I'm going to watch you drive out of the hospital, yes.'

'Fine. Look up the postcode of that pub while I get stripped.'

He did, and she got into her van five minutes later. 'I'll be there in forty minutes. He'd better be waiting.'

'They open at ten o'clock for coffee and don't close until midnight. And they have rooms. Don't leave the pub until you've seen Clarke.'

'You've lost the plot, sir.'

'You're not the first to say that, Tracey. Now go!'

As Tracey's van headed out of the mortuary car park, he was joined by Jepson. 'Milk, no sugar, right? I thought you might like a cup out here. To give you a chance to calm down and explain what on earth's going on. I've never seen behaviour like that in my operating room.'

Tom had half an hour to call Clarke. From what he could gather, although the man himself had probably been walking that dog of his since first light, the rest of his crew were not early risers. He owed it to Michael to share a little, and he could also find out if his worst nightmare were true.

He accepted the steaming mug of tea and was glad to discover it sported the crest of St Helen's Rugby League Club, and not the one with the brain on it. Jepson had kept that one for himself. Tom took a sip and said, 'You do all the unexplained deaths from Westmorland and Lancashire over the Sands, don't you?'

'My team does. This isn't a one-man band.'

Tom steeled himself to ask the question. 'Have you heard of the Union Assessors?'

It was Jepson's turn to blow on his tea. Tom kept his fingers crossed for the answer.

'I have. In my time here, two bodies have been slated for post-mortems but never arrived because a different doctor pronounced Natural Causes. After the first one, your Commander Ross went apoplectic. After the second one, they re-drew the boundaries of his Division. They only drew them back again this summer. Is that what this is about?'

'Didn't you kick up a stink, Mike?'

'Ross told me not to. He said it wouldn't do any good, and that we'd get a black mark when the contract came up for renewal. Not every man of principle can be a hero, Tom. I kept quiet for the good of my team and promised myself it wouldn't happen again.'

'Ross wants me to make sure it never does. Somehow. Oh, shit.'

'What?'

Tom pointed at the road. Coming along it was a battered Nissan X-Trail in forest green. At least he had the comfort of knowing that Tracey had gone south, in the opposite direction. 'It's a 4x4. Pretty much the calling-card for that lot.'

'Should I stay or should I go?'

'Stay for me or go inside for your team.'

The heavy vehicle bumped into the car park. 'I'll stay. It might be fun. I don't get out much, you know.'

There was no screech of brakes, and the driver urged the monster car carefully into a marked bay before getting out. He was older than the victim by at least a decade, and had a weathered, outdoor face. He was dressed more like a mountain guide than a law-enforcement officer, perhaps because his patch included a big chunk of the fells. His hair was a mess of dark curls and short bits, and Tom remembered that Matthew Eldridge had undergone brain surgery in the spring after an attempt on his life.

Eldridge locked his vehicle and walked across to them. He stopped at a distance, and Tom braced himself inwardly.

'I'm Matthew Eldridge. Have you got my brother in there?'

This was wrong on so many levels. Eldridge shouldn't know about this. He shouldn't be here. Tom stuck to his guns. 'Perhaps we could go somewhere else, Mister Eldridge.'

'I want to see him. I want to make sure.' He looked behind them, towards the mortuary doors. 'You need a positive identification. For all you know, it could be Tom, Dick *or* Harry in there. You wouldn't want to be investigating the wrong brother, would you?'

Clever. Very clever. And correct. Jepson stepped in. 'No matter who you are, Mister Eldridge, identifying a loved one is very painful. Allow us some time to prepare him.'

'I want to see him as he is. And his effects. I might be able to identify some of the items.'

Also clever. Tom studied the man. He had the pain underneath, the pain that always comes. Eldridge was – or believed he was – a professional, and he was channelling his pain into action. Tom couldn't see a man who wanted to cover this up. He saw a man who wanted justice.

'I'm afraid the items you're interested aren't here, Matthew. Do you mind if I call you Matthew? I've notified MI7. You know the ones. They're based in Merlyn's Tower.'

Eldridge frowned, the lines in his forehead like trenches in the desert. 'How in the name of the Goddess do you know them? And how did you know to call them in?'

'I worked with Conrad Clarke on the Blackrod case.'

Some of the lines faded as Eldridge relaxed slightly. 'Conrad Bloody Clarke. It would have to be him, I suppose, now he thinks he's lord of all he can survey from his bloody helicopter.'

It was a fair description, and delivered with resignation rather than malice. Tom tried to keep it light. 'That's the one. I don't think the world has room for another.'

'It doesn't. Not this world, anyway.' He nodded slowly. 'So be it. I prayed it wasn't Harry. It might not be, I suppose.'

'Do you have other brothers?'

'Not that I know of. When I'd finished praying that it wasn't Harry, I prayed for justice. And the Goddess sent Conrad Bloody Clarke. It shows she has a sense of humour.'

Tom risked a glance at Jepson and discovered that the pathologist had taken two steps back, towards the mortuary. Tom didn't blame him.

Eldridge looked up. 'If you give me a cup of tea while we wait, I'll tell you what I know.'

'Come round the front,' said Jepson. 'There's a family room there.'

Eldridge shook his head. 'I'll wait here, if you don't mind. I don't want to go in there until I have to.'

'Then I'll get the tea,' said Tom. 'And my coat.'

As soon as the door closed behind them, Tom got out his phone.

'There is no MI7,' said Jepson. 'And that man is bonkers, even by the standards of the Lake District. Am I still in bed, dreaming? Never mind, I'll get Mister Eldridge's tea. Do you want another.'

Tom held out his mug as Clarke answered the phone. Jepson took it off him and walked away.

'Hello, Tom,' said Clarke. 'Have you recovered from the match on Monday?'

'Conrad, we've got a problem.'

I liked it very much that Tom Morton had said *we* have a problem. He can be very conscientious, can Tom. Unfortunately.

And now his conscientiousness has landed a great steaming cowpat of misery in my lap. That's my metaphor, not his. When he's under stress, Tom has a tendency to mix metaphors like a bad barman. *We're up shit creek without a parachute* were his exact words. Me? I chose the cowpat image because where's there's a cowpat there are cows, and I was going to milk this situation to my advantage.

'Cordy! Scout! We're going out.'

'At least you called me first,' said Cordelia, emerging from the kitchen. 'I'm surprised you didn't whistle for both of us. Where's the fire?'

'Lakeland. DCI Morton has picked up a homicide in the Particular. A Mage, or at least a Mage's brother.'

I was on my way to the boot room and didn't notice at first that Cordy hadn't responded. I looked back and she was standing still in the hallway. 'So soon?' she said, and she wasn't talking to me. She shook herself. 'Coming. Are we heading straight up there? I'll get my stuff.'

'No. We're meeting someone in the village. I'll explain on the way. Can you take Scout's lead? I need to call the Boss.'

She fiddled with Scout's collar and wagged her finger at him. 'No jumping up, understand? And no trying to shag my leg. Are we clear?'

'Arff.'

I was still pulling on my coat when Hannah answered. 'What?'

I gave her the thirty second rundown and stood by the road waiting for Cordy and Scout to catch up. When I'm stressed, I tend to walk even faster.

'I … I don't know what to say,' said the Boss. 'I expected you to tangle with the Unions sooner or later, but not so soon, and not like this.' She paused. 'You'll come up against some powerful opposition if you try to take the case. It could wreck your career in the Watch.'

'What about yours? I'll leave it alone if you want me to. You don't need me causing avoidable trouble.'

'No, it had to happen sooner or later. We both know that the situation in Lakeland is wrong. I'll get on to Security Liaison. Is there anything else I can do to help?'

'Yes, there is. This is going to end up in court very soon. It would help if you got Cador Mowbray briefed and ready.'

'Good idea. I'll get on to it.' She tried to muffle the microphone rather than put me on mute. It didn't work, and I heard her shouting to Tennille to get Cador on the phone. 'I was expecting you to call me yesterday, Conrad. How's your new partner?'

'Standing next to me, ma'am. Scout has bonded with her already. Bonded quite closely, as it happens.'

'Ugh. Another picture I don't need. Got to go. Good luck.'

'Well?' said Cordy. 'Is the game afoot?'

The reason I hadn't called Hannah yesterday is precisely because she expected me to. I wanted to show that I could make my new partnership work with what I'd been given. Cordelia and I had talked quite a bit on the journey to Middlebarrow and afterwards. I'd seen her offensive magick in action, and although she was no Saffron or Vicky, she had more than enough to hold her own in most situations. Every time I tried to steer the conversation to her, her history with Raven or her situation with Rick, she changed the subject.

When she came downstairs last night after FaceTiming her children, it was obvious that she'd been crying. Of all my partners so far, she was the most self-contained. Karina had difficulty in social situations and in making small-talk, both of which Cordelia could handle, but when it came to sharing, Cordy was very sparing.

'We're meeting a mundane crime scene manager in the pub. Not something that happens every day.'

'Please tell me she doesn't smoke and that you won't want to sit outside. It's too bloody cold for that.'

'She doesn't smoke. We'll only go outside if there are crime scene photos to examine.'

On the way to the White Horse, I filled her in on what little I knew about the case and started to tell her about my previous adventure in the Particular. Unlike Karina, she hadn't had time to read all my files.

'Back so soon, sir?' said the landlord. I'd taken Cordy for a drink last night, and she'd smiled at everyone and talked to no one.

'Three coffees, please. We're expecting someone. There they are now.'

I'd like to say that Tracey Kenyon looked different without her white boiler suit on. Apart from wearing blue, not white, she was pretty much the same: large of frame, short of hair and loud of voice.

We were the only people in the pub, so we took a wing to ourselves. Tracey had brought one of her instrument cases inside, and held on to it tightly. We sat down, and she put it on her lap, ignoring her coffee for now. She cut straight to the chase.

'I'm only handing these over if there's a chain of evidence. If you really are a special, you'll have a collar number, and I can log it. The last time you were near one of my crime scenes, the body disappeared from the mortuary and no action was taken.'

'Believe me, Tracey, action was most certainly taken. One moment.' It was a good job I'd grabbed my best coat on the way out and not my dog-walking Barbour. I selected my L&W warrant card and laid it on the table for her to examine, and examine it she did. She even took it out of the plastic wallet.

'Signed by Ross. Counter-signed by a magistrate.' She turned it over and humphed. 'Why does it not surprise me that you're a licensed firearms officer. Let's see if you're on the system.'

She rested a tablet computer on the case and tapped away. 'You are, and you are now responsible for two exhibits. Sign there with your finger.'

I signed the screen and she opened the case. When I saw what she had, I held up my hand.

'Not inside, if you don't mind, Tracey. We'll do it outside later. While you're here, you might as well give me the full story.'

'Do I have to? Hanging man isn't my only case.'

'But it's your most important. I need to know as much as I can as quickly as I can, and DCI Morton is busy. I could ring Commander Ross…'

'Fine. As far as I know, it's like this…'

She told me everything she thought I would understand, and even agreed to show me some of the pictures. At that point we did adjourn outside.

Tracey had confirmed that all the signs were of murder elsewhere. 'There could be other explanations for the red back, but it looks lividity to me. He's been killed and laid on his back, then moved. Rigor mortis had been and gone, so he died sometime before dawn on Monday.'

We examined the pictures outside. Cordelia didn't seem bothered about looking – until she actually saw them. They were pretty grim. Mr Eldridge jnr had suffered a lot before he died, and what had been done after death was in some ways even worse. 'What's that wound?' I asked, pointing to the victim's chest.

'No idea. It's a straight cut down from his collar bone with a very sharp knife, just to the right of the sternum. Dr Jepson will be able to tell if it's pre- or post-mortem.'

I had a horrible idea about that. 'I don't want to talk to the good doctor, or question his thoroughness, but I'd be very keen to know if there's damage to the ribs other than a nick from the knife that made the wound.'

'Why?' said Tracey, and Cordy raised her eyebrows in agreement.

'I hope I'm wrong, so I'll spare you the details.'

Tracey looked at me for a moment. 'I'll email Dr Jepson, then I've got to go. You're not officially attached to this case, and until you are, I'm sending everything to DCI Morton first. Just so you know.'

'Of course.'

'Here's the evidence you've signed for. Will you be able to check for prints and log them?'

'No, I won't. What I can do is handle them carefully and return them to you for proper analysis. Thank you, and thanks for coming all this way. Safe journey.'

Cordy offered to take the cups back to the bar and I went for a wander. I was in no rush to go anywhere until the top brass had fought the first battle in the turf wars. I sent a text to Tom and asked him to call me when he could. I also needed to track down our missing Enscriber. Erin had had gone off with the manager of some boy band I'd never heard of. According to Mina, she'd tried for the lead singer and been rebuffed on the grounds that she was too old. I had to smile at that. I sent her another text, telling her to get her arse back to Middlebarrow.

'What next?' said Cordelia.

'In the absence of Erin, we – you – are going to examine this parchment.'

## 10 — The Late Harry Eldridge

'Here, take the biscuit tin,' said Jepson offering Tom a tray. 'I haven't put sugar in his tea. He doesn't seem the sort, but he needs something to sweeten him. And the sugar will be good for shock.'

'Thanks, Mike. We might be a while.'

'Fine. While I've got the technician here, I'll remove his clothes. We'll lay him in the viewing room after that. Obviously I won't start the cutting before Mr Eldridge has seen him.'

Tom nodded, and Jepson opened the door. In the grey light of a grey day, Eldridge was finishing a phone call.

'Are you sure you don't want to go to the family room?' said Tom.

'No thanks.'

'Then at least let's go round the front. There's a bench. This way.'

Tom set off and left Eldridge to follow. There was a sign by the public entrance that said, *South Lancashire Pathology NHS Trust* in bright blue letters. Underneath, in much smaller type, were the words *Liverpool Mortuary*. The bench had been deliberately placed with its back to the building, even though that meant facing a multi-storey car park. Tom handed Eldridge his tea and more or less shoved the biscuits in the man's face. He held it there until Eldridge took a couple of Jaffa Cakes. These must be Jepson's private stash. In no office that Tom had ever worked would Jaffa Cakes survive five minutes otherwise.

Eldridge ate one of the Jaffa Cakes and said, 'I've just had the Chief Assessor on the phone. She wanted to know what the hell was going on.'

'Is that your boss?'

'Sort of. I answer to my Union, not her, but she is our Chief, so yes, she is the boss. I didn't tell her about Conrad Clarke. It'll be a nice surprise. Do you know how this works, Inspector?'

Tom had a good idea and he wanted to know what Eldridge would disclose. 'Not really.'

'There is no assessor in Furness at the moment. The Chief would normally ring Barrow police station, but now that Ross is on the case, the Chief will ring the Union President. I imagine that Clarke is on the phone to the Peculier Constable. Will Hannah Rothman back him, do you think?'

'They're close. Very close. She trusts him.'

'You've met her? I know you're Entangled, Inspector, but I'm surprised they let you into Merlyn's Tower.'

'No. It was socially. At Clarke's place. Hannah beat me in a bridge tournament.'

The second Jaffa Cake froze half way to Eldridge's mouth. 'I'm sorry. Did you say she was in Gloucestershire? And playing cards?'

'She did Bollywood dancing last month. I've seen the video.'

Eldridge examined his snack. 'Well, well, well.' He popped it in his mouth and dispatched it quickly. Before he spoke again, he reached for another. 'In that case, Hannah will call Security Liaison. Round about the same time that the Union President calls the L&W chief constable, the Home Office will call him too. And he will tell the Union that this is very much a police matter.' He checked his watch. 'About eleven o'clock, I reckon. That's the mundane bureaucracy out of the way. The magickal one is another matter. Clarke won't have it easy.'

Tom had been in two minds when he rang Conrad earlier. Clarke had been shocked, of course, but his first reaction had been, *Are you up for leading this, Tom? It's going to need a top detective.* Yes, there was flattery there, but respect, too. In the Blackrod case, Clarke had let Tom do his job right up to the moment when Tom and Mina had been kidnapped by Gnomes. Tom had been very happy to let Conrad take over at that point. He shuddered at the memory of the chains holding him down and the shotgun pointing at Mina.

To Eldridge, he said nothing about who would be SIO. It was time to move the conversation away from politics. 'Do you have a picture of your brother?'

Eldridge brushed his hands and took out his phone, a battered Samsung Galaxy. He found a picture and blinked his eyes to keep away tears. Before he handed over the phone, he said, 'Did they damage him? Will you be able to tell from this photograph that it's him?'

Tom held out his hand. 'I'll be able to tell if it definitely isn't him. If it's not, we can spare you the ordeal.'

Eldridge looked lost for a second. 'In some ways that would be worse. It would mean that my mother had twins and gave Harry's brother away for adoption. DNA doesn't lie. Mostly.' He handed over the phone.

It was the victim, almost certainly. Or his twin. Tom didn't want to go there, though. Even identical twins have different fingerprints, so there would be that to sort out as well. At some point. Right now he studied the image of a confident young man on the top deck of a boat, smiling and squinting against the sun. It looked to be a few years old. Perhaps it was a favourite picture. He passed back the phone. 'Tell me about Harry.'

'He's thirty-one, and he will be for ever more, I suppose.' The tears were closer now. 'He was a lying, cheating, double-dealing sneaky bastard, inspector, but he was still my little brother. Have you got a black sheep in your family?'

'You're looking at him. I joined the police instead of becoming a barrister.'

'Your parents don't know how lucky they are.' Eldridge looked for more images on his phone, then put it down, at a loss for words.

'Where did he live? What line of magick was he in?'

'Does the name Waterhead Academy mean anything to you?'

'No. I only know what's in Conrad's reports and the odd juicy detail he kept out of them.'

'Some of them about me, no doubt. The Academy is a registered mundane private school. It doesn't advertise because all the students are children of parents from the magickal world. Mages, non-Mages and Gnomes all send their kids there. The Mages are helped through the coming of magick and have basic classes. I went there myself. A long time ago. It's at the very top of Windermere, just west of where the river Rothay flows into the lake.'

'You don't have to give me all the background, Matthew. I can get that from somewhere else. Just tell me about Harry.'

Eldridge frowned. 'This *is* about Harry. And now I've sat down, I find I'm not so keen to see him after all. I'd rather talk about him, if that's okay.'

'Please. We're both wrapped up warm.'

Eldridge managed a tiny smile as he looked at Tom's Crombie overcoat. 'You might want to swap that before you go to Lakeland. Anyway, there are two parts of the Academy. The part by the road is inspected by Ofsted. They don't know about the School House, the original building by the lake. That's where classes in magick are held, and where the sixth formers live. Non-Mages and Gnomes leave at sixteen to go elsewhere, while the Mages move into School House. They might do one or two A levels, but mostly the education is magickal.'

'And how did Harry fit in?'

Eldridge looked at him over his mug as he finished his tea. 'He broke his back when he was fourteen. Up to that point in his life, all he was interested in was horses, and the next seventeen years were second best for him. He got into sailing. He trained as an Enscriber. He bummed around the world of magick. He was always very good at numbers and finally he combined three of his late loves in one place.'

'Go on.'

Eldridge put his mug on the tray and put the lid firmly on the biscuit barrel. 'For the last five years, Harry has been living part-time on a houseboat moored next to School House, teaching Enscribing and maths at the Academy and running a book.'

It took Tom a second to understand. 'A book. As in bookmaking?'

'Correct. Harry was the official bookmaker to the Lakeland Chases and a number of other magickal events. If Quidditch were a real thing, he'd have run a book on that, too. Surely they must be ready in there.'

'I'm sure they are.' Tom led the way to the front door and showed his warrant card to the receptionist. Even DCIs have to be escorted, and they waited for someone to come through. 'You said he lived part-time on the houseboat.'

'It was full-time to start with. And then he met someone.' Eldridge looked out of the window. 'He wouldn't say who. Or why he was keeping her a secret – I know it was a her, and that she lived within reach of Ambleside. Harry didn't drive.'

Jepson himself came to collect them and took them into the family room. As government issue rooms go, it was tasteful, and fresh flowers sat on a side table covered with leaflets to inform the bereaved. Jepson had mentioned that the flowers came from the funeral director who had the contract for moving the deceased. There were two small couches facing each other and coffee table between them. The table's surface was clear of leaflets but showed many marks from hot drinks. None of that was what the visitor saw when they first walked in.

There was another room beyond the family room, separated by a big glass window. On the other side of the window were curtains, and beyond them would be the body. Eldridge walked straight to the window and waited, staring unfocused at the closed drapes. Like a metaphor made solid, the loved ones would be visible but out of reach. Out of reach to the mundane world. Would Eldridge be heading home later to do some Necromancy? That was not Tom's department.

Jepson handed Tom a form fastened to a clipboard. The form was for the South Lancs Coroner and was focused solely on identification, not investigation. 'Are you ready, Mr Eldridge?' asked the pathologist.

'No. Get it over with anyway.'

Jepson had heard the same words many times, and pressed a button by the window. A technician drew the curtains aside, and Eldridge moved forwards, pressing his hands to the glass.

'Can I go and see him properly.'

'It's best not to,' said Tom. He gave him a moment, then said, 'Mr Eldridge, is that your brother, Harry Eldridge?'

The assessor said nothing, and no one pushed him. After a long wait, he drew a ragged breath and turned away. 'Henry. His full name was Henry Neptune Eldridge.'

Jepson pushed the button again, and the curtains closed. 'I'm sorry for your loss, Mr Eldridge. Thank you. I'll leave you with Tom and ask the receptionist to bring more tea.'

91

'Tom, is it?' said Eldridge. Tom nodded, and Eldridge continued, 'You're going to cut me out, aren't you? Probably treat me as a suspect at first. That's why you wouldn't let me see him properly.'

'It's not personal, Matthew. The only exception we make is for parents of young children. Everyone else has to wait until later.'

'After the post-mortem, you mean.' He sat still for a second, then stood up. 'I need the loo. I promise not to sneak into the back.'

He wouldn't be the first to try that, and there was a rest room for families on the front side of the security door, not that a Mage would let a mundane door stand in their way. Or would they? Tom had no idea if overcoming digital systems was a regular thing in magick.

He waited in reception, and his gaze was drawn to a police car that had pulled up outside. What? Is that … yes. From the passenger side came his partner, DC Elaine Fraser, complete with walking stick and rucksack. She waved off the police driver and looked around. Tom hurried outside.

'Elaine?'

'Surprise, sir.' She did not look happy, and she checked to see if anyone was listening before she spoke in an urgent whisper. 'You've got a murder. A big one. A big one that might have magick in it and you want me to sit in a Manchester office trawling through passenger lists. I had to find out from Lucy where you were when I couldn't get you earlier. She thought I knew.' She lifted the walking stick for a second, and used it to point at him. 'You've not been taking my calls.'

'It's complicated.' He lowered his voice. 'There's a proper Mage inside, and his brother is the victim. I need to get back in.' He looked round. Eldridge was watching them from reception.

Before Tom could say any more, Elaine hobbled past him and through the doors. He hurried to intercept her, and introduced her to Eldridge. She gave the Mage her condolences and looked at the receptionist. 'Is that tea for me? I'm parched.'

Tom asked for another cup and led them back to the family room. Before things got totally out of hand, he passed the clipboard to Elaine. She accepted it without comment.

Eldridge assessed Elaine. 'Do you know Deputy Constable Clarke?' he asked.

'Yes,' said Elaine, 'but I don't get invited to his house. Unlike some. Don't worry, Mr Eldridge, I'm Entangled.'

'Could you confirm your brother's name for DC Fraser? She'll be taking notes.'

'Henry Neptune Eldridge. The "Neptune" is for his father, and I'll let Clarke explain why.'

'Is your mother alive, Matthew?'

'No. She died last year, and if she hadn't, this would have finished her off. We had no other relatives. I've filled that form out myself a few times, so I know what's coming.' He rattled off a date of birth, then smiled. 'Because he didn't drive or pay taxes, there won't be a single record of him on your system. I asked him once how he managed the money for his bookmaking business and he said that it was all online and all in the name of an occulted company.'

Tom risked a wry observation. 'Conrad can help with that. He knows a fair bit about money laundering. Will the school have records?'

'The Academy created a fake teaching agency to get round the magickal staff's lack of real qualifications. Don't get me wrong, the non-Mages are pucker teachers. Good ones in my experience.' Eldridge took a sip of tea. 'Before you ask, he didn't have many friends. He was close to Nicole Sanderson at the Academy, I do know that. And you have to speak to Aidan Manning at Sprint Stables in Longsleddale. And if he had any enemies, I don't know anything about them. I never went to another Chase after Harry's accident. I don't think I can take any more of this, Tom. Sorry. I'm going to go while I still can. Clarke's got my details, and if you give me the form, I'll sign it.'

'Are you sure you'll be alright to drive?'

'I'm not going far. I'll see a friend. Please.'

Eldridge was starting to sweat. Tom reached a decision. 'Just one thing, Matt. Your brother's mobile number would be a big help.'

Eldridge found the contact and gave Elaine his phone. She swapped it for the clipboard and said, 'There's still a few blanks, Mr Eldridge. If you want to get off, you'll have to trust me to fill them in.'

Matthew took the form and signed it. Elaine being Elaine, she had to push it a bit further. While Eldridge was writing, Tom saw her checking a couple of things. She didn't write down the late Harry's number, she took a picture of the screen.

Tom offered his card to Eldridge and accepted one in return as they got ready to leave. Tom finished by saying, 'We'll be in touch, Matthew. At the very least we'll need a statement. A mundane statement. And I'm sure that Deputy Constable Clarke or his colleague will need to talk magick with you.'

Eldridge paused a second. 'Vicky Robson, isn't it? A good Mage.'

'No, she was so good she's been promoted. I don't know who's replaced her. Have a safe journey, Matt, and I'm so sorry we had to meet like this.'

Tom watched Eldridge leave. He walked out and along the footpath before he realised that his car was round the back. He seemed to shake himself awake and waved at Tom before he headed round the corner. He should be safe to drive a short distance, and Tom hoped that the friend he was visiting was a good one. He asked the receptionist if he could use the family room a while longer and went to give Elaine a piece of his mind.

On the way back to Middlebarrow, I finally heard from Erin. 'Do we have to go to the Lakes today? Can't you go and feed your wolves or something?'

'Something's come up. Something serious. We've got to go soon. You don't have to come with us, but I could really use your help to look at a document.'

There was a pause. 'You're not just saying that to make me leave? You really need my help? Can't your new partner help you? Who is she? I presume it's a "she."'

'It's Cordelia, formerly of the Daughters, and yes, I do need you.'

'Cordelia? How about that, then, eh.' She chuckled. 'I'm in …' she spoke to someone else, 'Where am I? Altrincham. That's it.' She came back to the microphone. 'I'm in Altrincham. Is that on your way? If it is, just chuck everything in my bag and pick me up. Saves you waiting.'

It would save a lot of time if we did that. Erin's like a wobbly toy sometimes – she needs a nudge to get her back on course. 'That's a plan. Text me a location in the next ten minutes. It'll take us an hour to get sorted and drive up.'

'No helicopter?'

'Can't justify it, I'm afraid. Not yet. See you soon.'

Cordelia was trying to untangle herself from Scout's lead prior to unleashing him on the other side of the lodge gates. She was worrying at me in the same way that Scout worries a bone: what on earth was she doing here? What got to me, I think, is her passivity. We'd had nothing to do yesterday except get to know each other, and she'd been compliant in everything I suggested. Not once had she made a proposal to do something. In a raw recruit, I could understand that, but she's a proper grown-up. She's got kids and everything.

Saffron was only twenty-two when she got stuck with me, and right from the beginning, she got stuck in to the project. She asked questions, she challenged me and she wanted to learn. I couldn't decide whether Cordelia was simply passive by nature or whether she was *waiting* for something. What that could be, I have no idea. It was time to shrug and move on.

'Scout! To me!' He came, and I got out a doggy treat. I infused it with a little Lux and let him snarf it off my fingers. 'Find the magick, boy. Find it!'

He shot off down the track, sniffing and running from side to side. I went up to Cordy and said, 'We really are off this time. Picking up Erin on the way. Can you pack her bag?'

'Sure.' I waited to see if she had any questions. She looked at Scout, at the horizon and then at my rucksack. 'Do we really need Erin to examine that Parchment? Couldn't you give it a go?' She said it with a smile. Maybe she'd been listening to my thoughts. Did she not want to try? Magick was her job.

'Or you,' I replied.

'Or both of us,' she said reasonably.

'We've got time. Let's pack first, and I'll see you in the study.'

She headed through the Wards and down to the house, and I followed Scout to see what he'd do. After sniffing round the barrier hedge for a minute, he let out a bark and looked expectantly at me. I didn't need to check: he was standing on the Ley line from Nimue's spring. Quite impressive. I gave him a scratch and a treat. We followed Cordelia into the Haven grounds and I lifted the tailgate of my new car ready for loading.

Evie was at university today, doing her MA in creative writing, so I left her a quick note and put the kettle on before raiding the fridge for a few snacks. I left a pot of tea to brew and went to pack. Not that I'd actually unpacked much yesterday.

I helped Cordy load the cases. She'd reduced her baggage train a little, but we still had a full car by the time I'd squeezed in the dog basket. Scout hopped hopefully on to the back seat. 'Out, you. If you get mud on those seats, you'll clean it off yourself.'

'Arff.'

'It does make you look a little mad,' said Cordy.

'What?'

'Talking to Scout as if he understands you like a Familiar.' She smiled. 'Another thing I'll have to get used to.'

I grabbed some latex gloves and we adjourned to the study. There was a blank space over the fireplace with a picture hook at the top. There were a few places like that in the house, where my predecessor had hung his own choice of art, and the prime spot over the fire seemed tailor made for a coat of arms. An idea came to me, and I filed it away for later.

Evidence bags come in a variety of flavours. Some are anti-tamper and can only be used once. They're mostly used by police officers, and it means that laboratories can be sure that what was seized hasn't been meddled with in transit. Forensic technicians use re-sealable ones, like these two. I got out a plastic tray and wiped it with rubbing alcohol.

'What are you doing?' said Cordy. It was almost the first question she'd asked that related directly to our jobs rather than the social life at Elvenham.

'I'm a hybrid. Part Watch, part RAF and part L&W copper. If these get to the lab and they're contaminated with leather off the desk or dog-treats, they're useless in court.'

I reached inside the bigger bag and unfastened the map case. I put my hand inside and held it over the blank Parchment. No magick radiated from it, so I carefully drew out the paper, leaving the map case behind, and put it on the tray. This time I gave it a deep sweep and found two sources of magick: a small blob at the top and a bigger swirl in the body of the Parchment. The small blob was familiar...

'I think there's a Script Curtain at the top,' I said, unable to keep the delight out of my voice. I know it's one of the easiest Works of magick to deal with, but I'd found it all on my own. 'See?'

Cordy ran her hand over the Parchment. 'Looks like it.'

I waited. She did nothing. 'Go on,' I said.

'I assumed you'd want to do it,' she replied evenly.

Was this some sort of passive-aggressive insubordination? Not ten minutes ago I'd promised myself I wouldn't get hung up about her attitude, and now this. 'I thought I'd made it clear yesterday that our partnership works like this: you do the magick, I do the extreme violence. The rest we share.'

'Don't you think I'm capable of extreme violence? Because I know you're capable of more magick than you think you are.'

My jaw nearly dropped open. I blinked twice to bite back some of the obvious retorts – *How many people have you killed?* Being the most obvious. I also had to stop myself pulling rank. What would be the adult thing to do? Listen to her, I suppose.

I used my "magick" thumb (my left one) to rub away the concealing Work, and a small picture, like an ink stamp, revealed itself. It was circular, and featured the scales of justice surrounded by wavy lines. I peered closely, then stood back. 'Have you seen this before?'

She studied the symbol. 'No. Nothing like it.'

'And the other Work? I really have no idea.'

She checked the big swirl of magick again. 'Me neither.'

'One for Erin, then. We're obviously meant to find and recognise the symbol, so you find out what it means and I'll unfold the small piece.'

She hesitated for a fraction of a second, then got out her phone to take a picture. I wondered who she'd consult. The person I'd have gone to would have been Rick James. I doubt that he's Cordelia's first choice.

The other piece of paper was folded roughly, as if it had been crumpled rather than carefully stowed. I could just make out a series of black lines that looked nothing like writing. I checked the bag and it said *Found in right thigh pocket of trousers. Presumed too damp to open safely.* I put it back in the evidence bag and told Cordy that it also needed the attention of an expert. The last thing I wanted was to get on the wrong side of Tracey Kenyon. Again.

'Mmm,' said Cordy, staring at her phone. 'I'm waiting on someone getting back to me. They need to look it up.'

'Then let's get going. You'd better drive in case I have to take any calls.'

# 11 — Road Tripping

We hadn't made it to Altrincham before it all kicked off with conference calls and ultimatums. Or ultimata. Never knew which was right. After ten minutes, Cordy had to pull off the M56 to park up and get a reliable signal so that I could take a video call. I had no idea that the Lakeland Unions were capable of exerting so much pressure on the mundane authorities, until the chief constable of Lancashire and Westmorland threatened to suspend Commander Ross.

The UK has a well-oiled, national counter-terrorism command with its own hierarchy and HQ. They pretend to take an interest in far-right groups, but it's really all about Islamic threats. Beyond that, the secret state is much more of a patchwork, and the thread holding it together is the Security Liaison Office, in the shape of John Lake. I've come across him a few times, and I think he's okay, yet Tom Morton calls him the Angel of Death for some reason. I don't know how, but Hannah has managed to keep him away from becoming Entangled. How long she'll be able to keep it up is another matter.

Apparently, the climax of the showdown had been when John Lake held up his phone to the video camera and said, 'Chief Constable, do you really want me to call the Home Secretary?' The chief constable did not want that. Ten minutes later, I was on a three-way video call with Lake and the Commander.

The Commander of Cairndale Division, Allister Ross, is one of a disappearing breed – hewn from Aberdeen granite and a military veteran, he is lord of all crime-fighting west of the river Lune and south of Cumberland.

While they were waiting for my camera to spring into life, he stared unmoving at the screen in front of him, the gleaming buttons on his uniform a rebuke to every slovenly officer. The lights went green on the video toolbar, and I was live.

'Aah, Conrad,' said Lake. 'Glad you could join us.'

I nodded at the camera. 'Good morning, sir, morning John.'

Ross gave the curtest of nods in return. 'Good morning, Clarke. I hear you're a wing commander now.'

'Yes, sir.'

His eyes narrowed. 'That's a fine and marvellous thing, I'm sure, but that's not why I'm allowing you on to my investigation.'

Lake interrupted smoothly. 'If you remember, Commander, it was DCI Morton who called in MI7, and it's because of us that you've still got the case.'

Ross pointed his finger at the screen. 'You know and I know that there is no such thing as MI7. If you won't tell me who Clarke works for, then I can live with that, but he's coming here as a warranted officer of Lancashire & Westmorland. Is that clear?'

'Conrad?'

'Of course, sir. Without your help, I wouldn't have my firearms licence, would I?'

Ross looked wary. 'Are you trying to soft-soap me, Clarke?' He waved a hand in dismissal. 'Never mind. So long as you get these jumped-up vigilantes out of my division, I can put up with you. Who's with you?'

I moved the laptop slowly to show my partner to Ross. 'This is Lieutenant Kennedy.'

'That's me, Commander,' said Cordelia.

Ross stared at the screen. 'I look forward to meeting you properly, lieutenant. I'll tell my PA to make out a Visitor's badge. When are you due here, Clarke?'

I turned the camera back to me. 'Around lunchtime, sir.'

'We'll have a briefing in the secure conference room as soon as you and DCI Morton get here. I take it no one's spirited away our corpus?'

'No, sir. The post mortem is well under way.'

'Good. Until this afternoon, then.'

When I'd ended the call and closed the laptop, Cordelia sniffed the air dramatically. 'So that's what testosterone smells like. I've always wondered. Can't say it does anything for me.'

'Don't worry, Cordy. I'll keep your secret.'

A tiny glimmer of panic flitted across her face before she realised I was making a joke. 'And what secret would that be, *sir*?'

'That you think the Boss smells of testosterone. She wouldn't have behaved any differently. I'll text Erin and tell her we'll be there in ten minutes.'

Cordy started the engine and looked around for lorries. Whatever she was thinking, it didn't show in her face. When we were back on the motorway, she made an effort to lighten the tone. 'I wonder what she'll be wearing.'

'She had her stuff sent from the Manchester hotel in a taxi, so I doubt she'll still be in her going-out dress.'

'That's the Arden Foresters for you.' She said it with a disarming smile, but there was a hint of tension underneath. 'No one parties like the Foresters. Or so they say.'

When Erin skipped out of the impressive barn conversion where the music mogul lived, she was wearing an oversized tee-shirt featuring the boy band in moody black and white, her jeans and a smile. The multi-millionaire manager followed behind with a small suitcase and a big bunch of flowers. I wouldn't say that he was old enough to be her father. Uncle, possibly. It was hard to tell his real age under the Botox. I popped the boot open and took her case. 'I don't think there's room for the flowers,' I said dubiously.

Erin took them off the manager and gave him a kiss. 'I'll hold them. I presume I'm in the back? Fine. Thanks for everything.' She kissed him again. 'No need to see me off.'

He gave her a smile and a wink. 'If you're ever passing, you've got my number, yeah? See you around.' He left us to it and retreated to his barn.

I looked more closely at the tee-shirt. 'What's the writing? Have you been Enscribing?'

She gave me a strange look. 'Don't be daft, Conrad. The band signed it. I'm going to send it to Grace. She loves them. Look.' She twisted the shoulder round, and I could just make out the words *To Amazing Grace. You're the best. Love Liam. XXXXX.*

That's Erin all over. In the fallout from the murder of Lord Mowbray, a very young girl was left with no mother (until she gets out of jail). Erin was made the girl's magickal guardian, and instead of pocketing the fee and making three visits a year, she's found out what Grace likes and is sending the poor kid a gift beyond rubies. Yet she's also quite happy to disappear for two days.

'Aren't you going to put it away safely?'

She lifted the sweatshirt and showed me her assets. At least she still had her bra on. 'I had to swap it for my top.' She nodded at the farmhouse. 'He's a bit kinky that way.'

'A bit?' I shook my head. 'Get in.'

She got into the car and started chatting to Cordelia while I persuaded Scout to get into his basket. As soon as we'd plotted a course to Cairndale, I brought Erin up to speed on the broad outline. She's not part of the King's Watch, nor does she want to be ("I'd rather paint lighthouses in winter," were her exact words), but Erin is a trusted consultant. I twisted round in the seat to face the back and gave her the evidence bag. 'Could you have a look at that for us?'

'What about rubber gloves?' said Cordy, rather sharply.

'You should get out more,' said Erin. 'If the Daughters had a reciprocal arrangement with Salomon's House, like we do, then you'd have learnt about Macavity's Gloves.'

It was a challenge. Delivered with humour, but a challenge nonetheless. 'Macavity?' said Cordelia.

'As in *Cats*. Macavity is the master criminal who's never there. The Charm stops the grease on your fingers transferring to paper, so no fingerprints. It also makes your own ink stick to your fingers even more, which is a total pain, so I don't always use it.'

'Are we stopping on the way?' said Cordelia, abruptly changing the subject. Erin grinned and opened the evidence bag.

I chose to answer Cordy first. 'I'll text Lucy and ask her for recommendations. She'll have figured out all the best places to eat. I don't want to go into Cairndale nick until Tom Morton's there. What you got, Erin?'

'Your mum would appreciate this, Conrad,' she replied after a cursory examination. 'It's the magickal equivalent of public key cryptography.'

I looked at Cordelia. Surely this was a widely known technique, so why hadn't she spotted it? She blinked and pretended to be studying the traffic for a second. 'It was written with Urania's Pen?'

'You could say that.'

'That explains it. Enscribing was never my strong point, and I've simply never used one. I'd forgotten about it. I'm sorry Conrad.'

'Except it wasn't in the pen,' said Erin. 'It was in the seal. Old school. You write your message with any form of Enscribing pen, then put the stamp on it. Only the Master Seal will untangle the magick.'

What was going on here? Erin and Cordelia didn't speak much when we were in Cornwall, or not that I'd noticed. Erin had been busy and Cordy was pretty much chained to Raven, so what was this all about? It wasn't quite hostility, but it was going beyond banter. Put it this way: no one has ever said to me that the Daughters and the Foresters are enemies.

Cordelia took Erin's attitude in her stride and asked the question. 'Do you recognise the seal?'

'No. Sorry. Do you want me to find out?'

I stepped in. 'If Cordelia's source doesn't come up with the goods, I'll ask Francesca.'

Erin had strapped herself in behind Cordy because I always push the seat so far back that no one can fit in. Erin looked at me with raised eyebrows: *Why didn't you ask Frannie first?* I shook my head a fraction. *Don't ask.*

Erin re-packaged the Parchment and put it to one side with a shrug. 'Well, either way, you don't need me to unpack it, so what happens now? I don't want to be selfish, but the Batman and Robin stuff isn't my gig.'

'I hadn't forgotten that, Erin. As soon as Commander Ross releases her, Cordelia is going to take you to Linbeck Hall and protect you against the Sextons. She can drop you at Oxenholme station afterwards.'

Given her attitude so far on this trip, I half expected Cordy to complain. No. She just nodded in agreement and asked where we were staying tonight.

'I have no idea. Can I ask you a personal question?'

She flicked her eyes off the road for a second. 'You asked enough of them yesterday, so what's different?'

'They weren't personal. They were professional.'

'Asking about someone's magick is a very personal question,' she replied.

'Not to him,' said Erin. 'To him, magick is a skill, not the essence of your being like it is to us. You get used to it.'

'So I've heard,' said Cordelia. 'It's what everyone keeps telling me. So what does constitute a personal question for Conrad Clarke?'

This was too good a chance for Erin to pass up. 'Sex and money. Especially money. If he thought your sex life was relevant, he'd grit his teeth and ask anyway. He thinks that money is even more personal than sex.'

Cordelia doesn't have much of an accent. Sort of posh Hampshire. That sort of thing. She has, however, spent a long time around women who went to the best boarding schools. 'I can't wait,' she drawled.

I gave Erin a hard stare and she grinned back at me. I turned to face Cordelia and said, 'The expenses on Watch business are rubbish. I don't mind the Red Rose hotel, but I usually prefer somewhere more comfortable and pay the difference. Vicky couldn't afford it, so I subbed her. Saffron could afford it. In fact, Saffron would complain if the restaurant only had one Michelin Star.'

'Sounds about right,' said Erin. 'Saff does have expensive tastes. Not as expensive as your sister, from what I hear.'

What? Who's been talking about Rachael? Another time.

Cordelia gave the first truly bitter smile I've seen from her. 'Unlike the Foresters, the Daughters at Glastonbury really do believe in poverty and communal property. The only things I own that aren't in this car are in two cardboard boxes, one at my mum's and one in Rick's house. Rick had to give me some money just so I could get the train to Manchester.'

'We'll play it by ear, then,' I said diplomatically. Erin was going to come back, so I chucked her the other evidence bag to shut her up. 'That might be damp. Can you look at it anyway?'

'If it's on Parchment, sure I can.' She knows me well enough to launch straight into the explanation without any mind games. 'When they bond the fibres together, there's a connecting web of Lux. That's how it takes the magick. There's a Charm that energises the fibres and dries them out, and I'd use it now, but I don't want to tire myself out. If you've got any spare...?'

I held out my left hand and she reached up to take it, then stopped, her fingers inches from mine. 'I know you've done this loads with your comrades, Conrad, but this isn't life-or-death. Have you had a proper lesson in Subordination?'

'Can't say as I have. I usually rely on the other party to sort that out.'

She drew her hand back. 'And that's why Myfanwy and Vicky walk with a limp sometimes. When you're in a bad way, it kind of projects itself. The Goddess only knows what Eseld must feel.'

'Eseld?' said Cordelia. 'I know you helped her a lot in Cornwall, but I thought that was mundane.'

Erin totally ignored the signals I was trying to give her and pressed on. 'Oh, they've bonded alright. He doesn't talk about it because he doesn't want to make Mina jealous.'

'Erin!'

'Yeah, yeah. You're just good friends. I know. Mina says it's not her who should be worried about the bond, it's Eseld, so you're off the hook, Conrad.'

This time I drew my finger across my throat in a warning gesture, and Erin finally got the message. She moved her hand back towards me and said, 'It's not difficult. You pool Lux into your hand and let me draw it. So long as you keep it pure, there's no bond. And don't take any back from me, OK? Shoulders are best for this, but we know each other well enough to do it on my thigh.'

I nodded and closed my eyes, letting the warmth flow down my arm until my hand was hot and almost burning. I felt Erin gently take my forearm and move my hand until I felt denim. Then she clamped her legs together. That was not what I was expecting. Almost immediately I felt the Lux drain away from my hand.

'I said pure!,' she muttered. 'Less heat, please.'

'That's how I roll, Erin.'

'Whatever. Right. Let's see.'

There were rustling sounds over the engine noise, and the rate of transfer increased. I couldn't keep this up for long – I might be more accomplished in magick than I was, but I still have little stamina. I was running low and had to attempt something new: uncapping the reservoir in my tibia. I did the mental flick and felt the Lux flow round my body.

'Easy, tiger,' said Erin.

What?

'Okay, Conrad. Enough. Draw the flow back into your hand or there'll be a flashover.'

I felt something I've never felt before – the barrier between my personal space and another person's. I could feel where I stopped and where Erin began, and on the other side of that line things were very different. Instead of heat, there was … sound. Sound energy. Vibrations and noises. A total cacophony. Then the distance grew further and my hand was just a hand. Clamped between her thighs.

'If you could let me go?'

I opened my eyes and she was flushed red from neck to hairline. She opened her legs, and I drew my hand out. Before I could say anything, she shook her head and took a deep breath. 'The paper's dry, now. Give me a few minutes and I'll analyse it.'

I turned around to face the motorway, and the Satnav told me that we'd be there in forty minutes. I checked my phone and saw a message from Mina. Funny how coincidences can creep you out. The message said:

*We've stopped for lunch, and by Ganesh's tusk, I'm missing you. I wanted to throw myself in your arms and let you take the strain after this morning, but all I had was Annelise. She doesn't have the same effect on me that you do. It was tough in the witness box. The barrister for Clan Flint is a total windbag. Tell Erin that we're going to go with the Save-the-Date option. I love you. XXXXX.*

To which I responded:

*I wish you were here, too. Or I was there. You'll tie them in knots, love. You do that to me, so they stand no chance.*

And other things I won't repeat here.

'Erin? Mina says, and I quote, "We're going to go with the Save-the-Date option." Does that mean anything to you? Because it means nothing to me. Not that it's my wedding or anything.'

'Oh. Right. Thanks. I wonder why she didn't tell me directly.' She paused. 'Aah. I get it. She wants me to explain it to you. Mina can't decide whether to have the legal ceremony at the Cheltenham registry office or at St Michael's.'

'What! In the church!'

'According to Mina, the church has to marry you if you live there. And there's no reference to Jesus in the vows, just to God. They've always been flexible like that.'

'I'm sure that the Allfather would find it highly amusing. I'm not sure about St Michael himself. Getting struck by lightning was not part of my plans.'

'Mina said you'd say that. The problem is that if you go to Cheltenham, there's loads of logistics and Myfanwy can't go, can she?'

'It's not her bloody wedding.'

'Mina said you'd say that, too. I won't tell Myfanwy, Conrad, even though she is my best friend and she did pull your sorry arse out of the fire.'

'I think perhaps this is a conversation I need to have with Mina.'

'Whatever. Do you want to know about this Parchment or not?'

What I really wanted to do was send a sternly worded text to my fiancée. I paused with my fingers over the keys and realised that this was not what she wanted to hear. And then another thought struck me: one I'd have to research later. I turned back round. 'Go on, Erin.'

She showed me a piece of scrappy parchment, torn roughly along one edge, and covered in crossings out. 'What's underneath?' I asked.

'What do you mean?'

'He's crossed something out, hasn't he? I presume this is the victim's work.'

'Probably, given that it was found in his pocket. No, he hasn't crossed it out. He's done some dynamic magick.'

'Isn't that difficult?' said Cordelia. Her silence during the marriage discussion had been eloquent.

'Mmm,' said Erin. 'I think this is a Lattice Ward. It's the only thing that makes sense. No other pattern of magick looks like that. See the way the lines are bent to make an opening here? I think he used the Enscription as a focus to distort the Ward and get through it. To answer your question, Cordy, it would be nigh-on impossible for me because I can't write fast enough. If you're quick on the draw, it's not so challenging.'

'Is there anything else you can tell us?'

'It's Sexton's paper. So was the other one. No surprise there, given that they have a monopoly in Lakeland. I think the encrypted one was done with a brush, not a pen. Until it's decrypted, I've got nothing else. Sorry.'

'Thanks, Erin, that's been most useful.'

I lapsed into silence as we passed Preston. Erin got out her phone, and I remembered that I had to text Lucy. When I'd finished, Cordelia said, 'If I'm going to the Sextons this afternoon, I need to know why they've got a grudge against the King's Watch.'

It took most of the journey for me to tell the story, with sarcastic interruptions from Erin not helping. I was getting a headache when Lucy said that we should go not to Cairndale but to Byford Mill, just up the Cowan Valley from the town. *And tell me what the service is like. I'm thinking of buying it.*

All right for some.

'What am I doing while you're in conference?' said Erin. 'I doubt there are any shopping options in Cairndale.'

'There's a nice park,' I replied. 'Scout will love it.'

She groaned. 'Tell me you're joking.'

## 12 — A Meeting of Minds

Today has already been a day of surprises, and I got another one when DC Elaine Fraser got out of Tom Morton's car. She gave us a heroic smile, then nearly fell over. Deep tissue wounds can do that to you. She retrieved her walking stick, and I introduced my new partner in magick to my partners in the police.

'Elaine foisted herself on me,' said Tom. 'I think it's because Rob's in Scotland and she doesn't fancy looking after herself.'

Cordy gave me the raised eyebrow.

'Rob's a pro rugby player. Plays centre for Scotland. They've got a full schedule, haven't they?'

'Another month!' said Elaine. 'And minimal time off under this new coach of theirs. Expects them to live like monks.'

'Shall we have a pre-meeting?' I asked Tom.

He pointed to the CCTV cameras. 'Better not. Ross will know we're here.'

'Can I put this bag in your boot, first?'

He gave me a dark look and opened his boot without a word. He had a good idea what was in the bag.

We set off towards the HQ building, and I said, 'I think you and I will be going off together. Cordelia has to deal with Watch business for a couple of hours and needs my car.'

'Fair enough. Let's take the short-cut through the custody suite.'

The HQ for Cairndale Division was built at a time of higher budgets and optimism. The architect wanted to pioneer low-energy technological solutions, so instead of air-con, the windows are barely visible because of reflective awnings. It looks very Blade Runner, a point I made to Tom.

'Spanish,' he replied. 'The architect was Spanish. With all due respect to Sofía, they have different weather down there. Allegedly the architect assumed the rainfall figures for Westmorland were a mistake.' We all stopped to look at the greying sky. 'For fifteen days a year, it's brilliant. For the other three hundred and fifty, it's like a concrete bunker.'

'Eurgh,' said Cordelia when we exited the custody suite. 'That was disgusting. Are they all like that? The smell of despair and bleach is inhuman.'

I let Tom answer that one.

'You should try Earlsbury – it has added stale tobacco. And the smell is all too human, I'm afraid.'

The secure conference room was a windowless space with endless whiteboards attached to bare concrete walls. At least they'd spent money on decent lighting: the recessed LEDs wouldn't give me a headache. Ross was waiting, and so was a much friendlier face.

'Welcome to Cairndale, Lieutenant,' Ross said to Cordelia. 'This is your Visitor's Badge, and this here is PC Smith, on secondment to CID.'

'Call me Barney,' said the solidly reassuring figure. I went to shake his hand after Cordelia had finished, and he couldn't suppress a grin. 'Good to see you again, sir.'

'And you, Barney. New suit?'

'Does it show?'

'Later,' said Ross. 'Dump your stuff and sit anywhere.'

We all jumped to obey, and naturally turned to face the still standing Ross.

'As of an hour ago, I have replaced myself as SIO and allocated DCI Morton. This is, however, a Divisional investigation, and that means we sink or swim together. Are we clear?'

I wasn't. What was Ross's game here? Tom seemed happy enough, though. 'Yes sir.'

'Good. This is your case, Tom, and I don't interfere. I expect you to give me enough to brief the press office. At the moment, interest is minimal because we've lied our arses off and said it's a suicide. I can sit on the PM report until tomorrow, but it's going to have to go public as a murder.'

'I understand.'

'Then I'll leave you to it. Oh, one more thing, Mr Clarke. I won't insult you by using your police rank, because I know you're more than that. Up to a point.'

'What point would that be, sir?'

'Up to the point where a serious incident occurs or a firearms operation is necessary. At that point, I am your Gold Commander. My adjutant is on holiday this week, would you believe. Until he gets back, you can report directly to me. Right. I'll leave you to it. You've got my number, Tom.'

'Sir. Thank you.'

He left us alone, and we all breathed out. Especially Tom. It took him a few seconds to realise that we were now looking at *him*. 'What? You don't need me to tell you where to sit, do you? If that's the case, we're doomed.'

We gathered around one end of the room and unpacked our bits and pieces. When we were settled, Tom took his stance. Tom Morton is one of the smartest dressed police officers you'll ever see, if you consider hand-made three-piece suits and Crombie overcoats to be smart. It's not just a sartorial affectation, he was once in a situation where good Yorkshire wool saved him from serious injury. I kid you not.

He'd already taken off his suit jacket, and he stuck his thumbs into the armholes of his waistcoat. I'm sure he learnt that at a very young age, watching his father do the same thing in court. He looked first at Barney and then at Elaine. 'There are some serious security aspects to this case, Barney. I won't sugar coat the pill, but you'll be out of the loop on a lot of stuff. Sorry.'

'I'm still on my first murder enquiry,' he said. 'That's more than I'd get back at Barrow. If I get bored, I can always go fishing in the Cowan.'

'I might join you,' said Tom. 'As for Elaine, I'm afraid that you're staying here.'

'Yeah, I know. I'm going to take time off for physio. They have the best sports injury faculty in the north at ULIST, and I'm going to use it.'

'Good.' He unhooked his thumbs from his waistcoat and picked up a marker. I saw rather than heard Elaine draw breath. Tom flipped the marker in the air like a baton and caught it cleanly. Elaine sighed. I don't think she cares if he makes an arse of himself – this was more like he was casting the runes, a prayer for good omen. Clearly she was satisfied that the gods would smile on our venture. If only it were that simple.

'We'll start with the victim,' said Tom. He wrote *Henry Neptune Eldridge, 31* on the board and continued, 'Harry's brother – half-brother – told me you'd explain the middle name, Conrad.'

'Me? I don't know why he's called Neptune.'

'Family lines,' said Cordelia unexpectedly. She looked at the mundane members of the team and tried to work out how to explain it, especially with Barney not being Entangled. There was going to be a lot of this. 'Some of the families in Lakeland are very old and very … cliquey. They use a set of names going back generations to show their lineage. And it helps to manage the gene pool.'

'Oh. Right,' said Tom. 'Thanks. We'll park that one for now. On to the autopsy.' He paused, and his eyes moved to a place beyond Cairndale, then he shook himself. 'Harry was a fit and healthy man. Mostly. He'd broken his left arm at some point, and according to Dr Jepson, he'd been very lucky: there had been a serious spinal fracture, exactly as Matthew told us.' He looked at me. 'According to the doc, there was evidence of neurosurgery around the spine, but no evidence of incision. I told him that it was experimental microwave surgery and he accepted that. He didn't believe me, of course. Following the original trauma, there has been considerable ongoing damage, scar tissue and swelling.'

Tom fiddled in his pile of papers. 'Before I get to the gruesome stuff, that reminds me.' He offered me a slip of paper. 'These are your HOLMES2 credentials, Conrad. Unfortunately they're no use without a secure laptop or terminal, and everything has to go on to HOLMES. I'll do any joint stuff, but would you mind if I gave them to Elaine? She can pretend to be you. Strictly against the rules, but I don't see another option.'

Elaine pointed her pen at me as if it were a rapier. 'I am not your secretary. You write the reports, check them and email them to me. Understand?'

I held up my hands in surrender and said nothing. Cordelia's face was impassive. Barney looked at the desk and tried not to laugh.

'Moving on,' said Tom. 'Harry died sometime around noon on Monday, with a possible window from 08:00 to 15:00. I'm afraid he was being tortured, and died from stress. Subject to various tests, Mike – the pathologist – expects to find a fatal dose of adrenaline. His hands had been bound behind his back for hours *before* he died, and there were bruises to his torso, legs and face. Cover your ears, gentleman, because the poor man had been beaten so badly in the genitals that one testicle was ruptured.'

Barney and I winced in sympathy. Cordy shook her head at something, and only Elaine spoke. 'Very, very nasty.'

'It was,' continued Tom, looking at me. 'Why did you ask about damage to the ribs? You were right, by the way. The long cut was administered just before death, and there was a big notch taken out of the top rib.'

'I'm not surprised he died,' I said quietly. 'The last thing he saw would have been a pair of giant bolt cutters coming to sever his ribs. And that's only the start.'

'Please tell me you're joking,' said Elaine plaintively.

'I'm afraid he's not,' said Cordelia. 'Harry willed himself away from there.'

Everyone had gone pale. Tom cleared his throat. 'Is this a Clan thing?'

He meant Gnomes. I shook my head. 'Not in their repertoire. And I think we know what happened.' I slid the smaller Parchment over to Barney. 'Tracey can have this back now. It's got the schematic for an alarm system on it. I think Harry was caught breaking and entering.'

'Very interesting,' said Tom. 'It's a line of enquiry, but we must not jump to conclusions. Let's move on to what else we know.'

Over the next twenty minutes, we shared information, and Tom slowly filled a second whiteboard with Actions. The capital letter is a police thing. Another board was headed T.I.E. for *Trace, Interview, Eliminate*. Also a police thing. By the time we'd finished, it had three names: Matthew Eldridge, Nicole Sanderson and Aidan Manning.

'Do you think the brother is a suspect?' said Cordelia. 'Really?'

Tom looked at Elaine. 'Everyone and no one is a suspect until we prove otherwise. I doubt very much Matt had anything to do with this, though. We still need to interview him again once the shock has subsided.'

There was also a line connecting Matthew to the Actions board, linking his name with Action One – Encrypted message.

In police speak, Action is a noun, verb and predicate. People, things and police officers are all Actioned. And I thought the RAF was opaque sometimes. In normal language, this is what we ended up with:

Tom and I were going to Waterhead Academy as an Urgent Action, both to search his houseboat and interview the staff, especially the Principal, the Housemaster and Harry's friend, Nicole Sanderson.

Barney had already requested Harry's phone data and was going to start going through it, with a focus on finding the mystery girlfriend. Elaine was going to start on data entry and getting background on Sprint Stables and anything she could glean on the plantation where Harry had been strung up.

'Thanks, Barney,' concluded Tom. The PC knew when he was being dismissed, and headed out, closing the door firmly but gently behind him.

'Over to you, Conrad,' said Tom. 'What have you not told us?'

'Almost nothing. I could get technical about the encryption, but it functions exactly like a mundane one, which is why I mentioned it when Barney was still in the room. There is one thing, though. The Chases. They are exclusively magickal, and all his punters would be magickal or entangled.'

'Is that why they're called Sprint Stables?' said Elaine. 'As in Sprite? Do they have a secret name?'

'No. Rather boringly, they're named after the river that flows through Sleddale: the Sprint. England's fastest river, I believe. Good name, too, and a good location. It's totally the back of beyond up there.'

'Then let's get going. Elaine, can you copy down the whiteboard then clean it? Thanks.'

We packed up and met Barney in the corridor. 'I'm sorry, erm, Cordelia. We need to go out through the front so that you can have your picture taken.'

'Good,' said Cordy. 'That's where Erin's waiting. Oh, Conrad, who's looking after Scout? Because I'm not.'

Tom gave me the raised eyebrow.

'We need him,' I said. 'He's specially trained, so either he comes in your car or you hand it over to Cordy and we'll take mine.'

'Will he chew my seats?' asked Tom balefully.

'No.'

'Fine. We'll need to swap stuff.'

And that's why we all ended up outside, and that's how I introduced Barney to a rather flustered and wind-blown Erin while the others headed round the back.

'You're not part of this lot, are you?' said Barney with a smile, hooking his thumb in my direction while they shook hands.

'No chance,' said Erin. 'I'm barely a consultant. What they get up to is nothing to do with me. Honest.' She tried to run her fingers through her hair and tipped her head to one side. 'Are you going to be attached to this case permanently?'

'I hope so.'

'Then I might see you later. Better go.'

Barney disappeared, and we headed for the cars. 'I didn't think he was your type, Erin,' I said, 'given that he's not a Mage.'

'He's got nice eyes and big shoulders. What's not to like?' She shook her head. 'Who am I kidding? He's probably on his second wife.'

I said nothing until I'd sorted a blanket for Scout to save Tom's leather seats. When Erin started to get into my car, I said, 'He's never married, and he's currently single. Have a good trip.'

She stuck her tongue out and muttered, 'Yeah. Right.'

It wasn't that Tom didn't want Conrad (or his dog) in the car, it was more that every time he got in a vehicle with one of the Elvenham crew, something bad happened. Like nearly dying in a helicopter. Or being kidnapped. That sort of thing. He joined the traffic on the A6 north and was going to start a conversation, but Conrad beat him to it.

'You've been to Elvenham, Tom, and you've conducted a lot of searches. If you were Mina, and you wanted to hide something from me, where would you put it?'

That was not what he was expecting. Not at all. They were driving up to search a murder victim's home, and Clarke wanted to talk about *this*? 'I'm not sure I should answer that question.'

Clarke rotated his frame again, and tried to push the seat further back. He found another inch and twisted to look at Tom. 'You have to. The girls stick together, and we have to as well.'

Tom knew he was joking, and that took out enough of the sting for him to ask what she was hiding and whether it could be in her wardrobe.

'Short of wardrobes, I'm afraid. And I do a lot of her ironing. I've seen in her bedside cabinet, too. It's about the size of two box files but can be broken down.'

Tom cast his mind's eye around the many nooks and crannies of Elvenham, all of which Conrad was likely to wander into at any time. Except one.

'Erin's bedroom. Because it's grace-and-favour, it's not really Erin's private space.'

'Excellent. You're right. I haven't set foot inside it since it was opened up and decorated. Thanks.'

Clarke got out his phone and made a call. 'Ben! You're staying with Myvvy while we're gone, aren't you ... No, I'm not calling to warn you off the brandy cellar ... Of course you can, if you want ... Listen, I want you to go into Erin's room and look around for something ... No, it's not trespassing unless you poke in her drawers ... Myfanwy says it's a total pigsty ... Just look around for a stack of bridal magazines … Yes, bridal magazines. Text me if there is more than one British magazine … No, you fool, I don't mean French, I mean Indian. There are loads of copies of *Bollywood Bride* and *Your Hindu Wedding* lying around downstairs. I want to know if Mina has a stash of British magazines … Yes, I'm relying on you. Talk later.'

He looked at Tom and said, 'I'll explain it all if my hunch is right. And yours. Thanks, by the way.'

'Right. Your turn to answer a question. What's your biggest priority, Conrad? Justice for Harry Eldridge or disrupting the Unions?'

Clarke didn't hesitate. 'My first priority is to keep the team safe. You, Cordy, Barney and Elaine's survival is Number One always.'

It was said with such utter conviction that Tom knew why women – and men – would follow Clarke into the jaws of Hell if necessary. Was he born with it, or did he learn it?

'That's good to know. Which is your *bigger* priority, then?'

'They're the same. If I honestly thought Harry would be better served by me stepping back, I would. And it's the assessors, not the Unions I have a problem with. And so should you.'

'Believe me, I think it's wrong as well.'

Clarke had spoken of justice with the same authority he spoke of survival. Of course, just because Clarke believed he was best placed to achieve it, that didn't mean it was true. That could wait, however, because Tom knew that without Clarke, he had no chance of achieving anything, and having seen what was left when Harry's trousers were removed, Tom would move heaven and earth – and hell – to find who had done that to him.

'Why not bond your phone?' he suggested. 'In case you have to drive.'

Clarke fiddled with the devices until he'd succeeded, and they were starting to plan their tactics for the visit when Clarke's phone actually rang. The display said *The Boss*. Tom thought it might be Mina, but no, it was the Constable. Clarke took the call and told Hannah that she was on speaker.

'That was a smart call in getting Cador Mowbray on board,' she said. 'The Grand Union have lodged a petition in the Cloister Court. At Hawkshead. Thankfully, the judge there knows when a hot potato has landed in his lap. He's turfed it to the Old Temple on condition that Judge Bracewell hears it urgently. The Union counsel is getting the train down tonight.'

Clarke nodded to himself, and seemed content, but Tom had a question. 'So what's our legal position?'

Hannah gave a laugh. 'Bizarre. Mundane law always trumps magickal law, with one exception. You can't try a Mage in the mundane court if the crime involves magick.'

'Can we arrest them?'

'Under mundane law, yes. And you can hold them in police custody, but if Conrad tries to arrest them under magickal law, they might fight back and claim self-defence because he has no jurisdiction. That's what's going to court tomorrow.'

'I understand, ma'am,' said Clarke. 'I'll be very careful.'

'You'd better be. What's the latest?'

Clarke looked at Tom, who said, 'You tell her. I'm driving.'

When he'd finished, Hannah was silent for a while. 'Are you sure this doesn't smell of Gnome?'

'No. Their messages are private, not public, and the Blood Eagle is not their preferred method of torture. If we'd found Harry minus a few limbs and dumped on Matt Eldridge's doorstep, then I'd be making a call on Clan Skelwith. This is human. Or Fae.'

'Then good luck.'

They were off the motorway now, past Kendal and threading their way through the edges of Windermere town. Clarke had received a text during Hannah's call, and he opened the message to read it.

'Shit. It's Matt Eldridge. He says, "I hope you're on your way to Waterhead Academy, because I can't hold the line much longer. Hurry the fuck up." Does your car have those built in blue lights, Tom?'

'No. It's a private vehicle. Hold on and I'll do my best.'

'I'll tell him we're on our way.'

Tom decided to take the Troutbeck roundabout legally, then put his foot down and his hand on the horn. The chance of being reported to the police was quite high – the chance of there actually being another copper nearby was remote. When the control room ran his index, they'd send a message to Ross in the first instance. If only it wasn't half term and the roads full of families...

At least he didn't have to worry about his human passenger freaking out. Clarke leaned left to see round right hand bends, and said, 'No,' at one point when Tom was tempted to overtake. They had to wait again at the lights by the Waterhead Pier, then they were round the lake and turning into the almost hidden entrance to the Academy, just beyond the rugby club.

Tom couldn't help it – he was arriving at England's only school exclusively for pupils from the magickal world. Of course he expected Hogwarts. And naturally, he was disappointed.

The very real Waterhead Academy was composed of five two storey buildings, one of which was obviously a gym and two were accommodation. The largest one, in the middle, did at least have a small clock tower. They were all modern, all unassuming and all designed to blend in.

'There's Matt's car,' said Tom, pointing beyond the buildings to where a small car park nestled against a small wood. There were only three other vehicles present, and there had been no sign of life in the school. Tom pulled up next to Matthew Eldridge's monster vehicle and killed the engine. Clarke was already half out of the car.

They grabbed their coats from the boot, because it was bloody cold here by the water, and rain would be with them shortly. Tom looked left, down the line of trees. The campus was large, but only had a tiny frontage on to the lake. A substantial, unbroken post and rail fence separated them from the woods, so the action must be elsewhere. He set off towards the main building.

'Tom,' said Clarke. 'Hold on.' Tom stopped and Clarke stood next to him, clutching Scout by the collar. 'I'm sorry, but the School House is through the wood. The Occulting is so good, you have to know it's there to realise.'

Tom turned round and stared hard at the woods. No matter how hard he looked, they were still trees on the other side of a fence. He turned back and waited.

'I'm going to try a shortcut,' said Clarke. 'When I let Scout go, look down and look only at him, not at me and not at where you're going.' He clipped a long lead on to the dog and took out a treat. He held it in his hand for a second before feeding it to the excited dog. 'Go on, boy. Find the magick.'

Tom stared hard at Scout as the dog started to snuffle the ground in random patterns. Being a Border Collie, he jumped manically from side to side, and at one point Tom barged into Clarke, who gave a grunt of pain and held his leg. Somehow they both managed to focus on the dog, and after half a minute, they were moving in a straight line.

When Tom realised they were on a path, he thought they were heading away from the woods, and then it went dark and he nearly looked up. Two seconds later, Clarke said, 'Here we are.'

'Now that's more like it,' said Tom.

They were at the far edge of the woods, and Scout was going crazy. To their right was the real McCoy, a hulking great Gothic building in grey stone with tall, thin windows and a baronial entrance. There were graceful turrets at the corners and a clock tower in the middle, now obviously seen as the original on which the modern version beyond the trees was based. Tom wanted to gawp, but the action wasn't at the School House, it was down by the lake.

They started quick-marching towards the water, where a long, modern jetty projected from the end of a banked up dock. The near side of the jetty had two sailing boats and a couple of dinghies tied up while the far side had a bulky, clumsy, top-heavy boat moored to it. The whole thing must be fifty feet long, and it was proportioned like a modern cruise ship, with the superstructure overwhelming the original hull.

As well as a solid block of living rooms, the top had a big space with railings and a ridged awning. Tom hadn't been on many boats in his time, but he wouldn't want to be out on the lake in that if there was a storm. They got closer, and Tom realised that the entrance to the jetty was a scene of conflict. They got closer still, and it wasn't a conflict, it was a siege. Standing in the way, defending the jetty, was Matthew Eldridge, and it didn't look like he could take much more of whatever was going on.

Clarke slowed down and spoke the scariest words Tom had heard since a mad Irishwoman pointed a shotgun at him. 'Over to you, Inspector.'

Shit.

The siege had abated now that they'd been spotted, and all eyes were on the new arrivals. Eldridge was facing off against three opponents. Or two opponents and a spectator. The lead antagonist was a middle-aged woman in a green coat; her sidekick was a young man, very young. Barely into his twenties, the lad looked like Clarke's team of new recruits – Vicky, Saffron and Karina, but without their spark. The spectator was male, in his forties and had his face hidden by a tweed cap. He was standing well back from the two aggressors.

Against those two, Matthew Eldridge was collapsing. He had aged another five years since this morning, and he was leaning against a wooden pole at the entrance to the jetty. His eyes were swollen and red from the crying he'd done in private or with his friend. Tom was surprised the bloke had made it all the way back here in one piece.

Tom unbuttoned his coat and reached for his warrant card, but it was Eldridge who spoke first.

'Thank the Goddess you're here. Where in her name have you been?'

'You know where I've been, Matt,' said Tom with as much compassion as he could muster. Eldridge flinched, and the woman spoke out, completely ignoring Tom and almost spitting at Conrad.

'Begone, you. This is no place for a Witchfinder. You have no right and no law here.'

With total deliberation, and the barest flick of his eyes towards Tom, Clarke got out his cigarettes, taking it very slowly. Aah. It was a cue.

'Put those away, Constable. You're on duty,' said Tom sharply, then turned to the others. 'DCI Morton, Lancashire and Westmorland Police.' He showed his card. 'And you are?'

The woman frowned. Tom could almost see her brain re-booting. Close up, she was older than middle-aged, and had a lined face that had seen a lot of living. She looked again at Clarke, who now stood in brace position, his right hand at his side, Scout's lead in his left and his face impassive. When she got no response from Conrad, she turned back to Eldridge.

'What's going on, Matthew? What is this pantomime.'

Eldridge slowly folded his arms and leaned even harder on the pole.

'Madam, are you with the school?' said Tom.

She finally let her eyes rest on him. They were blue, a watery blue, and slightly blurred from contact lenses. 'No. I'm Philippa Grayling, Chief Assessor of the Lakeland Union. My colleague is Assessor for Eden Valley.' She paused to weigh him up. 'You're a senior detective, yes?'

He thought of giving her the same silent treatment. No. That wouldn't work, and it wasn't his style. 'I'm a chief inspector. Technically not a senior officer, but I am the SIO in this case.'

'And you have crossed the threshold?'

'If you mean I'm Entangled, then yes. I am.'

'Then why in the name of all you hold holy are you letting the Witchfinders pull your strings like the puppetmasters they are?'

It was a good question. It was why Tom had asked Clarke about his priorities. 'I answer to Commander Ross of Cairndale Division, Ms Grayling. In police matters, Conrad answers to me. That's the beginning and end of my role. If you're not happy with the way I run the investigation, I can give you Commander Ross's number.'

The anger in the Assessor's face burned brighter in a flare-up of rage. 'You are so wrong, Inspector. So, so wrong. They want to destroy us and wipe away a thousand years of liberty. The Lakeland Particular is a lesson from the past and a model for the future. You can pretend it's about a murder if you want, but if you truly believed that, you'd let us do our job. Let those who know this world put it to rights.'

A flicker to Tom's left made him turn before he answered her. Matthew Eldridge had stood up straight and unfolded his arms. 'And if that were true, Philippa, I'd let you get on with it. We've become a joke, you know. There's no Assessor in Furness, and one person is covering both Eskdale and the Western Waters. If you'd backed me to investigate, I would have made a stand, but with all due respect, Philippa, the Assessor for the Eden Valley is not up to investigating my brother's death. He had to call in reinforcements for the Appleby Horse Fair,' he said, not looking at the young assessor as he damned him.

Philippa Grayling looked around her, the classic tell of someone seeking a way out. 'I'm suspending you, Matthew. With immediate effect. I was going to let you go on compassionate leave, but not now.' She snorted with laughter. 'I never thought that three *men* would bring me to this. Hopefully Justice Bracewell will sort this out tomorrow and we can make finding Henry's killer our top priority instead of engaging in a pissing contest.'

She turned and marched off, the young man following in her wake. When Eldridge had insulted him, he'd looked down at the cinder path as if he knew what the older Assessor was saying was the truth.

Tom had forgotten about the man in the flat cap. He moved smoothly to fill the gap left by the Chief Assessor, and smooth pretty much summed him up. For one thing, he wanted to shake hands. 'Good afternoon, Chief Inspector. I'm Martin Hoggart, Bursar at the Academy. I was the only member of staff here when the Chief Assessor arrived. I still am.'

Tom shook hands and stood back. The Bursar was a short, stocky and slightly overweight man. Three inches shorter, and Tom would have had him down as a Gnome. Hoggart glanced uneasily at Eldridge and said, 'Do you need a warrant to search poor Harry's boat?'

It sounded like an open question, an enquiry not a threat. 'No. Harry was the victim of a crime, so we don't need a warrant to search his home.' Tom took another look at the brooding mass of the School House. 'Technically, we would need one to search his work room, classroom or locker. Unless the Academy invites us in, of course.'

The Bursar took off his cap and ran his hand through thinning hair. 'I'd have to speak to the Governors about that.'

'Well, before you do, I'll need to see you anyway. I'll need to see Harry Eldridge's personnel file, details of payments and so on. Of course, I might need to call in Ofsted if there are child protection or professional issues.'

Hoggart put his cap back on. 'You might need to call them?'

'Only if I felt there was a need.'

'I understand, Inspector. My office is in the new building, but I'll wait in the foyer of School House until you're finished.'

'Thank you, Mr Hoggart.'

'Glad to help.' The Bursar took half a step away, then turned back to look at Matthew Eldridge. 'I won't stand in their way, Matt. Harry wasn't an easy man to deal with, but he was a good one. I won't let the Academy forget that. Let me know if there's anything I can do.'

And then there were three. Hoggart's footsteps were loud on the cinder path and Tom felt the stress drain away as the Bursar retreated. He was still watching the man's back when Clarke sprang into life.

Clarke walked up to Eldridge and offered his hand. 'Matt, I'm sorry we have to meet again like this. I can't imagine how you're feeling.'

Eldridge shook his hand. 'Do I have to call you Lord Guardian now, or will Dragonslayer suffice?'

Clarke slid a glance at Tom and smiled. 'Either is better than being called "Constable", but I prefer "Conrad." I take you've been doing a Horatio impression.'

'Less heroic than that.' Eldridge turned to Tom and Clarke stepped back. This time, when Conrad took out his cigarettes, Tom didn't argue. Eldridge shivered from his curly black hair to his walking boots. 'Don't worry, Tom, I haven't set foot on the boat. It's all yours. I'm going home if you don't mind.'

'Thank you, Matt. We're very grateful for what you did. I'll need to see you again soon, but I do have one question. We found some Parchment on Harry's body, and the message was encrypted. Do you have a copy of the Assessor's seal we could borrow? I'd rather not approach Ms Grayling.'

Eldridge summoned a smile from somewhere. 'Philippa is going to find that her authority is less extensive than she thinks. She can't suspend me – only the Langdale and Leven Union can do that, and the chairman has already put me on compassionate leave. Good job, or I'd have to hand over the seal. You can't borrow it, I'm afraid, but I'll happily use it on the Parchment.'

It was a compromise Tom was willing to make. 'Thank you. Is there someone who can be with you tonight? I'd offer the services of family liaison, but we're a bit short handed.'

'My apprentice lives in. She was itching to come here with me. It's not far home. I'll get there.' He forced himself to stand straighter, and set off on the path to the woods. By the time he was half way there, his shoulders had slumped again.

Before Tom turned back to the boat, he took another look at the School House. He'd felt it before, and it was stronger now: *something* was watching them. A person? A ghost/Spectre? The House itself?

Conrad was standing at the entrance to the jetty, staring at the boat.

'What do you reckon?' said Tom. It was a vague enough question. For all Tom knew, Clarke had gleaned all sorts of magickal insights during his showdown with the Chief Assessor.

'I reckon that it's time for you to stay here, Tom. Just until I've got on the boat. Don't worry, I've come prepared.' Clarke turned round and gave him a flat smile while he held up a pair of police issue latex gloves.

'Are they proof against booby-traps?'

'There aren't any. If there were, Matt would have told us. He'd rather we succeeded with his help, but he certainly doesn't want us to fail.' Conrad wrapped Scout's lead around the wooden pole where Eldridge had been leaning and gave his dog a scratch. 'Won't be long, lad.'

If Clarke was so certain that it was safe, why did Tom have to wait on dry land? Even a week ago, it was a question he'd have asked out loud. For now, he took it on trust.

117

## 13 — Where he Laid his Head (Part One)

I don't think he bought it. In fact, I'm pretty certain Tom knew that I was worried about surprises on the boat. Not Wards set by the late Harry Eldridge so much as booby traps from his killers. It had been well over two days since he died. More than long enough to visit.

I couldn't detect anything from the dock, and a confident march down the jetty showed nothing either. As I got closer to the houseboat, the first thing I saw was the name: *Thunderer*. A name like that covered a lot of bases in the world of magick. He may even have inherited it with the boat.

There was a small gangway on to a narrow walkway round the deck. Before crossing, I checked out a wooden cabinet at the end of the jetty and found the utility connections – water, electricity and an Ethernet port. A very well connected boat. The connectors were all in place, but water and power were turned off, in compliance with stern warning signs about leaving them switched on when the boat was unoccupied. It would be dark inside the cabins, so I flicked the switch for power and turned my attention to magick.

Nothing at first. I closed my eyes and spread my arms. That does nothing in itself by the way, it's more of a cue to the brain, and it's an old Circles trick. Cordy taught it me yesterday. See? I'm always looking to learn.

Still nothing. Or nothing protecting the boat. There was the faintest flicker up top, but that was it. 'Clean so far,' I shouted to Tom. He gave me a thumbs-up, and I set foot confidently on the gangway and then the deck. I breathed out when both feet were on the boat.

It was deserted, and I opted to walk round the deck to take a quick look at everything. I have no idea what this tub was once, and the superstructure had been bolted on roughly, with little attempt to integrate it. Big holes had been cut in the steel sheets for windows, and although I glanced at them, every one was covered by curtains. I didn't bother trying the door into the accommodation section: the padlock spoke volumes.

The old wheelhouse at the back had been raised to see over the cabins, and I got nothing from there either. I returned to the gangway and waved Tom to come aboard. Scout barked and strained at his lead, then stood there giving me a wounded look. Tom jumped on to the deck and looked around.

'There's a faint trace of magick up top,' I said. I forced myself not to suggest we start up there, because I'd given my word to the Boss, to Commander Ross and above all to Tom that he was the SIO.

'We'll start up there, then,' he said. 'After you.'

'Are you sure?'

'Of course I am. I got Mina to give me chapter and verse on Anciles when we were kidnapped, and when it comes to magick, I am in your shadow. Literally and metaphorically.' He gave me a smile with his eyes. 'Which is how you feel with your partners, I imagine.'

'Harsh but fair, Tom.'

I climbed the narrow stairway to the top deck and let out an involuntary, 'What the fuck?'

Tom emerged, took a look round and said, 'You're not wrong there. I wonder if Matt even knew about this.'

The top deck was protected by a canopy with a pitched roof (that was about to be tested for rain), and steel panels to hip height. Underneath was what can only be described as a private casino.

An oval table was the biggest feature, and it was covered with a heavy cloth, except where one edge hadn't been secured properly and had blown up to reveal an immaculate green baize surface. Around the edges of the top deck were some cupboards, and at the back was a bar, hidden in the gloom of near dark and rainclouds. Something had been going on recently, because someone had tidied but not cleaned up.

The canopy was supported by metal poles, one of which had a waterproof switch box attached half way up. Tom lifted the cover and flicked switches. Lights came on, and infra-red heaters started to glow. We both took another look around.

On top of the bar were two ice buckets with four sparkling wine bottles neck down. Next to them were dirty glasses and a couple of full ashtrays. 'Give me a second, Tom.'

I opened my Sight again, and narrowed down the magick to two sources, both in the middle of the room. One was a case, lying on the table, and the other was the table itself. I told him what I'd found and he motioned for me to go ahead while he skirted the room, checking everything else.

There were actually two cases on the table. Before I touched either, I checked out the green baize. 'This is an Artefact of some sort,' I announced. 'I can tell that it's dormant, but that's it. Oh, and I didn't feel a Ley line coming on board. They're very difficult to run across water.' Tom nodded, and I looked at the mundane box. It was made of aluminium and shaped a lot like my gun case. Or a camera case. I flicked the latches and found it full of casino grade gambling chips. I left the lid open and looked at the other one.

The magickal box was made of lacquered wood decorated with Japanese scenes, mostly of women talking under cherry trees. The detail in the blossom was stunning, and I couldn't help running my fingers over it first. A little Work of magick pulsed and drifted away.

'What's that?' said Tom, looking around him.

'What's what?'

'That music. Sounded oriental. Chinese or Japanese.'

'I really must get my hearing checked, you know. I think it came from the box.' He watched me open it and turn it to show him: several decks of cards in their wrappers, two buttons saying *Big Blind* and *Small Blind* and a wooden pagoda, about four inches high. With the lid open, I could tell that that little trinket was the most magickal thing on the boat. 'Dealer's button. I'm not going to touch it.'

'We'll take it. Come and have a look at this.' Tom had reached the bar, and pointed to the glasses. 'Nine glasses, eight with lipstick marks. All the cigarette butts have lipstick, too. And what on earth are these?'

He offered me a pile of greeting cards, shoved inside each other. The biggest one wrapped all the others, and it was a fortieth birthday card in questionable taste (there was a joke about a certain part of the male anatomy which I'm sure isn't relevant and which was stomach churning, given what had happened to him).

Some more tasteful cards completed the set of nine, and all had been written in girlish hands. Or part of them had. There were greetings to "Sir" or "Mr Eldridge" and variably legible signatures (I could make out Willow, Iolanthe and Perci, amongst others). That was odd enough, but it was the bit in the middle that really interested me.

'Is that Enscribing?' asked Tom.

'Yes it is. Or was.'

Between the salutation and the signature were messages written in thick black ink. The sample from "Willow" was typical (if neater and more polite):

*Thank you for organising the Floating School again, and for letting me come back!! Looking forward to winning this year instead of losing my blouse (again). My bid for the buy-in is £400.*

They all finished with a bid of some description, from £300 to £1,250 (from Iolanthe). I do have a tendency to jump to conclusions, so I handed back the cards and kept to the facts. Clearly Tom is having a good effect on me.

'I've seen enough of Erin's work to recognise a quill pen in use, and the ink is always thicker. I'm guessing they were handed over with a minor Work on them, because there is absolutely no Lux left now.'

'Nine cards, eight glasses with lipstick. I … What's up with Scout?'

I rushed outside to see what was causing him to go mad. I half expected it was another dog, but he was straining on the lead and *barking at the water*. His focus was hidden by the bow of *Thunderer*, and I debated vaulting the railing to get closer. Then it went darker because the lights had gone off. We dashed to the starboard and realised something very disturbing.

'We're moving,' said Tom with a disbelief I completely shared.

'Shit. Get down, I'll look aft.'

I belatedly activated my Ancile while Tom crouched next to the table. I squeezed past the bar and into the corner. From the stern, the mooring rope stretched out over the lake. It had been joined to another rope, and at the end of *that* rope was … water. 'Stay there.' This time I did go over the railings, sliding down rather than jumping to the deck.

We were starting to move at a slow but steady pace, away from the jetty and on to the open water. I grabbed the mooring rope in my left hand and looked down the length of it. I kept hold of the rope and closed my eyes. I sent pulses of Lux down the rope, expanding my Sight until I felt resistance. Something was pulsing the Lux right back at me and changing the shape of it, like a distorted echo. I opened the channel to my tibia-battery, and drew enough Lux to shape it into … what would be good here? A torpedo. That would be good.

Using the rope as a guide, I fired a torpedo of energy down the line and a burst of magickal light lit up my retinas.

'What the fuck was that?' shouted Tom.

I opened my eyes and the concealing Glamours were gone. At the other end of the rope was a cabin cruiser, large by lake standards, and with no Silence, the engines roared out, screaming as they pulled the Thunderer.

I squinted at the boat, trying to see who was crewing it. I got the impression of a woman at the wheel, and two masculine shapes at the back, both in waterproofs with dark caps covering their faces. It was a bloody long way, but I got out the Hammer and took aim. The men ducked, and one of them grabbed the woman by the leg. She ducked, too, and moved to the side. She kept hold of the wheel, though.

I stowed the Hammer and reached into my tibia for more Lux. I am rubbish at offensive magick – using compressed air like a weapon, mostly. But this was a sitting target, under tremendous strain. I focused on where the mooring rope was fastened to the stern and tried to create an axe of magick. I braced myself and used my arm to help the Work come into being, closing my eyes and bringing my arm down, discharging the Lux and thinking of nothing but hot, sharp steel.

There was an enormous *clang* of metal on metal, and I pitched forward into the railings, dropping to my knees to avoid tipping into the water. A human scream sounded over the roar of outboard engines, and I saw that the cruiser pilot had fallen off her perch into the two men. I rubbed my knee and limped round to the stairway. When I got upstairs, Tom was staring out towards the cruiser as it shot across the lake now there was nothing holding it back.

He turned round and said. 'That was awesome, Conrad. Truly awesome. How did you conjure an axe out of thin air?'

'An axe? It was just compressed air. That's all.'

'That's not what it looked like from here. Why didn't you shoot? Too far?'

'I doubt that they were towing us away for an early birthday party, but our lives weren't in immediate danger. You heard the Commander.'

'So I did.'

'I drew my gun to see if they ducked. Because they did, it means they don't have the upgraded Anciles.' A blur of movement over his shoulder caught my attention. The cruiser was circling round. 'Shit. They're coming back.'

He wheeled round. 'Who are?'

'Can't you see the boat?'

'No, but I can hear something. What does that mean?'

'Fuck knows, but if they come within range, this time I will shoot. Let's go.'

On impulse, I grabbed the black lacquered box and pile of greeting cards from where Tom had dropped them on the table. He was already standing by the stairway.

'Go where?' he said.

And that was a good point. We'd come a fair way from the jetty and we were now well into open water. In the distance, Scout was howling like a wolf.

'I'd rather not be up top,' I said. 'Go forward and circle away from the sound. Watch out for something coming close to the boat. I'll track them round.'

He jumped down the stairs with me hard on his heels. He went left, I went right and watched the cruiser turn again. The woman set a course that would bring them very close to our stern and put most of their boat between me and the crew. On dry land, with somewhere to brace the gun, I can shoot much more accurately than you'd believe with a handgun. On a bobbing boat against a bouncing target, I stood no chance. They'd have to be right alongside before it was worth wasting ammunition.

I dropped to one knee as they got closer and tried to look like I meant business. The pilot crouched as low as she could, and at the last moment, the two men leaned out from behind the cabin. Out, but not far enough for me to shoot.

As they passed, the starboard guy pointed at the *Thunderer* and great gouts of water splashed up around our port side. The boat rocked to starboard, and I didn't realise what their other guy was doing until Tom shouted, 'We're on fire. And we're sinking.'

'And they're coming back for another go,' I shouted back.

This time I had to risk it. On their approach, I fired at the windshield. This was a vanity cruiser, with big windows to aim at, and one of them shattered. I'd missed the crew, but it was enough. Although they put another couple of holes in our starboard side, they didn't come close enough to let us have a full broadside, and then they sped off in a straight line.

I jogged round to the starboard side, then retreated. Smoke was billowing from the smashed windows of the accommodation section, and roaring fire from above said that they'd got the gaming deck, too.

Tom ran round and joined me at the stern. 'Have they really gone? Did you get one of them?'

'Yes and no. That was serious offensive magick, Tom, and Pyromancers like that are few and far between. If they manage a proper ambush, we could be in serious trouble.'

'You mean we weren't then?'

'They wanted to destroy the boat, not us. This time.'

*Thunderer* lurched and rolled. 'Looks like they succeeded, Conrad. Do we swim for it?'

'And ruin your coat? Not if I can help it. Give me a hand with this.' I had spotted the small life-raft on my tour before. These things are only required on sea-going vessels, and I'm now guessing that *Thunderer* started her life as some sort of fishing boat. I just hoped that the life-raft had been maintained.

'We used to drop these from the chopper on air-sea rescues occasionally. All we have to do is get it in the water and pull on the line, then wait for the boat to sink enough to jump in.'

Tom grabbed the other end of the huge plastic canister. 'What about the fuel?'

'Right at the bottom in a sealed tank. Not a problem. On three. One ...'

We heaved the canister over the rail, and I managed not to let go of the rope. With a few tugs, the compressed air did its job and a small red life-raft burst from the pod like a butterfly. I pulled it round to the gangway opening and waited for us to sink a bit more.

'Look,' said Tom. 'On the jetty.'

It was the Bursar. He was shouting something that I couldn't hear, but Tom could.

'We're fine!' he responded. 'A rescue would be good!'

'Excellent. After you, Tom.'

He braced himself on the railing and dived into the life-raft. I pulled it closer and followed suit after I'd stowed the greeting cards in the box and chucked it to him. I didn't have the advantage of someone holding the rope, and landed with my feet in the lake and my top half on top of DCI Morton.

'Providing a soft landing is not in my job description,' he muttered. 'Get off, Conrad. I don't like you that much.'

'People never cease to amaze you, do they?' I observed to Tom as the portly Bursar expertly moved a small boat up to the life-raft and grabbed the line. 'I had him down as a golfer, not a sailor.'

'You know you're still barred for life from Cairndale Golf Club after landing that chopper on the green, don't you?'

'Good.'

We sailed regally towards a flat part of the lakeside, and Hoggart let us loose to float ashore.

'I'm already wet,' I volunteered when it seemed clear we weren't going to beach unaided. I jumped out of the raft and tugged it in. 'Shame you're not Mina. I could have made jokes about the Birth of Venus.'

In the distance, Hoggart, flat cap still firmly in place, was already tying up his boat on the jetty. I lit up, and Tom said, 'Who do you think they were?'

'It could be the killers, trying to hide evidence. But why now and not on Monday?'

Tom ran his hand through his hair. Lucky devil. 'The world of magick is small, and everyone in Lakeland knows everyone else anyway. Is it possible they didn't know who he was when they killed him?'

'Only if they've never been to the Chases. A bookmaker would be a memorable figure.'

'True. In that case, who the hell would want to sink a murder victim's boat and then set it on fire?'

'I hate to say this, but it could be Harry's friends. What do you suggest we do now?'

He'd been giving it some thought, and surprised me by saying, 'How about we split up? You handle the School House and follow up on what Harry was doing with a bunch of girls on his boat as well as the other lines of enquiry. I'll go and see Matt.' He looked around the lawns of the School House and the shoreline before gazing at the building itself. 'You know what we want, don't you?'

'Bank details, records, contact info for Nicole Sanderson and an interview with the Housemaster. Personal effects. Oh, and any gossip. I can get Cordy to pick me up here. Pass me the greeting cards.'

Hoggart was walking in our direction now, and he did something very brave: he unhooked Scout from the jetty. The mad mutt raced at me and practically knocked me over when he leapt up.

'One more thing,' said Tom. 'Ask if that place is haunted. I'm sure we were being watched. Thanks, Conrad. That wasn't what I was expecting this afternoon.'

'Me neither, Tom. Oh, and give Barney a call. Tell him to look for a boat called *Merry's Delight*. Sometimes Mages are so cocky, they don't think plods like us will check the blindingly obvious.'

'Will do. See you later.'

SIX FURLONGS

Tom waved his thanks to Hoggart and walked off; I wasted no time in thanking the Bursar properly.

'Least I could do, Mr Clarke. What the hell happened out there?'

'If you have a source of heat and a mug of tea, I'll tell you.'

He smiled. 'I think I can stretch to that.' We started walking (or squelching in my case) towards the School House, and he continued, trying to inject a lighter tone than he probably felt. 'Are your lot going to do salvage on the boat?'

'Sorry, no. It's got no evidential value and we've got no budget for a magickal salvage operation.'

He winced. 'The governors will go potty when they hear that.'

'Sorry. What a beautiful building.'

'Most people find it a little intimidating. Or tasteless. Or both.'

'I think Gothic revival is seriously underrated. It's not haunted, is it?'

He gave me a sideways look. 'You don't think we'd allow Spirits of Spectres on site with a bunch of young Mages, do you?'

'Yet you're happy to let Harry run a poker school for girls. Do tell.'

'Aah. I half hoped that would stay under wraps.'

We had reached the steps to the grand entrance, and I started to unlace my boots. 'Can Scout come in?'

'Only into the foyer or the admin office. It's on the right, behind the hatch. I'll go and put the kettle on.'

I tipped water from my boots and squeezed hard to wring out my socks. The trouser legs would have to dry naturally. The granite had sucked the remaining heat out of my feet, and I hopped eagerly up the steps and through the grand doors.

I wasn't disappointed inside, either, and I wondered if all magickal buildings suffer from envy of Salomon's House. They'd got the twisty staircase going up to a cupola, they'd got the carvings and the detailing, but the original purpose of the House was given away by the floorboards – nothing ages quite like a wooden floor in a school. You could even see where the Victorian passion for games had resulted in dints from the metal studs. Next week, I imagine it will be warm and cosy, probably with a real fire in the baronial fireplace, but right now it was bloody freezing.

The right hand wall was pierced by a large glazed opening, as seen in the porter's lodge of Oxbridge colleges, and the door next to it was half open. I called Scout to heel and went through.

'Bless you, Martin,' I said. The Bursar had switched on a fan heater, and I went straight over to warm my feet. Scout joined me and didn't like it one bit. He backed away from the blast of hot air with a bark and went off to sniff the waste paper baskets.

The rest of the office had barely made it into the twentieth century, never mind the twenty-first. Or perhaps it had skipped over the last century – there

125

were no computer monitors, for example, and no metal filing cabinets. Everything that could be made of wood had been, and all of it stained dark. Nice to look at, but perhaps not to work in every day.

Hoggart emerged from a side door at the back with two mugs of tea and pulled out a chair so that I could sit down next to the heater. I grabbed a bin and put my socks over the edge for them to get a share of warmth, too.

'So, Martin, tell me about the floating poker school.'

He dug in a couple of drawers until he found some coasters (expensive wooden ones). He placed one within reach and put my mug down.

'I'd rather not,' he said after a long pause. I gave him a raised eyebrow. 'I thought the Housemaster was away for half-term, but she's back. Or she never left. I got a voicemail when I was rescuing you, and she's on her way here. Shouldn't be long.'

Should I steam in and challenge him or should I mark it down for later? What would Tom do? I think he would have steamed in and checked for discrepancies when he spoke to the Housemaster. I was too cold for confrontation, so I left it and tried something else. 'When did you find out what had happened to Harry?'

Hoggart made himself comfortable. 'I don't know what happened to Harry, other than that the poor bloke was murdered. First thing I knew was when I saw Matt's car come on site and drive to the far car park. I was inspecting the playing fields.'

'You know Matt?'

'Of course I do. He's our Assessor.'

Of course he was. Stupid Conrad. Hoggart had more. 'When I say Assessor, I don't mean he's responsible for the school. He had to drop that when Harry joined the staff.' He gave me a smile over his mug of tea. 'We may be a small world, but even the Particular wouldn't allow Matthew Eldridge to inspect Harry Eldridge's teaching, or the school where he worked. The students were a different matter.'

'So who is the school inspector?'

'Was. You met Petra, didn't you?'

'I did. A memorable woman.'

'And she'd hate you for saying that. She'd say she was memorable, full stop. They're still arguing over who should replace her. Perhaps it'll be Matt, now.'

'So, Matt arrived and disappeared. Did you know Harry was AWOL?'

He shook his head. 'He left on Friday when school broke up for half term. I wasn't expecting him back until next Sunday night. I honestly thought I'd be the only person in the whole school today. Even the site manager is having two days off, and yes, I followed Matt. He was already on guard by the jetty when I got here. He was also on his phone. Don't know who to. By the time he'd finished, Philippa Grayling was steaming down the path like a battleship. All Matt had time to tell me was, "It's Harry. He's dead."'

We both sipped tea. 'What happened next?'

'They got right into it. I've never seen one Assessor speak to another like that.' His face went neutral. 'Not in front of the staff, anyway.'

'The Clerk to the Watch has no magick, you know. I buy her cream cakes when I'm in town.'

He nodded. 'Do you know how I got this job? My mother was chair of governors and the Witch of Blea Tarn. I've spent fifteen years trying to prove to the governors that they made the right choice and ten years trying to prove to my mother that marrying a Daughter of the Earth hasn't brought shame on the family, so you'll forgive me if I'm a little reticent.'

Blimey. Talk about getting your version in first. I couldn't speak to his professional qualifications, but marrying a Daughter of the Earth is unusual in the world of magick. As you know, Gnomes produce a huge surplus of human girls, and they're known as Daughters of the Earth. A good number of them marry Gnomes from other clans; the ones who don't mostly escape to a mundane life. Okay, perhaps *escape* is a bit loaded.

Hoggart wasn't finished. 'They're good enough for the staff, though. Most of the New House teachers have Gnomes for a father.' He gave me a smile that could almost be wicked. 'Trouble is, who else is going to apply? They have to be Entangled *and* a qualified teacher for New House.'

I put my tea down and gave my feet a good wiggle. They'd gone beyond the pain barrier now, and were pretty much back to normal. I was still dreading putting my wet socks and boots back on. 'Trying to fit in is a bugger, isn't it?' I offered, to show I'd been listening. 'And a good way of not telling me what the Assessors were arguing about.'

'What?' He looked genuinely surprised. 'They were arguing about you, of course. And the Inspector. Except that Philippa wouldn't even acknowledge his existence. I can give you the edited highlights if you want.'

'I'll pass. How about some boring stuff instead? Tom Morton will want all the paperwork.'

'I hadn't quite finished getting it together when I heard your dog howling and came to see what was going on. Won't be long.'

I used the couple of minutes grace to send a message to Cordy and text Mina and the Boss together. Saves time and arguments about who I contacted first:

*Victim's boat sunk and burnt. Tom & I OK. Unknown attackers. Matt Eldridge faced down Chf Ass. on our behalf. Conrad. (X for Mina).*

'Here you are,' said Hoggart. 'They're tube socks, so they'll fit even your enormous feet.'

'They're also bright pink, but thank you. That was very thoughtful.'

As well as the socks, he had an armful of papers. And bits.

127

'The socks were all I could find in lost property that weren't girl-sized. Right, here we go.' He sat so that there was a desk between us and started to go through papers, handing them over as he went. 'Here are all the financial records of payments, under Harry's randomly allocated cover name. Here are the equally bogus contracts. All of that stuff is from my office in New House. This one is another matter.' He showed me a fairly thin folder and a large, stout brown envelope. 'This is Harry's file from School House. I can't hand that over without getting in serious trouble, but I wouldn't want you to think that we were going to redact it.' He slid the file in the envelope and laid out his bits: a small spirit burner, a piece of sealing wax and a seal. 'Can I borrow your lighter? Thanks.'

While he lit the lamp and prepared the wax, I suddenly remembered a question that Tom would expect me to ask. 'Just for the record, where were you on Sunday and Monday?'

'With my in-laws, getting away from the whole Samhain circus.' He looked up and smiled. 'My wife's father is the third son of Henry Octavius, and your ears may have been burning on Sunday evening. There was a fair bit of talk about the inauguration of a First Mine for Clan Salz and your role in it.'

I thought he'd been keeping something back. From the moment that we'd been left on our own at the jetty, he'd treated me like he knew more about me than he should. I thought he was a friend of the Sextons or something.

'Is your wife related to any of the Clan who defected?'

'No. They're from a completely different House and line to the Octavius family. From what I hear, Henry thinks it will be good for Clan Blackrod to have some competition.'

'Interesting. Thank you. And the rest of your mini-break?'

'We went to London Zoo on Sunday afternoon, dinner with the in-laws on Sunday evening, and we travelled back Monday afternoon.' He looked down again. 'We may want to avoid Samhain, but my wife can't afford to miss the half-term trade. She makes and sells jewellery in a little shop in town. There you go.'

I felt a flash of magick as he applied the seal. 'You must really hate the Housemaster.'

He blinked once and paused to show that he wasn't going to deny it. A door banged in the distance, and he stood up. 'Anything else?'

'Harry had a "friend" in Ambleside. You must know who.'

'Friend? He had a part-time job at the Britannia Hotel. Everyone knew that. His heart was broken when he was younger, or so he said. I've never seen him express an interest in women.'

The door to the office opened, and the Housemaster walked in. She barely glanced at me, reserving her anger for the Bursar. 'Martin, what the hell is going on here, and why did you allow a Witchfinder on the premises?'

Oh dear. It was going to be one of those.

# 14 — Coming to Terms

Tom had a vague memory that Matthew Eldridge lived in Great Langdale, and so he turned left out of the Academy while he waited for Elaine to pick up the phone.

'How's it going, sir?'

'Not good. Where does Matt Eldridge live?'

'Hang on … Chapel Stile. Blackburn House. He gave me a note: *Turn left before the Wainwrights' Inn and follow the road for half a mile*. What's the problem?'

He brought her up to date as he made the short trip from Ambleside to the start of Great Langdale, a wide valley that thrusts its way into the fells and is the jumping-off point for any number of challenging walks. Or so the guidebooks say. Fell-walking was not Tom's thing. 'Any news your end?'

'Barney may have a lead on the mystery woman. There are a lot of calls to the Oak Tree Hotel in Ambleside, and they're nearly all on Monday to Thursday. He sent very few SMS messages, so it looked like most of his texts were on an encrypted App.'

Tom was entering the village, and slowed down. 'Thanks. I'll call later.' He looked left and right, and was about to get his phone out to check when he saw the Inn on his left. It was named (indirectly) after the famous Alfred Wainwright, the man who did more to popularise fell-walking than anyone else, to the point where the Lake District summits over 1,000 feet are collectively known as "Wainwrights". A tiny country lane just short of the Inn was signposted, but only negatively. *No Access to Burlington Slate Quarry*. Fair enough.

Tom fretted about his paintwork as he drove over a rickety bridge and up the steep, narrow lane. No wonder Eldridge owned such an indestructible vehicle if he lived here. It always takes much longer to do half a mile at that speed, and Tom forced himself not to panic. The way that Conrad had seen their attackers this afternoon while Tom had been totally blind was yet another unnerving demonstration of the powers of magick to hide itself. And surely an assessor would want some privacy?

No. There it was. The lane twisted right and got even narrower as it became purely a farm track. On the bend was a short length of stone wall with a battered black sign announcing Blackburn House. He rumbled over a cattle grid and on to a grit drive. Eldridge's house was to the left, with his car and a second vehicle to the right in a flat space probably culled from a prehistoric predecessor to the modern quarry: there was a lot of exposed slate here, and much of it might have gone into Blackburn House.

It was long, low and made entirely of slate or wood. Tom parked next to a small Audi Quattro and got out to have a proper look. He was still trying to decide if the windows were too small when a young woman came round the far side and stood with her hands on her hips, guarding the front door. For one jolting moment, he thought that Elaine had teleported to be here, then he saw that the colouring was wrong.

She had Elaine's wiry frame and thin face, and followed her taste in ponytails and footwear (maroon DMs), but this woman's eyes were brown and her hair a much darker shade than Elaine's. As he got closer, he saw that there were purple streaks in the hair, too, something that the police did not yet encourage.

'You must be Mr Eldridge's apprentice,' he said. 'DCI Morton of the L&W Police.'

'Yeah. I'm not sure he's up to visitors.' She looked down the lane and cocked an ear. 'Where's the other one? The Dragonslayer?'

One of the first things they drummed into you at the police academy was not to let witnesses take over the conversation – a lesson that Conrad should learn. 'Is Matt about?' he said.

'He's had a terrible shock, and that confrontation with the Graylord hasn't helped. What do you want him for?'

'Perhaps you could tell him I'm here.'

The front door opened, and Eldridge himself appeared. 'No need. I knew you were here the moment you crossed the cattle grid. Come in, Inspector.' He smiled at the young woman. 'Perhaps some tea? It might stop me hitting the bottle for a bit.' She turned on her heel and went back the way she'd come, leaving Tom to go through the open door after a retreating Eldridge.

There was a short passage with the biggest shoe racks Tom had seen outside a youth hostel, and as many pairs of walking boots. Or climbing boots. The Apprentice's similarity to Elaine went even further, with several pairs of specialist rock-climbing boots in vivid colours. Tom bent down, unlaced his shoes and popped them in an empty space.

Beyond the passage, he thought he'd entered a living museum, centred on a Viking longhouse. 'What a beautiful home, Matthew. I'm impressed.'

The room was designed to make a complete feature of the floor-to-ceiling windows opposite that gave views across the valley to rugged peaks, now topped with cloud. The slate floor was covered with a whole series of rugs, some hand-made, some oriental, and all in muted colours. The wall to the right had a big fireplace with a fire just starting to take hold of the logs. The furniture was arranged to take advantage of either the view or the fire, and nowhere in sight was there a television. Or a desk. What it did have, on the wall opposite the view, were many, many bookshelves.

About half the building was taken up by the long room, and there were doors at either end. Eldridge waved him to a seat near the fire, and Tom was forced to sit with his back to the view. Reluctantly, he took his coat off and settled down. Opposite him, Matthew had the classic bachelor's nook, with a comfy chair and two side tables. One had a stack of books, the other a decanter of whisky and an empty tumbler. The Assessor removed them and put them on top of the mantelpiece, underneath an oil painting of a very big river with snow-capped mountains.

'Not the Lakes,' said Tom. 'In the picture, I mean.'

'What? No. It's the Rhine. Most people think it's a piece of tat, but I inherited it. I've got something for you, Tom. I am still allowed to use your first name, aren't I?'

'Of course. Before you do, I need to tell you that Harry's boat was attacked shortly after you left. With Conrad and I on it. I'm afraid it was set on fire and sunk, out in the lake.'

'What? Is he okay?'

'He is. A little wet, but unhurt.'

Eldridge sat down with a bump. 'Who did it?'

Tom shook his head. 'We don't know. Conrad uncovered their ... Glamour?' Matthew nodded. 'He broke through the magick, but they didn't come close enough for him to see them. I'm sorry to have to tell you this on top of everything else.'

Eldridge shook his head. 'This day gets worse and worse. Where is he now? Getting changed?'

And there are times when you need to take people into your confidence. 'Only his feet got wet. I decided to leave him at the Academy. If people are taking action, I think we need to move more quickly.'

The Apprentice came through with a tray containing two mugs, one of which she gave to Matt. 'Sugar, Inspector?'

'No thank you. Are you in training to be an assessor?'

She laughed. 'Not bloody likely. I'm an apprentice in Wards, not that Matt's much of an expert himself. Beggars can't be choosers, though, and this place is handy for the crags. Do you want anything else? If not, I'll do the tea. Beef casserole. You need to keep your strength up.'

Tom didn't know that there was a working class in magick – apart from Vicky Robson, they all seemed to come from money. The girl's words and accent both said that she was from an ordinary local family. 'Thanks,' said Eldridge, and she left them alone.

The Assessor reached for something behind his pile of books. 'I've got the seal, and I also have this. It's a couple of years old, but I can't imagine he'd update it and not tell me.' He offered Tom the stiff white envelope that he instantly recognised from his days as a solicitor. He didn't need to see the cursive script on the front to know that it was Harry Eldridge's Last Will and Testament.

He accepted it and saw that it hadn't been opened. The Will is a public document, and it would be rude not to open it here. He broke the seal and scanned the text with a practised eye. Matthew was named as executor, with a firm of local solicitors as backup. The bequests were simple, and Tom couldn't keep a wry smile off his face.

'What?' said Eldridge.

'I'm afraid that you've just inherited a complete liability. "To my brother, Matthew, I bequeath my boat *Thunderer* to induce a love of the water in him."'

'Bloody typical.'

'There is better news. You will also receive an item described as *Our mother's Japanese workbox and its contents.*'

'Now at the bottom of the lake.'

He looked to be on the verge of tears when he heard that, so Tom quickly said, 'No it's not. It's in my car. Conrad saved it. It was the only thing we did save, and I'm afraid it's evidence at the moment, but it's safe.'

Eldridge did start to cry now. 'Thank you, Tom. And thank Conrad Bloody Clarke for me if I don't see him myself. You'll never know what that means. Excuse me.'

Eldridge left the room, and Tom sipped his tea while he re-read the will. When the Assessor returned, carrying a wadge of kitchen roll, Tom folded the document and put it back in the envelope. 'The bulk of Harry's estate may also come to you, Matt, because it's been left to "Any children that are acknowledged as my own." Does that have a special meaning in magick?'

'It does. It means he's been sowing his wild oats in the Circles and he may have children out there that he knows nothing about. For them to inherit, the mother has to acknowledge them while he's still alive. I've had to adjudicate a few of those in my time, and as far as I know there are none on the Union register. That doesn't mean they haven't been acknowledged privately, though. What the lawyer wrote is a standard formula, and I'd be surprised if any came to light.'

'Why's that?'

'You remember I told you about his accident?'

'I do. The post mortem found some serious injuries.'

'That was bad enough, but he was head over heels in love with a Witch called Lara at the time. She was a couple of years older than him, and much more secure in her magick. They were riding together and she went for a serious jump. He didn't make it, nor did his horse Thunderer.' Eldridge looked over Tom's shoulder at the mountains. 'It'll be dark, soon. I can't wait.'

Tom waited a second. 'Go on.'

'Sorry. Well, I blamed her. Loudly and publicly. Harry and I fell out then, as you can imagine. She stayed with him, got the best healers to work on his back and there was talk of weddings. And then she died. Tragically, as they say. I say it was poetic justice.'

'What happened, Matt?'

'Harry had taken up sailing. He was good, and she followed him on to the water. They were racing, and her boat broke up. The stupid cow hadn't fastened her safety line properly, and got dragged down.'

Calling your late brother's greatest love a *stupid cow* was harsh. Very harsh. Yet Matthew meant it completely. He continued, 'Her boat wasn't the only thing that broke up. Harry had to go into rehab with a mental breakdown and an addiction to painkillers. It was only then that we started talking again.'

'Just one more question, Matt, then if you could use your seal, I'll leave you in peace.'

'Just one more question? I'm so full of bloody questions I don't feel like I'll ever have an answer again. Sorry. Too much time on my own.'

'Just your movements from Sunday evening to Tuesday morning.'

'Sunday evening and Monday evening I was here. My Apprentice can confirm that. Here's my journal for my work on Monday if you want to take a picture.'

He took a leather bound book from the stack and opened it to where a blue silk bookmark held the place. Tom got out his phone and took a moment to scan the contents. *Meeting with Ch. Ass ... Follow up with A. Jenkins ... Inspection of LL XIV ...* And so on. He took the picture.

'I hope you got breakfast with the Chief Assessor. Rather early for a meeting. And what's *LL 14*?'

'We did have breakfast, and *LL* stands for *Locus Lucis*. That one is near Haverthwaite. The Warden there isn't on the phone.'

That was convenient for Matt: it was right on Harry's time of death. Checking the alibi would go on the Action Board, but Tom wouldn't be giving it a high priority. Not with so much else on the go. 'Thank you. I've got the Parchment and a pair of gloves here.'

'Don't need them. The seal isn't bothered by mundane evidence bags.'

'Are there magickal ones?'

'Of course there are. Merlyn's Tower doesn't have a monopoly on innovation, you know.' The bitter smile was back. 'If we ever have a moment at the end of this, I'll show one to Conrad or whoever he's got minding him at the moment. Who is it, by the way?'

It wasn't a secret. 'Cordelia Kennedy. She's got two small kids, so keeping Conrad in line shouldn't be a problem.'

'A mother? In the Watch? That'll be a first, then. I wonder what Nimue will say about that?'

Now that was way above Tom's head. He handed over the evidence bag, and Eldridge took a tiny case, like a pocket watch, from his stack of bits. He clicked it open and dropped a lump of gold into his hands. Tom couldn't help drawing breath – it was huge. 'Not something I'd want to carry around,' he commented.

'It's not solid gold. Has a silver core and you can't lose it.' He didn't amplify the last comment, and Tom didn't want to outstay his welcome. Eldridge moved the seal slowly over the bag, and black writing suddenly appeared on the Parchment.

It was upside down, of course, and Eldridge tilted it up to look at it. Fresh tears appeared in his eyes, and he whispered, 'By the gods, Harry, what have you done?' He thrust the bag at Tom and fumbled the seal back into its case.

Tom took the Parchment and turned it round. In large letters was a simple message. *BY THE LAW, SO DIES A THIEF*. What the hell?

'You've got a problem, Inspector Morton. A big problem. This is what used to happen to thieves, under the old law. Landowners could hang them.' Eldridge made eye contact, the tears running slowly down his lined face. 'It was done away by the de Quincey Agreement. The one that let in the Cloister Court. Only some families never fully accepted it. Philippa had a couple in her time as an Assessor, and I don't think she ever got to the bottom of who did it. She might not want to talk to you, but Conrad should think seriously about notifying her. And you should all be very, very careful.'

So Clarke's hunch was right: Harry Eldridge had been up to no good. 'Thank you for the warning, Matt. And thank you for the tea. No need to see me out.'

'No need for anything anymore.'

Tom had learnt not to argue with grief. He left the longhouse, the picture window now as dark as its owner. When he got outside, he found that it was raining, too.

The Bursar stood his ground admirably, and of course I had backup: Scout appeared from round the corner and barked at the Housemaster. He knows an enemy when he smells one.

'Here boy. Good dog.'

Hoggart kept his face bland. 'This is PC Clarke of Westmorland Police. The senior officer was called away. Conrad, this is Dr Judith Yearsley, Housemaster of Waterhead Academy.'

Wherever the Housemaster had been, it looked like it had been quite a do. She was wearing a dress that my mother would have described as *Old money county set*, and a pair of court shoes that had splashes of water on them. Being a true countrywoman, she also sported a waxed jacket even more battered than mine. When Hoggart made the introduction, a look of genuine incomprehension came to her face.

'What are you on about man? Senior officer? Has the Peculier Constable been here as well?'

The Bursar's lips set in a line: he'd handed over to me.

'The senior officer is DCI Morton, Dr Yearsley', I said. 'We're here as police officers, and here's my warrant card.' I showed it to her and added to her confusion by throwing in a magickal reference. 'Martin has been gracious enough to offer the Academy's hospitality.'

The Housemaster looked like she was going to burst a blood vessel. As well as the dress, she'd gone to town on the makeup, so her anger showed in the tide of red visible on her scalp. Her blonde hair was thin, quite short, and had been disarranged by the hood of her coat.

'We'll continue this conversation in my study in five minutes,' she said curtly, then left without waiting for me to follow.

A sly grin spread over Hoggart's face. He pointed to my steaming footwear. 'Leave that here and I'll keep the fan on it. If your masculinity won't be threatened by wearing pink socks, that is.'

I shoved the dainty hosiery on to my feet and looked at Scout. He was watching the door. 'Will you be here long? It wouldn't be fair to leave him outside.'

'I'll be here until you're finished. You don't think she'd lower herself to lock up, do you? Don't forget to take the envelope.'

I stood up and collected it. 'Where's the Housemaster's study?'

'Where would you expect the spider to be? At the centre of the web.' He paused. 'Down the long corridor. Can't miss it.'

'See you later, Martin.'

I nipped outside and stood under the shelter of the Gothic portico. A single lamp illuminated the front, barely a beacon in the darkness that had descended over the lake. There was another single light by the jetty, and I couldn't see anything else because it was now raining, a steady Lakeland rain that was absolute hell to fly in and could turn remote moors into tarns in minutes. A fellow pilot once landed on grass near Scafell to do a rescue and by the time they'd loaded the patient, his wheels were underwater.

Sometimes I like to tell myself stories about people. I could just see a young Martin Hoggart as a student here, his lack of magick disappointing his mother and his lack of height pushing him into the arms of the real Gnomes of Lakeland. And now he was amusing himself by getting one over on everyone else. I was tempted to ask if he'd been at school with George Gibson, the only Gnome of Clan Skelwith I've actually met. I didn't say anything because, for all his desire to co-operate and undermine the Mages of Waterhead, Martin could still be lying through his teeth.

I padded back through the foyer and down the long corridor. Magickal light had come on and cast a yellow glow over the serried ranks of honour boards. My old school has them, mostly for sporting achievement (yes, I'm there as captain of the 1st XI). I hadn't expected to see any sports here, given that they'd have no one to play against, and I was nearly right. What they did have was a list of Old Boys and Girls who'd won the Waterhead Chase. I scanned the names for a second, to see if I'd come across any of them. One of them I did recognise: Nicole Sanderson, Harry's friend, had won it eight years ago. There was another, too. Right at the beginning was a name that haunted me: Lucas of Innerdale. I must tell Scout about that.

More prominent were lists of magickal trophy winners – Skelwith Scholarship for Artificery, Lord President's Award for Excellence. That sort of thing. I passed them by and nearly missed the last set of boards before the corridor ended. Interesting.

I walked into what must be their Great Hall, only it wasn't very Great at all. If this had been the original school, there can't have been many pupils here. What it lacked in size, it made up for with ostentation, and if it had been better lit, I'm sure the carvings would be even more lifelike than the ones in the Salomon's House Receiving Room. From the right, across the hall and next to the raised platform, a large door stood ajar, proper light flooding out. The spider's lair.

I felt totally creeped out as I crossed the space, limping round old tables and fighting the urge to look over my shoulder. I had to force myself not to burst into the Housemaster's study after I'd knocked politely.

'Come,' she said.

Now if I were top dog here, I'd want a room at the front, with Lake views. This one had big windows, but whether she could see the fells, I don't know. It was moot anyway, because her desk faced away from the darkness outside. I did take a mental note of the room, in case I ever get to see Dean Hardisty's study for comparison.

The Housemaster was standing behind her desk, fingers pressed to the wood either side of a large smartphone. She'd taken off her coat and pulled a brush through her hair in my absence, and was now fully in control of her anger.

'I've just spoken to the Chief Assessor,' she announced, 'and apparently it's true: you've enlisted Commander Ross and some plod to lever your way in here. I might have known that Hoggart would enjoy that, and I shall be speaking to him later.'

'Don't worry, Dr Yearsley. I won't tell DCI Morton that you called him a *plod*. I'll let him make up his own mind about you. Unless you co-operate, in which case he won't have to meet you at all.'

'Philippa has told me *not* to co-operate until the Court has sat tomorrow. Your welcome here is just about at an end.'

I stood at ease in front of her desk and took the files out from under my coat. 'Didn't you wonder why Martin let me in?'

She didn't answer that. The Housemaster would not want to wash her dirty linen in front of me.

I put the sealed envelope on her large desk, leaving it well out of her reach, then I gave her my senior officer smile and held up the printouts. 'He was thinking of the Academy, actually. Especially the part where you employed a ... Jon Williams to teach lower school maths. I wonder if the University of the South Downs will have a record of him? Regardless of the Court's decision, we can still bring in the school inspectors. Martin decided that it was better to co-operate with the police in the shape of me than risk a confrontation with the mundane authorities. After all, I presume you want Harry's killer found?'

'I've met Constable Rothman, you know. She didn't strike me as the sort to go to war over a dead Enscriber. If you try to burst open the Unions over this, she won't back you.'

'Your call, Dr Yearsley. Don't forget that Colonel Rothman was a copper long before she was a Mage, and dead people of all descriptions deserve justice in her eyes. And then there's your Head Girl, Willow. I saw her name on the board outside.'

I left it hanging, and she blinked. 'What about her?'

I took out the greeting cards. 'We recovered these from Harry's boat. Admissions to the floating poker school. I'd like to ask Willow about that. And possibly her parents. Do they know it goes on? Do the governors, come to that?'

Bullseye. The shock was so severe that she had to sit down.

I pressed home the advantage. 'It had her family name out there, too. Is her father the Secretary of the Duddon and Furness Union?'

The Housemaster licked her carmine lips. 'Grandfather. Her family live nearer to Whitehaven. They were all eighteen, you know. This isn't a prison, and we have a responsibility to the town. They got to dress up and test their boundaries without putting themselves or the mundane population at risk.'

If that what she told herself, who was I to argue? There was a question that no one had asked yet, and I was going to keep it in reserve: How come they let Harry moor his boat there? It was an ugly monstrosity in a beautiful setting. Why did he get away with it, and what hold did he have over the

Housemaster? My school turned a blind eye to a lot of what we got up to in the upper sixth, but if a teacher had organised a poker school, they'd have sacked him if they found out.

'It was all above board,' she continued. 'Harry isn't interested in girls.' She looked down. 'He wasn't interested.'

'If that's true, I'm sure that Willow will confirm it. Call her and get her to ring me. Urgently. I'm sure you've got the Head Girl's mobile number in your contacts list. If you do that, and show me his teaching room and other spaces he used here, I'll be on my way. Oh, and this.' I leaned forward to put my finger on the envelope. 'It's Harry's folder from School House. Martin sealed it for me.'

She stared at the envelope. 'That's all you want?'

'Nicole Sanderson's number as well. And if none of the evidence points at the Academy, none of the evidence will leave our files. Here's my card.'

She looked at my card for a second; I'd chosen the RAF one. 'Take the file. I'll do the other stuff now.'

She started to use her phone, and I opened the seal on the envelope. Harry's secret file was almost as boring as his fake file under the name Jon Williams. Letter of application. Job offer. Ooh. There's a familiar name.

There was a photocopy of his certificate of Mastery, awarded on completion of his apprenticeship. It was a shame it was in black and white, because it had been crafted by a truly great Enscriber: the late Tuulikki Sexton, inventor of the Staveley Stitch. I almost sound like I know what I'm talking about, don't I?

I checked the small print. *Class of Award: Satisfactory*. Ouch. That must have hurt. My phone pinged, and the Housemaster said, 'That's Nicole's number. And mine, of course. Are you going to notify her about Harry?'

'Won't she know?'

'How could she? I only found out when Martin left the voice message.'

She was telling the truth. It looked like the leak of information hadn't been as widespread as I'd first thought. 'Were they close?'

'In a platonic way, yes. There was a mutual love of horses. Bit of a waste, in my opinion. She should be doing so much more than driving Harry round like a chauffeur. Backwards and forwards to the stables and race meetings.'

'Rather a lot of contact for a platonic relationship. My fiancée only lets me drive round with young Mages because they're my partners.'

'You'll have to ask Nicole about that, but from my observations, she's more interested in fillies than stallions.'

I think that was supposed to count as a joke, so I gave it a knowing smile. We were very short-handed as a major incident team. Word would get around from now on, so I gambled on an olive branch to follow Dr Yearsley's attempt at humour. 'She's your colleague. If you know the best way to break it to her, then I'd be grateful if you could.'

She nodded. 'Willow will be in touch later, I'm sure. Now, let me show you his teaching room, such as it was. You can examine his armchair in the common room, if you like, but he didn't have a locker or anything like that.'

It wasn't far to the broom cupboard that Harry had been allocated as junior teacher of Enscribing: the mystery of his appointment and mooring perks deepened when I discovered that there was another Enscriber who handled the hard stuff, and that Harry didn't' work at all on Fridays. At least the room had a couple of windows.

'The materials are all what you'd expect,' she announced. 'If you're familiar with a Scriptorium, that is.'

'Oh, I keep an Enscriber in my stables,' I said casually. 'She's not as tidy as this, though.'

It didn't take me long to exclude everything but a small cupboard that was locked. 'Good job I have the master Stamp,' said the Housemaster. She took the coded brass strip in one hand and felt the lock with the other. The cupboard popped open to reveal half a dozen books, an oak box and a bottle of Bourbon. The Housemaster sniffed at that but said nothing.

I opened the box and found an exquisite set of calligraphy pens. I put them on the desk and reached for the books.

'Before you start,' said Dr Yearsley, 'I should say that most of them will be school property. There will be a bookplate inside the cover.'

She was right. I laid four books in one heap after a quick flick to the front. Harry wouldn't be leaving anything interesting in a school textbook. I turned my attention to the other three, and discounted the largest one: it was his Apprenticeship workbook. The next one was a present from his brother. *Congratulations, Harry. Good luck in the job, Matthew.* It was entitled *The Little Book of Wards* and the author was none other than Matthew Eldridge himself. I placed it on the workbook and looked at the last volume. It was the most well-thumbed and annotated of all of them. It was also hand-written.

I read the title out loud. '*Lord Galleny's Guide to the English Chases.* Is this the original manuscript or did someone copy it?'

Her distaste was even more evident. 'Unless I'm mistaken, Harry copied it himself. He must have spent a long time in the Prince's library.'

'Prince?'

'Lord Galleny is now Prince Galleny of the Borrowdale Fae.'

'The Queen of Keswick's people?'

'Mr Clarke! If you really want to carry on getting up people's noses, then by all means call her that. Her preferred name is Queen of the Derwent. Only offcomers call her that.'

'I stand corrected. I really would like to see his armchair as well. You never know what he's dropped down the side.'

'Really?'

'Really.'

The building may have been huge by most standards, but a lot of it was given over to prestige spaces, and of course to bedrooms. The senior common room had chairs for a dozen staff and still had a whiff of tobacco to it. Probably from the furnishings. There was nothing down the sides of Harry's mouldy armchair, either. I did spot something on the draining board, though.

'I'll take his mug, if that's OK. I presume that only he would have one with this message.' It was blue and said, *Old sailors don't die, they just get a little dinghy.*

'What on earth for?'

'I've got all of Harry's possessions from the school. Some we need to examine. All of them will go to Matt in the end. He might throw the mug away or he might keep it forever. Either way, if I left it here, it wouldn't get collected. Thank you, Dr Yearsley.'

'You're welcome. There's a shortcut this way.'

There was a surprise waiting for both of us in the foyer: Cordelia *and* Erin. It would have to be Erin who spoke first.

'Loving the socks, Conrad. Your little secret, are they?'

The Housemaster frowned when I introduced her to Cordy, and Cordy blinked hard in return. 'If there's nothing else, I'll be going,' said Dr Yearsley. 'I'm sure that Willow will be in touch soon. If you meet up, you can give her the socks back. They were an unwise choice from a fancy dress day last year, unless I'm very much mistaken. Good day, Mr Clarke.'

When the great doors had closed behind her, Erin said, 'Proof positive that boarding schools are a very bad idea if you ask me.'

'For once, I agree,' said Cordy. 'For further proof, look at Conrad.'

'Arff!' said Scout from inside the office. Hoggart let him out for a reunion and brought my boots and socks with him. I sat on a hard chair to put my boots on. Out of stubbornness, I left the pink socks in place and stuffed the (almost) dry wool ones in my pocket. While I was doing the laces, the Bursar asked where we were staying tonight.

'Don't know yet.'

'Well, if you're not going back to Cairndale, there's room at the Little Langdale Lodge. And a welcome.'

I stopped tying the knot. 'How do you know about that?'

'Natasha Bickerdike is a cousin – one of the few relatives who still speaks to me. And Andrea Forster catered for our northern wedding.' He paused, then added, 'The big do was in Essex, but that was mostly Clan.'

'Oh, yes please,' said Erin. 'Count me in. Mina said it was lovely.'

I shrugged. 'Looks like we'll be in the Lakes tomorrow, so it makes sense. Don't know about Tom and the others, though. And you'll be on your own for dinner, Erin.'

The Bursar smiled. 'I'll call her back and tell to keep a couple of rooms.'

'Thanks, Martin.' I passed him my card and asked him to text me with his number. 'Just in case we have any follow-up questions. We'll be in touch about the boat, as well.'

We left on a round of friendly handshakes, and made our way into the rain. 'Let's go somewhere warm and dry before we talk.'

I guided Cordy to a little known car park in the town centre, and then to a small café that was popular with the mountain rescue teams (and therefore welcomed hyperactive dogs). To Cordy's disgust, I ordered sausage rolls and cake. 'You never know when you're going to eat again during an operation,' I informed her.

'Sometimes it's better not to eat at all,' she replied. 'Especially when the goods have been going stale all day.'

'I'm with Conrad,' said Erin.

Tom called at that point. He said he was on his way back and that he'd taken a unilateral decision: he was moving the HQ to Ambleside. Barney and Elaine were ringing round looking for a venue.

'What are you doing here, Erin?' I asked. 'Please don't tell me you're in pursuit of poor PC Smith.'

'No. Well, yes, but that's a bonus. I'm going back to the Sextons tomorrow on some private business.'

'Fair enough, but that's a bit awkward.'

'I know. I do get that a murder investigation is top priority. One of the national car hire chains has a branch in Kendal, and they deliver. I've got to be at the Salutation in half an hour. Is it far?'

'Nowhere is far in Ambleside. That's good, because I've got a job for you.'

'Hey! You're not my boss. If you ask nicely, I'll think about it.'

'This is a commission. An actual job where I pay you money. I'll tell you later. In the meantime, could you do me a real favour and have a look at this stuff?'

'Oh. Right. Get me another sausage roll and I'll think about it.'

I bought all the remaining stock on the basis that Tom would be hungry, too, and Erin started going through the haul from the School House. While she did, I took Cordy through the afternoon properly.

'You've made a friend in the Bursar,' was one of her few comments.

'You must be joking. You don't make friends with a spider.'

'I'm sorry?'

'He said that Judith Yearsley was a spider in the centre of the web. That's not where you find the spider, that's where you find their prey. The spider lurks in a safe place at the side.'

She frowned at me. 'That's rather reductive, Conrad. He seemed very nice to me.'

'He is. He also has a vulnerable position to defend and a long-term agenda to promote.' Erin had finished with the goods and was doing something on her phone. 'What do you reckon?' I asked her.

'The pens are good quality, but nothing that special. I can see why he only passed as Satisfactory from the evidence in his workbook. He did everything he was asked and not a lot more. Apprentices are supposed to push the boundaries a bit and take risks, you know? It's only at the end, when he works on betting slips, that there's a flicker of genuine originality. Without that, he'd have been Adequate, and no one wants to be Adequate.'

'And the manuscript?'

She looked thoughtful, which is not something you often see on Erin's face. 'Can I get back to you on that one?'

'By … Hang on. That's Barney.'

I took the call and heard the sound of speaker phone. 'You're on conference with the boss,' he announced. 'I mean, the Inspector.'

'Get on with it,' said a very crackly Tom Morton. I motioned for Cordy to listen in and put the phone between our ears.

'We're on our way up,' said Barney. 'My sister's mother-in-law works at Charlotte Mason College. You know the place?'

I did a quick Smith family tree in my head. Not a close relation. 'The teacher training college north of Ambleside?'

'That's the one. They're the only place that's quiet this week – they do half term for most of the students. I've bagged us a room with Ethernet and Wi-Fi at mates rates. We'll be there in half an hour.'

'Excellent,' said Tom. 'Good work. I'll go straight there.'

'What about tonight?' I asked.

We sorted out the accommodation with everyone at Little Langdale except Barney – much to Erin's disappointment. Tom was going to ask Lucy to join him as well. At the end of it all, the café owner was cleaning the floor and about to turf us out.

'I'll walk Erin to her new car and give Scout some exercise,' I said. 'Could you take the car to Charlotte Mason and call the Little Langdale, Cordy. And take a break to Facetime the kids.'

She looked down and muttered, 'Thank you, Conrad. That's very thoughtful of you, but I spoke to them earlier. I will call my mum, if that's okay.'

Erin saw the look on my face and shook her head. I led us out of the café and we went our separate ways.

## 15 — Where he Laid his Head (Part Two)

'What's up with Cordy?' I asked Erin as we headed for the main road.

'Dunno. She made sure that the Sextons weren't going to kidnap me then begged their Wi-Fi code and went outside to call Rick. She wasn't happy after that. I asked if the kids were having fun, and she said, "It's possible to have too much fun, Erin." I didn't know what else to say, so I rattled on about laterally entangled fibres and the evils of bleach.'

We were at the pub in no time, and waited opposite, outside the Post Office. 'About this job.'

'Oh, yes. You've got me intrigued, Conrad.'

'You do heraldry, don't you?'

A playful smile spread over her face. 'I do indeed. Are you coming over all aristocratic?'

'A powerful friend suggested it might be a good idea to have a coat of arms. He suggested gyronny.'

'For the rotor blades of a helicopter. Good choice. It would have to be red and white – red for battle. Any other ideas?'

'Do I have to follow the rules or anything?'

She shook her head. 'Only if you want it to be registered by the mundane heralds. If it's occult, just send it to Iain Drummond with a cheque for one hundred guineas.'

'Iain? I know his office is called the Curator of Heraldic Law, but I thought that was a cover name.'

'He does both. Well, he delegates the heraldry to his uncle.'

'Well, I'll be. Right. Could you perm any combination from a book, a sword, the Plough constellation with Polaris included, an eagle, a defeated Dragon, a molehill, a mattock...'

'You have been thinking, haven't you? I'm sure there's a special badge for Dragonslayers, but if you leave it with me, I'll knock something up tonight. Here's my car. I think.'

It was her car, and I waved her off. Ambleside goes very quiet very quickly. A few restaurants were lit up for early service but Scout and I soon had the place to ourselves. I found a bin for the poop bag and then a shelter so that I could follow up on one of the texts I'd had.

'Can you speak?' I said to Ben.

'Yeah. I'm in the library doing a report.' He lowered his voice even further. 'You were right. Big stack of bridal magazines. About two thirds were traditional Indian wedding magazines. The one on top had coffee stains on it and was really battered. It was called ... hang on ... *Today's Bride: A Fusion Special*. What's going on, Conrad?'

143

'Tell you later. Thanks, Ben.'

The next call was to Mina. 'What happened? Is Tom okay?'

It's what I'd have asked first, too. I think. 'He didn't even get his feet wet. I did.'

'Thank goodness for that. I wondered why Erin had messaged a picture of you wearing pink socks. Where did you get them from?'

'I haven't got long, and it's a bit of a tale. We're setting up a new incident room in Ambleside and I've taken some time out to walk Scout. And call you, of course. How was the afternoon?'

'Tedious. Apart from Marcia losing her temper. It was like I'd been tipped out of bed and dropped straight into the Emperor's box at the arena. Clan Flint may need a new barrister tomorrow, and talking of tomorrow, I'll be there for the hearing into the Particular.'

She wouldn't be allowed to speak, and her presence would make absolutely no difference to the outcome, but it cheered me up no end. 'Thanks, love. Listen, you could have just asked if you wanted.'

I could hear her go on her guard. Her chin lifts when she does that, and her eyes narrow. Her voice drops and octave as well. 'What do you mean, Conrad?'

'If you wanted a church wedding as well as an Indian one, you should have just told me. I think you'd look ravishing in an ivory silk gown.'

'You have no idea what you're talking about, do you?'

'About the dress, no. It just sounded good. I know you wouldn't wear white because of Miles.'

She sighed. 'You do know me sometimes. Sometimes. It was just the cost, that's all. You know I spent all my savings on getting this bloody Ancile tattooed on my chest.'

'We won't starve. Have you booked the church yet? I'd be surprised if you haven't.'

'Ha! I have enquired, but I haven't booked it because Nell Heath's mother is one of the churchwardens, and she's an even bigger gossip than her daughter, if that were possible. As soon as it goes in the diary, everyone in Clerkswell and the three counties will know.'

'Well, that's your evening sorted.'

'I am taking Sofía out for a meal. There's a Gujarati restaurant north of Hyde Park that looks good.'

I felt a surge of pride and happiness for no real reason. 'Have a great time. Got to go, love. I'll call you later.'

'Take care.'

When I got to Conference Room 3 at Charlotte Mason College, there were sausage roll crumbs everywhere. And more tea, thank goodness.

'Thanks for those, Conrad,' said Tom. 'Total lifesaver. Cordelia has been telling me about life in a Coven. The others will be here shortly, and Lucy's on her way. Oh, and you're sleeping in a Yurt tonight. They're new for this year but no one's booked them since September.'

'Why me? I was looking forward to a night of luxury.'

He pointed at the splash marks on the wall from where Scout had shaken himself. 'That's why. They've booked out all the dog-friendly rooms in the main hotel, and you're clearing that up later.'

It took a while to unload Barney's car (they'd brought two secure computers with them), and even longer to get everyone updated across the various strands of the enquiry. Elaine and Barney went first, as Barney wasn't staying long, and we'd decided to exclude him from most of the Academy lines of enquiry.

'That posh school?' he said. 'I know it's got a big red warning sign on it: all cases to be referred to the Assessors. Now I know why. Look, I know my place in this investigation, but if there are child-protection issues…?'

'There aren't,' I said decisively. 'Their post-16 curriculum is a little unusual, that's all.'

'Fair enough. I found out a bit more about the Oak Tree hotel. Or Elaine did.'

'Oak Tree? The Bursar said he worked at the Britannia. So why was he calling the Oak Tree, and why does Martin Hoggart think that, "Everyone knows it's the Britannia."?'

Elaine looked at Tom. 'You taught me well, sir: follow the money. Harry Eldridge may or may not work at the Oak Tree *or* the Britannia, but owns half of the Oak Tree.'

'What?' said Tom sharply.

'It took me a while, but Harry was no expert at hiding his money. There are two shell companies, and once you told me the name of his boat, it was obvious: Thunderer Holdings and Investments was a giveaway. We were less successful on the woods where he was found.'

'That's right,' added Barney. 'Those woods could be owned by Vladimir Putin or Lord Lucan for all we could find out.'

'Keep on it. What about the other half of the Oak Tree?'

She checked her notes. 'A company called Kyiv-Ambleside Investments. That in turn is owned by Z and A Zinchenko if they're not fake names.'

'Let's find out,' said Tom, suddenly grabbing his overcoat. 'Conrad, with me. Cordelia, could you look at that box and then help Elaine make a start on the statements.'

'My leg's feeling a lot better tonight,' said Elaine hopefully. She looked at Cordelia (who was equally unimpressed by her given task), and continued heroically, 'It would be good experience for Lieutenant Kennedy.'

Tom started to fasten his buttons. 'Nice try, Elaine, and I love the sisterly solidarity with a woman you've barely met.'

'Erm, Tom?'

I actually lifted my hand in the air. Like I was back at school. The impact of my visit to the Academy. Or that's what I'm telling myself.

He paused mid-button and looked at me. 'Yes?'

'That's not a bad idea, actually. This was Harry's mundane bolthole. So secret that Matt didn't know about it and the school thought he worked at the Britannia, a completely different hotel. You and I have got to brief our COs. Cordy can even drive to just outside the hotel to save Elaine's leg.'

He let go of his buttons. 'The hardest part of being a DCI is letting go. You're right. I'd prefer to call Commander Ross sooner rather than later. And they can get the pizzas on the way back.'

'Pizza?' said Cordy. 'Please tell me you're joking, sir.'

'He is,' said Elaine. 'I never settle for less than Chinese.'

'Aren't there a whole load of wholefood restaurants in Ambleside? One of them must do takeaways.'

'Welcome to the police service,' said Tom. 'A land where sausage rolls are considered haute cuisine.' He took his coat off. 'Why are you still here?'

Elaine struggled to her feet. 'Ha bleeding ha. Sir. Cordy, does Conrad's car smell of smoke?'

'Smoke, no. Dog, yes.'

Elaine grabbed her stick and waved a goodbye.

Tom and I were preparing reports for our bosses, when Cordy called. I put her on speaker.

She spoke quietly, and Tom and I had to put our heads together to hear. 'He's got a family here. A girlfriend and a daughter. The girlfriend is Zinayida Zinchenko and A. Zinchenko is her brother. Anatoly. I'm just on my way to get him from the kitchens. He's the chef.'

Her voice dropped even further. 'Zinayida is pretty much in denial. Says that Harry didn't have a brother, only a sister who drowned, and that he didn't work at a school. They named their daughter after her. Lara.'

'Lara?' said Tom. 'A sister called Lara?'

'That's what she said. Showed us the picture and everything.'

'Get a copy of that picture. And one of ... Zinayida, was it? And check to see if Harry left anything behind that wasn't dirty washing.'

'Right. Yes, sir.'

'That changes things a bit,' said Tom when Cordy had gone.

'Does it?' I asked.

'For one thing it means that little Lara inherits half a hotel. Harry may have kept Zinayida a secret, but he was there an awful lot. They were part of his life. It helps us understand what motivated him.'

'Does it? It looks like he kept the Zinchenkos well away from magick, and it was magick that killed him.'

'Even so,' said Tom. 'Even so.'

We hastily amended our reports, called our bosses and waited for the girls to come back. My stomach rumbled, and I said, 'Is it evil of me to hope they didn't forget pizza?'

'No,' said Tom. 'It shows how dedicated you are.'

Neither Ross nor Hannah had much to say. Hannah is essentially on tenterhooks waiting for the court decision tomorrow, though she did smile when I told her that Mina would be there. And then the girls were back, and Scout woke up as soon as he smelled fish and chips. So did I.

'Poor woman,' said Elaine. 'That really sucked. She was just ready for evening service when we called. She'd put her daughter to bed, got dressed up in her national dress and done her face. She was just waiting for the babysitter.'

I glanced at Cordelia, and she'd been crying. She was trying to hold it together, distributing the fish and chip bundles and sorting out some items they'd removed from the hotel.

'Thank you, Elaine,' said Tom. 'And you, Cordelia. If I'd thought there was a family there, I'd have done it myself.'

'You're a DCI, not a martyr,' said Elaine. 'We got what we could and left them to it. Told them we'd be back tomorrow.' She hung her stick off the back of the chair. 'Look, sir, do you mind if we eat first? I don't think I can concentrate with that smell in here.'

'You and me both,' said Tom. 'Which one's got the mushy peas?'

We ate in near silence, reluctant to pick over the remains of Harry's devastated family and guilty at our hunger. Only Cordelia looked like she was forcing down the food. Perhaps it's because she's the only parent of the group.

When the wrappers had been disposed of and tea dispensed, Elaine did some transfers to the secure laptop, then hitched it to the data projector. The first picture was of a smiling Harry standing between the Zinchenko siblings. Anatoly was in gleaming chef's whites, his arms folded in defiance of the camera. On Harry's right was Zinayida in her red and white national dress. She had her right hand curled across her chest to rest on Harry's shoulder. 'Opening day after refurbishment,' said Elaine. 'The press picture didn't have Harry in it, and she told us she'd just found out that she was pregnant. Have a look at this. It's supposed to be Harry's sister, Lara. And according to Zinayida, Harry didn't have a brother. According to his actual brother, he didn't have a sister.'

It was impossible to tell how old it was, but the picture looked to have been taken with a camera, not an early phone. It was summertime, and the girl was wearing a sleeveless top. The wind was blowing her hair everywhere as it escaped from an Alice band, and she stared right into the lens with a look of playful devotion, accentuated by the fact that her lips were gripping the pendant from a chain round her neck. A horseshoe charm? I'll tell you one thing, my sister Rachael has never, ever looked at me like that girl was looking at Harry.

Either way, even I spotted something: ignore the hair, focus on the bone structure and the lips, and this girl could have been a teenage Zinayida.

Tom cleared his throat. 'There's something in my full report that I didn't mention earlier because we're focusing on the present. Matt told me that Harry's great lost love was a Witch called Lara. She drowned in a sailing accident, and Matt had little time for her.'

Elaine spoke first. 'Zinayida could be Lara's older sister. She could *be* Lara, older and blonder. And now his daughter's another Lara.'

The repetition of the name kicked my synapses into gear. 'Lara Dent,' I blurted. 'On the Honour Board in School House. Lara Dent won the Waterhead Chase and the Union Chase Trophy when Harry would have been seventeen.'

'I know. Creepy isn't in it.' Tom drank some tea. 'I don't know about you, Conrad, but my gut instinct says we don't tell her. We tell her that Lara was actually a step-sister, and we get Matt to do the same. And Matt is the only person we tell in the world of magick. It seems the right thing to do.'

'It's the right thing and the safe thing.'

Tom nodded slowly. 'Anything else?'

Elaine killed the data projector. 'According to Zinayida, she last saw Harry on Saturday morning. He left saying that he was going to the race meeting at York and then Scotland for a few days. She was getting worried, yes, but only in the gaps when she wasn't running the hotel and looking after an eighteen month old child. Cordelia?'

'Um. Yes. We asked if Harry had left anything, and she said no at first. She knew he was a bookmaker, and said that since Easter he's been running his Book on a laptop. Then she remembered that his old Book was in the safe. Anatoly and I retrieved it, and as far as I could tell, the only magick in the whole building is in here somewhere.' She placed a leather messenger bag on the table and slid it towards me. My first thought was that she should examine it, and then I saw her face. She really didn't want to.

I took the bag and removed a black leather book, about nine inches by twelve. The book as a whole wasn't magickal, but I could feel a trace inside it. I flicked through it, trying to make sense of the figures. At least it wasn't in code. There were headings for the different chases – Langdale, Patterdale, Upper Eden, Lower Eden, Swaledale … a few in Scotland. And dates. I kept flicking right to the end, and after the last race, I got a flash of magick. On an empty page.

I ran my fingers over the blank lines, releasing a touch of Lux. Oh dear. I showed Tom the book, and he squinted at it. 'I can't see anything.'

'Oh. Hold my left wrist and stare at the page. It might not work, but it's worth a try.'

I closed my eyes and released Lux, imagining the drawing coming to life.

'Shit. Fuck me,' said Tom.

'That's what I thought.' I removed my hand from the page. 'Can you still see it?'

'No.'

This time I tried it with my eyes open, so we could both focus on Harry's drawing. It was done in red Enscribing ink, blood red on the page. Appropriate, because Harry had drawn a lake scene, with mountains in the background and some water, but mostly it was foreground, and the foreground was a cemetery. A cemetery with cartoon gravestones, each one headed RIP, and as they got closer to the water, they got smaller and older.

From oldest to newest, the inscriptions read, *RIP Thunderer, RIP Harry the Horseman, RIP Lara, RIP Martha*. The nearest was much larger and had the most lettering. *RIP Harry Eldridge, Ind. Bookmaker.*

'Poor sod,' said Tom. He took his hand off mine and blinked at the newly blank page. 'Cordelia, could you do the same for Elaine?'

Cordy didn't try to hide her distress when she saw the graveyard, and she didn't give Elaine as long as she'd have liked looking at the vision.

'Ten minute break,' said Tom, 'while I give this some thought.'


When we reconvened, he started by having a good natured dig at me. At least, I think it was good natured. Hard to tell with Tom.

'I bloody hate you, sometimes, Conrad,' he stated, waving Harry's Book in the air. 'Because of what you did at Fylde Racecourse, I had to go over the accounts of several bookmakers looking for discrepancies.'

Cordy was all ears, as you'd expect. I opened my arms in a *What can I say?* gesture.

'As the only one here with a prayer of understanding this, I'm going to devote hours of my life to going through it. Hours I won't get back. As for the rest, I think it is time you got out, Elaine, but not on your own, and not far. You and Barney can go back to the Oak Tree tomorrow and get their statements and the rest. After that, follow the money.'

'Great. I get the grieving family and the bank accounts. Yeah, yeah, I know.'

'I know it's a lot for you to handle, Elaine. That's why I've been on to South Lancs and borrowed Hazel Cotton.'

Elaine groaned loudly. 'Why her? Is there no Family Liaison officer in Westmorland?'

'Commander Ross says not one he'd trust.'

'You can't trust Hazel, either! If Lucy finds out, you'll be in deep shit. Sir.'

Whatever this Hazel Cotton's track record, it was a surprise to see Elaine be so open in the incident room. Normally she reserved her full and frank opinions for when she and Tom were alone. Or so I've been told. And Tom didn't even frown at her.

'That's my problem, Elaine. Hazel will behave, because she thinks that I've still got the voice recordings of what she did.'

'Have you?'

Tom gave his Sphinx smile and ignored the question. 'What's more, her kids are with their dad for a few days, so she'll be at the Oak Tree first thing.' He rubbed his left arm, then his jaw. 'I want her to handle Matthew, too. Bringing them together will need an experienced hand.' He looked at Cordy and me. 'Joking aside, you two, Hazel Cotton can dig into your personal lives like a rabid mole if you let her.'

'Tom,' I said. 'Have some respect for moles. Is she that bad?'

'Yes. No matter how hard she tries, tell her nothing.'

'Understood.'

'Conrad, why don't you and Cordelia kill two birds by seeing Nicole Sanderson at the stables tomorrow. You said she'd text you?'

I pulled my lip. 'She has. And I've just had one from Willow, the Academy head girl. Nicole has suggested we meet in Ambleside at ten o'clock, which is late enough not to be suspicious, but early enough to stop us going to the stables first.'

'What's your point?' said Tom.

'I'd like to go to Sprint Stables first thing. Without Nicole.'

'The last time you went to a stables in the Particular unannounced, you got shot, didn't you?'

'Strangely, I hadn't forgotten that, Tom.'

'Fine.'

Cordy groaned. 'How early is early?'

'If we leave at seven, we should get there at eight, so not too early.'

'You don't have to put up with this,' said Elaine. 'How about we swap?'

'Shut up, Elaine,' said Tom. 'What about Willow?'

'She's staying with a friend over at Coniston and doesn't have a car.'

'Fine. Get over when you can after the stables and Ms Sanderson. If nothing else comes up. Anything else?' We shook our heads. 'We'll give it another hour tonight. If we don't, the paperwork will overwhelm us all. Don't be afraid to leave things for Barney tomorrow. Conrad, a word outside?'

'So what do you reckon?' he asked, standing upwind of my cigarette.

I took a moment to get my thoughts in order. 'I reckon that we're missing something in Harry's relationship to the Academy. It's totally unbalanced in his favour. Even his part-time wages were well over the odds. He didn't pay mooring fees or charges for power.'

'I agree, but there are so many gaps in our understanding of his life ... How would you proceed?' he asked.

'I can't. Not until after the hearing in court tomorrow.'

'What time's the hearing?'

'Ten. Another reason to think that Nicole Sanderson's timing is suspicious.'

He grunted, acknowledging the point. 'At least poor Zinayida has given us a story for the press briefing: Harry Eldridge, local hotel owner and father of one. That's going out at ten o'clock, too.'

'And that reminds me. I'm going to hold my nose and call the Chief Assessor.'

'Fine. See you inside. And no trying to dodge the paperwork.' He grinned. 'Unless you can legitimately delegate it.'

I called Philippa Grayling and I was surprised when she took my call. I was less surprised at the abrupt, 'What?' that greeted me.

'Out of courtesy, I wanted to let you know that Harry Eldridge had a mundane life, with a business and a family that he went to great lengths to conceal from Matthew.'

There was a pause, and she dialled down the anger a couple of notches. 'I see. Are you going to inform Matthew'

'We are. A trained Family Liaison Officer will handle it.'

'Have you seen him since … since we met at the Academy? How is he?'

It sounded like genuine concern. 'DCI Morton visited. He said that Matt was pretty much as you'd expect. His Apprentice is going to keep an eye on him.'

'Hmmph. Thank you. I heard about the attack on Harry's boat. Why are you telling me about Harry's other life? I presume you're not telling me anything else.'

'I'm not. I'm telling you about Zinayida Zinchenko because it's going to be in the press release tomorrow morning, and I know Lakeland. It'll be all over social media by lunchtime. The Zinchenko siblings, and Harry's daughter, are innocent. I'd be grateful, on their behalf, if you could put the word around that we've cleaned out all of Harry's possessions from the hotel.'

'What are you saying, Mr Clarke?'

'I'm saying that the Assessors leak like a sieve. Whoever attacked the boat didn't find out that Harry was dead from my side, did they?'

There was another pause. 'Thank you for calling Mr Clarke. Our positions may change after the hearing tomorrow. Good night.'

So, I'd been promoted from "Witchfinder" to "Mr Clarke." Small victories and all that.

At the end of our hour's paperwork, Tom said that he needed to brief Commander Ross. I had to call the Boss as well, so he asked Cordy to take Elaine to the hotel, and we all started packing up. After a last check on the laptop, I announced (mostly to myself) that there was high pressure building in the North Atlantic.

'Another thing for your list,' said Elaine.

151

'What list?' said Tom.

Elaine grinned and sat back, massaging her leg. 'Cordelia has a list of things about life with the Dragonslayer that she has to get used to. She can add "Random weather forecasts" to it.'

Cordelia took it in her stride. 'Actually, I won't. He's just told me that it's going to be dry but cold for a few days. Good to know. I have, however, added "Terrible diet" and "Caffeine overload." And that's just the last three hours. Let's go.'

Erin and Lucy were waiting in the bar when we finally got there. I wouldn't say that we crept into the Little Langdale Lodge, but they didn't roll out the red carpet. Fair enough – I didn't want a red carpet, I wanted a drink and time to call Mina before crashing out. At times like this, you have to rub your head to remember that you'd never heard of Harry Eldridge when you woke up this morning.

Lucy disappeared with Tom. We were going to unpack and meet for a work-free bottle with Cordy and Elaine. Erin was keeping the seats warm for us.

When Lucy was gone, she said, 'I've got something for you. What do you think?' She passed me a piece of paper and explained, 'I sweet-talked Andrea into letting me use the hotel's printer. She's lovely, isn't she?'

'She is.'

'This is just the shield, the most important bit. I'll add the rest later. Oh, and you'll want a motto, won't you?'

I stared at the design. 'Yes, please. I thought I'd change it slightly: "Our Word is Binding". This is perfect. Thank you, Erin.' I leaned down and gave her a kiss. 'How much do I owe you?'

'I'll give you a 50% discount if you tell me where Barney's going to be tomorrow. Just so that I can, you know, casually bump into him.'

'It's no secret that we're based at Charlotte Mason College. I'll tell you what, I'll message you when we stop for lunch, if he's going to be around, that is.'

'You're useless, you are.'

'Oh, one more thing. Was there anything in that book on the Chases about Longsleddale?'

'There was, actually. Harry had left a few blank leaves at the back, and added some notes. Look.' She had the volume in her Enscriber's case, and opened it to the back. 'Does this mean anything to you?'

There was a drawing – a sort of conceptual map of the valley – and various jottings. The annotations rang a bell, and I checked the next few pages. Harry had done similar work on a couple of other stables (including the Blackthwaite Stables near Millom, where I'd been shot). I passed it back to her after another look at Longsleddale. 'You need to show that to Tom, and tell him to cross-reference it with Harry's Book. Capital "B". If you turn up at the incident room before nine tomorrow, Barney should still be there, but Tom definitely needs to know. Okay?'

She shuffled in her seat, a little shuffle of anticipation. 'I always aim to satisfy our public servants.'

'You're worse than Scout, you are. Talking of whom, I need to go and light a fire in my yurt.'

She couldn't resist it. As I limped across the lounge, she called out to my back. 'You can light a fire in my yurt any time, Conrad.'


The clouds did clear, and I got my call to Mina under a beautiful black sky, a glass of malt whisky in my hand and my faithful dog at my feet. I could even see the reflection of the moon in the tarn. Yes, it really was that good. Most of what we talked about you either know or is best left to your imaginations. Early on in the conversation, Mina did tell me that Sofía had pumped her for gossip on Kenver Mowbray.

'I think he has asked her on a date, and she doesn't know whether to say yes.'

'I'm not going to say anything, because she'd never forgive me for interfering.' I let that sink in. 'You, on the other hand, have no doubt given her your expert opinion.'

'I have. Why else do you think she asked me? It's what girls do. I told her to think carefully, because Kenver is only a boy. It would also ruin her chance of going out with Cador, who is a much better prospect.'

'Is he? How do you work that out?'

'If Kenver is as good a Mage as his father, Sofía will always be in his shadow. If she is a better Mage than him, he will resent her for that. But with Cador, she will always be the Mage, no matter how high he flies in the law. These things are important.'

They are, and I couldn't argue with Mina's brutal calibration of the weakness of the male ego. 'I think you're forgetting that Sofía is only nineteen.'

'Which is why she must act decisively. These Mowbrays will not be on the market for long.'

She said it in a half-mocking tone that was meant to deflect criticism, and in others it would work. I know her too well. She was being entirely serious.

'You're right, up to a point,' I replied. 'Her best option would be Eseld, though. Sofía can trail along on her coat tails and then dump her in a few years.'

There was a silence over the line while she computed that. 'No. I have Rachael lined up for Eseld. I think they will make the perfect couple.'

It was my turn to have my mind boggled. It totally rejected the idea of Rachael and Eseld. 'How was the food?'

The last thing I did before I turned in was have another look at my new coat of arms. I'll sleep on it and show you when I've made a final decision.

# 16 — Bookmaking

Tom hadn't really appreciated the Lodge last night, because he was shattered and they'd arrived in the dark. He'd appreciated the comfortable bar and the cosy room, and he'd very much appreciated going to bed with Lucy; the rest, not so much. He did, however, take Conrad's advice about getting out early for a walk.

You could barely see the Lodge from any angle, so cunningly had it been dug into the hillside above the tarn. A few slate walls at the top made it look like a cave because the roof was completely grassed over. He left the front door and headed left, following an obvious footpath down to the water.

He stopped half-way down because his breath had been taken away. The beauty of the small tarn lay in its simplicity – just water with reeds, grass, ripples and a view of the other side of Little Langdale beyond it. He drank it in until the cold breeze drove him down to the water's edge.

He walked through a complex garden that mixed ornamental features with kitchen produce, and that was when he realised just how *different* the world of magick truly was. Yes, the garden was bare now, but no one should be planting that stuff at this altitude or latitude in England. Yet they did, and it grew. He shook his head and walked round the tarn to a terrace. Even from here, where every bedroom in the Lodge had a window, it didn't look out of place. On the bottom level, the whole width of the hotel was glass – the restaurant. One of the panels had a discreet sign saying *Entrance*, and he went through. Breakfast was upstairs, in the bar, and he found Lucy studying the menu.

'I could get used to this,' she said. 'This place is registered and it has planning permission – don't ask me how – but it's nowhere on the internet. Nowhere. You only get to come if you know someone. I can see why Conrad thinks it might be a good place for a short honeymoon.'

'Don't tell me you're getting wedding fever.'

'Who, me?' She smiled archly. 'Only a bit.'

'And Conrad wants to put a spanner in the works. This place wouldn't exist if the Unions didn't have a whole bunch of strings to pull. Talking of pulling strings, Hazel Cotton's on FLO duty at the Oak Tree this morning.'

Lucy looked up and thought for a moment. 'Good. It will frustrate the hell out of her knowing that she's being kept out of things. I hope she pulls her mangy hair out. You're going for the Full Westmorland, aren't you?'

'I am. No idea when I'll get another meal, but I promise you we'll eat here before we leave.'

'Good.'

Tom had underestimated Hazel Cotton's ability to get in where a draught wouldn't. When he and Elaine arrived at the incident room at eight thirty, she was already there, browbeating Barney Smith.

'The one bloody day she's early,' muttered Elaine.

'Morning, Boss,' said Hazel. At least she had a clean blouse on. The cardigan might have seen a washing machine, too, because the stains now looked baked in rather than fresh. 'So who's our silent partner, then? MI5? MI6?'

Barney gave Tom a beleaguered look of mute appeal.

'MI7,' said Tom. 'And you don't want to mess with them.'

Hazel had the invulnerability of someone who believes that they've already suffered the worst than life can throw at them, and laughed. 'I'll look on that as a challenge, then. I've already made the tea.'

'She has,' said Elaine, putting a mug on Tom's desk. 'Wonders will never cease.'

'Thank you, Hazel,' said Tom. 'I wouldn't bother hanging around. They're on an operation and won't be coming in until much later.'

She considered whether he was bluffing and decided he wasn't. 'Fair enough. I'll just finish me tea and get off, then. It's within walking distance, yeah?'

'Yes. If you're staying, Elaine can brief you on the line we're taking about Lara Dent. I'm going to call Matthew's lodger.'

The Apprentice at Blackburn Cottage said that Matt had been okay this morning, and had been up before her to stride round Lingmoor Fell. So far so good. He gave the Apprentice Hazel's number and asked if Matthew could call the FLO when he was ready. He'd barely disconnected when Hazel said, 'Aye aye, who's this then?' and Erin Slater breezed in after barely knocking once on the door.

'Thank you, Hazel,' said Tom. 'I'll catch up with you later.'

The moment's diversion was enough for Erin to reach Barney's desk and plant her backside on the edge in front of him. It was like watching an avant garde film, where one half of the screen had been speeded up and the other slowed down. Hazel took an age to gather her stuff and leave, while Erin Slater worked as fast as she could to entice Barney into her web.

Tom mentally kicked himself for using the *spider* image. Conrad had assured him that there was no such thing as a love potion in magick. All manner of potions to lower inhibitions and increase libido, yes, but nothing to make the river of love flow in directions didn't want to go. Barney could look after himself.

That didn't excuse Erin shoving herself into his investigation, though.

'Can I help you?' Tom asked.

'I've got something,' Erin replied with a lazy smile.

'Really?'

'Yes. I'm not just a pretty face, you know. Conrad said I should show you this so you could compare it with something called, "Harry's Book." Especially the annotations.'

Tom suspended judgement and looked at the manuscript. Conrad was right – these would help a lot. 'Have you finished with this?'

Erin waited until she was sure that Hazel Cotton wasn't eavesdropping. 'Not quite. There's something bothering me about ... this technical thing. Do you want to take pictures?'

'Please.'

Job done, he escorted her out of the incident room and on to the steps of the modern, slate finished extension building. The original college building was round the corner, somewhere, and he promised himself a visit later.

'Thanks for that, Erin. I presume Conrad told you to bring it here when you saw him at half past six this morning, before you embarked on a ten mile run?'

'What are you trying to say, Tom?'

'Nothing. Nothing at all. Are you staying over again tonight?'

'Probably. See you later.'

Tom took great delight in putting on a bland face when he returned, and Barney searched in vain for a clue to Tom's thoughts on the merits of the effervescent Erin Slater. 'Can you leave it ten minutes before you spring into action. I want to check with the solicitor about that will.'

Greening and Whitecross, Solicitors and Commissioners for Oaths were exactly like the Little Langdale Lodge: almost no online presence. Tom had to resort to the Law Society index to find their number, and the secretary put him straight through to Mr Whitecross when he announced himself.

'Aah. I've been expecting a call, Chief Inspector.'

'And why's that?' said Tom, more to test the waters than because he thought he'd get an answer.

'Because of the will. With Matthew Eldridge supporting your side, I knew you'd get the will first.'

'We're all on the same side, Mr Whitecross.'

'If only that were true, life would be a lot easier. I think we can agree that we're all playing by the rules. So far. And I shall continue. Young Mr Harry Eldridge left us when he formed a relationship with a mundane partner. His new lawyers are over the little estate agency on Church Street. Can't miss 'em. He did so because he needed commercial expertise that we can't provide, given that we mostly deal with magickal law. In fact, my partner will be robing up in the Cloister Court around now.'

'Is he acting for the Chief Assessor?'

'She. Yes she is. I have something else for you, Chief Inspector. Harry made a new mundane will, but he also left a Statement of Guardianship. It names Matthew as the magickal Guardian of his daughter. I believe that Matthew is also joint trustee under the mundane will.'

'Thank you, Mr Whitecross. You've been most forthcoming.'

The lawyer chuckled. 'You mean you thought I'd stonewall you. Well, I don't want Matthew to get caught in the crossfire. Being obstructive is in no one's interests.'

'Ha. If only all the solicitors I dealt with felt the same way. Would it be okay for one of my officers to collect a copy? We're going to be bringing Matthew and Harry's family together later.'

'By all means. I shall have them ready.'

Tom put his phone down. Conrad had told him that the Chief Assessor was worried about Matthew. Whitecross was concerned, too. It seemed genuine, and it helped Tom understand why Conrad had once risked everything to get justice for Rod Bristow. The ill-fated Mr Bristow had been a mundane farmer with aspirations to breed horses. He had been taken out in a cold-blooded hit and his home had been burnt to the ground. When he was killed, he had only been truly missed by a teenage stable girl. Whitecross hadn't wanted Matthew to be *caught in the crossfire*, but he hadn't said anything about the Zinchenkos. They looked after their own in the world of magick.

Tom picked up Harry's Book and discovered that Conrad was right: the drawings from Erin made total sense of the headers for each race, and Tom now knew what it all meant. On the drawing of Longsleddale, a section of practice course had been broken down – LS1, LS2 and so on. The same was true for Blackthwaite Stables in Millom, and either Harry himself or an associate had timed the various horses over those sections, and these were the headers for each Chase.

As the date of the race approached, Harry would sometimes scratch a horse or add a note on one that was coming in from outside the Particular. And then there was the Book itself: the balance of wagers made and odds given. For example, if there were £8k on the favourite at 3:1, so long as the wagers on the rest of the field added up to £24k, the book balanced. And until the end of winter, it did.

There were only three Chases after the Langdale in January: two short ones in February and then the final race of the season on the night of the Equinox: the *Grand Wasdale Cup* sounded fairly impressive, even if it didn't have the prestige of the Langdale.

According to Conrad, the reason the Langdale stood out on its own was the length and brutality of the course and the fact that it was restricted to horses and riders from the Particular. Over those last three races, something had gone badly wrong with Harry's Book.

Tom laid out some lined paper and started to put the figures in an order that made sense. Despite his moaning to Conrad, Tom really loved the challenge. This was almost a treat for him, and took him back to his days in the Economic Crimes unit at City Police. He put his phone on charge and chose one of his favourite playlists, the Quintessential Thomas Tallis. It was only when he got thirsty and went to put the kettle on that he realised the time: quarter to ten. What were Conrad and Cordelia up to, he wondered.

While the kettle boiled, a slew of text messages came in from Elaine and Hazel. His team had arranged to meet Matthew on neutral ground to break the news; Matthew wanted to see them regardless of the outcome in the Cloister Court. All the business of the wills had been handled, too, and Zinayida was starting to accept Matthew's existence – given that he was the trustee for little Lara's inheritance. Satisfied, Tom treated himself to a Hobnob and went back to his figures.

He had to go and check some dates, and dig out the encrypted file on Conrad's dealings with Sextons. It looked like Conrad had been indirectly (and innocently) responsible for Harry's fall from grace. Tom put together a timeline, and it went something like this:

- February – A horse from Blackthwaite Stables wins one Chase and is placed in the other.
- A horse from Ireland fails badly in another of the Chases.
- Harry starts giving shorter odds on the Blackthwaite horse for the Grand Cup and longer ones on the Irish horse.
- March – Vicky Robson breaks Diarmuid Driscoll's leg, and Conrad arrests him.
- Shortly after, Driscoll is murdered. His stable is closed down. Harry has to refund the bets on the Blackthwaite horse. His book no longer balances.
- Conrad arrests multiple members of the Sexton family. Rowan Sexton pulls out as a rider.
- Harry makes a desperate attempt to balance his Book. He fails, and is totally cleaned out when the Irish horse wins the Grand Cup.

Tom summarised the losses and left them for Elaine and Barney to follow up. If Harry had had any capital, he could have ridden out the crisis, but he didn't. His capital was all in his share of the Oak Tree Hotel.

He walked over to the whiteboard and wrote,

*Who bailed out Harry? Who gave him the laptop? Where is the laptop?*

Getting to know Erin had taught him that young Enscribers might be as addicted to their phones as any other young person, but the important stuff always went on paper, so what had made Harry switch to digital bookmaking?

He was trying to work out other questions when his phone rang. He was expecting Hazel, but it was an unknown landline number.

'Hello?'

'Sir, it's Cordelia.'

'Hi. How did you get on?'

'Erm, Conrad's on his way to the hospital…'

## 17 — At the Gallops

'How was the yurt?' asked Cordelia when she slipped into the front seat of my BMW, which is not to be confused with Tom's BMW. Perhaps I should tell him to get an Audi.

'The yurt was remarkably comfortable and warm until I got up this morning. Outside the furs, it was bloody freezing, and I'm saying nothing about my naked dash to the shower block. If the hot water hadn't worked, you'd be doing this on your own.'

'No I wouldn't,' she said, adjusting some of her layers and testing to see if the car heating had come on. 'Partly because I'd be traumatised by the image of you running naked through the lodge grounds, and partly because I haven't a fucking clue what we're doing. Sir.'

I joined the main road down the valley (if you can call it a main road), and risked a glance over to the east. In the shadow of the fells, it was still pitch black. The sun wouldn't be showing his face for at least half an hour. 'You've mastered the sarcastic use of "sir", so figuring out what we're up to should be a doddle.'

She frowned. 'Do *you* have a clue?'

'We're going to see a man about a horse. That's it.'

'I've got my notes, and I know that we need to talk to Aidan Manning, but you didn't explain what Erin found in the manuscript.'

'I'm about to tell you now because we'd both had enough last night. If you were that desperate, you could have asked her.'

'Not my place.'

'Plus the fact that you really don't like her, do you?'

'She's not someone I'd choose to hang around with, no.'

'Is it her, or is it the Foresters you don't like?'

She got a little agitated. Just a little. 'I didn't say that. I just wouldn't choose to hang around with her. Or with the Foresters in general. They have different values to the Daughters of the Goddess, and I'm not sure about their choice of friends.'

That was close to being a judgement, something she's stopped short of up to now. 'What do you mean? Which friends?'

'The Prince of Arden more or less *owns* the Foresters, like ...' She cast round for a simile. '... like a Russian oligarch who owns a football team. He lets them get on with it and enjoys the fun, until he gets bored and sacks the manager.' She drew a deep breath. 'Not that I'm implying anything about Erin. You trust her, and the Constable wouldn't have asked her to work on the Warden elections if she didn't trust her, too.'

We'd joined the (proper) main road that led into Ambleside, and I still hadn't seen another vehicle. Cordy waited until I'd shot round the lake and caught up with a delivery lorry at the traffic lights. We'd both cast a look at the Waterhead Academy as we passed.

'You're not going to tell her what I said, are you?'

'Erin's a mate. She rents my stable. She spends most nights in my house. She's Myfanwy's BFF. But she's not my partner. You're my partner. What you say to me stays with me. I didn't think I needed to spell that out.'

She sighed. 'Maybe it's because the partners I've had before weren't as old-fashioned as you are.'

'I prefer *timeless*, but there you go. About those drawings.'

'Yes, please.'

'Do you know anything about horse riding or racing or training?'

'No. Not beyond what the Boss calls the *bleedin' obvious*.'

'It gets under your skin. If you can afford your own horse, it can become an obsession. It was for me, until I couldn't afford the horse any more and I joined the RAF. If you get to ride or work with horses for a living, it becomes your world. The early morning gallops, the sound of horseshoes on cobbles, the smell, the camaraderie. And the risks. The adrenaline. Harry might have given up riding, but he didn't give up the horses, did he?'

'No, he didn't.'

'And we haven't spoken to a single person who shared that world with him yet. That's why we're going to Sprint Stables. From what I saw of Harry's Book yesterday, he used to go up Longsleddale regularly to time the horses over the gallops. That's what the drawings were: short course, long course, course through woods. And plane-shifting. Lots of that.'

'Right.' Perhaps emboldened by what I'd said about partners, she went a bit further. 'You used to hunt, didn't you?'

'I did. For a while.' I risked overtaking the delivery vehicle as we passed the Lakes School (the local state school), then I continued. 'The hunting ban had come in not long before I got my own horse, and I must admit I sided with the hunters at first. I enjoyed my first few hunts.'

'What changed?'

'Two things. One is that I got a holiday job with the servants. As a terrierman.'

'Working with the dogs?'

'Oh no. Our job was to go round stopping the earths. So the fox couldn't go to ground. I was only a teenager, but it still made me think.'

'I didn't know that. The Daughters have a lot of land, but we hadn't used to get involved with hunting one way or the other. If our tenants wanted the hunt over their farm, that was their business. I honestly didn't know the fox had nowhere to hide.'

'The next time we rode out, I couldn't help thinking about it, and then I saw the looks on some of the faces. They knew the fox had no chance, and they didn't care. I think it gave me an early idea of what a psychopath looks like. I switched to point-to-points after that. Mostly. Still went to the social events, though. Look, that's Windermere School, the local private boarding school. I bet they've had a few of the Academy's sixth formers go there.'

Just past Windermere town, the countryside opens up, and we could see that dawn was getting nearer. We had to go nearly to Kendal, through scrubby and scrappy fields of sheep, before we could turn and follow the Sprint up Longsleddale. There really is only one way in and one way out of that valley. Unless you're on foot, of course. Or a horse.

'People who didn't know her used to say that Raven was a psychopath,' said Cordelia. It was the first time she'd mentioned her former boss/partner/lover properly. There had been references to her job as Raven's Page, or asides about things they'd done together, but this was the first time she'd talked about the giant Witch as a person.

'I knew she wasn't as soon as I met her,' I said. 'What made the others say that?'

'She didn't care what most people thought about her, and those people mistook that attitude for lack of empathy. No one cared more about the ones she loved than Raven. Are we going to get breakfast?'

'Yes, but not until we've finished. Did you see that sign for Staveley a while back? Wilf's does a brilliant breakfast, but they don't open until later. I have energy bars in the glove compartment.'

'Ooh, goody.' She flipped the catch. 'You also have packets and packets of cigarettes. There we go. Excuse me.'

She'd changed the subject to breakfast, he thought, because she'd butted up against a painful fact: when Raven died, she'd already stopped loving Cordelia in the deep sense. I know that because I was there when Raven renounced the Order and quit the Daughters. Cordelia was not there, and Raven didn't give Cordy's feelings a second thought.

We stopped at the tiny hamlet of Garnet Bridge for a break. I needed a smoke, Scout needed to run around, Cordy needed to see the map, and we both needed coffee. As partners go, Cordelia is geographically somewhere between Vicky and Karina. By that, I mean that Karina would have memorised the map in advance and that Vicky wouldn't have bothered because it might as well have been in Russian for all she could understand it.

'So the stables aren't occulted, then?'

163

'Not fully. From what I can tell, it's based in these old buildings, here. I think they might have been outposts of that farm, there, from the days before tractors and quadbikes. I know maps aren't updated that often, but Google Earth isn't showing much more, either. You can't run a stables in something that size.'

'And where are we going?'

'The route that Harry drew curves east, then west, over the road and over the river Sprint. Then it follows that ghyll, there.'

'What's a ghyll?'

'A steep valley, usually with a powerful stream and woods. Harry didn't ride. I hope he didn't have the loan of a quadbike. I think he was driven to this point, here. There's a short farm track. And then he walked to this ridge. Not far. About ten minutes.'

'Won't we be seen?'

'This valley has no through road. Apart from a few serious walkers, no one comes up here. Let's go.'

The earliest runners and walkers had already passed through the valley, and the school bus wasn't due yet. We drove up Longsleddale without seeing a single human being. If you compare it to some of Lakeland's bigger, grander valleys, it's a bit underpowered, but what it lacks in dramatic sides and width, it makes up for with a greener landscape and intimacy. And peace. Perfect, soul restoring peace, which my three litre diesel engine had no doubt ruined for some people.

Cordy kept a careful eye open for Sprint Stables. It was easy to spot because of the new wall and new entrance. The old entrance led straight on to the buildings, and it had been replaced by stones and a mound of earth with young trees that shouldn't have grown that quickly. From the new entrance, nothing of the stables was visible, and only the smallest sign announced its presence.

'Plenty of magick there. It positively thrums with it.' She turned round to comfort Scout, who had jumped out of his basket in the luggage section and sat whining on the back seat. 'That's okay. Good boy. We'll go and sort out those naughty Mages, won't we?'

'Arff.'

'What's up with him?' I asked.

'You don't get many Wards designed to discourage animals. They've got one.'

'Here's the track.'

There was evidence of a lot of vehicles – why else would they stick a gravel turning space up here. In mundane racing, it's both legal and encouraged to watch horses over the gallops. It looks like the same rules applied in the world of the Chases.

I opened the back of the car and debated the likelihood of danger. I glanced at Cordy fastening the laces of a new pair of boots and decided on caution. I took my sword, Great Fang, and strapped it on my back. Better safe than sorry.

It wasn't quite ten to eight, and I'm betting that the serious business of training starts at eight. It was a beautiful morning now that the sun had chased the mist away, and I could just see the woods poking out of the ghyll ahead of us, gloriously orange in autumn splendour, with splashes of green from the firs. 'We're heading over there,' I said, pointing to a shoulder of the hills. It was a short but steep slope. 'We'll take it slowly and have some fun.'

Cordy looked around. 'Fun? Where's the fun in a wet field with nothing in it?'

'Got it in one, Cordelia.' I slipped the lead. 'Scout! Away! Let's go.'

I started walking, and Scout headed for the corner of the field. Cordy shook her head and took out her phone. 'I'll call the actual kids and tell them Mummy's got a new big kid to look after.' We ambled slowly towards the hill for a while, as I called out instructions to Scout, and then Cordy started holding up her phone. 'No signal. None at all. What network are you on?' I told her. 'Damn. so am I.'

'We might get lucky with a bit of height. Reception's at its worst on the valley floors. Come by! Come by!'

We hit the hill, and I called Scout to heel. 'Good dog.' I gave him a treat and we stretched our legs. With a little slipping and sliding, we reached the vantage point.

'Whoo!,' said Cordy. 'I need to start working out.'

We were both short of breath, and took a moment to enjoy the view up the ghyll and down Longsleddale. From here, we could see a marked track running over grass to the start of the wild fells, where the dry stone walls ended and open country reached up to the top of the hills. We could also see the back of Sprint Stables.

She looked around, shielding her eyes for a second, then looking at me. 'You bonded with Vicky quite early, didn't you? In a magickal way, I mean. And not much with Saffron.'

'Yes.'

'I saw what you did with Erin yesterday. I'd like to try something more structured so that we can see through the Glamours together. If that's okay, Conrad.'

I looked down at her, and she smiled back, the lines around her eyes creasing up. She was making an effort here, and that touched me. Her Goddess braid was a well-disciplined one, with no stray hairs, and a pair of diamond studs glinted in her exposed ears. I still had no idea what Cordelia Kennedy was doing in the King's Watch, but she'd surrendered an awful lot to be on a hillside with me. I stretched out my left hand. 'Eyes closed or open?'

'Closed to start with.'

Her small hand took my ham fist, and I closed my eyes. Her fingers were warm and got warmer when they tingled with Lux. I got a vision of green and black swirling in front of my eyes, like someone had turned the Jamaican flag into a kaleidoscope.

'Let's have a look, shall we?'

I opened my eyes and stared at the stables. The two tiny stone buildings shimmered, and then they were seven. Three modern, steel-sided structures appeared. They were low, and one of them faced us; you could clearly see that it was divided into stalls. The original farming sheds were revealed to have been extended at the back and had a domestic look to them. The last two buildings were also new and steel, but they were round, with slightly conical roofs. A bit like last night's yurt. In the centre was a concrete yard, and in the yard were horses. And people.

'There's still a barrier,' said Cordelia. 'Something's not right.'

The people were getting ready to mount up, and I tried to work out ages and sexes, but although I could see a tap in the yard clearly, I couldn't make out their faces. Magick.

Cordy turned to the right, up the ghyll. 'Bloody hell. Look at that.'

I turned my head. 'Why are the trees glowing?'

'Plane shift. It's leaking. Here they come.'

One of the horses walked out of the yard, on to the grass, and others followed. The lead horse started to trot. And then it disappeared. In ten seconds, half a dozen horses were gone from our sight. Or should that be our *Sight*. 'Can we do anything to track them?'

'Not right this second. Let go?' I withdrew some Lux from my hand and released her fingers. I was childishly pleased to see that she didn't wipe them on her trousers. It has happened. 'Let's walk up there, towards the trees. I might be able to effect a transition.'

We set off, up another slope, this one with less grass and more rocks. 'That was excellent,' I said. 'You've been hiding your light under a bushel.'

The middle of her forehead made a micro-frown. 'Not me. Don't forget that I lived and worked inside a plane-shifted Grove for years, so all senior Daughters know the basics. That ghyll place has a very soft border, with a fair bit of Lux leaking out to help the transition. I wonder if that's for the horses and riders.'

We were walking slowly, parting and rejoining to avoid the outcrops, and the conversation broke up. Scout thought it was great fun. 'I thought that's what the saddles were for.'

'Sort-of. Do you reckon the stable hands are all Mages? Living and working out here?'

'Grooms. They used to be called *stable lads*. Of both sexes. In a lot of places they still are, and no, I don't think Mages would put up with the hours or the pay. What are the implications?'

'A couple of Artefacts might help, but to transition like that, the liminal margin must be huge. At Glastonbury, it's as thin as a knife edge. That's why we have access portals. This should do.'

We had arrived on something like a ledge, with the ghyll starting to form below us. The more I looked at the trees, the more the brown leaves flashed with hints of silver. In the golden autumn light, that was just wrong.

Cordy wiped her forehead and looked at the slope down to the beck. 'We're close to the edge here, but the liminal margin is sharper. I'm going to try turning this rock into a liminal step.'

'Sounds good.' She gave me the Look. Every Mage does it sooner or later, and I try not to take it personally. It's the Look that says *you don't a clue, do you?* And I don't. 'Enlighten me.'

'Necromancy is quite close to plane shifting, in some ways. To talk to Spirits, you need to occupy both planes at the same time, and that's an important part of the craft. I'm going to try doing that on this step, then move to occupy just the higher plane. I'll do it on my own first, then try to drag you with me.'

I stood back and called Scout to put him on his lead. She stared at the step, then shrugged off her coat and gave it to me rather than leave it on the still-wet grass. She hitched up her hiking trousers and wiggled her hips to make them more comfortable. 'Let's do this,' she said to herself. I'm glad that I'm not the only one who does that.

She spread her arms and spoke an incantation to the Goddess, and that's one of the big differences between the Circles and Salomon's House: we Chymists don't go big on incantations. Or proper Chymists like Chris Kelly don't. I offer lots of silent prayers to Odin, but that's mostly because I haven't a clue what I'm doing. Cordelia does have a clue, and her incantation wasn't a prayer, it was a focus to put the magick in the right place.

The rock started to glow with warm yellow light. Very promising. She brought her hands together and it glowed brighter still. Then she climbed on to it, started to fade and freaked out.

I could only see the barest outline of her now, like a transparency. 'In the name of the Goddess, who walks here?' Although her voice was faint and far away, I could hear the authority in it. I could also hear the nerves. Scout could hear her, too.

He'd sat down for a rest, and jumped up with a bark, straining at the leash. I moved towards the rock just in time for her to vanish completely and for the step to become stone again, bereft of magick. Shit.

167

Mark Hayden

Scout is not a scent dog. Until recently, his training has all been about movement and following commands. That doesn't mean he can't smell, though. I shoved Cordelia's coat into his nose. 'Find Cordy. Find her, boy!'

He raced up to the rock and jumped to where she'd been standing. His tail was up and he lifted his nose as if he were modelling for a sculpture. 'Arff!'

'Thanks, Scout. I could have worked that out for myself. Come here, you daft dog.' He jumped off the rock and bounded over. Cordelia was right behind him, and I breathed a sigh of relief.

She was looking over her shoulder at something, then shook her head and focused on me.

'OK?' I said.

'Yeah. I think so. There were three Spirits watching the course – it really does look like a race track on the next plane. I had to transition fully to speak, and when they saw me, one of them said, "It's her! The Fury!" Then they scattered like the wind.'

'Three of them?'

'Yeah. They were in pure form, so just blobs of light.' She looked back again and shrugged. 'Perhaps they just like horses. Whatever. It's an easy transition. Shall we?'

We could have just gone straight to the stables. We could have. We didn't do that for two reasons. First, I wanted to find out as much about the Chases as possible. Second, Cordelia was itching to bring something to the party.

'Absolutely. Can Scout come?'

She looked dubious. 'If you carry him. And if he doesn't jump out of your arms. I'll go first, then you've got about three seconds before the step reverts.'

Have you tried to carry a frisky Border Collie who doesn't like being carried? And then performing magick? I tied him to a sapling and got ready to follow my human partner.

The step glowed red, and Cordy disappeared again. I counted *one* and followed her.

Every molecule, every atom, every muon and gluon in your body has to change, ever so slightly, when you transition to another plane. It doesn't happen all at once, and for a micro-second, less time than it takes to shiver, the electrons in your nervous system have a meltdown. It's like being slapped all over, inside and out. And then it's gone.

And so had the ledge on which we were standing. 'By Odin's eye, Cordy. What a place. Well done, Cordelia. That was pretty damn seamless.'

'Thanks. This is a bit Gothic for me,' she replied. I could see why.

Off to my right, I could see a Fae wood. It was obviously a Fae wood because the trees were still in leaf. They don't drop until after the winter solstice. Those trees, and the magick with them, can distort our world in strange ways. For one thing, they can pull rain onto their plane ("Even in

168

Spain" – Chris Kelly). Enough to make a little brook that ambled through meadows, woods and through ruins. Yes, ruins.

The depth of the ghyll had been replaced by a more gradual slope that suddenly plunged to our left to re-join the lower plane's level. It was like having your own little cloud paradise. You knew you were standing in mid-air, but the ground felt real enough. Just to make sure, I knelt down and touched it. Oh, and it was warmer here.

'Where are those from?' I said. There were a good dozen or so bits of construction – walls, half-houses, arches and a tower with a gateway arch.

Cordelia stepped away, across the grass, towards a clear track that led from up the valley where the stables would be. 'You know what, Conrad, I think they're deliberate features. Look at the pattern.'

She was right. The arrangement was too linear. No conceivable settlement would have this pattern. 'Yes, of course. The real Chases no doubt have real ruins to negotiate. Someone's gone to a lot of trouble.'

'They have.'

I passed her coat back and looked around again. 'I feel a bit exposed here. Shall we …'

'Conrad! They're coming!'

'What?'

'I can fucking hear them!'

'The bushes. Over there.'

We sprinted across the grass to some overgrown gorse and ducked. Just as we got out of sight, I heard tiny shrieks and whoops, and high pitched animal noises. What the hell?

And then they came, galloping and swerving down the track. Tiny unicorns being ridden by little creatures with green wings. My mouth dropped open and my brain shut down.

'By the Goddess, I never thought I'd live to see that,' said Cordy in a whisper.

A pony is not a small horse, and these were not ponies. A pony is stockier, has a thicker coat and a different shape. These unicorns were much smaller than ponies, and had a horse's proportions. They were all white, with white horns and long flowing white manes. Holding on to that hair, because there was no saddle or bridle, was a small, naked child. With green wings. And a manic look on its face.

They were racing hard, following the track except where they tried to pass each other. The unicorns leapt over rocks as their riders fought for advantage. One mount baulked and threw its jockey. The little child flexed its wings, and although it didn't fly, it did come down for a soft landing. It emitted a shriek of annoyance as the others disappeared down the slope, and it cried out in a language I've never heard before. Now it was standing, I could see that it looked like a boy from the body shape, but had no external genitals. It

169

whistled, and the unicorn stopped still. With a flick of its wings, it was back astride the mount, and then it was off, crying and keening encouragement.

'Sprites,' I said. 'They must be Sprites.'

'Of course they're Sprites. What else would they be?'

What else indeed? I've met young Fae and old Fae, but never thought I'd see a Sprite. When a Fae Queen lays an egg (yes, they really do do that), it hatches into a Sprite, and they are almost never seen outside the sídhe. The one I'd seen most closely would be about three feet tall. Much taller and they shed their wings and grow to human size. Or so I've read.

'What about the unicorn foals?'

'Foals? They're fully grown,' said Cordy. 'Didn't you know?'

'Clearly not. Why aren't they huge?'

'These are common unicorns. That's as big as they get.' She gave me the Look again. 'High Unicorns are only slightly more common than Dragons. Shh. There's something else coming.'

We crouched again, trying to peer through the gorse. I picked out louder voices. Adult female voices. And big hooves and …

'Oh no,' said Cordy, scrambling to her feet. We were right in the way.

The Sprites and their tiny mounts had followed the track because they couldn't negotiate the walls and obstacles of the faux settlement. Not so the next two.

They jumped and flew over the walls, and one of them took an outside route, putting it on collision course with us. Cordy made the mistake of trying to stay hidden instead of just getting the fuck out of the way. I reached to grab her. Too late. The giant beast saw us or sensed us and it tried to swerve the gorse plantation. The rider pulled hard on the reins and it reared up, just short of where Cordelia was trying to hide.

The beast's smell washed over me, and it wasn't the honest sweat of horse: this was the smell of magick. Of something that shouldn't exist in nature. Of a High Unicorn.

It was huge, as big as a Belgian draft horse, a mountain of pulsing muscles, veins distended on the glistening white coat. And then it lowered its head, and the jagged bone of its horn was pointing at me. All I could do was grab Cordelia properly and backpedal away from it to give me time to do something. Anything.

I was so focused on the serrated horn that I'd ignored the rider. A black gloved hand reached forwards and touched the beast on its cheek, steadying it and trying to turn its head. I looked up and nearly fell over. Riding the unicorn was Lara Dent, and she was staring back. With fear.

'Walk on!' she cried, urging the unicorn with her knees. I glanced left, and saw that the other unicorn had pulled up and the rider, another girl, was watching. Lara got her beast in motion, and in a second she was away, over a wall and lost to view. At that point I realised that I still held Cordelia's hand. I let go.

'Oww, Conrad. You've got a grip like a vice, did you know that? And did you have garlic last night?'

'You watched me eating fish and chips. That was our mini-bond in action.'

'Sorry?'

'When Nimue nearly drank all my blood, her parting gift was the ability to smell non-human creatures. High Unicorns smell of coffee and garlic.'

'Oh. I think I'm in shock.'

'No you're not. You're just high on adrenaline. We need to get to the stables as quickly as possible. Which is faster: the way we came and the car, or straight down the hill? I know it's a lot closer, but we have to transition, don't we?'

'The hill. The transition will be a lot quicker that way, and we did take a very long route coming.'

'Good. Off we go. Slow jog or we'll collapse. Keep talking.'

'I can't believe it. Two High Unicorns. Two! And racing Sprites. Saffron did say something else.'

'Oh yes? Do I want to hear this?'

'I said, "What's it like working with the Dragonslayer?" And she said, "You get used to it. Apart from the weird shit. You don't get used to that." I thought she was exaggerating. Now I think she's right.'

There was nothing to say to that. Of course, no one asks how I feel, do they? Apart from Mina. We made a steady pace along the cinder track. How do you get cinders on to a higher plane, I wonder?

'Was it her?' said Cordy cautiously. 'It looked like Lara Dent, didn't it?'

'It did. It wasn't her, though. I've never met Lara Dent, and whoever it was recognised me. What are the Fae doing with two High Unicorns?'

'Must be breeding them. There's a whole world the Fae keep to themselves. Including Sprites racing on unicorns. I had no idea that existed.'

'And that's rather worrying. I've seen what the Fae will do to keep their secrets. Is this the transition coming up?'

It was like coming to the edge of a cliff on a foggy day. You knew there was something there to worry about, but couldn't see it. My auto defence mechanism kicked in, and I slowed to a stop. Cordy had been keeping pace with me and tried to give me an encouraging smile. 'I don't like to do this bonded, but it might be easier. The edge is very blurred here, even though it looks worse. Part of the challenge, I expect. And try to do it with your eyes open.'

We joined hands and started jogging again. Ahead of us, the grass sloped gradually at first, then I saw the wall of smudge. All browns and greens together, and the same when I tried to use my Sight on it. Cordy tugged gently to keep me going, and I stretched out my legs. And then we were through.

Blackness blotted out the sun, a great *whoosh* of sound filled the air, and I tripped over my own feet just as something smacked me in the face.

'Hey, Conrad. It's okay. Nothing happened.'

I sat up. 'Whaaaaa? Why has the sun moved? Where's the bird?'

She looked away. 'What bird?'

'I could have sworn…'

'Time difference,' she said, interrupting me. 'Much slower up there. And without a mobile signal, our phones won't update.'

I may have a built-in compass, but not a built-in clock. I looked at the sun's position over the hills. 'At least nine, I reckon. Not to worry. So long as it's still Thursday, we're good. Give us a hand up, will you?'

I was back on my feet, and we were only one field away from the stables, now a blur of activity. We started jogging again, and Cordy looked over her shoulder. 'The horses!'

The mundane beasts we'd seen leave earlier were on their way back, coming through the transition and galloping across the meadow. The lead riders hadn't expected us to be there, and they had to cut hard to avoid us. Seven riders, five young women and two young men, thundered past us and into the yard, casting curious and worried glances as they went. When we were a hundred metres from the stables, I told Cordy to slow down and activated my Ancile.

At the end of a hard gallop, the stable grooms should be checking their mounts, hosing them down and giving them the attention an elite athlete deserves. Instead, they were being shouted at by a large man in a flat cap, and – horror of horrors – the horses were being left to mill around the yard with their saddles still on while the staff were sent into one of yurt-like structures. As soon as we got to the concrete floor of the yard, I felt the tingle of magick.

'What are we going to do?' said Cordelia.

'Play it straight. And try not to get shot.'

The man in the flat cap, the one in charge, was having an argument with another man who sported a purple Merseyside United baseball cap. Flat cap pointed after the other grooms, but purple hat turned his back and ran to the horses, who had all sought out the water trough and were now steaming profusely.

The yard was laid out in a rough triangle, and we had come in at the apex. The right hand side of the triangle was formed by the two round buildings and the long stable block was on the left. Facing us, the two cottages converted from barns made up the base. Flat cap man took up a position near the right-hand cottage. Cordelia remembered my briefing and moved three metres away to my left. I held up my warrant card in my left hand; my right hand rested on the Hammer.

A lot of my training at the Met Firearms Unit had been about de-escalation. About *avoiding* the use of lethal force. 'Constable Clarke,

Westmorland police. We just want a word with Aidan Manning. That's all. Are you Mr Manning, sir?'

'What do you want with him?' said flat cap.

'It's about his friend, Harry Eldridge. We're not here about anything else.'

Cordy murmured out of the side of her mouth. 'Manning is over there. Purple cap.'

At that point, the Lux flowing through the yard swirled a little, and my nose got the earth-and-sawdust smell of Fae. Cordy probably knew as soon as she'd seen him. 'I'm sure it won't take long, Saerdam.'

'I am the Count of Force Ghyll. This is my domain, and you are not welcome here.'

It was a magickal statement: clear off.

'I'm not here as Deputy Constable of the Watch, my lord. I'm here as a police officer.'

'What about Harry?' Manning had left the horses and come half way across the yard.

The Count of Force Ghyll glanced to his left. 'Get back to the beasts, Aidan. Don't let Scipio overheat.'

'Have they told you he was found on Tuesday, Mr Manning? Murdered, I'm afraid.'

'What the hell?' said Manning, coming a little closer. It was clear from his face that he had no idea about Harry.

'Look to your duty!' barked the Count, lacing his order with a twist of magick. Manning reeled back, holding his neck, then turned and staggered towards the animals.

'Look out, sir,' said Cordy. 'From the roundhouse.'

The sides had been pulled further open, and a full posse came towards us. The seven stable grooms were in a bunch, and they were being driven on by two slightly blurred figures at the back. The smell of more Fae came across.

'They're armed!' said Cordy.

And they were. The grooms had picked up a variety of knives, poles and even a scythe. None of them looked like they'd ever used them in anger, especially the shortest girl who trailed a jockey's whip in her hand. There was more noise from the roundhouse: beasts in distress and those keening cries.

I kept my focus on the approaching posse and the Count until the eruption behind them made me look away. The Sprites and their unicorns charged out of the doors, veered left and headed out of the yard and on to the trail that led to the transition. The two High Unicorns came next, struggling against their riders. One of the beasts got his head sorted and started to trot, then gallop, and I got a good look at his teenage rider – a wiry looking girl who was strangely familiar. The other High Unicorn pulled up, and Lara Dent dismounted.

The Count stepped back a pace, and the posse surrounded him. He stepped back further and he was next to the other Fae. They dropped the distorting Glamours and I got a good look at them. One was male and had gone for the ninja vibe, with a loose, black combat outfit and a red scarf pulled up over his nose and mouth. The other one was female and looked like she'd come from the gym, with leggings and a cropped top. Not something you wear round a stable yard. She was even carrying a gym bag. I was starting to get a very bad feeling about this.

'Tell them we come in peace,' hissed Cordy.

It would get us out of a sticky situation. Probably. It would also end any chance we had of compelling an interview with Aidan Manning. I was weighing up my options when gym bunny opened her bag and took out a pump action shotgun. She handed it to the Count and dropped the bag, putting her hands on her hips and giving us the Fae smile, the one where they seem to have too many teeth. Ugh.

'We come in peace,' I said, 'and in peace we will depart.'

The Count was keeping the gun pointed down and his finger wasn't on the trigger. As far as I could tell. He'd put himself half behind the stable lad with the scythe, a sure sign that his Ancile wasn't proof against my gun. And also a sure sign that he knew who I was.

'Too late,' said the gym bunny. 'They've seen it all. They can't leave now. Think about it. Kill them now and who will know?'

That bad feeling I told you about? It just went red.

For a horrible second, the Count actually thought about it. I think he was working out what his seigneur would do to him if we walked away.

'Do a deal. It's not too late. His word is backed by the Allfather.' I'd forgotten that Lara Dent was still here. The Fae hadn't even noticed.

The Count whirled round and roared at her. 'Get on Keraunós and get the fuck out of here!'

Lara stood her ground. She was uncannily like the pictures of Zinayida, except for the unruly brown hair. She had an open-necked shirt on, and I could see – more than see, I could *feel* the horseshoe pendant round her neck. 'No. It'll ruin everything if you break the King's Peace here.'

The Count shoved his shotgun into gym bunny's hand and rounded on Lara. 'Don't you dare say those words here, you cheap whore!'

Lara quailed. Her right hand flew to her face and the blood drained from her cheeks. 'For Harry's sake. Please.'

'I'm going to shut your mouth,' said the Count. He made a lightning grab for Lara's face, and in doing so his hand grew and turned into a monster's clawed foot that raked and dug into her cheek, her chin and her neck. With his other hand, he ripped off the pendant, and there was a flash of magick. Lara shimmered and collapsed in heap of bright red hair.

The Count retrieved his shotgun and moved back behind his human shield. He spoke to the posse of grooms. 'Attack them together. Get in their personal space and hack them to pieces.'

They shuffled, but didn't rush us. I reached my left hand over my right shoulder and drew Great Fang, revealing it to the audience in the process.

'You can do this,' said the Count. The kid with the jockey's whip was barely five foot tall and couldn't have been more than seventeen. The whip fell out of her hand and she took a step back.

'Pick it up and get ready.'

'I ... no.'

The Count fired into her chest from two metres. She was dead before she hit the ground.

He didn't wait for the stunned silence. He grabbed the ninja Fae by the wrist and shoved him into the posse. And then he stood on one foot and pirouetted, and when he stopped turning, there were three Counts moving along the back of the posse. Damn. As soon as one of them did something significant, the Work would be broken, but until then...

'On the count of three, charge them. All together. Remember, I'm right behind you and I've six more shells in here. One ... two ...' I drew the Hammer and took aim at the ninja Fae. He took something in his hand.

'... Three!'

The Fae didn't wait for me to shoot. He threw down a stone and it went off like a thunderflash, blinding everyone and blowing the eardrums of half the posse.

I couldn't see. Not a thing. Not good. I dropped the Hammer and switched to the Ancile in Great Fang, taking great sweeps in front of me and stepping back towards the stable block. I caught a movement in what was left of my peripheral vision and poured all my Lux into sharpening the details. Like a curtain going up, my vision came back, just as the ninja Fae tried to jump me. His hands were on fire, great gouts of flame rising from blackened skin. From a great distance, I heard a muffled *boom* and screaming. Lots of screaming.

He jumped, holding out his hands to grab me, to grab me anywhere, so long as that flame touched me. Fae fire is like phosphorus. It *is* phosphorus. You don't want that on you. I couldn't strike him and dodge those hands, so I pivoted, and he flashed by, rolling on the ground and coming back up.

I had half a second, so I glanced round. Another stable lad was down, and of the remaining five, three were patting down fires on their clothing. A boy and a girl were closing in on Cordelia, both with big agricultural cutting hooks.

Back with me, the ninja – sorry, the *Firefly* – came forwards, weaving his hands like a kung fu master, just as the Count shoved scythe boy in the back and sent him to join the party. I looked over the Firefly's shoulder and saw the two hook-wielders approach Cordelia. A look of infinite pain crossed her face and she made a slashing move with her hand. The boy's legs went from under him as if he'd been hit by a car, and I was grateful for the ringing in my ears.

And that was my cue: now that Cordy had proved herself, I could leave her to it. I feinted at the Firefly and turned right, running at scythe boy. He lifted the scythe for a backswing and opened his body right up. When I stabbed at him, I pulled the stroke before making contact. It was a good call. He flinched backwards and fell over. My path to the Count was clear.

I jumped past the lad and took two more steps. The Count was holding his ground, staring me out. I lifted my sword and pivoted on my bad leg. You didn't think I'd forgotten the Firefly, did you?

I didn't pull this stroke, and slid Great Fang under his ribs while he was preparing to strike. Another half second, and he'd have had his balance, and I'd have been toast.

Another pivot. The Count had dropped his shotgun and taken out a dagger that bristled with menace. I took a moment to feel for magick and saw the look in his eye. Naked fear.

'Lower your weapon and I'll make it quick,' I said. 'Otherwise, we'll be taking you prisoner. Now that *is* a promise.'

A step. A glance round. Another step. He lowered his dagger, and I kept my promise.

The gym bunny had kept a safe distance from the blood. Wouldn't want to get that on her outfit, would she? She looked around the yard and looked at me. 'Oops. That didn't go well, did it?'

She actually *winked* at me, then turned and ran. Like a sprinter. I have never run that fast in my life. Not even when I was eighteen.

'Cordy!' I shouted. 'Can you fix my hearing?'

# 18 — *Judgement Call*

Tom's every muscle locked, gripping the phone. 'What?'

'He's fine. He's gone with a casualty, and we've got more here. He says you need to field this one when it hits the police system.'

'My God, Cordelia, what's happened?'

'A lot. Have you got a pen?' He could hear trembling in her voice, and he knew what he had to do.

'I've got one, Cordy. Take it steady and we'll get there.'

'Right. Okay. First, call Erin and get her arse into gear.'

'Is that a direct quote?'

'Yeah. You shouldn't deal face to face with anyone until she's with you.'

'Right.'

'Then call Mina, or text her and get her to call you. Tell her that I'm okay … I mean, tell her that Conrad's okay. She needs to tell the Boss that there has been a serious breach of the King's Peace by the Fae. In those words.'

'… a serious breach of the King's Peace by the Fae. Got it.'

'Then call Eseld. Tell her that we've found Morwenna and that she's on her way to Preston Royal Infirmary by chopper. Conrad will get in touch when he can. He'd do all this but we've no signal here.'

'Are you both unhurt?'

'Yeah.' He heard her draw a shaky breath. 'If you could make it up here with some help, that would be great.'

'Are you in danger?'

'No. Probably not. But I have got a bunch of pissed off grooms, several wild horses and a unicorn to look after.'

Of course she did. What else did he expect?

'I'm on it, Cordelia.'

His first call was to the L&W control room. They had received notification from the air ambulance of a suspicious incident, and Tom put himself down as responding. He didn't call Erin next: he called Elaine and told her to be on standby. After that, he worked his way through Conrad's list as best he could.

He could tell that Mina was holding a lot back when she took the message, and she didn't give any more away than a curt, 'Please keep me updated.' How she put up with it, he had no idea. Eseld didn't take the call, and he had no option but to text and move on. He was struggling to remember who

Morwenna was – the name rang a bell, but Conrad's reports were long and had strategic omissions. His call to Erin had been the weirdest, though.

'I'm only doing this as a favour,' she huffed. 'He's not the boss of me, damn him. In fact, I'm only doing this to see the Unicorn. If it really exists. Fine. Meet me at the Gateway Inn, Plumgarth, and I'll follow you.'

The shit didn't start hitting the fan straight away. Tom and Elaine speculated constantly after he picked her up at the Oak Tree Hotel, and the only thing they could agree on was that they would form a united front: Clarke was doing *all* the paperwork on this one.

Erin was leaning against her car, enjoying a little warmth from the sun when they got to the Gateway Inn.

'That was a quick change,' said Tom. 'She was wearing a short skirt and low cut top at the incident room earlier.'

'And now she's gone all pre-Raphaelite,' observed Elaine. 'Why?'

'You were so preoccupied with disliking Hazel this morning that you didn't see the way she made sure that Barney got an eyeful. Presumably this outfit is more suited to her professional role.'

'And it's very unprofessional of you to gossip like that, sir,' she said, rather primly.

'Sod off, Constable. You're just annoyed that you missed it, and talking of Hazel, you reckon that she and Barney can handle bringing Matthew Eldridge on board?'

'Yeah. It might have been different if Hazel had got to go to Matt's place, but with him coming into town, it should be okay. Erin's coming over.'

'Any news?' said Erin. The long velvet dress looked like it had been designed for someone slightly taller and thinner, and she'd had to lift it over a couple of puddles on the way from the car.

'I'm afraid not,' said Tom. 'The air ambulance will have landed by now, but I've heard nothing yet.'

'And they're both definitely alright?'

He assumed she meant Conrad and Cordelia. 'He left a detailed list of instructions, and you know what he's like. If he'd been hurt, he would have told us. For operational reasons, of course.'

'Of course. Not that anyone would actually care about him.'

It should have been delivered ironically, but there was a slight edge to Erin's words. Tom needed Erin, and only full disclosure would do. 'The injured party is someone called Morwenna, who's known to Eseld Mowbray. Ring any bells?'

She looked stumped for a second. 'Well, the missing Mowbray is called Morwenna, but it can't be her, can it? What in the name of the gods would she be doing up here? Shall we go? I'll lead.'

'Missing Mowbray?' said Elaine when they drove off.

He shrugged. 'There was nothing in the report on Lord Mowbray's murder.'

The console screen lit up with a call: Hannah Rothman.

After five minutes of crisp questions, some swearing in Yiddish and a curse aimed at Conrad, Hannah realised that there was nothing she could do but ask for an adjournment in the Cloister Court and sit by her phone. Tom knew how she felt. She also said that dealing with Commander Ross was, 'Up to you, Tom. So long as you don't use the *M* word.'

'Did you notice?' said Elaine. 'She asked if we were sure about Conrad four times, in different ways. Twice I could understand...'

'I think that's what makes her such a good boss. God, this is a windy road to nowhere.'

The road wound further up the valley than Tom thought was possible, until Erin slowed down, then suddenly sped off. Tom barely had time to accelerate before she slammed on the brakes again.

'That's Scout!' said Elaine.

Tom put on his hazard warning lights and jumped out to see what was happening. It *was* Scout, but why was he pulling half a tree behind him? And what was he doing out here? Erin was doing her best to calm him, so Tom walked up and started untangling the lead from what was actually a whole tree – a sapling, complete with roots.

'Poor thing,' said Erin. 'He must have come a long way. And there's special Wards to discourage animals, so he's been stuck here, knowing he needs to go on, but unable to move forwards.'

'I know how he feels. Where was he going?'

'We've just driven past the stables and you didn't even notice.' She turned serious for a second. 'This is a big case. Conrad shouldn't have brought you in and not given you a Mage to work with. Oh, and by the way, I am not that Mage. I'm doing this as a favour.'

Tom looked around. 'I think that's his car, up there. Through the gate. And in Conrad's defence, he probably has an overinflated idea of my powers. He thinks that because I cornered him once, I must be a superhero.'

Erin frowned. 'Nah. He just likes to recruit people. If he started a cult, he'd be bigger than the Scientologists in no time. Right. We'll park up there then all get in my car. Scout included.'

The moment they went through the Wards on the way back was like being plunged into feeding time at the zoo. Scout went mental and jumped out of Tom's arms; Elaine bounced up in her seat and screamed when her leg spasmed, and Erin started shouting, 'It's a Unicorn!' like a teenager at a boyband concert. As for Tom, he just thought they were going to crash into a brick wall.

Erin was out of the car before Tom had processed that they were in a large yard, and Scout flew through the open door after her. Elaine was massaging her leg and didn't look up until she realised how quiet it had gone.

'Tell me that's a prosthetic. Please tell me that's not real.'

'Oh, it's real alright. You wouldn't make a prosthetic out of sharpened bone, would you? Come on.' Tom paused to remove Erin's keys and went to see what was going on.

The Unicorn was half in, half out of a roundhouse building and was being attended by two young women plus Cordelia and now Erin. One of the young women – stable grooms, he supposed – had no coat and her right arm covered in torn sheets as dressings. The beast himself (and it was most definitely a *he*) had no saddle, bridle or rope, and looked as if he were there of his own free will.

'Meet Keraunós,' said Cordelia. Did the hairs on Tom's neck prickle when she spoke the beast's name. 'It's not every day someone gives you a High Unicorn as a gift.'

'What?' said Erin. 'No way.'

Cordy gestured at Keraunós. 'Right of plunder. Conrad seized him and gave him to me for obvious reasons.'

'I'll buy him!' said Erin. 'Just name your price.'

Cordelia fished a piece of paper out of her coat and passed it to Erin. 'Item seven.'

Erin squinted at the text. 'You should go on an Enscribing Course, Cordy. Your writing's crap. Here we go. "Item 7. Do not sell the unicorn to Erin, no matter what she offers you." Story of my life, that. Thwarted by Conrad Clarke at every turn.'

Elaine was leaning heavily on her stick, but still in awe of the gleaming animal and its rippling muscles. She tentatively reached a hand forward then dropped it and said, 'Did you get it because you had a unicorn pencil case at school, Cordelia? Because otherwise, it's not at all obvious to me.'

'Or me,' added Tom.

Erin took it on herself to answer. 'High Unicorns will only let themselves be handled or ridden by females. Not virgins or any crap like that: mature females. Of any species.' She turned round. 'You know what that means?'

'Fae Queens.'

'Correct. Having a High Unicorn is about the biggest status symbol a Queen can have. He's a beauty, isn't he? Come on, Keraunós.'

And they'd lost her. Tom shrugged.

Cordelia was only just holding it together. She rubbed a hand across her hair, pressing down hard to stop it shaking. 'I'm so glad you're here. All of you.'

'What happened, Cordy?'

'Come and have a look.'

She led them to the other roundhouse. The doors were barely open here, and Cordelia went in sideways, then Tom. As soon as she saw what was inside, Elaine staggered back out and vomited.

Four bodies made a line on the concrete floor, dimly lit from the high Perspex roof. The outer two were young. So young. The girl should still be at school by rights. Both had their eyes closed and hands crossed on their chests. The girl had a torn sheet of tarpaulin over her torso, under her folded hands. It must have been bad in that case.

The central pair were worse, though, because they were dissolving. Two male figures were starting to leak, and Tom realised that they'd been placed either side of a drain. When he saw that the larger one's head was no longer attached, he'd had enough.

Blood rushed to his face and he spoke through gritted teeth. 'I was not brought here to be the cleaner in Conrad Clarke's charnel house. What did he do to them?'

'No, no. He tried to stop it. He tried to leave. It was the Count. That one. He shot two of his own people to make the others attack us.'

Tom couldn't believe it. 'He did what?'

'He stood behind the grooms and told them to attack. When they didn't, he shot the girl. The lad tried to run away, so he shot him, too. Conrad couldn't get to the Count in time to stop him.'

'Did you take care of the other one?'

She wiped tears away with the back of her hand. 'No. He was a Firefly – he could produce liquid fire from his hands. It would have been him who attacked you on the boat. Conrad killed him, too. All I did was break someone's legs. An innocent lad. He may never walk or ride again.'

Tom gave the two human victims a moment. He even found himself making a prayer in his head: *Whoever you are who watched over them, look after them. Amen.*

He gathered Cordelia into his arm and was about to usher her outside when he heard a clicking and scraping coming towards them. A shadow in the door. A black and white shadow.

'Arff.'

Cordelia slipped away and dashed over to the dog. 'How did you get here, eh? Don't worry, boy, he's okay. He's okay. Let's get you outside.'

Back in the bright, fresh air, Tom took a deep breath, held it, then breathed out.

'Over here, sir.' It was Elaine, calling from a bench near one of the barn conversions. Erin was sitting with her, keeping an eye on things. 'There's tea on the way, if we promise to be quick after.'

They walked over to the bench. 'Why's that?'

'There's two with serious burns inside who need medical attention. Apparently two people went to hospital with Clarke.'

181

'Morwenna and the lad whose legs I broke,' added Cordelia.

'I think you'd better start at the beginning,' said Tom.

She did, telling them about the plane shifting, the Sprite racing, the confrontation in the yard and the aftermath. She added that Aidan Manning had been a close friend of Harry's, was a Mage, and that the grooms had loved him. Still loved him: Manning had disappeared and ridden off on Scipio, the best horse in the stables. Other than the unicorns, of course. And it was the unicorn jockeys who needed the most explanation.

'The one who fled was Persephone,' said Cordelia. Telling the story had calmed her down and put some of it into perspective. At one point, Erin had leaned over and given her a big hug, telling her Rick didn't deserve her and had never deserved her. Not having met Rick, Tom didn't know what to make of that. 'Persephone is also known as Perci,' added Cordelia meaningfully.

'As in the floating poker school,' said Elaine quietly.

'Looks like Conrad was right,' added Tom. 'The answer to Harry's death has four legs and walks on two.'

'Sir,' said Elaine. 'Metaphor alert.'

'What? Never mind, Cordy. Carry on.'

She gestured to the right, where the confrontation had taken place. 'The surviving grooms didn't hesitate to drop the Fae in it. This whole operation really belongs Prince Galleny. The Count didn't even have any Knights in service.'

Erin sat up. 'Ooooooh. Shit. Fair enough, Tom. Conrad was right to call me in. I can 100% make sure you don't die first. Maybe even fourth or fifth.'

Cordelia snapped back. 'Shut up, Erin. If you've got nothing useful to say, then shut up.'

'Yes, Mum.'

Talk about a love-hate relationship. Elaine stepped in with, 'So did this Prince guy kill Harry, or what?'

'No,' said Cordelia. 'We're not certain, because Manning ran off and the other witness … well, all I know for certain is that Harry Eldridge became the Prince's bookmaker, race course fixer and croupier at Easter. If Harry had tried to steal from the Prince, he would have been punished, yes, but not like that. Never like that. The grooms only stopped threatening mutiny when I convinced them that we wanted the truth, too.'

'What about this other witness? Presumably the other Unicorn jockey.'

'Mmm. She dismounted and tried to stop the Count from attacking. It was Lara Dent.'

'What? You mean she never died?'

'She died alright.' Instead of looking at Tom and Elaine, to her right, Cordelia turned to Erin, on her left. She took out a blood-stained handkerchief and peeled back the bright red layers. She held it on her palm and almost shoved it under Erin's nose. 'It was a Deathbinding. Here's the amulet.'

'Ugh. Take it away. It was nothing to do with me, Cordelia. What do you think I am?'

'You tell me, Forester.' Cordy turned to her right and showed them a broken gold chain with a gleaming gold horseshoe pendant. The hairs were definitely prickling now. After the Gnomes' underground Needle, this was the most powerful magickal Artefact Tom had seen, and he'd seen it before, round Lara's neck in the photograph.

Cordelia folded the handkerchief and put it back in her coat. 'Lara was the Prince's jockey. She rode his mounts in the Chase, and she could ride Unicorns. Then she quit to be with Harry. Part of her was bound to that horseshoe. A Deathbinding. The Spirit of Lara Dent, and all her skills were bound into that amulet, ready to be poured into a Vessel.'

At first, it seemed like the idea wasn't something that Erin could accept. 'There's no such thing. Vessels are just a myth. No one's ever seen one outside of a library.'

'So how come there's one on the way to hospital?' shot back Cordelia. 'Conrad didn't know what to look for, but I did. At some point in her childhood, Morwenna was turned into a Vessel.'

'No,' said Erin emphatically. 'Not Morwenna Mowbray. Please not her.'

Cordelia didn't look round, and her smile was grim. 'Oh, yes. It means that you become mostly someone else, Tom. For a while or forever. In this case it was only partial, which is why Morwenna/Medbh recognised Conrad and pleaded for us to be left in peace.'

'What happened?'

'The Count lost it. He warped his arm into a monstrous thing and ripped into her face. And throat. Then he tore off the Deathbinding amulet.'

'By the twin gods, no,' said Erin. 'And she's alive?'

'Thanks to Conrad. It was horrible. The claws missed the artery, but … So much blood, Tom. And she may never speak again. Conrad held her, bound her throat and did something to stabilise her.' Her eyes flicked around the yard again, reliving the moment. 'I think it's because of his relationship to Eseld. You know, Morwenna's sister. And the floor. He drew on the Lux underneath us. I couldn't have done that. Anyway, he had to go with her to hospital.'

Everyone took a moment to digest this. Tom immediately knew that the Mowbrays hadn't done this, so who had? At first glance, it sounded very much like something that could be an issue for his researches on the Codex Defanatus, but until the Mages had sorted out the *what* and *how* could Tom worry about the *who* and *where*.

183

Erin shifted uneasily and hitched up her dress for the umpteenth time; Cordy stared into the distance, and Elaine looked at Tom. She'd been very quiet, and Tom gave a tiny nod for her to go first.

'Did Harry know about Lara's reincarnation?' she said.

Erin stood up and walked four paces away, then span on her heel and swished back to the bench. 'Why else would he become the Prince's bonded servant? Because that's what he was.'

'Money,' said Tom.

'It's always about the money with Tom,' added Elaine. 'Why, though?'

'While all this was going on, I discovered that Harry got cleaned out in the spring. Hundreds of thousands. The Prince must have baled him out, and that was well before Medbh became Lara, if you met her in the summer, Erin.'

'He knew about Lara,' said Cordelia. 'Before Morwenna lost consciousness, it was the one question she asked. She used her phone to type it: *Is it true abt hary?* I saw the look in her eyes when Conrad told her. She'd been with Harry as Lara, and she'd fallen for him.'

'Shit, shit and double shit,' said Erin. She started marching up and down in front of them, tearing at her collapsing blond curls. Scout sat up and whined at her distress. She stopped, facing the bench, and looked at each of them in turn. 'So, we've got a dead Count, a Prince who's been a naughty boy, and now you're in possession of his stables, most of his horses and one of his Unicorns. Furious doesn't even cover it.'

'We have a window that's probably closing,' said Cordelia. 'All of them escaped on to the higher plane, and I'll bet they went all the way to the high fells. The time difference will have put them well behind us.'

'I read that list of orders,' said Erin. 'Number three was to notify Eseld. Have you done that, Tom?'

'Only by message. She was probably teaching.'

'She'll be on her way before long, then. Like an avenging Fury.'

Cordelia jerked her head at the word *Fury*. What was that about?

'Did the Prince turn Morwenna into a vessel-thingy?' asked Elaine. 'I take it that's a bad thing.'

'Very bad.' Erin sighed and collapsed back on to the bench, swinging her feet up and dropping them again. She started scratching Scout without really noticing. 'It's a very bad thing, but Prince Galleny didn't do it. That would have happened in Ireland. He still used her, though. What a fucking mess. What are we going to do?'

'Are you included in that?' said Tom. Just to be sure.

'At the moment I am, yes. How long for is another matter. I'm not going to sit here and star in my own version of the Alamo, though.'

A young man appeared, looking very worried. The front of his shirt was soaking wet. 'Katya's started to sweat badly. The book said she needs urgent medical assistance now.'

Elaine jumped in fright when Cordelia's pocket rang out a tune. Cordy fished out a small handset from a cordless landline phone and answered it. She listened for a second, then pressed a button and passed the phone to Tom. 'I'll go and look to Katya. You'd better talk to the Prince. I've put it on mute.'

# 19 — Families Valued

It was the blue that saved her. Mowbray blue. The colour of the sky over Cornwall on a cloudless summer's day. I'd thought she was dead at first, which is why I hadn't rushed over. After Cordy had done something to my hearing, and I'd corralled the stable grooms under Cordy's supervision, I went to check who Lara Dent had become, and that's when I'd seen the blood still oozing out of her neck. I'd also seen the inside of her trachea. Poor Medbh Mowbray.

Stemming the blood had been the easy part, and then I'd touched her cheek and heard the scream inside her, wordless and soundless to everyone else. I'd closed my eyes and dived in.

An Imprint is not your soul. It's more a record of what makes you who you are. People have said that it's like a computer program printed on paper: a schematic of what will happen when animated by Lux, and there's some truth in that, but the human body is not a computer. A real live human being is more than the sum of their Imprint, their body and Lux. A real live human being is a person, and Medbh was about to become an ex-person.

When I dived into Medbh's closed world of pain, I'd needed some help to cross the barrier. What she'd done was give me a little of her Gift, and her biggest gift is to be able to open herself to others. How else would she have absorbed the Spirit of Lara Dent? I know they call it being a *Vessel*, but that's not the best image. Think *Sponge* instead. Not such a good word, though, is it?

I found myself in darkness, with the only light coming from *me*. I was glowing. Please don't tell anyone else about that. If Vicky finds out I glowed in a vision, I'll never hear the end of it. My left hand was still touching Medbh, but either my arm had grown or my eyes had become fisheyes, because she seemed so much further away. And so ... naked. And dying. I could tell that from the red leaking out from great patches of browny-green skin. Weirdest of all, the great wounds in her face and throat weren't bleeding at all.

I've held dying people before. Some have acceptance in their eyes, and some have the pleading, imploring gaze that says *help me* more than any words could. Medbh was pleading, and there was nothing I could do. Or nothing I knew of.

'How do I fix this, Medbh? Help me out here.'

She reached up her left arm and touched a spot on my chest, right where you put your medals. When she drew her finger away, it had Mowbray blue gunk on it. She smeared it on one of the patches over her shoulder, and the patch seemed a little firmer. I looked down at myself, and my body had patches of its own. Not patches like hers, which looked like repairs to the skin, but more like veining in marble. I won't tell you about the others, because I have no idea what they mean, but there was a little blue, funny-shaped blob on my chest. I touched it, and some of it came away, like dipping your finger in lip balm.

The patches on Medbh's skin were more than just patches. It looked like she'd been badly repaired. With earth-toned plaster of Paris. It was on her arms, her chest, the area around her right eye, and there may have been some on her neck, I think. And they were all leaking redness, and there was a lot of them. I couldn't do all that at the current rate of production. I needed a bigger source of Mowbray blue. There was the reservoir of Lux in my leg, but even that wouldn't be enough.

I looked down, beyond Medbh. There was darkness all around when there should be light. We'd gone into this vision in a yard with underfloor Lux, so where was it? I knew that my real eyes were closed, but what if I had to close my inner eye to access my own magick? Worth a try.

It's hard to think *down*. I'd closed my inner eye okay, and I felt a bit warmer, so where was the Lux? I tried to focus on my left hip and thigh, the bits that had been touching the ground. Warmer still. I moved my right hand and anticipated the floor. There it was.

Owww. Bloody hell, that's hot. Got power, though. Let's move it to my chest. There. I dipped my finger in the pot of pectoral blue and hovered it over Medbh. What do I do now?

She took my wrist in her hand and moved my finger to somewhere. Contact. I felt the leaking patch of bark and smoothed the edge down with Mowbray blue. Better.

How did I know it was bark? Where had that come from? No, not bark … carapace. WTF? Whatever. More blue, more healing.

After that, it was just a question of stamina and whether I could withstand the pain. Yes, is the answer. Just. Finally, Medbh guided my hand to my side and tapped me with her fingers. I opened my inner eye, and she looked a lot better. Horribly patched, but no longer dying. Except for one tiny leak, by her right wrist. She took her left hand and gathered some of the ectoplasm.

Ectoplasm?!!

She started to write, but only made it *MOR* before the leak got so bad that I stopped her and sealed it. I'd got the message. She wasn't Medbh any more, she was back to being Morwenna.

And I was back to the stable yard.

'OWWWWW.' Bloody hell. 'OWWWW. My sodding leg! OWWWW.'

187

'Are you okay, sir?'

It was a girl with second degree burns on her arm.

'Just a muscle spasm. I might need your help shortly.' I looked at Morwenna, and her eyes blinked open. I carefully withdrew my left hand and nothing bad happened. I rolled away from her and lay on my back for a second.

'I think she's trying to tell us something,' said the girl.

I looked right and Morwenna was tapping her thigh and making texting motions with her thumbs.

'Is she going to live?' asked the girl with burns.

'Yes she bloody well is, and she can hear you.' I got up on my knees and pulled Morwenna's phone out. She typed a question about Harry, and seconds later, she passed out. 'Cordy! Get a pen and paper and come over here!'

Amazingly, one of the roundhouses had a stretcher in it, and between us we got the wounded to the field next door while we waited for the air ambulance. I could tell that even with my police warrant card, the paramedic didn't buy the explanation of *agricultural accident*, and I don't blame her.

When the A&E team came to the chopper at Royal Preston Hospital, I had one more thing to tell them before they whisked her away. 'She's in early stage pregnancy.'

'Are you …? Right. And the only name you know is Maeve? No surname.'

'Not Maeve or Medbh. The operator must have got it wrong. Her name is Morwenna Mowbray.'

And then she was gone, and I was left next to the air ambulance with more adrenaline than a platoon of charging infantrymen and not a fucking clue about what to do next.

The chopper pilot found me still standing there, staring at the aircraft a few moments later.

'Are you okay, sir?'

'Yes thanks. I was just wondering what she was like in a crosswind. I've never flown one of these.'

He looked me up and down, especially the blood all over my shirt. And probably my face, too. 'It can get interesting, that's for certain. Would you like a cup of tea while you wait? There'll be one on the go.'

'That would be very kind. Thank you.'

The tea was provided by an older man with a bushy grey beard, a volunteer who took one look at me and said, 'I'll put a few sugars in it. Are you a relative? You can go into A&E, you know.'

I sat down at a tiny table. 'Police.'

He put the tea down and took the other chair. 'Looks nasty.'

'It was. She should pull through, but, you know: *life changing injuries*. That's the phrase they use, isn't it?'

I drank deeply from the sweet tea. I hadn't realised how much I needed it and closed my eyes for a moment.

That was a mistake. I was straight back to the blood-soaked stable yard and the gaping wound. I blinked and took another slurp.

'Is someone coming to get you?' he asked.

'Not until I turn my phone back on.'

He drank some of his own tea. 'Do your family know you're alright?'

'Hopefully. Via a colleague.'

'Then I'd make that your priority. If they know something's wrong, they won't rest until they've heard from you.'

He was right. I owed it to them all to get back in touch. I fumbled in my coat pocket, and the volunteer put his hand on my arm.

'They can wait five minutes. Finish your tea and you'll be in a better place.'

'Thank you.'

A phone rang. A woman answered it. 'RTC on the M55 near Blackpool. Right. Thanks.'

That wasn't the order – it was confirmation. I could already hear the engine starting up outside.

'It doesn't get any easier, does it?' he said.

'I should hope not. Then I really would be worried.' I finished my tea. 'This was a particularly bad one, though. Thanks again. Much appreciated.'

As I walked back out, the chopper was about to lift off. 'You can donate via the website,' said the volunteer. I lifted my thumb in approval and headed for the opposite corner of the landing zone.

On the way over, I switched on my phone. The only messages were from Eseld:

*Is this true? WTF Conrad?*

And later

*Of course it's true. I'm clearing out and going home. Call me as soon as you can. E. X.*

I thumbed Favourites and hit the top entry: Mina.

Tom took the phone from Cordelia and looked at Erin and Elaine.

'Don't use my name, please,' said Erin. 'Not if you don't have to.'

He nodded and pressed first the loudspeaker button, then the unmute. 'Hello? This is DCI Morton of Westmorland Police. Is that Prince Galleny.'

Mark Hayden

'Prince of Galleny Falls, People of Borrowdale to be precise. Are you really a policeman?'

The voice boomed and honked like a cross between a foghorn and an angry goose. Tom felt like saying *And are you really a monster?*

'Yes, I am.'

'Is the Dragonslayer there, or have you come to drag his corpse back to Merlyn's Tower?'

Tom toyed with continuing the farce that Conrad was *PC Clarke*, but the bodies in the roundhouse had moved matters well beyond the polite fiction of mundane policework. 'Deputy Constable Clarke is alive, but not here.'

'Hunh. Well, Mr Policeman, I've just had my head lad on the phone with the most tremendous cock and bull story about the Count of Force Ghyll running amok. Shooting people and killing my favourite filly, if you can credit that. Can you shine any light on this murky business?'

Favourite filly? Did he really care more about a horse than anything else?

Conrad's advice from their last case echoed in his mind: *When dealing with the Fae, play the straightest bat you can, and expect them to cheat. Don't, whatever you do, try to outsmart them.*

'I've only just arrived, sir, but as I understand it, the Count and another of your people are dead, along with two of your grooms. There are also serious injuries. None of the horses or other beasts was hurt.'

'Other beasts, eh? Well, I hope you've got a Witch looking after Keraunós. I suppose my gamekeeper got away, did she?'

'One of your people who appeared female did escape, yes.'

There was a burst of laughter down the line. 'Talking like that, you really must be a policeman. Shame about the firefly. Bigger shame about Medbh.'

It clicked in his head: Medbh was the filly. 'If you mean Medbh Mowbray, also known as Morwenna, then I have good news. She's alive but seriously injured. Mr Clarke accompanied her to hospital.'

For the first time, there was silence. 'How do you know who she was?'

Who she *was*? Tom's grip on reality, severely challenged by meeting a unicorn, was starting to loosen even further. He looked at the two women, hoping for some reassurance, and got nothing from Erin. She looked like she'd rather be anywhere but here, and she was showing nerves rather than fear. He did better with Elaine, who was staring intently at the handset, doing that Zen thing she did when about to climb a rock face. Focus. That's what he needed. Straight bat.

'The victim's family are well known to Mr Clarke. He has met Morwenna before.'

There was an explosion of air, straight into the Prince's microphone. 'Hell's teeth, man, are you serious? You'll be telling me next that the Mowbrays know where she is and what she's been doing!'

'As with all victims, notifying the family is a priority.'

Prince Galleny roared with laughter, and Tom was grateful that he didn't have the handset next to his ear. 'So what the fuck are you doing there, and when can I have my stables back? Oh, yes, and who's looking after Keraunós?'

That was a very good question. What the hell was Tom doing half way up this valley on the road to nowhere? Nothing, that's what.

'We're about to leave, sir. We'll arrange for your staff to get medical attention. What about the parents of your grooms?'

'Damn, yes. There'll be Weregild to pay. Don't worry, Mr Policeman, I'll pay up promptly.'

Elaine hissed through her teeth. It was the first time she'd had even indirect contact with the Fae. Before Tom could ask who would do the hard part, the notification, the Prince interrupted him.

'Never mind about the grooms, who's looking after Keraunós?'

'Watch Officer Kennedy has that in hand. I can see from here that ...' He tried to say the name *Keraunós*, and found the syllables wouldn't form in his mouth. '... that your mount appears quite happy. I'm sure he'll be fine.'

All three of them sat back when the Prince spoke again. Gone was the roaring squire, and something far older spoke in its place. 'If anything happens to Keraunós, all of you will be held personally responsible. You're wrong about one thing, Mr Policeman. He's not mine, he's the Queen's, and I'd better go and face the music. Good day.'

The line went quiet, and all three breathed out. Tom found himself rubbing the scar on his arm. Damn. It was the first time in days he'd done that. Thankfully, Elaine was still staring at the phone, and Erin didn't know what it meant. She had a fistful of velvet dress in her hand, and the hand was white at the knuckles. Tom forced himself to pick up the handset and look at the display. He passed it to Elaine. 'Make a note of that number, would you? We might need it. What about Cordelia, Erin? Will she be at risk if she stays.'

Erin blinked rapidly. 'No. Probably. We'll all be at risk if she goes.'

Tom stood up. 'We'd better get going. Elaine, could you talk to the grooms. Get names and contact details. Including their colleagues in the roundhouse.'

'Sir.'

They gathered around the vehicles for a temporary goodbye. The two stable grooms with burns were loaded up, one of them in their friend's car and the other in Tom Morton's. Erin was taking Conrad's car, leaving her rented vehicle behind. Erin had told Cordelia that it was the best option, given that Scout was going with her, and it meant that Erin could wait for Conrad at the Sextons' place near Plumgarth.

Cordelia thought it had more to do with Erin not wanting the wounded grooms bleeding on the seats or leaving horse shit behind in the hire car.

They drew together, and Cordelia saw Erin fussing with the skirt of her dress and checking the side seam. 'I can't wait to get this off before the damn thing splits. I am so going to have to go on a diet.'

'Why didn't you take it back and get a bigger size?' asked Elaine, never one to shy away from a pointed question or to worry about its effect. Cordelia quite liked her for that. She was quite jealous, too.

'It's not mine!' said Erin. 'It's ... well, it's a long story, and one that Conrad needs to hear first. So, I'll see you all at Charlotte Mason when I've collected the Dragonslayer, shall I?'

Tom Morton straightened the bottom of his waistcoat and shot the cuffs in his sleeves. 'We could deliver your car to you, Erin. Save you the bother.' He had a smile on his face when he said it. What was so funny?

'Oh no, no bother,' said Erin breezily. 'And you'll need statements and stuff, won't you?'

Tom's smile turned solemn. 'We will, though it's a shame that only someone Entangled can take your statement.'

The penny dropped. Tom and Elaine thought that Erin was interested in Barney Smith. By the Goddess, Erin was incorrigible. Talk about inappropriate. Cordelia shook her head.

'Let's go,' said Tom.

And then Erin came to give her a hug. 'You'll be out of here soon, Cordy. See you later.'

She remembered Saffron's judgement. *Mostly lovely*. She forced herself to hug Erin back. In a moment, the convoy was out of the drive and gone.

She wasn't alone at Sprint Stables. The two uninjured grooms – the gawky Jake and the mousey Flora were with her in body if not in spirit. Cordelia's first act after the cars left was to return the pair's mobile phones. Unlike Team Conrad, they'd chosen their network so that they got a signal of some sort out here, and they went off to tell the world of magick what had happened. There was non-human company, too, in the shape of Keraunós. Just thinking of him made her drift back to the yard.

When it comes to High Unicorns, you've either got it or you haven't, and Cordy had got it. She could bring alive the magick in the sound of his name and feel what it meant when she stroked his mane.

Keraunós. Thunderbolt.

She'd had to stroke him before, to calm him while the grooms had cooled him off, and she'd felt it straight away: the pounding heart, the twitch of stretched muscles and the whiff of death in the air.

Keraunós had been leaking his senses to her, sharing what he felt at a visceral, sensual and muscular level. And more – he had been taking something back. What, she didn't know, but he was immediately less agitated.

And now, an hour later, he was much calmer. Almost sleepy, no longer sharing himself, and ready to go back to his stall, a step that had been too far before. She moved her hand to his neck and turned him, guiding him into the roundhouse and towards the royal suite to the right. She grabbed a carrot and held it in her open hand, walking slowly backwards until they were outside his stall. She backed in and Keraunós followed. When she'd turned him again, she let him snaffle the carrot and stepped out of the stall, closing the door behind her. On the outside was a gold plaque. Real gold. Alchemical Gold. And on it was written *Keraunós* in Fae script.

She should have known that this couldn't be hers, that the Goddess would not drop such a gift in her lap so easily, especially after she'd crippled that poor boy. Women who break people's legs are not given High Unicorns as a gift from the Goddess.

She ran her fingers over the plaque and snatched them back. That was Fae magick at its most impenetrable. And most corrupt. She walked out of the roundhouse and back into the sunshine. If she was going to do it, now was the time. With no witnesses. She took a deep breath and walked quickly into the other roundhouse.

Conrad hadn't cared about the rest of the stables – he'd been too focused on saving Morwenna Mowbray. And the other injured, to be fair. He'd issued Cordelia with instructions to check for other enemies and corral the grooms. When he'd finished his advanced healing (and how had that happened?), she'd lied to him. Again.

'No one else in the stables, sir.' The fact that it was technically true didn't alter things. There was life, but not in the stables.

Inside the roundhouse, she skirted the rapidly disintegrating bodies of the Fae and addressed the heavy doors that sealed off most of the building. Conrad hadn't even looked in here, and Erin had shown no interest, either, even though she must have known what was to be found.

The sídhe of the Count of Force Ghyll was the heart of Sprint Stables. It was where the Sprites lived, where the little unicorns were stabled, where

Keraunós had been born and where other things might be done, and she had to know what. She had to tick it off the list.

Only the Count could secure the sídhe properly and he hadn't had time before the confrontation, so Cordelia opened her magick to the doors and they blazed with silver patterns. She didn't have time to appreciate the door-art, and felt for the difference: one set were on this plane, one on the next. She found the higher designs and focused on them until the others faded.

Unlike the violent transition on the gallops, this was more of a tingle. If Tom Morton had stuck his head in, he'd have seen her fade and vanish, nothing more. And now she was with the sídhe, and she pushed the doors open.

She walked a little way down the slope and turned round, closing the doors and putting a twist into the magick. Raven had shown her how to do that, and it should give her some privacy, or at least a warning of another Fae approaching.

The drop was shallow. In such a rocky and unforgiving place as the Lake District, a deep sídhe wasn't possible, and this one barely descended below ground level. She walked down the ramp, and the others, the ones who had to be here, stood waiting.

Every sídhe has its quota of Hlæfdigan, the neuter Fae who look after the sídhe. And provide *Amrita*, the Lux-laden liquid without which the Fae cannot grow or transform. There were five of them here, a huge number for a mere Count, and they clung together for protection. Two were dressed normally, the other three in rough overalls.

'Your Count is dead. You have no protector,' said Cordelia, trying to keep the loathing out of her voice. Unless she butchered them all where they stood, everything she said would find its way back to Prince Galleny. She had to try and keep it official.

The older Hlæfdige in a dress knelt down. 'Have mercy on us, my lady.'

'Tell me what business is done here and has been done. If you tell me truly, I may be merciful.'

They started, tumbling over each other to tell their story. Cordelia interrupted them, saying, 'Tell me of the birthings. All of them. Since the sídhe was built.'

When they told her, she swore out loud. She'd been convinced it was here, but they denied it, and the naked fear in their faces confirmed that she was in the wrong place. Some of the things they *had* confessed to would have seen the Count of Force Ghyll in court many times over, but she would have to look elsewhere for what she wanted.

'Go in peace,' she said.

They all got down on their knees. 'In peace, we thank you.' Cordelia turned around and left.

When she'd transitioned back to the core world, her hands flew up in a defensive posture. The Knight who'd fled, the one the Prince had called his *Gamekeeper* was standing over the bodies.

'Who's a clever little girly, then?' said the Gamekeeper.

Cordelia was well aware of how others saw her small frame and elfin face, and where possible she used it to her advantage. The creature's insult was nothing new, and she casually turned it back on her. 'It doesn't say much for you, then, does it? Kept out of a sídhe by a mortal girl.'

The Gamekeeper attempted indifference. 'I didn't want to risk the Hlæfdigan, so I left you to it. It will be mine soon anyway, so there's no rush.'

Cordelia stepped round the bodies, and for the first time since she'd left the Daughters, her hands went to her thighs to lift her robes over the mess. It was a little thing, but it showed she needed to depressurise soon. It was tempting to fire a parting shot, but too dangerous.

Outside the roundhouse, standing well back but watching closely was Flora, the stable lad.

'Are you okay?' asked Flora. 'She didn't try anything, did she?'

'She wouldn't dare.'

'Aidan and the rest should be back in half an hour,' said Flora. 'I've just made some tea.'

It would be Cordelia's fourth mug on an empty stomach. 'Sounds great.'

Flora led the way to the kitchen. 'You've really got a way with Keraunós, my lady. I've only seen Lara handle him so naturally before.'

'The Goddess held my hand,' said Cordelia, and Flora smiled back.

She might only have half an hour, but Cordelia wasn't finished at Sprint Stables yet. 'Tell me about Ronnie. It helps to talk, Flora. I should know.'

Flora cast a last look at the roundhouse. It was where her soulmate, Verona, was lying covered with a tarpaulin. If anyone could be squeezed for more, it was Flora.

## 20 — If you know what's good for you

Judgement was due at three o'clock, and now that I had my secure laptop back, we could all watch it in the incident room. That wasn't the only news I was waiting on. I sat on the steps of Charlotte Mason's conference block and watched the sun sinking over the western hills beyond Windermere, smoking and drinking coffee, and waiting for Eseld to call.

She'd managed to catch the eleven thirty express to Preston, and we'd talked on and off during her journey, amidst all the other voice calls, video calls, messages and emails that had flown around after I'd turned my phone back on.

There hadn't been much to smile about since I'd left the helipad, but I have to share this with you.

When we'd first got back to Ambleside, Hazel Cotton's eyes had gone on stalks when she saw my uniform (there was nothing else clean in the car). 'I'd say I love a man in uniform,' she'd observed archly, 'but everyone knows about my ex-husband. Why the change, Conrad?'

I shrugged. 'Bloodstains. I had to wear my coat on the train or they wouldn't let me on.'

'Hop it, Hazel,' said Tom. 'Now.' When the ever-curious Ms Cotton had left, Tom stared at me. 'You'll pay for that later, Conrad.' He turned his attention to Erin, who'd been looking around frantically and was all set to start opening cupboards in search of something. Or someone. 'I've got a special mission for you, Erin.'

'I'm all out of missions,' she replied.

'Oh? I was going to ask you to go to the Oak Tree Hotel and make sure Hazel doesn't sneak off. She'd get past Barney easily, but with you to keep her in check, we should have the afternoon to ourselves.'

Erin stopped in mid twirl. 'Is that where PC Smith is? The hotel?'

'Oh yes. Between the two of you, Hazel shouldn't be a problem. It would be a special favour.'

'Right. Yes. As a special favour, then. See you later.'

Erin quick marched out of the door, and Cordy slipped behind to have a word outside. I wonder what that was about?

'Is Erin always this transparent?' said Elaine.

'Yes,' I replied. 'Just because she's obvious about her intentions, it doesn't mean she's less successful.'

Elaine had shaken her head and had started to take a sandwich order. I didn't tell them about what Erin had said in the car – that she needed to talk to me in private. After the judgement.

And there was also a lot that I hadn't told Eseld. That was partly to spare her the pain, and partly because I thought it was Morwenna's to tell. I'd stuck to telling Eseld the two simple facts: Morwenna had become a Vessel and Morwenna had been seriously injured. The rest would come out in the end. Or not.

Eseld rang at ten to three. 'How is she?' I asked straight away.

'Good. Out of surgery and in recovery. She should be in critical care in an hour, but she'll be heavily sedated until tomorrow.'

'That's good, Eseld. That's good. Would the surgeon talk to you?'

She tried to lighten the mood. 'I'm a Mowbray. Of course she talked to me.' She took a breath, and I heard her strike a match. 'They were able to save part of her larynx, so she'll be able to speak. She might have to move to the bass section, but there's scope for magick in normal conversation. Maybe. The facial wounds were actually worse, and there was gouging. That's going to be a long road.'

'She'll have help. I know you won't desert her, Eseld.'

'You know more than I do, then.' She sighed. 'Dammit, Conrad. What a fucking mess.'

'Have you told Kenver yet?'

The late Lord Mowbray had two wives. The first was Isolde, now a Daughter of the Goddess, who is Cador and Eseld's mother. His second wife was Aisling, and she had died in a terrible accident when Morwenna was nine and Kenver was five. Morwenna had disappeared for many years after that, and Kenver had doted on his big sister ever since he'd discovered that she was still alive.

Earlier this afternoon, we'd discussed how it was that Kenver hadn't spotted that Medbh (as she called herself) had become a Vessel. Eseld thought that it was because Medbh had simply refrained from using magick. When their father had been murdered, Medbh had fled, probably to avoid being exposed. And now she was back again, and she wanted to be Morwenna.

There was a lot more to it than that, and Eseld had decided to hold off telling Kenver about their sister until she'd seen Morwenna for herself, and now she had seen her, she couldn't put off making the call.

'He's in Wales with Chris, so not too far away. I'll tell him now. And thank you again, Conrad. The Mowbrays are in your debt.'

'Keep me updated.'

While we were saying goodbye, Cordelia stuck her head outside. 'We're on in two. How's Morwenna?'

I got up stiffly and shook out my leg. 'Alive. In recovery. Let's learn our fate.'

The data projector showed the imposing bench of the Cloister Court in the Old Temple and nothing else. I half expected Mina to run in front of the camera and jump up to wave at me, but the Cloister Court does not encourage jumping and waving.

Instead of Mina, we got the top half of Stephanie Morgan, Bailiff to the Court. Complete with Axe. 'All rise.'

The Honourable Mrs Justice Bracewell appeared and settled into the enormous red leather chair under the Royal Arms. Stephanie bowed to her and placed the axe in a holder to the judge's left.

The judge settled her papers and looked off camera. 'Is the technology working?'

'Yes, my lady,' said an off-screen usher. 'We have confirmed links to Ambleside and Keswick.'

We were the Ambleside connection, while the Chief Assessor, the Union President and probably some of the Fae were the ones in Keswick. The judge turned back to face the front.

'Having considered the facts of these various matters, I have reached my judgement. We begin with the complaint that Deputy Constable Clarke deliberately tried to subvert the Occult Law by acting as a Watch Captain in Longsleddale.

'I find that because he is a warranted police officer, and worked within the mundane law, this court has no jurisdiction. I make no judgement as to his motives at this stage. However, if he were to persist in using civil authority when he has no prospect of making an arrest, and did not immediately hand over all the evidence to the appropriate magickal authority, I would reconsider my opinion.'

That was clear enough: no penalty for involving Tom and Elaine. No comeback from what we'd done so far. At least not on that issue. The really big question was this: *Who is the appropriate magickal authority?*

The judge turned her pages. 'In deciding jurisdiction for this case, I have followed these principles. First, that despite counsel for the Union's assertion otherwise, the Cloister Court and Occult Law takes priority over the whole of Albion. The so-called de Quincy Treaty was made under Occult Law and does not supersede it.

'Furthermore, the Deputy Constable is also the deputy constable for the whole of Albion, despite arguments to the contrary, and his powers apply as much in the Particular as they do in Land's End or John O'Groats.' She smiled at that, leaving it open as to whether my powers had much weight anywhere.

'However, I can make no ruling on Mr Clarke's status as Lord Guardian of the North. That is an honour bestowed by Nimue herself. If the Unions want to drag our lady of the waters to this court, they are more than welcome to try.'

Now that was interesting. I had no idea what it might mean, but I wasn't going to say no to a little extra-judicial authority. Not yet, anyway.

'Moving on, the compact in the de Quincey Treaty is very clear: the late Harry Eldridge was a Mage, and the Unions have the power to investigate crimes against Mages. They also have the option of requesting assistance from the King's Watch under Article Seventeen. The fact that they chose not to do so is their concern. This immediately makes the Unions the appropriate authority.'

Damn. That couldn't have been any clearer, but the judge wasn't finished.

'The King's Watch also has the right to petition on the victim's behalf if the Unions have failed to investigate.' She paused to stare at one of the off-screen lawyers. 'Ms Greening's assertion that the Unions are accountable only to themselves has no place in this century.'

That would be the partner of Mr Whitecross in Ambleside.

'However,' continued the judge, 'because the Assessors have not yet begun investigating properly, I cannot rule that they have failed. This ends my judgement.'

She picked up her papers and got ready to rise. She looked into the camera one last time and said, 'That such a tragic death as Harry Eldridge's should end up as a legal football is not the finest hour for either the King's Watch or the Unions. I hope that the investigation can now proceed uninterrupted and reach a successful conclusion.'

'All rise.'

Ouch. That was painful. The honourable Mrs Bracewell doesn't often express personal opinions, and that one couldn't have been clearer: I had acted within the law, but I had acted rashly.

I had also acted to support Tom and Commander Ross, and do you know what? I don't regret it for a moment.

Cordelia spoke first. 'What do we do now?'

Tom looked at me. 'I presume you're going to follow orders, Conrad.'

'Yes.'

'Then as far as the police are concerned, this investigation is closed. I am not going to proceed in a magickal investigation without support from the King's Watch. We'll update the files and get ready to hand over.'

'Sir?' said Cordelia to me.

'You heard the judge, Cordy, and you know Hannah's motto.'

'Which one? "Conrad Clarke will be the death of me?"'

Elaine could sense the temperature, and tried to lower it. 'Is that your CO's motto? I'm inclined to agree with her, tbh.'

It didn't work. Cordy barely looked at her.

'Close, Cordelia, and it was me who inspired it. Her motto is, "Part of the solution, not part of the problem." If Harry's going to get justice, he won't get it by us breaking the law. And besides, we're not finished yet, are we, Tom?'

'We aren't,' he agreed.

'Then what?' said Cordelia. 'Oh, hang on, that's Erin.' She checked her phone and then stabbed her finger towards it. 'We're nearly there. Erin's confirmed that Harry really didn't drive, and the only person who Zinayida saw giving him a lift was Nicole Sanderson. Every other time he slipped off, he was picked up somewhere else. Or he took the bus to Keswick, and that fits with what Flora told me at the stables this morning. That creature, Prince Galleny's gamekeeper, also acts as his driver sometimes.' Cordelia was getting worked up now. 'We know he stole something. Either Nicole or the Gamekeeper must have taken him there. We should question them.'

Tom nodded supportively. 'That's excellent work, Cordelia. If you look at the Actions, you'll see that I've already written *Driver ????* Thanks to you, we can fill that in. And the Assessors can follow it up. I don't often agree with Conrad, but in this instance we are as one: we retire and keep a watching brief.'

Cordelia blinked a couple of times. She was trying to control her emotions, and I couldn't work out whether it was anger, frustration or pain she was keeping in check.

'We shut out the Assessors before,' she said. 'They'll do the same to us.'

'And that's our challenge,' said Tom. It was his turn to get a phone message that couldn't be ignored. 'Better sharpen up everyone. They'll be here at six.'

We were about to settle down again when distant thunder exploded over the town. 'Fireworks,' said Elaine. 'I'd forgotten that it was Guy Fawkes night.'

Scout had woken up and looked worried. Poor dog. 'Can you help me with a Silence for him when it gets bad?' I said to Cordy.

'You can do a Silence,' she replied rather stiffly.

'Yes, but if he can't hear the ambient noise, he'll get just as upset. We need one around this room, and I can't do that on my own.'

'Of course,' said Tom. 'A silence around the room. That's what we need.' We looked at him as if he'd started speaking in tongues. 'Elaine, message Hazel and Barney. Tell them to be here at six. We'll hand over the files in their presence and give the assessors some hard choices they have to make without discussing magick.'

Cordelia's work on that Silence thing had the desired effect on Scout, and the actual fireworks didn't get in the way of their frantic preparations. Just before Hazel and Barney were due, they moved the dog to an empty room next door.

The metaphorical fireworks started when Chief Assessor Grayling and her sidekick arrived. Tom had seen from the email that his name was Kian Pike, the Assessor for the Eden Valley, and he didn't look any more inspiring tonight than he had yesterday afternoon.

The Chief Assessor looked slightly smug when she came in. Not too much. Just enough to let the King's Watch know that she considered hers to be a righteous victory. One thing that hadn't changed was that she ignored Tom and focused her triumph on Conrad Clarke. She didn't even glance at the new arrivals to Tom's right.

They all stood up, and Tom made the introductions. 'This is Lieutenant Kennedy RMP and DC Fraser. They've been working with Conrad and I on the sensitive aspects of the case, while DC Cotton and PC Smith have handled the more mundane aspects of the enquiry.'

His emphasis on the word mundane was subtle enough to fly under Hazel Cotton's radar and score a direct hit on Ms Grayling's expectations. He gave her a second to let it sink in. 'Let me take your coats. Tea?'

Grayling did her best to fight back. 'Tea would be nice, thank you. I presume that your colleagues know that there are ... security aspects to this case?'

'They do. We've put all that in the written reports. Sit down, please.'

Conrad likes to move around, and likes to show that he's not above domestic duties. He and Barney passed round the tea and took their seats again. The police officers were on Tom's right and the Mages to his left. Tom and Conrad had taken a walk around the steeply sloping college campus earlier and discovered they'd been thinking along the same lines. As they stretched their legs (and Scout cocked his leg), they'd agreed on a lot of things, including the keeping of their bosses in the dark. When Conrad then agreed to Tom's particular stipulations, Tom couldn't help but wonder if Clarke weren't keeping his powder dry for some nefarious plan of his own. As Tom sat facing the assessors, he couldn't hide a smile at the idea of Clarke keeping his powder dry on Guy Fawkes Night of all nights.

Tom had a stack of folders in front of him on the table, along with a USB drive. There were more cartons on the table behind. He steepled his fingers and rested them on the documents. 'Hazel has been working very hard with the family all day, so her reports are a bit sketchy. I thought it best for her to give you a verbal summary and be available for questions. Hazel?'

Hazel had never worked in Westmorland before, and she hadn't even heard of the Union assessors until this morning. Her questioning of Barney had apparently been relentless on the topic. No wonder he'd been glad when Erin showed up.

Hazel opened her notebook and gave the assessors a smile. 'The big issue is going to be the inquest in Kendal tomorrow. Zinayida is in no fit state to go anywhere, but Anatoly wants to attend on her behalf. And Barney will need to go.' She looked up and pointed to her right. 'That's Barney.'

'Who are these people,' said Philippa Grayling, genuinely confused, 'and why haven't you listed the inquest for the special coroner in Keswick?' She'd looked at Clarke again when she spoke. At least she hadn't called him Witchfinder. Tom mentally compared Philippa to some of the other born Mages he knew – Eseld, Chris Kelly, Tamsin and Sofía. The difference was that for them, magick was the main thing in their lives, but not the only thing that mattered. Philippa was *all* about the magick.

Kian Pike had started to look very uncomfortable during Hazel's remarks, and he checked his phone. When he spoke, he had a deeper voice than Tom had expected. 'That's the Zinchenkos, right? From the Oak Tree?' Hazel nodded, and Pike spoke to his boss. 'The mundane connection is all over the local news sites. All of Ambleside and half of Westmorland know about Harry the family man.'

Tom had gambled that Philippa Grayling simply wasn't plugged into the mundane news world and had no idea about the implications of the Zinchenko connection. He was right.

While Philippa was taking this in, Hazel carried on. 'There wasn't much press or public intrusion today, but there'll be more after the inquest, and the boss reckons that there might be more from Harry's other life – the one I know nothing about because he won't tell me. Oh, and I promised Zinayida that I'd text her tonight with the name of the new FLO.'

'I see,' said Philippa.

Conrad had told him that Occulting after the fact was very difficult, and that one of the Unions' best Occulters was actually Matthew Eldridge. The Unions were well beyond putting the genie of Harry's mundane family back in the bottle.

The next step was one of Tom's sticking points. Conrad had wanted to wait, but Tom had said no: give them everything up front. When Tom had suggested using Erin to create a bit of theatre, Conrad had given that feral grin of his and said, 'I like your style.'

Tom took an envelope from the top of his stack and passed it to Cordelia, who reached over and gave it to Philippa. 'This is the headline summary of our investigation,' said Tom.

Philippa opened it and took out the blank piece of paper. For a fraction of a second, her face said, *They've got nowhere.* Then she felt the magick. She turned the paper so that Hazel and Barney couldn't see it and used her Sight to read the message that Erin had Enscribed for them.

*Harry Eldridge was killed as a thief under the old law.*

*Harry was heavily in debt to Prince Galleny.*

*Harry was driven to an unknown location on Sunday night.*

*The driver was probably Nicole Sanderson or a Fae Knight in the Prince's household.*

Philippa passed it to Kian Pike without a word. Pike's eyes bulged and his mouth twitched as it sank in.

It was time to make them an offer.

'Ms Grayling, we have hidden nothing and are happy to answer any questions, but it's time for some of us to go. That is, unless you want to ask for our help. I suggest that DC Cotton and PC Smith should continue their work in family liaison under your supervision. You can ask DC Fraser and myself to co-ordinate if you wish. You can request intervention from MI7.' He paused to let the options sink in. 'So long as Matthew, Zinayida and Lara get justice for their loss, it doesn't matter who works on the case.'

Philippa Grayling let the paper rest in her hand on the table as she looked around the room, from her left to her right. This time her gaze stopped at Tom and didn't get as far as the King's Watch.

Tom didn't hold his breath and didn't rub his scar. No lives were at stake here, and he would still be a DCI no matter what the Chief Assessor decided.

It was different for Clarke, though, and Tom still had no idea what the man's endgame really was. On the surface, Conrad was impassive; his partner was a different matter.

Whatever was driving Cordelia Kennedy was much closer to the surface, and she leaned forwards with her hands under the table so that no one could see her fiddling with a black bracelet.

Philippa lifted the paper. 'Are you sure about these conclusions?'

'The first three, yes. The last one is our main line of enquiry, so that's not a conclusion as such. And it links with something that Wing Commander Clarke needs to talk to you about.'

'Then thank you for your offer, Mr Morton. It would be much better for Harry's family if your officers could continue working with them. They can report to the police inspector in Barrow. The Lakeland Unions can handle the rest of the investigation, and I will lead it myself.'

She couldn't bring herself to ask for Conrad's help, could she? She simply couldn't swallow it. The most obvious reaction was from Hazel, who groaned out loud and didn't care who heard it. Barney looked worried, as well he might be, given how much he'd pissed off the Inspector in Barrow. Conrad and Elaine gave nothing away, but Cordelia bent and twisted her bracelet with white knuckles. Whatever that bracelet was made of, it was no material that Tom had seen before.

'As you wish,' said Tom. 'We'll leave you to it, then. Conrad has a couple of points first.'

Conrad cleared his throat. 'If it's okay with you, I shall be seeing Matthew Eldridge in the morning to return some property and pay my respects properly. I didn't have a chance to do it yesterday. I'd be more than happy for Mr Pike to accompany me.'

'What property?' said Philippa.

'A box. A family heirloom we recovered from the boat. It has no bearing on the case.'

'Boat!' said Hazel, cutting across everyone. 'Sorry, sir. It slipped my mind when I was writing the report, but Matt said something about a boat called Thunderer.'

'Oh?' said Tom. 'And what did he say, Hazel?'

She flicked through her notebook. 'He says that he's going to employ some firm called Clan Skelwith Ltd to salvage it. He said that would mean something to you.'

That meant the Gnomes. Right up their street. 'Thank you, Hazel. Sorry, Ms Grayling.'

Philippa looked at Conrad with a curled lip and tipped up nose. She wasn't doing herself any favours with that attitude. 'Do you agree not to discuss the case with Matthew?' she asked him.

'No more than is necessary for his role as executor of Harry's estate,' said Conrad.

'Fine. Kian will have better things to do tomorrow than babysit you, Mr Clarke.'

'Good,' said Tom. 'Hazel and Barney, thank you for your time and your contribution. I won't forget it. Enjoy the evening. You both know what you're doing.' He made a point of looking at the assessors. 'Their Actions are all in the folder, and Hazel is actually staying over at the hotel rather than going back to Wigan.'

Philippa gave a formulaic smile, and the two constables headed out. From the look that Hazel gave to the back of Philippa's head, the Chief Assessor was in for a Cotton-shaped headache at some point.

It was Conrad who spoke next. 'That Fae Knight was part of a group that attacked DCI Morton and myself on Harry's boat. She needs to answer for that.'

Philippa nodded, clearly expecting this. 'And I have your answer, sworn by the Prince's Counsel. The three who attacked you were the Count, the Firefly and the Gamekeeper. The Prince sent the Firefly and the Gamekeeper to work in the Count's household, they acted under his authority and you have had mortal satisfaction from the Count. You also killed the Firefly.'

Conrad had warned Tom that this might happen. Neither of them thought the Count was on that motor yacht.

Conrad nodded. 'Convenient. The boat belongs to Matthew now, so he will need compensation, too.'

Philippa kept a straight face. 'Understood. Kian, sort that out will you?'

The young assessor nodded and added something to his phone.

'And then we come to what happened at Sprint Stables this morning,' said Conrad.

'We've already covered the stables business. The Gamekeeper is a witness in *our* enquiry,' said Philippa with an air of finality.

'Mmm, but I'm talking about the murder of the two stable grooms,' said Conrad. 'Both mundane civilians, and therefore very much my business. I need to question the Gamekeeper for inciting the Count to murder them.'

The Chief Assessor had looked on Conrad with enmity and contempt so far, and now she added incredulity. 'Are you mad? The Count lost himself to the darkness, and you dealt with it. Whether that would have happened if you hadn't stuck your nose in where it didn't belong is another matter. I've already spoken to both sets of parents, and they are not happy with the King's Watch over this. If I were you, I'd slink away and hope they forget your involvement.'

'We're not in the habit of slinking away. However, I don't want my case to impede your case. I'll hold off from seeking a reckoning until you've finished with her. Just let me know.'

'I will do no such thing. Given the Cloister Court's decision today, I was going to overlook your actions, and now you've forced me to make a formal complaint.'

Conrad wasn't finished. 'As you wish. I shall also be visiting Morwenna Mowbray eventually. When she's well enough to receive visitors.'

'Under no circumstances. She is a witness.'

Clarke was unfazed. 'A witness in both our cases. Again, out of courtesy, I'll steer clear of discussing Harry's death, but the Mowbrays are friends.'

Philippa cut right back at him. 'I'm not going to waste resources trying to police you, Mr Clarke. I have more important things to do, but all of this is going to the Vicar of London Stone tomorrow. If you reconsider and withdraw overnight, I'll hold my fire.'

'That's your prerogative, Ms Grayling. Now, if you'll excuse me, my dog is in a quiet place to protect him from the fireworks. You've got my number.' He paused. 'We all want justice for Harry. Please remember that, and may the raven guide your search.'

Only Tom heard the hiss of breath from Cordelia when he said the word *raven*.

## 21 — His Brother's Keeper

I wouldn't say that Cordelia flounced out of the meeting with the assessors. Or stormed. If you can *seethe* out of a meeting, that would just about sum it up. She caught up with me while I let Scout run round the trees before we set off for the Little Langdale Lodge. There was a lull in the fireworks after the back garden parties and before the big public display at the lake.

'You said they'd buy it, Conrad. You said the assessors would ask us to finish the job.'

'I said, "sooner or later. Probably sooner," if you recall. And they bought Tom's idea of Barney and Hazel staying to work with Harry's family.'

'Why is that important?'

'Cordy. You of all people should know that.'

Her anger was close to the surface. 'Is that because I'm a mother? That doesn't define me, Conrad.'

'Of course it doesn't, but it should help you understand. Philippa Grayling hadn't even heard the news. She had no idea that Harry's family had been publicly linked with his death, and now Hazel is in there. You know what she's like. She'll be at that police inspector in Barrow 24/7 to find out what's going on. It's more pressure on the assessors. And after tomorrow, they'll have Matthew on the case, too.'

She'd calmed down a little when she thought it through. 'Why did you tell them you were going to see Matthew and Morwenna?'

'To put my cards on the table. I promised not to discuss the case, so I can see Matt on his own. And she can't stop me seeing Morwenna without risking a serious problem with the Mowbrays.'

'You're right. It's just I wish it could be a bit sooner.'

'Sooner could be as soon as tomorrow night, which is why Mina is joining me for the weekend at the hotel. I'm happy to pay for you as well, or you can clear off any time after breakfast and go to London for your Badge of Office. Besides, the assessors were never going to give us the case straight away after going to court over it, were they?'

'But it was our case!' She caught herself and breathed through her nose. 'Sorry. I sound like my youngest, there. It was my first case in the Watch, Conrad. I wanted to follow it through.'

I can imagine that it's very difficult to say no to Cordelia sometimes. She was doing it now – sticking her little nose up in the air and smiling. She's tried everything today: reasoned argument, professional pride, appeal to my ego and using Erin as a bargaining counter.

I suppose I should be flattered that she saved open flirting as a last resort because I'm solid with Mina. Either that or she finds me so repellent that she couldn't bring herself to do it before now.

'As Saffron said, Cordy, you get used to it. Here, boy! Good dog!'

On the way to Little Langdale, she came to a decision. Of sorts.

'I need a car, Conrad. This is ridiculous.'

'You're right. I bet you've got no credit history, have you?'

'None.'

'I'll lend you the money.'

'You barely know me,' she said quietly. 'They say you shouldn't lend money to friends.'

'You're not my friend. You're my partner, and that's what partners do. Besides, I know Rick's good for it. Not that I'd dream of telling him unless I had to.'

'I don't know whether to laugh or cry, Conrad. Laugh that I could have a new car tomorrow or cry that I'm still reliant on a man I was once married to. I won't find one round here, will I?'

'Kendal has a full range of dealerships. Even a Porsche one, but I'm not lending you enough to buy a Porsche. Tom can drop you there in the morning if you're not going to London.'

It was too twisty and too dark to risk looking at her. She was silent for nearly a minute, then said, 'Thanks, Conrad. Thanks very much. What's the mainline station called again?'

'Oxenholme Lake District. It's just east of Kendal.'

'I'll ask Tom to drop me there and go to London, then work my way back up the country over the weekend via Middlebarrow. And yes, I would like a loan. How much interest?'

'Shall we say half a dozen walkies for Scout per month and a bottle of Laphroig 25 at the end?'

'Deal. Are we expected to eat together tonight? I'm not sure I can face it.'

'You seemed to get on well with Elaine and Lucy last night. You might find it helps. You have got something to wear, I take it?'

'I despair of you sometimes, Conrad. You think that the only reason I wouldn't go is that I've got nothing to wear?'

'No. But I haven't met a woman for whom that wouldn't be a major issue. And tell me if I'm wrong.'

'Sod off.'

'That's better. What sort of car do you fancy?'

'I haven't a clue. I might need to get a man to show me round.'

She said it light-heartedly enough. I could have had a go back at her, but Cordelia had been through the mill today. The attack at Sprint Stables was not a good introduction to the King's Watch for her, and it deepened her engagement to the cause of Justice for Harry. The problem is that I can't help thinking that she's got another agenda going on that isn't necessarily linked to it.

'Do you know your salary?'

She did, and we spent the rest of the drive trying to work out how much she could afford per month, then gave up when we realised that we were both too tired for mental arithmetic. 'I think a bath then dinner sounds good to me,' was her conclusion as we drove through the gates. Followed by, 'Why is Erin standing out there, and why has she borrowed someone's parka?'


Erin made a great fuss of Scout when he ambled over to her, and Cordelia took the hint, saying she'd see me later. She cast a backward look as she went through the doors, and I shrugged to her.

'What's up, Erin?'

'Can we talk? I've got a hip flask here. I thought by the tarn?'

'Of course. I'll grab my hat.'

'Nice walk for you,' she said to Scout. He actually looked like he'd prefer a log fire. He did pull up a tree and chase across the countryside this morning. Probably had more exercise (relatively speaking) than any of the humans. He's a good dog, though, and fell in with us when I'd put on an extra layer.

While we wandered down the path, I filled her in on the meeting with the assessors. We sat on one of the benches away from the hotel and she gave me the hip flask. 'Drink the lot if you want. It's malt whisky. Urrgh.'

'Cheers.' It was a buttery, warming Highland malt. Very tasty.

I waited patiently for her to get round to it while she fussed with the borrowed coat. 'Remember last Sunday, yeah? When I arrived at your place in a bit of a state after Samhain?'

'I'm surprised you didn't redecorate the inside of the Smurf.'

'It wasn't just the drink.' She shuffled on the seat. 'You know the reason I first turned up at Elvenham?'

I cast my mind back to the days after the hunt of the Phantom Stag. 'You said you wanted to see a real life Druid, and I had one in captivity.'

'That was just an excuse, really. I came because I half fancied you. Then I met Mina, and I don't have a death wish.'

'Vicky hinted as much. You've been a really good friend to Myfanwy when she totally needed one. You can't have fallen out, though. No one falls out with Myfanwy.'

'No. And we'll always be friends, but there's other stuff going on. You know I got kicked out of the Scriptorium in Stratford?' I nodded. 'When I started renting off you, the Countess invited me to tea. She wanted to know all about Elvenham House.'

No wonder she wanted to talk out here. In the dark. By the lake. The Prince of Arden is a massive figure in the Fae world. In some ways, he's more powerful than his Queen, and the Countess of Stratford is his Consort and fixer.

'This was months ago, Erin. Why are you telling me now?'

She turned her head to face me. There was some light from the hotel and a couple of Lightsticks in the garden. 'Don't you want to know what I said?'

'Only if you want to tell me.'

'When the Fae invite you to tea, it's like being asked to go for a party in a minefield, Conrad. I had to give her something, so I told her everything she could have learnt by hanging out in the village shop and everything she could have seen for herself by knocking on the door.'

I wasn't surprised. The fact that Nell Heath of the village shop has never had cause to say, 'Someone's been asking about you,' only proves that we haven't been visited by lesser Mages or Fae. A powerful Mage or Fae Count wouldn't leave a trace.

'And since then?' I asked.

'The next time she asked, I told her that it was my turn, and that we'd love to have her come to Elvenham when you were there to show her the respect she deserved.'

I laughed. 'Neat. Thank you. So what's changed?'

'Samhain. We went into the Prince's sídhe to party, and he made a beeline for me. And he gave me the Rapture.'

It was so quiet by the tarn that we could hear the diners in the restaurant, way over to our left. It's said that you can't understand the Rapture until you've experienced it, and when you have, you can't describe it. It could start with anything – a dram of whisky after a hard day, scoring a goal, getting to the top of a mountain with a clear view. Whatever little moments of pleasure you have in your life, the Rapture can turn them into something out of this world.

However, the Fae are not known for climbing mountains or playing football. Mostly, they deliver the Rapture during sex. I'm guessing that's what had happened to Erin.

'He didn't want anything,' she said. 'Yet.'

I sighed. 'The long game.'

'Yes. In a way. I think he was making me choose, and he didn't expect me to choose to spy on you. I think it was more to get me out of the Circle. Someone – could be Fae, could be human – didn't want a Friend of Elvenham inside the Arden Foresters.'

She could be right, and I had never doubted that Erin would choose Myfanwy over the Prince of Arden. 'You're leaving the Foresters?'

'Yes. And I think the Goddess stepped in to help me.'

Erin is not a great believer in providence and divine intervention, so this was a surprise. 'How so?'

'By sending me to the Sextons with Cordelia as a minder instead of you. Cordy turned on the charm and had old Evelyn Sexton wrapped round her cute little finger in no time.'

The Sextons might be dysfunctional, but they are also rich in resources. After Vicky and I sent Diana and Guy Sexton to jail, the semi-retired matriarch, Evelyn, had taken over the family again. I'd heard nothing from them since then.

'How is Evelyn?' I asked.

'She's fine. She nominated Pihla to be the next Guardian instead of Rowan. Diana heard about it and now Rowan has left Linbeck Hall.'

'I see.'

Diana is in the Mage's prison, the Esthwaite Rest, and doing four years for murder. The chances are she won't survive unchanged. She certainly lost the chance to be a major player in the Particular. I drank some more whisky and lit another cigarette. At my feet, Scout started to snore.

Erin continued. 'That puts Pihla in a vulnerable position. She's only a year into her apprenticeship, and there's a whole Scriptorium in trust for her. A big prize. Evelyn offered me the job of apprentice master.'

I sat up straight. 'Here?'

'Mmm.'

'And Pihla?'

'She didn't want to be used either. If they chose an Enscriber from the Particular, it would give them a lot of influence. This way they stay neutral, and they know I don't care about politics. Not like that. It's a win-win.'

'You don't sound very enthusiastic. Are you worried about Myfanwy?'

'Yeah.'

'She'll miss you, Erin. No point pretending otherwise. Especially when the cricket season starts again, but I think you know that things have changed. When you first met her, she was completely alone, and much as I love her, I'm still her jailer. That's why you were so good for her. She's got Ben now, she's got a little Druid on the way, and she's got friends in the village. And there's nearly always a Mage around these days for her to talk magick with.'

'Thank you, Conrad. I needed to hear you say that.'

'There is one thing, Erin. Do you really fancy Barney, or is it just a hangover from the Rapture?'

She stood up. 'He's single, he used to play rugby, he's got a proper career, and have you seen the size of his guns? What's not to like?'

I bent down to scratch Scout's paw. It's the kindest way to wake him up. He gave me the evil eye (the blue one), then got up and did a superb downward dog with yawn.

'I know you keep saying I'm not your boss, Erin, but think very, very carefully before you Entangle Barney.'

She leaned over and gave me a kiss. It was too cold to hug. 'I won't argue with that.'

We set off up the hill. 'When are you going to tell Myfanwy?'

'I'm signing a contract tomorrow morning, then I'll head off to Elvenham. It's good that you're not there this weekend.'

We were nearly at the doors when Erin stopped me. 'You've never completely trusted me, Conrad. I get that. But you've never doubted me or suspected me of anything. Very few people have done that. I'll never do anything to hurt you, because that would hurt Myfanwy. See you in half an hour.'

It took me, ooh, ninety seconds to get changed, and I used the other twenty-eight and a half minutes to talk to Mina. Mrs Justice Bracewell had decided this morning that the Flint Hoard hearings would be adjourned until Tuesday, so Mina was going to take the early train to Chester tomorrow and pick up a couple of things from Middlebarrow Haven. Business over, the rest of the conversation was pleasure.

It had taken Cordelia a lot longer than ninety seconds to get changed, and she was wearing a beautiful black silk scarf/pashmina/thing. It was the first time I've seen an item of magickal clothing.

If I'm struggling to describe it, that's because it actually shifted and metamorphosed during dinner, from plain black square to something more like a feather boa. She said that it only worked in venues with an undercurrent of Lux, and she wanted to practise using it.

I'm sure she did. I'm also sure that she wanted to make a subtle statement: I am not just an ex-Daughter and part-time mum. Message received, Cordy.

Erin loved it, and straight away asked where she'd got it. 'A gift,' is all Cordelia would say.

And I was right about Cordy getting on with Elaine. At one point they were even talking about steam locomotives. I know.

I got a message to call Eseld during dinner, and did so when I took a break before coffee. 'Why didn't you tell me about the pregnancy?' she asked, with more curiosity than anything.

Eseld had been allowed to see her sister for five minutes on the critical care ward. Only Vicky would have spotted the foetus with magick (it's a Gift), so Eseld had found out the old-fashioned way: reading the notes. It was in big letters on the front, to stop some ignorant junior doctor prescribing the wrong drugs.

'Not my story to tell. When she stopped being Lara Dent, she might have changed her mind.'

'She didn't. Before she passed out, she must have used magick to hide it. Good job she told you. Got to go – Kenver's on the line.'

Morwenna hadn't told me about the pregnancy. I'd felt it when I was patching her up. To be accurate, I'd felt *them*. Morwenna is going to have twins. I think. One for another day.

'Do you see this sort of thing as a message?' said Lucy. I think that's what she said. It was hard to tell, given that all I could see of her face was her eyes. The rest was covered with a knitted hat and scarf combo that clashed slightly with the orange down coat and brown boots.

I'd been out giving Scout his morning constitutional and found her on the terrace by the tarn.

'What sort of thing?'

She used a matchingly gloved hand to move the scarf away from her mouth. She must feel the cold as badly as Mina. Not that it was that cold. 'The impenetrable fog. Is it a message from … someone?'

'No. It takes a huge amount of energy to control the weather – which is why the gods had a reputation for lightning bolts. Much easier to manipulate. Lightning and avalanches.'

She nodded, taking my answer a lot more seriously than I'd intended it. 'That's good to know.'

'You could see it as a metaphor instead of a message,' I suggested.

'Eh?'

'A metaphor for the impenetrable nature of this case, because Tom and I are groping about in the fog. That sort of thing. Or you could see the fog as a result of high pressure, a clear night and being in England's wettest county.'

'I'll go for the metaphor,' said Lucy, returning the scarf to her nose. 'You have to get used to them living with Tom.' She started walking towards the entrance. 'You know, he once said that Hazel Cotton could make a dog's dinner out of a sow's ear.' She stopped with her hand on the door. 'How can something so wrong be so right?'

I rubbed Scout's neck. 'What do you reckon, lad? Pig's ear for dinner?'

'Arff.'

'Doesn't he get in the way?' asked Lucy.

'He does sometimes, which is why I'm sending him with Erin this morning. The Oak Tree is not a dog-friendly hotel.'

Lucy's words about pig's ears came back to me an hour and half later as I wandered along Ambleside's main street, killing a bit of time before my appointment with Matthew Eldridge at the Oak Tree, and what triggered a repeat of the metaphor was the pair of bright blue earrings on display in a well-lit boutique.

The window had been segmented into themes, and on the left was a section with a black backcloth. A transparent Perspex head dominated the scene, and jewellery had been added – nose stud, lip ring, necklace and earrings. And the earrings were … ears. Worked in silver, they were small ears which in turn were pierced with another ear hanging off them. You get the idea. I smiled to myself and glanced up at the interior of the shop. Woah!

Inside, four women were staring hard at me, and I took a step back, and that brought the name of the shop into view: The Daughters of the Earth. No wonder they were staring. With a shop run by the wives and daughters of Gnomes, no matter how little magick they had, there were bound to be Wards on it. I bowed and pointed to the door. Four pairs of eyes tracked me as the bell tinkled and my scant hair told me that magick had happened.

'Forgive me,' I said. 'I was drawn here for no other reason than the quality of your work.'

One of the women was leaning on a counter. She was slightly larger than the others, and wore a vivid tunic in autumn colours over black leggings. She smiled at me and held out a hand. 'The quality of our work and the Attraction Ward on the shop. I'm Eleanor Octavius Hoggart. You met my husband Martin yesterday.'

'The Bursar. Of course.'

'You are welcome in peace, Dragonslayer and friend to the Clans.'

'In peace, I am honoured. I am also on my way to an appointment, so please excuse me. I hope to return with my fiancée.'

'Oh? What sort of jewellery does she like?'

'She's of British Indian heritage, so…'

'Bling,' said Eleanor. 'Lots of gold. Now that would be a challenge. Safe journey, Dragonslayer.'

'Conrad, please.'

I left the shop with an even bigger smile on my face. Not everyone in the Lakeland Particular hates me. The smile died when I saw Matthew Eldridge outside the hotel.

He looked haggard. His hair was all over the place, and he'd cut himself shaving. The black suit he was wearing under a specialist outdoor waterproof already looked crumpled. The skin on his hands when we shook was dry as sandpaper. I offered my condolences, and he gave me a bare nod in return.

'Do you mind if we go to White Platts park?' he asked. 'It's just down the road. Zinayida doesn't need any more strange policemen in her home.'

We started walking. 'And I'm a pretty strange policeman.'

'Not as strange as our Family Liaison Officer. She could make the standing stones give up their secrets, that one. She's very good with Zina, though. She made her have a bath and get changed last night. Even looked after little Lara for a bit.' He made eye contact. 'After she'd enjoyed a free dinner, of course.' He looked down at the pavement again. 'I still can't believe that Harry hid all of this from everyone. Here we are.'

The fog had lifted over the town, leaving everything soaked and dripping. There was going to be no autumn sun today, and Ambleside looked like

213

something from a horror story – all the majestic fells were hidden and the little town was cut off in its own little world.

White Platts is more of a recreation ground than a park, with a bowling green, tennis courts and crazy golf. A single family of tourists were about to embark at the first hole, and Matthew led me to a bench well away from them.

'How is Zinayida?' I asked.

'She swings between denial and anger, and I'm not helping much, because according to Harry I didn't exist. I wasn't cut out to be an instant uncle and shoulder to cry on. I took a family album this morning, and she's looking at that. Of course, she wants to know where Lara is in the pictures. What a fucking mess, Conrad.'

I said nothing and waited.

'You're not going to tell me anything, are you?' he asked. The light in his eyes was a little clearer now, the sharpness was half-way back. 'The Grayling made you promise, didn't she? I'll bet that can be a burden sometimes, having to keep your word.'

'Which is why I try not to give it. Seeing you was more important, though. Here's the box. I got my partner to have a look and she's none the wiser.'

Matt took the extra-large padded envelope and withdrew the heirloom. The lacquer was so highly polished that even on this dull day it gleamed. He ran his hand across the scenes of gossiping geishas and the smile that passed across his face looked like it had been wrenched from his heart with a pickaxe.

He stared at the box for a while. 'This means nothing unless you're an Eldridge, and I shouldn't have it. It should have gone to a sister, but I don't have one of those, Lara Dent notwithstanding.' He opened the box and took out the little pagoda. 'Most would see this as the prize. It's unique in this country and one of only half a dozen in the whole world. It's a sort of magickal robot: you can program it. The gods only know what Harry used it for.'

He looked up at the mist over the fells, and I looked down. The intrepid golfers had reached a particularly decorative hole, and a boy of about seven was lining up to putt his ball through a slate recreation of the famous Bridge House. 'C'mon, Jason, you can do it,' said his father encouragingly. 'There's a hot dog if you get this in one.' I have no idea what the family were going to do with the rest of their day, but right now they were one hundred percent into their game.

'There is something I can tell you, Matt.'

He tuned back in. 'I can't tell from the look on your face if its good news or not.'

'It could be either, but you need to know. In thirty-nine weeks, you could become an uncle all over again.'

His face creased up even more. 'Sorry?'

'There's a girl who's pregnant. Harry's the father. I'm really sorry, but I've promised someone – not the Chief Assessor – that I'd keep their identity a secret.'

One of the good things about being an habitual liar who has to keep his word, is that you can lie about having made a binding promise. It's the act that counts, not talking about it.

'I have to ask. Are you sure?'

'Yes.'

'And the fucking mess gets worse. They'll have a claim on Zina's share of the hotel. I'll have to get a mortgage and buy them out. I can't let Zina lose the hotel. My stupid idiot brother saves the best until last.'

He'd only met Zina yesterday. He'd only *heard* of Zina yesterday. That was impressive loyalty.

'Don't worry, Matt. Her family are rich enough and nice enough not to throw a spanner in the works. They won't bother Zina or Lara.'

'A Mage?'

'Yes.'

He suddenly looked at his watch. 'I have to go, Conrad. Thank you for what you've done. I don't know what happened at Sprint Stables, and I know you can't tell me. Doesn't matter. I know you, and I know you'll make sure that justice is done. One way or another.' He looked over his shoulder at the café, toilet and ticket blockhouse. 'There's someone coming who wants a word.'

I didn't turn round until we'd shaken hands and he'd gone. Coming down the path, carrying two takeout coffee cups, was another Matt Eldridge – but shorter. It didn't take long to see through the Glamour and recognise George Gibson, a Gnome of Clan Skelwith. Once he'd sat down and handed over a coffee, the magick dissipated completely. 'Better safe than sorry,' he said, offering me a cigarette.

'Am I so toxic, George?'

'It's both of us I'm thinking of.'

'But mostly the clan.'

'Mostly.'

'Does your wife work in the jewellery shop? I found myself drawn there earlier.'

'No. She's a photographer, actually. One of the Chief's daughters works there. She's the youngest.'

'Mmm. Much as I appreciate the coffee, I'm sure that's not why I'm here.'

'I'll keep it simple. The clan wants good relations with the Guardian of the North. But not openly and not yet, and we don't think it would help you to get too close to the Children of Mother Earth just yet, either.'

'I won't take it personally.'

He gave me a strange look. A lot of people think I'm an empire building politician, for some reason. They're completely wrong. I'm just trying to stay one step ahead of the slavering pack and do my job.

'We'd like to offer support. Anything that won't come back to bite us on the arse.'

A plan I'd been knocking around since Mina messaged me this morning came into shape, but I'd start with some information.

'Tell me about the Queen of the Derwent and Prince Galleny.'

It was George's turn to go off on a tangent. 'When you became Lord Guardian, our Chief summoned me – because I'd actually met you. He asked me to compile a report as best as I could. I discovered that the Keeper of the Esoteric Library has been a guest at your house at least twice.'

'She gets about a lot, does Francesca.'

'Quite. You should ask her to let you borrow the manuscript copy of a book called *Reflections on the Wild Hunt of Trafalgar*. There is a printed version, but it was so heavily edited that it's mostly lies.'

'A bit like my reports. If you rely on those for intelligence, George, you're screwed.'

He laughed. 'I had heard that, and we haven't hacked the Merlyn's Tower network. *Reflections* has all the historical stuff, but to cut a long story short, Her Grace of the Derwent loves to hunt and chase, and Prince Galleny is her Consort and Master of the Hunt.'

'So they're close.'

'And she keeps him close because he's not fit for much else. In our opinion. Her senior Prince is Harprigg, from near Kirkby Lonsdale, and she has another in the Eden Valley. I would go a long way to avoid dealing with them.'

'Good to know.'

'And that reminds me. Last time we met, you accused me of stealing water from Nimue's spring. In a polite way, of course.'

It was true. George Gibson has a spectacular grotto near and below Windermere, and taps water from a magickal source. He also channels it to a public fountain for any Mage to drink from. 'I was just asking a question, George.'

'You should know that we are the only clan who has a relationship with Nimue. Ask her about it, but not here. Not on Windermere or the Windermere catchment.' He turned on the bench to face me fully. 'I know you summoned her at the Wray Repository, but please, for your sake, don't do it again until you know a bit more.'

'Noted. Now, about giving me some help. I need an Occulted location, fairly central, where I can come and go without anyone knowing. Come and go by road and air.'

'Now you're asking. We'd be happy to do that if we had somewhere suitable.' He suddenly snapped his fingers. 'I know. The Windermere Haven Hotel. Do you know it?'

'I've seen it. On the east bank, just north of Brockhole. What's your connection?'

'The Chief's eldest daughter's daughter runs it with her wife. They're both Witches. They have a field that would do. It's not fully Occulted, but if they know you're coming, they can muddy the waters a lot.'

'And they'd do this?'

'They would. I'll talk to them and get in touch.'

'Thank you. Who should leave this secret meeting first?'

'Me.' We shook hands, and I turned away to avoid interfering with his disguise.

I'm sure you're dying to know, so I'll tell you. The young lad had failed in his bid for a hot dog at the Bridge House hole, but I sat and watched him get it two holes later, while I was talking to Mina.

'Will you be able to get a pilot at such short notice?' she asked.

'I'm sure of it. It'll save you having to take the train back to Manchester. Just get the stuff from Middlebarrow Haven and head to Chester airfield.'

'I'm not sure I want to be flown by anyone but you, Conrad.'

'He's good. And highly rated.'

'You're right about the train. I would do a lot to avoid that. I'd better go.'

An hour later, I met Erin (and Scout) at the Two Sisters café in Plumgarth. 'How are the Sextons?'

'Fine. They didn't change their minds overnight, and I am now Pihla's Apprentice Master, as well as trustee of the Scriptorium. She's a good kid, even if she does have terrible taste in clothes.'

'You what?'

'You never saw me at Sprint Stables, did you? Perhaps for the best. When she interviewed me yesterday, she insisted I wear one of her dresses.'

'Why on earth was that? She didn't strike me as being more bonkers than any other Mage.'

'I think she wanted to see how far she could push me. Having got me dressed up like an extra from a vampire film, she offered me Fae wine. When I said no, she said I'd do. To be honest, Conrad, I think all the Sextons are bonkers pretending to be normal.'

'And you're normal pretending to be bonkers? Pull the other one, Erin.'

She struck a pose by the car and put on a theatrical accent. 'You wound me, Conrad, and you'll miss me when I'm gone.'

'I might still be here on Monday. If I haven't been ambushed.'

She leaned in to her rental car to wipe some muddy paw prints away. 'Why? Who's got it in for you now?'

'You're going. Tom and Elaine have gone. Cordy's gone. It's just me and Scout up here now.'

'And Mina. Forget about it all for a while. I would.' She twisted the cloth in her hands. 'I'd better go. I have to be in Cheltenham to hand over this car before six. And then I have to face Myfanwy.'

'She'll be thrilled for you. So long as you promise to come back and bat next season.'

We hugged, and she bent down to say goodbye to Scout.

'Take care, Conrad. And have some fun.'

'I'll do my best.'

## 22 — *Scramble*

Barney hadn't always been a good lad. He'd once broken an idiot's nose at school, and he knew what it was like to sit outside the headteacher's office. At least she was going to spare him that.

He knocked on the open door, and Police Inspector Gibson looked up from the letter she was reading. Had she always worn glasses? Was it new? She blinked and took them off. Reading glasses, then.

'Come in, sit down and close the door.'

PI Gibson had two things in common with Commander Ross: immaculate uniform and the ability to reduce junior officers to a state of fear simply by looking at them. Granted, Ross's buttons had an extra gleam, and he could project authority over the phone as well as in person, but he was older and four rungs further up the ladder.

Gibson didn't have her scary face on today. Not yet. Somehow, that was even more worrying.

'Thanks for coming in on a Saturday,' she said. 'Then again, you get overtime, so you should be thanking me.' She paused. 'That was a joke, Barney.'

'Yes, ma'am.'

She held up the letter and two email printouts, put them back down and placed her hands flat on the desk. 'So, DCI Morton thinks you're the bees knees, Barney. And Commander Ross commends your work for the division. Even the Lakeland Unions want you to carry on working on what I now know to be a murder enquiry.'

The last time he'd felt this disoriented was getting off the waltzers at Ulverston Fair. Was she going to rip into him now? God forbid that she was actually nice. He couldn't cope with that.

'How did you do it, Barney?' she asked. 'What did you take to the party?'

How the hell should he answer that? Talk about a loaded question. This was more loaded than those guns that Clarke carried around and no one seemed to notice. He thought back to when he'd broken Darren's nose. He'd avoided being expelled by telling the truth.

'Hard work and keeping my mouth shut, ma'am. Especially the latter.'

She nodded, as if he'd given the right answer in a secret test. 'What's he like?'

'Who, ma'am?'

'Scout the bloody dog. Who do you think? I'm talking about Clarke.'

'He's very tall, ma'am. Makes an excellent cup of tea and doesn't hog the biscuits.'

'Very droll, Barney. You liked him, then?'

'I barely saw him.' Barney very nearly dropped himself in it by adding *this time*. His last encounter with Clarke wasn't in any of the Westmorland Police records.

'And his sidekick? What's her name again? Watch Captain something?'

Another test. There was no way that PI Gibson didn't know who Cordy was. 'Lieutenant Kennedy, ma'am. I saw even less of her. She has very long hair.'

PI Gibson looked at him as if she were looking over the glasses she'd just taken off. She shook her head slightly and blinked. 'What have they got you doing at the weekend, then?'

Barney relaxed and felt his shoulders creak as the tension left them: Gibson wasn't going to rip into him or put him on prisoner escort duty.

DCI Morton had told him to play it completely straight from this morning. Everything in the open as far as PI Gibson was concerned. 'I'm to check in with the family and be on hand, so I'm basing myself in Ambleside. The FLO will be back on Monday. While I'm there, I'm going to work through CCTV and a few other jobs suitable for uniformed officers on secondment.'

He delivered the last line with a slight raise of the eyebrows, something he thought Gibson would appreciate. She did. 'Oh, the racing pulse of detective work. Now you know why I stayed in uniform. Don't forget your eye drops: they're part of the risk assessment for CCTV work.'

He shifted his weight to his knees, ready to stand up, but Gibson wasn't finished. 'And all this is for the assessors?'

'Them's my orders, ma'am.'

She nodded, and he was dismissed. At least her office wasn't overheated, or the trail of sweat down his back would have been a river. Talk about a lucky escape. He headed for the street door and his car.

What he'd left out of his explanation was that Commander Ross had refused to delete their investigation from HOLMES2, so DCI Morton would be able to see everything once Barney had logged it on the system. After all, Morton was still the SIO, wasn't he?

He found the victim's brother, Matthew Eldridge, still acting as gatekeeper for the Zinchenkos when he got to Ambleside. He'd known Eldridge for years, of course, because Eldridge was the local assessor, and had poked his nose into numerous police investigations. Grief had aged him and changed him. He was being very solicitous about his brother's family, despite their existence being a total surprise. When Barney arrived, Eldridge closed the door to the private quarters behind him and spoke to Barney in the hotel corridor.

'Zina's a bit more together today,' he said. 'She felt up to having the funeral director come round, so that's what we're doing now that the coroner has released the body. It'll knock her out when he's gone, but once it's done, it's done.'

'I'll leave you in peace, then. I'm only up the road if you need me.'

Barney treated himself to an extra-large baguette from his favourite sandwich shop and settled down in the incident room. He sniffed the air a second. Smoke? No. Wet dog. Had Clarke been in this morning? The door had been double locked and nothing had been disturbed as far as he could tell. He shrugged and put the kettle on.

Ambleside is a very small town by national standards, and mostly very quiet. At midnight last Sunday it was about as dead as you can get. Except for the A591.

That road runs straight north-south through the Lake District and a fair few overnight delivery waggons use it to get from Keswick to Kendal, and it was Barney's job to sort the wheat from the goats. As DCI Morton had put it.

Westmorland Police only had two CCTV cameras in Ambleside, both covering areas where students or hen parties were likely to get out of hand and, ooh, maybe sing songs at one in the morning. The permanent residents of Ambleside do love their beauty sleep.

By accident or design, the cameras also caught the two parts of the A591 as it split, but he wasn't starting with CCTV. He was starting with ANPR – number plate cameras which recorded vehicles going in and out of the town. Most passed through or went home, and Barney started work on the two lists, ticking them off if they passed through or cross-referencing them if they were locally registered vehicles. What was left would be the anomalies.

After his sandwich, Barney remembered the AudioVisual system, and synched his phone so that he could listen to music. Then he went for a walk. Then he carried on. Then he phoned his mum. Then he got a call from Erin. He sat up much straighter at that point.

'Hello you,' she said. He loved her Bristol accent, sort of seductive without making her sound like a country bumpkin.

'Hello back. How's things?'

'Not so bad. I've got a big strong man with me. That always brightens my day.'

That was Erin all over. She loved to say provocative things. From what he'd learnt so far, anyway. He slid his legs under the desk and leaned back. 'Well, if you can't have me, I suppose you'll have to settle for second best.'

'Mmm. Let me see.' She took the phone away from her mouth and shouted, 'Myfanwy, Barnabas says that your Ben is second best.' He heard the distant words of a woman with a lilting voice. 'Myfanwy says you're to come here and say that. Doesn't matter, he's helping me pack so they can get rid of me. It's all happening down here.'

221

'So you're definitely moving to Westmorland?'

'I am. Van's coming on Monday morning. Have you had your shifts for next week, yet?'

'Nope. Still on this case, so it'll be daytimes unless I'm taken off. I'm still free to take you round the fleshpots of Bowness on Tuesday night.'

'I can't wait. Message me if anything changes.'

'Will do. Take care, Erin.'

Five minutes later, he realised that his mouth hurt because he'd been grinning. And if he was honest, his mind had been wandering a little. Erin could be very distracting, even when she was two hundred miles away.

He looked at the printout and forced himself to go back half a page and do it again. That was when he hit the anomaly.

An Audi A4 (according to the index number) had come in from the north but was not shown leaving on the southbound, data-only ANPR camera, and the car was registered in London. Could be a tourist who'd gone to the Theatre by the Lake in Keswick and come back to their holiday rental. He watched the CCTV for the relevant time and nearly missed it. There. Same registration number, different car.

He double and triple checked. He was right. A small hatchback with fake number plates that should be on the Audi had entered the town and then disappeared, the visual image giving the lie to the data. He quadruple-checked, and just before it went off the camera, it indicated left. It was going up the Kirkstone Road, either to a house up the hill or to the Struggle, the windy road that led almost vertically up the fell and crossed over to the Kirkstone Pass.

DCI Morton had said that none of this was urgent, and Barney's eight hours were nearly up, so he took a walk back to the hotel and was told by Anatoly Zinchenko that their parents were flying out from the Ukraine tomorrow.

'Matthew is very kind,' said Anatoly. 'He will go to collect them from Manchester Airport. Can you come here at lunchtime?'

The next morning, Sunday, Barney went back to Charlotte Mason and picked up where he'd left off, rewarding himself with a cup of tea and a biscuit. He quickly cross-checked a camera near the A66, north of Ullswater. Another hit. And again in Keswick.

So, a hatchback with false plates had left Keswick, arrived in Ambleside and left via the Struggle/Kirkstone Pass, returning to Keswick after a trip through the village of Glenridding and round Ullswater. He got out a calculator and worked out the average speed. Bloody hell. Lewis Hamilton would find it hard to top that.

Barney had one more job to do. He looked through all the police reports for Monday in both Westmorland and the neighbouring county of Cumberland, given that the car had travelled through both counties. It was almost time to report to the hotel when he found the only thing that might be relevant: an expensive rowing boat stolen from a mooring on Ullswater some time on Sunday night/Monday morning. And it had been found drifting on the lake on Wednesday.

If – and it was a big if – Harry Eldridge had been picked up in that car, then why had it gone back via Ullswater? The only sensible answer was to drop him off somewhere. And if he'd stolen the boat then been abducted, it would explain his captors setting it adrift on the lake.

Barney logged it all on the system, then re-wrote it in an email for the assessors. He also included updates on how the Zinchenkos were doing. In the email, he put his findings last. The assessors might read the whole email or they might not. He closed down the computer and picked up his coat.

On his way to the Oak Tree, his mind turned to Erin (and not for the first time that day). He loved the way she'd sat on his desk the other day and smiled at him. That thought took him all the way down the hill to the town, and then he remembered that she'd parked her handbag next to her. Barney was about as far from being an expert on handbags as it was possible to be (unlike DCI Morton, for some reason). Even so, he couldn't help noticing the gold Aspinal tag, and how could a calligrapher and letter artist afford a £1,000 handbag? Even more to the point, how could she afford *two*? In different colours?

Erin's public social media posts were thin on the ground, but one of them definitely had the plum version of the green bag he'd seen on Thursday. It was funny how someone as open as Erin could clearly be hiding so much.

'Why are we going for a walk, Dad? We went for walks allllll week!'

Cordelia stood by the back door watching Rick zip up their daughter's coat until she was snug against the lingering chill outside. He stayed squatting down in front of the little girl and put his hands on her shoulders. 'What happens tomorrow, angel?'

She hated that he called her *angel*. She had a perfectly good name. A name they'd agreed when she was born. It was one of the many things she could have a go at him about. If only the kids didn't look so bloody happy.

Her daughter frowned, drawing the dark freckles across her face into a new pattern. 'We go back to school?'

Rick stood up. ''Sright. And we want you both tired out tonight so you go to bed.'

'Well, I'm not going to be tired. I'm going to save all my energy.'

Rick opened the back door and propelled the girl gently through it. Her older brother followed and pulled her hood over her head with a practised yank.

'Hey!' said the girl and went to hit him, but he was gone, jogging down the drive. She set off in pursuit screaming, 'That hurt!' Within minutes they were deep into the countryside and the children were expending enough energy to power the National Grid. They would definitely sleep tonight.

Cordelia looked around as they started the descent towards the stream where no doubt her daughter would make every effort to push her son into the water. She loved it here, with rolling hills and grass that still looked green. Unlike Ambleside, where the mountains crowded round you like jailers and the lake taunted you with visions of escape, or the Lodge by the tarn, where the grass was tussocky and oncoming winter had robbed the landscape of colour.

'Any emergencies while you were away?' she asked. While Rick had been on holiday, Vicky Robson had been covering his patch. In theory. As Rick explained.

'No. Vicky decided she could do the job from London, so it's a good job no one ram amok. To be fair, she dealt with everything she needed to by phone. It's only Conrad who seems to walk into trouble wherever he goes.'

She'd only worked with him for a few days, but Cordelia was instantly moved to defend her new partner. 'If you're going to be fair, Rick, it's Hannah who sends him there. He didn't find Harry Eldridge's body. Or the Count of Canal Street.'

He grinned. 'Fair comment.' He checked that the kids were well out of earshot before he dropped his bombshell. 'I've been on to admissions at the Cathedral Prep School. I've reserved two places for January.'

She stopped dead in the middle of the field and raised her hand to her chest, where all the pain of leaving the Daughters had gathered. 'You had no right!'

There is a primary school near Glastonbury where most of the children's mothers are members of the Daughters of the Goddess. Where most of the staff are members, too. It was half an hour's drive from Rick's house north of Wells. Not much, unless you have to do it twice a day.

'The school bus comes past the road end every day,' said Rick, stealing into her thoughts. 'And I haven't signed anything yet. I haven't mentioned it to them, either. Yet.'

The children had disappeared round a hump in the hillside, and Rick started walking quickly to get them back in sight. Cordelia reached down to lift her robes and swore to herself. No robes. At least she wasn't wearing wellingtons, and ran to catch up her ex-husband.

He was standing on a rise above the stream, watching the children start to explore. 'Now you've got your Badge of Office, you're properly one of us,' he said. 'You might stay with Conrad, you might not. Whatever happens, the kids can't stay at that school. Not for long.'

She was glad that she was out of breath for a second. It meant she could bite back the retort that had come to her lips, because he was right. Unless she went crawling back to the Daughters, her children would have to move schools, and he was giving her time to sort her head out. Being nice again. She hated it.

She balled her fists and closed her eyes, taking a deep breath. She could do this. She could get it all sorted by Christmas and find a new home for her and the kids. Or she'd be dead, and the Cathedral School no doubt had excellent counselling services.

'You're right,' she said. 'About moving. The schools in Chester are pretty good, too.'

He didn't turn to look at her. 'We'll see. Shall we go and look at what's in the wood, before there's a drowning?'

Cordelia's phone started vibrating. She nearly ignored it, then remembered that the King's Watch are never off duty. Rick had interrupted quality time often enough in the past. Payback. And then she saw the CallerID: Flora, from Sprint Stables.

'Hi. Everything OK?'

The girl replied in a half whisper. 'They're installing the Gamekeeper as the new Count of Force Ghyll tonight.'

Instinctively, Cordelia started walking back towards the house. Rick's house. 'Remember what we talked about. We're not finished with her yet.'

'I know, I know, but that's not why I rang. They're having a hunt first, and they're bringing in the Queen's Hounds.'

Behind Cordelia, Rick whistled to summon the children, like Conrad whistled to summon his dog, but the Queen's Hounds weren't dogs. They were Dual Natured Mannwolves, and Flora had something else to say. 'A van came last night, and I saw them taking food into the roundhouse this morning.'

Cordelia's stride lengthened further. 'Food?' She hoped she'd misunderstood. 'They take food in all the time.'

'Not human food, they don't. Can you get a warrant or something? You might catch them red-handed. Before it's too late.'

But it was already too late. She was down here, in Somerset, and Conrad was on his own in Little Langdale, miles from the stables. Not that it mattered where Conrad was, because Flora had even more bad news. 'The Madreb from Kirkby Lonsdale always seals the valley when she comes here.'

Shit. Shit, shit and double shit. Why had she agreed to stop over last night? She could have been there. To confront the Queen. The spasm of guilt and anger passed, and she forced herself to remember her duty of care. To Flora. 'I'll do what I can, Flora. I really will, but you have to be strong. You have to remember what happened to Ronnie. You have to stay quiet. Do as you're told. All of you.'

'You're not coming?'

'I'm not in the Particular. I'm going to make some calls. See what I can do. I'll be there late tonight. Sit tight, Flora.'

The girl's voice shrank even further. 'Right. Gotta go.'

Ten paces behind Cordelia, Rick stood with the children on either side of him. How often had she stood like that while Rick took a call before dashing off. 'Trouble?' he said.

'Yeah.' She focused on her daughter. 'Can you help daddy throw all my stuff in the case? All of it, mind. Quick as you can.'

The children ran off towards the house as she pressed Conrad's number.

'Worth it?' I asked when we got to the summit. If you can call Orrest Head a summit.

Mina had started the walk out of Windermere Town in full penguin mode: coat, scarf, gloves (and thermals – I'd been there when she got dressed this morning). She'd started shedding layers as we walked up the short but steep path that led to where the young Alfred Wainwright had had the epiphany that led him to fall in love with the Lakeland Fells. Apparently. By the time we got to the top, I was carrying more of her clothing than she was wearing. I was even tempted to try loading some of it on to Scout.

'It's certainly popular,' said Mina. We were not alone at the viewing point. If we had been, I think she might have taken her trousers off, too. Not that I'd be complaining. Having made her point, she turned round to soak in the view.

Is it the finest view in England? It must be in the top five, especially on a clear day like today. The perfect combination of lake, mountains and blue sky was simply stunning. It must have been stunning: for once, Mina was quiet. I felt her fingers interlace with mine, and neither of us took our eyes off the prospect before us. I felt like the luckiest man on earth. She gave my fingers a squeeze to seal the moment.

As if sensing that we'd got what we came for, Scout started pulling on the lead, eager to leave his mark on the panorama stone.

'Have you been here before?' she asked. 'To this exact spot?'

'No.'

'Good. That means it's something we have together.'

'That's what I thought. And it's easy access for people with bad legs, short legs and four legs.'

'Hah! What's on that stone?'

A family moved away from the panorama, and we took their place. A piece of slate had been etched with an outline of the distant fells so that you could work out which they were, together with the quotation from Wainwright: 'Those few hours on Orrest Head cast a spell that changed my life.'

'It must be truly stunning in winter. With snow,' said Mina.

'It is. Much more dangerous, though.'

She traced her fingers over the outline of the fells on the stone. 'Which ones have you landed on?'

'That one. That one, twice. On that one we were too late.'

'Give me my coat. It's cold when you stand still.'

'That bench is free. Tea?'

'Why thank you, kind sir. After that breakfast this morning, I didn't think I'd feel hungry again.'

We sat down and I got out the Thermos. 'Good job I brought cake, then.' I shifted myself to take the weight off my phone, hoping it didn't ring just because I'd thought of it.


It didn't ring at Orrest Head, but it did ring in the end. By then we were back at the Lodge, and I was helping Mina to get out of her thermal underwear. Her hand was nearest, and she picked up my phone. I could tell by the look on her face that there was a good chance that she'd reject the call. I rather hoped she would.

'Who's Kian Pike?' she said.

'That assessor I told you about. I'd better take it.'

Mina took it on herself to answer. She often does that.

'Conrad Clarke's phone …' She looked down at me and gave an evil grin. 'The Lord Guardian is busy. Can I take a message, or is it urgent? … Hold on.'

She passed me the phone, shaking her head slightly and shifting round to get off the bed. Damn. Damn and blast it.

'Clarke here.'

'Lord Guardian, erm,' His voice squeaked with panic, and he cleared his throat to try and get a grip. 'I'm sorry, but there's no one else I can ask for help. The Fae have kidnapped a member of one of the Families. My Family.'

Mina had already slipped off the bed, heading for her dressing gown. I sat up straight and massaged my leg. 'Are you sure? Why?'

'Yeah, I'm sure. They took her yesterday. I was trying to find out what had happened when they called me just now.' He took a deep breath. 'They told me she was responsible for what had happened to Harry and that they were going to treat her the same. Then they told me to stay out of it.'

My mind was already running in ten different directions. I started looking around the room for some clothes to put on and saw that Mina had taken a call, too, and that she was heading into the bathroom. I closed my eyes and pinched my nose to put some order into things. I decided to start with the Family – capital "F". They're pretty loose collections, but they are also the main blocs of human power in the Particular. The Sextons used to be an upper-mid ranking Family until I put a spanner in their works.

'Which Family, and how are you connected, Kian?'

'The Ripleys. I'm only a fringe member. It's Saïa they've taken, but I know she didn't do it! She was with me. By the Goddess, I swear it.'

My heart got a lot heavier, not because Kian might be involved with his cousin but because he thought that her guilt was a factor. 'It doesn't matter what she did, Kian. Where is she?'

'I don't know! She could be anywhere – Borrowdale, Kirkby, Shap. Anywhere.'

Mina sat next to me, still on the phone. 'Does he know where she is?' she asked.

'What? No, he doesn't.'

'I do. This is Cordy on the line. The girl is at Sprint Stables. Cordy says something about a hunt, sealing the valley and Werewolves.'

'Shit.' That was me.

'No!' That was Kian. He'd heard what Mina said.

'What does Philippa Grayling say?' I asked.

'I can't get hold of her,' he replied. His voice was edging up again. 'Her phone's off.'

I turned to look at Mina and raised my eyebrows. She closed her eyes and nodded her head. Her mouth twitched in what would be a prayer to Ganesh.

'Here's what's going to happen, Kian. You're going to get in your car and go to the Windermere Haven Hotel on the A591, just up from the Langdale Chase Hotel, because today is your lucky day. If it was Saturday, you'd be out of luck.'

'What? I don't understand.'

'The Peculier Constable doesn't answer her phone on Shabbos, Kian. If, and only if, the Chairs of three Unions call her and request help from the King's Watch under Article Seventeen of the de Quincy Treaty, then I'm sure the Constable will agree it.'

'They'll never do that. You're sentencing Saïa to death.'

I looked at Mina when I answered. 'If I go in without authority, we'll all die. If I have authority, there's a slim chance we can do something. You know the Union Chairs. Just find two who'll go on the record, and I guarantee that Langdale-Leven will follow suit. But only call them last, when you've got the others. Understand?'

When I'd finished speaking, Mina got up and went to talk to Cordy.

'I understand,' said Kian, 'and I'll do my best. What do I do when I get to the hotel?'

'Park your car in the staff area, then look for a border collie tied to a gate. Untie him and go through the gate. Now get off the phone and get moving.'

Mina handed me my combat uniform. 'Are you actually taking Scout?'

'Yes. I don't have a lot of choice of partners today, do I?'

The pre-flight check was nearly complete when we heard barking from across the scrubby field at the back of the Windermere Haven Hotel. Kian looked as if he could barely hold on as Scout dragged him across the grass. I closed the access hatch and wiped my hands on a rag before Scout leapt at me.

I took the lead from Kian and introduced him to Mina.

'Hi,' said Kian. 'I've heard a lot about you.' He cast a nervous glance around the field. 'When are the others getting here?'

I pointed to Scout. 'You've just brought him.'

He swallowed. 'What about Cordelia Kennedy? And the other one you tried to hide from us?'

'You mean Erin? She only hides when there's an ex-boyfriend around. Anyway, she's in Clerkswell, and Cordy is on the M5.'

He looked beseechingly at Mina. 'Are you coming?'

A smile twitched at her lips, and she shook her head.

'Mina's job is to keep working the phones and let people know what's going on. And if I don't come back, her job is to exact a bloody and terrible revenge on my killers.'

'This is true,' said Mina, 'but I don't think it's what Kian wanted to hear. I think he would prefer it if you had a plan.'

Kian nodded, trying to stop the panic spreading down his face from his eyes.

'We don't have plans; we have objectives, and today's objective is to stop the blood hunt of Saïa Ripley. That was her name, wasn't it? And how are you related, exactly?'

'Yes. Saïa. Her mother was married to … what does it matter, Mr Clarke?'

I pushed the button to start the Smurf's many electrical systems and stood back. 'Call me *sir*, now that you're assisting the Watch. It matters because I want to know how high up she is in the Family. I take it she's a Mage.'

229

'She is. Her mother went away and now she's back, and Saïa might be Senior one day. Is that enough?'

'So the rest of the Ripleys might be gathering right now?'

He nodded rather than risk saying an answer.

'Now you know why I wasn't going to go in there unauthorised. Well done, by the way, on getting four Chairs to call in. It'll stand you in good stead during the aftermath.'

He blinked. 'What do you mean?'

I glanced at the display. 'All self-checks complete. Fuel at eighty percent, other levels at optimum. That's it, love.'

Mina tapped the iPad a few times and scrawled a red nail over the box at the bottom. She passed it to me, and we kissed.

'I will see you later, my love,' she said. 'Until then, Ganesh will be at the threshold.'

'And the Allfather has your number,' I replied.

If you think that sounded a bit like a formula, you'd be right. We talked it over yesterday, when we heard that Morwenna Mowbray had had a relapse and was back in surgery. Mina had said that she couldn't bear the thought of ever saying goodbye to me, and we'd agreed never to do it.

She wrapped her cold fingers around my wrist for a second, then turned to walk away.

'In you get, Kian. Sit there and put that headset on. Oh, and you're in charge of Scout. He's not the world's best flier.'

I climbed into the cockpit and switched everything ready. 'Can you hear me?'

'Yes. Sir. What did you mean about the aftermath?'

I pushed the button to start the engines and held my finger on it. The noise was sweet and even. If Ganesh had wanted to stop me, he'd have squeezed a fuel line or something. No going back now.

While the engines continued to climb up the scales, I spoke to Kian. 'Your boss is in on this. She knows what's going on and turned off her phone. The modern version of turning a blind eye, I suppose. If you stand your ground and they don't sack her, you should quit and join the Watch.'

Perhaps he had no answer to that, or perhaps he muttered it. Either way, I heard nothing except the roar and howl of the Smurf as he got ready for action.

## 23 — *Choose your Enemies*

Kian finally spoke while I was executing a slow and safe turn to head south. 'What's that lake?'

'Haweswater. It's hard to miss. We'll start to descend when it's behind us.'

'Where are you going to land?'

'Nice field next to the stables on the north side.'

I couldn't see his face, of course, and most of the nuance was lost from his voice, too. 'How are you going to get through the Wards? If their Madreb has sealed the valley, how will you even find it?'

'What's a Madreb?'

'The Fae word for the Mage who looks after the Queen's Hounds.'

I had one of those. My pack of Mannwolves call her *Auntie*. Sounds nicer, somehow. 'Bit late to ask how I'll find it, Kian. What would you do if I told you that was your job?'

'I ... I don't know.'

I left it a second before I answered. Up here, far from ground-based magick, the navigation system knew exactly where we were and how to get to the co-ordinates I'd given it. I stared at the theoretical path and let the computer put us on the right course. Then I disengaged it. At some point, the bloody thing would fly us into a hill if I didn't. That's Occulting for you.

'I've been to the stables before, Kian, and that's how I'll find it. It's my thing, and that's all the answer I've got for now. You can get out here if you want.'

He had no comeback for that. Shame. I was trying to needle him into anger, to engage the fight reflex. Ah well.

'Right. Final instructions. Bite Scout's lead if you have to, but don't say another word until we're down. No matter what you see. Understood?'

'I think so.'

'And when I say *Get out*, I mean it. Quick as you can. And run towards the stables. Here we go.'

I fixed my eye on Blea Water, just to the left of High Street summit, and dropped as low as I dared to follow the scree slopes down into Longsleddale. At least there were no trees to get in the way.

Good Occulting sends out a completely false visual image that's totally non-magickal. It's why Sprint Stables looks like a shed from Google Earth, and why Merlyn's Tower looks like a section of wall. There's nothing about the image that's inherently magickal, so no detector can tell the difference. The only way to see through a Glamour is to reach *behind* the image and find the magick. On its own, something I'm quite good at. Unfortunately it's more of a challenge when flying a helicopter.

It would be down there somewhere in the green foreground. Reach out. Find the magick.

Bloody hell.

'Mmmmmnngghhhh,' said Kian from behind. It was the noise you'd make if you were biting a dog lead and scared to death.

It was like flying towards the Great Wall of China from the side. A huge great glittering barrier of magick surrounded Sprint Stables in a semi-circle. If I'd come at that head-on, we'd be heading back to Windermere with our brains scrambled. Or dead on a hillside.

There was a tiny gap between the wall of piss-off magick and the side of Force Ghyll, and I had to bank so hard to squeeze between them that Scout fell off Kian's lap. I battled the Smurf into a solid landing, hit the shutdown switch and grabbed Great Fang from the co-pilot's seat. 'Get out, Kian. Let's go.'

I didn't look round until I was nearly up to the wall that surrounded Sprint Stables. Kian and Scout were catching me up, and Kian looked a little more focused. Good. I stopped three metres short of the wall and ducked, beckoning Kian to join me. If someone looked, they'd see us, but for another minute the turbos would drown out our noise.

'Any booby-traps in the wall?' I asked.

'I can't see any.'

'Good. Neither can I. I'm going up to the wall. If I don't see any danger, I'm going over. When I go, unclip the lead and chuck Scout over the wall, then follow.'

'Right.'

It was a much higher wall than normal. Dry stone walls don't hold together well above five foot, and this one was about my height. I activated my Ancile and took a run at the wall, digging my boot into a big gap and lifting myself for a quick scan before dropping back.

Nothing unexpected. No one manning a defensive position. Good to go for now. I motioned Kian forwards and started to climb the wall properly.

I got up, rolled over the top and dropped on to the rough grass, scanning constantly.

'Arff! Owwwl!'

Kian couldn't quite get Scout over the wall in one go, and the daft dog ended up standing on top, barking loudly. 'Come here, you.' I reached out to get him, and he just leapt into my arms, knocking me over and putting me in a heap. To add insult to injury, he slurped his big pink tongue over my nose. Never work with children or animals is what I say. I heaved him off and rolled into a crouch. Still nothing.

'Oof.' That was Kian. 'What now?'

'Hold your fire. Don't start anything, okay?'

'Right.'

'I'm going round the corner. Follow when you see my hand go down.'

I raised my left arm, put my hand on the Hammer and walked round the corner. At a steady pace. Looking unafraid. It's a good job my heart wasn't connected to a loudspeaker, though. That would have been a giveaway.

'There he is!' said a young girl. Her fellow grooms turned in my direction, took two steps forward, then stopped when they remembered what had happened last time I was here. I lowered my arm and walked into the yard. It was a reception committee, but not a hostile one.

'Are you Flora?' I said to the one who'd spoken. There were several I didn't recognise, and it looked like they'd dragged in all the staff and volunteers for the special occasion.

Scout shot round the corner and stopped just in front of me, on guard. Kian wasn't far behind.

'Yes,' said the girl. 'I'm Flora, and you came, but you're too late. They've gone.'

'Gone where?'

She pointed to the field that led to Force Ghyll. 'On to the course. Out of this world.'

That was not good. That was not good on so many levels. 'It's never too late, Flora,' I lied. 'We're here now – this is Kian Pike, by the way. He's the assessor, if you didn't know.'

'Was it her?' said Kian unhelpfully.

Flora didn't understand what he was on about. 'Show her the picture,' I said.

Kian fumbled out his phone and held it up. At least he'd put Saïa as a screensaver, so that saved a few seconds. Flora nodded and nearly welled up with tears.

I moved to interrupt Kian before he went off on a tangent. 'Flora, tell me who was here and who has gone through the barrier.'

She took a deep breath, wiped her eyes and sniffed hard. 'Right. The Prince and the new Countess came here first thing with two Knights. They call them the Whippers-in. Then the Prince Harprigg. I hate him even more than I hate Prince Galleny.'

Flora was losing it again. 'Who was with him?' I asked, trying to keep it conversational.

One of the others took over. It was the girl with burns to her arm. She had hard eyes edged with determination and looked like she'd been a believer until the Count's rampage.

'Harprigg came last,' she said, correcting her friend. 'The Queen's Hounds and their Madreb came first. The Queen herself and her party aren't coming until later.'

They could be on their way already. 'What about the Sprites?' I asked.

'In the sídhe,' said Flora. 'They don't hunt.'

233

'Good. Now tell me who went through the barrier, in what order and when.'

'We should get going,' said Kian. 'Every second counts.'

'It does. But not as much as finding out what the fuck is going on.' I turned to the girl with burns. 'What's your name?'

'Inge, Lord Dragonslayer. My mum said you were in the jewellery shop on Friday.'

'I was, Inge, now tell me who's in there.'

She looked at Kian and pointed to his phone. 'What's her name?'

'Saïa.'

'At half past two, they brought Saïa out of the roundhouse and made us watch. All of us. Prince Galleny put her to the question. He accused her of killing the Bookmaker. When she denied it, they said they'd try her by hunt.'

Trial by combat is not unheard of in the world of magick, but trial by hunt?

'Is that a Lakeland thing?' I asked Kian.

'It's a Fae thing. The bastards.'

'Go on, Inge.'

Her face was locked in a rigid grimace. Flora was sobbing and had started to lean on a beanpole lad who was way too tall to be a jockey (a bit like me). Inge spat out the next part of the story. 'The Gamekeeper said the Hounds needed a scent. She stripped her to the waist. Totally. Top, vest, bra. And Artefacts.'

'Come on!' said Kian. 'Let's go.'

But Inge wasn't finished. 'And she filmed it. Or one of the Whippers-in did. The Gamekeeper had an hourglass, and when she turned it over, she told Saïa to run. Then...'

Kian grabbed my arm. 'She could be dead by now!'

The first two times, I put it down to desperation. Now I was beginning to wonder. 'Tell me, Inge.'

'The Gamekeeper went into the office with her phone. There's a computer with proper broadband. She said, "I wonder what the little ones will make of this." She meant the Ripleys.'

Kian had let go of my arm and stepped back, towards the stable block. When he saw the look in my face, he turned round, but there was nowhere to run. I had him in two steps, grabbed his jacket and slammed his face into the wall. Twice.

'Whose side are you on, Kian? Who put you up to this?'

'Mnaaagh.'

I pulled his head right back. 'I'll keep going until there's a new window in here. Now talk.'

He spat blood. 'No one! I'm doing it for Saïa! The Prince knows it wasn't her, but she was the only one he could get to. He took her to force the Family to act. They'll come round the back way and Saïa will be caught in the middle.'

'Why me?'

'No one else wants to know. Philippa said it would be a lesson for us. The Ripleys.'

I bent his arm up his back, took out my pliers and removed his Artefacts, chucking them away. I forced him on to the ground and turned round. 'You. Lanky. Take his phone, tie him up and sit on his head. Flora, call Cordy and tell her what's going on.' I pointed to one of the others at random. 'Go and get the clothes that Saïa was wearing and bring them to me. Inge, get me a horse and a plane-shifting saddle.'

They moved half an inch, then stopped, and Flora spoke. 'I said it was too late. They've severed the bridge. An ordinary saddle won't be enough to transition.'

'That's my problem, not yours. Now move!' This time, they moved.

I lit a cigarette and followed Inge across the yard to the smaller stables next to the two roundhouses, calling Scout to come with me. A couple of the other grooms had jumped to help Inge, and they were already in the stall of a large but rather elderly stallion. The plate on the door said *Agrippa*. And the prize horse was *Scipio*. I'm sensing a theme here.

'Is he fit for hunting?' I asked.

'Don't push him too hard,' said Inge. 'The others are too young. It takes a lot to get a horse used to plane shifting. He knows the score, don't you Marcus?' She rubbed the horse's nose and smiled the smile that goes with being a truly besotted animal keeper. 'Marcus Vipsanius Agrippa. Father of the stable.'

'So I can expect to meet Prince Galleny, Prince Harprigg, The Gamekeeper, the Madreb, Two Whippers-in and how many of the Queen's Hounds in there?'

'Four,' said another of the girls. 'But you've forgotten Aidan and Perci.'

'Don't worry about them,' said Inge. 'They'll be right at the back. Violence isn't their thing, but steer well clear of Perci, obviously.'

'Not obvious to me.'

'She's riding Hipponax. The other High Unicorn.'

'Right. Tell me about the course.'

'Where did you come in last time?'

'By some fake ruins.'

She nodded. 'That's near the end. The flying finish. After that is the steep wood. Saïa could be hiding in there, it's on the shoulder of the hill. Once you get up to the top, there's only one part left. The Gauntlet.'

She paused to make a final adjustment. 'The Gauntlet is six furlongs of hell. I'd tell you what's there, but it changes all the time. There we are – all set.

I'm not a Mage, but I know magick. How the fuck are you going to get on to the course at all?'

I started introducing myself to Agrippa, making sure that Scout could see me and learn. 'Friends in low places, Inge. Why have you lot turned on the Fae? You'll all be in deep shit for what you've told me.'

She grinned, and I could see her Gnomish heritage coming out. 'We're going to quit. En masse. After what she did, none of us would work for the Gamekeeper. She can muck out her own shit. Good luck, Dragonslayer.'

She led Agrippa into the yard and over to the mounting block – she'd seen my bad leg and knew I'd need one. The other groom, the one I'd sent for Saïa's clothes, appeared. 'Put them down,' I said. I called Scout and got him to give them a good sniff. The poor thing wasn't happy – these clothes had already been turned over by the Queen's Hounds, and he could smell wolf as well as human. Dogs can very easily get mixed messages. I stood up and got ready.

Inge patted Agrippa's cheek and held him ready for me to mount. I swung on and took the reins. Across the yard, Flora was wiping Kian's bloody nose for him. There were going to be a lot of reckonings today, and I wasn't finished with the little shit yet. Assuming I came back, of course.

'Walk on, boy. Walk on. Scout! With me.'

Barney had planned to let the Zinchenkos have some space. He had figured out that the internal system at the hotel was able to distribute Sky Sports to any TV, and thought it might be nice to catch the early game behind the desk in reception. If he was really lucky, someone might bring him one of those amazing hot beef rolls.

There had been some arguments about whether to close the hotel completely. Anatoly might be great in the kitchen, but he was no hotelier. Then Zinayida had said that they needed to keep it open, 'For Harry.' Unfortunately, she was in no fit state to participate in actually running the place. As a sort of compromise, they'd closed the restaurant to all but residents, and weren't taking new residential bookings for a week. When Barney said he'd man the phone, if they didn't mind him having the TV on, Anatoly had jumped at the chance and scurried back to the kitchen.

Merseyside United had taken a 2-0 lead at half time, and Barney was ready to stick his head in the kitchen to see if everything was okay (and beg for food). He'd just stood up when the agricultural rattle of Matthew Eldridge's X-Trail sounded outside. Barney grabbed the phone and punched the number for Zinayida's extension. 'Zina, your parents are here. I'll go and help with the luggage.'

By the time he'd got outside, the luggage and two bewildered parents were already on the kerb, and Matt was halfway up the steps.

'I've got to go,' said the assessor. 'There's a situation at Sprint Stables.'

The stables was one part of the investigation that was completely closed off to Barney. No one had said anything about Clarke and Cordelia's visit there on Thursday, but that hadn't stopped him checking the logs and discovering that the air ambulance had been called out.

'A situation, sir?'

'Yes. Clarke is in way over his head. I've got to go and help him. Or pick up the pieces.' Eldridge's face said that he was close to breaking down again. 'There's no one else. No one.'

'I'll come,' said Barney. 'I'll do anything I can, if it would help.'

Eldridge looked at the hotel and at Mr & Mrs Zinchenko, huddled on the pavement. For a second, he was lost in whatever nightmare the true story of Harry had generated, then he shook his head and laughed. 'Why the fuck not, Barney? Here.' He chucked some keys in the air. 'You can drive. It's going to be one hell of a ride.'

## 24 — On the Scent

The angry strike of horseshoes on concrete gave way to the deep thump of grass. Agrippa had been this way before. Probably every day of his adult life. He knew where he was going, and at first I let him head for the end of the field where the liminal margin began.

Half way across, I turned him and made for the corner of the field nearest to Force Beck. The grooms knew what they were talking about, and if they said that the bridge was closed, it would be. I needed to find another way, and for that I needed help.

On the way to the beck, having got used to Agrippa's rhythm, I tried out the magickal attributes of the saddle by touching the saddle horn and closing my eyes. Back at Elvenham, I think that Eseld may have delayed explaining the saddle for another reason than sheer devilment: I couldn't have worked it without the knowledge I'd gained completing the Ley line from the well. I had to draw the two ends of the circuit together, and that image gives the wrong impression. Two ends of an electrical circuit want to be complete, but Lux does not. You have to draw it across the gap and shove the two together. I gathered the strands of heat gave them a twist with my wrist and strapped them across the pommel. Voilà.

'Easy boy, easy,' I said to Agrippa. The transition was a lot less painful than earlier, but it was still a shock, and the poor horse hadn't been expecting it. I pulled him up and looked around. The most startling thing was that it had worked. I was nowhere near the gallops, but I wasn't in a field any more.

Instead of grass, all around me was grey emptiness: light grey sky, dark grey ground and fade to grey between them. It was as if the whole world of Longsleddale, Sprint Stables and Lakeland had disappeared into a CGI glitch: I could see the foreground, but nothing else. And now my legs were aching. Badly. And it was deafeningly quiet, with no wind noise or barking dog to break the silence.

I twisted round and discovered that there *was* something. Behind me rose a cliff of grey splodges, and on top of the cliff was vibrant green grass. I could see the gallops, but my visual cortex was telling me that without Salomon's House quantities of Lux, I wouldn't be transitioning up there on my own. I gripped the saddle horn again and reversed the flow of magick.

'Arff, Arff!' said a very distressed dog who was wondering why that great horse had disappeared in front of him.

'Walk on, Agrippa. Walk on.'

Once he was moving, I pushed him through his paces into a gallop. I needed to know if the old lad could clear the wall safely before we went any further. He did, and we were out of the cultivated bottom of the valley and onto the wild fellside. I slowed him down and chose a spot near the beck with a nice hump of rock where I could re-mount later. I slipped down and summoned Scout so that I could fasten a very long rope to his doggy harness and tie it to the saddle. Now for the hard part.

I made my way to the beck and rolled up my left sleeve. There are several scars there, including the teeth marks of a lion and a pair of punctures from a Nymph. To become Lord Guardian, I'd been bitten by Nimue and nearly died of blood loss, and now I was going to summon her again. Voluntarily. There is no discipline of blood magick as such, but there aren't many branches of the Art where a little of the red stuff won't act as a lubricant. I've even had lessons in cutting myself precisely for this reason.

I'd got as far as reaching for my knife when Scout went bananas, barking and pulling so hard on the lead that poor Agrippa started to follow him. My head snapped around, and then I felt it: something was changing upstream. I jogged with a limp towards Scout and Agrippa, and the feeling got even stronger.

There was no hope of getting on Agrippa's back now, so I grabbed the reins and yanked on Scout's lead to pull him in. 'Easy boy. What can you smell, eh?'

'Arff.'

I closed my right eye and held up my left hand to try and focus on the landscape ahead. It was definitely shimmering, and I felt the same feeling that had come on me when Cordy created her step up to the higher plane. 'Come on you two. I'm not going to look this gift horse in the mouth.'

I moved towards the margin as quickly as I could whilst leading a horse, restraining a dog, limping and trying not to fall down the rocks into the beck. As I got closer, I could feel it begin, and more than that, I could feel a presence. This wasn't a random act of magick – there was someone there enabling it. I pushed through the transition, dragging the animals with me, and tried to recover as quickly as possible. I hadn't ignored the possibility that I'd been brought here to be captured or killed.

A younger horse would have bolted and dragged me under his hooves. Agrippa reared and pulled, then stood snorting while I looked around and tried not to trip over Scout, who was going even more bonkers than usual. The presence was still there but hidden.

'Here, boy. Calm down you mad mutt. Good dog.' I straightened up. 'Whoever you are, thank you for that.'

We were on a green slope that became a very steep drop to my left and ended at the spirit version of the beck, because that's where we were: the Spirit Realm, and you have to have names for these things, even if only for reference.

The world I was born into, the world that most of us live in full time, I've decided to call *Mittelgard*, in honour of the Allfather. The man himself lives on an even higher plane: Asgard, home of the Aesir. A lot of Mages refer to where I am now as the Fae Realm, but that sticks in my throat. The other main residents are Spirits, so Spirit Realm it is.

Away to the right was the green turf of the flying finish, where Cordy had brought us and where I'd seen my first Unicorn. Only a few metres away, a disintegrating wall would make the perfect mounting block. 'Let's go, boys. Clock's ticking now.'

If you're wondering why I hadn't shown the same urgency at the stables, it's because of the time difference. I knew that whatever was going on up here would be happening very slowly relative to Mittelgard, but now that I'd crossed the boundary, time was very much of the essence.

On the way to the wall, Scout started pulling and barked. Surely he couldn't have found a scent here. I looked for fresh hoof prints and saw none; what I did see was the thinnest silver thread leading away to the west, towards the woods. As good a place to start as any.

Agrippa seemed happy to be back on the move, and I let Scout follow the Lux in a straight line through the obstacles until we got to the trees, then I pulled him in. So this was a Fae wood.

The mundane woods of Mittelgard lost their summer finery weeks ago, with only a few sheltered specimens keeping their leaves. Not in the Spirit world. We humans gather our Lux from each other, mostly, harvesting the energy in Collectors and shunting it round through Ley lines. The Fae use trees. Special trees that live entirely in the Spirit Realm and photosynthesise Lux somehow. There's a Fae Wood on 'my' land at Elvenham, and exploring it is on my to-do list next time I'm home.

The silver line led into the woods, well away from any defined tracks. If Saïa had her magick, I'd have backed her to hide in here. Without it, I'm betting she'd have run as fast as she could, going for distance and praying that the rest of the Ripleys managed to breach the defences and rescue her. So where did this line go? It had to be connected to whoever had helped me get here, and in the absence of any other clues…

'Walk on.'

Passing through the wood, following the trail, was like walking down a road in Kabul, something I've done only once. The way was empty, but you knew that the trees of Force Ghyll and the houses of Kabul were hiding dangerous things, and that those things were watching you. I survived Kabul by having a mullah with me, and I think only survived the wood by sticking close to that line. It was not a place I was in a hurry to explore again.

'Whoa, boy. Easy.'

There was brighter daylight ahead. A thinning of the trees and a change of surface from spongy soil to rocky outcrops. In the glow of the sun, I could see that the line faded away. I dug my heels into Agrippa's flanks and urged him into a fast trot. We emerged from the trees, and Agrippa nearly threw me off when he changed his gait and launched himself over a tiny hummock of grass like he was at a steeplechase. In the air, I felt it again – another transition. We were into the Gauntlet, and Agrippa had known the only safe way to get there. Boy did this horse deserve a basket of mixed fruit when this was over.

There was no element of surprise, because Scout howled loud enough to let the whole world know we were there. In this case, the whole world was three riders facing a narrow defile in a cliff. A cliff? Where the fuck had that come from?

Down in Mittelgard, we would be on top of the watershed between Kentdale and Sleddale, a typically bleak bit of the fells. Up here, we were in wonderland and anything goes, starting with the sides of a gorge like something out of an old Western, all dry rocks and dust, and leading to a narrow gap at the top end. In the Gauntlet, anything goes and nothing is quite what it seems.

I spurred Agrippa on towards the riders and decided that it was time to untether Scout. His rope was a loop, and I unhooked one end to let it run out. He went straight to the left to circle round the back.

I held up my right hand and slowed down as I approached the group. They were here for a reason – either to stop me or because they were holding back. When I realised that one of the beasts was a High Unicorn, I knew they weren't here to ambush me. That didn't mean that they wouldn't attack though, especially when I saw the sword.

The girl on the Unicorn was trying to hide behind Aidan Manning and the Fae noble who took the front. His horse was a magnificent beast, his saddle had silver chasings through it and his sword glowed with magick as he lowered it to rest it across the saddle in front of him. In his person, I'm guessing a great age, because he wasn't afraid to wear green and sport a pair of pointed ears. It's no more natural to the Fae than any other shape, but it's how they present themselves when they hunt. Or so I'm told.

'My lord Prince Harprigg, unless I do you dishonour,' I said.

'A strange meeting, Lord Dragonslayer. Or would you prefer *Protector*. You have almost as many titles as I do.'

He was in no rush. Unlike me. Behind him, Aidan kept turning round to look at the girl on the Unicorn, and she was watching the defile. I was about to push Prince Harprigg when in the distance, somewhere down the defile, a horn sounded urgently. The Unicorn stamped his hooves and the girl – Perci, I presume – struggled to hold him back.

'That's for us,' said Perci. Her vowels were flat and she made *us* sound like *uz*. She was as local as you can get. She also sounded nervous and excited.

'My Lord Prince,' I said, grasping at straws. 'The grooms of Sprint Stable are in revolt. Surely it would dishonour your Queen if she wasn't given the reception she deserves.' It was a load of old tosh, but it was all I had. Rule Three of dealing with the Fae is always to offer them a way out with dignity, no matter how scant the fig leaf.

He gave me a grin. A human grin. No extra teeth. 'And would you be so good as to see what Galleny is up to, Lord Dragonslayer?'

'A pleasure,' I replied.

He turned round. 'Come on you two, let's go and deal with these revolting grooms.'

'But Hipponax needs blood training,' said Perci. Aidan had moved aside and I got a better look at her. Where the hell had I seen her before? There was something in that jawline…

'He does,' said the Prince curtly. 'But the Queen doesn't want the blood to be his blood.' He sheathed his sword and took the reins. 'Walk on.'

He turned and left, in the certain knowledge that the others would follow. Aidan turned his own mount to block off the path to the defile. 'This is no place for us, lass. Nor for Hipponax.'

I left them to it, galloping towards the defile and wondering if the real ambush was in there. After all, they didn't call this place the Gauntlet for nothing.

The journey was perfectly normal until they got near Sprint Stables. Normal, that is, if you ignored Eldridge shouting into his phone about *Queens* and *Princes* and not giving a fuck who was going to be there when they arrived. At one point, Barney was sure that the assessor had said that his driver wasn't *Entangled*. Driving up one of Lakeland's many dead ends made Barney feel pretty tangled up in something.

The madness started when Eldridge told him to pull in at a passing place and said, 'Do you really fancy that Enscriber?'

Barney went redder than the dye on the sheep's fleeces in the next field. It was the first thing he'd seen, because he'd rather look anywhere than at Eldridge. What the hell was he doing asking that question, and why now?

'Do you mean Erin, sir?'

Eldridge barked out a laugh. 'I'll take that as a yes. Well, today is your lucky day, constable. I'm going to give you a unique insight into her world. You can thank me later. Now, lower the window, open the tailgate, and when we drive off, go slowly. No more than ten miles an hour, Barney.'

Eldridge was out of the car before Barney could open his mouth to complain. He pushed the button for the window and heard Eldridge shout, 'Tailgate,' from behind him. He scanned the buttons and pushed one for that, too. He heard the assessor rummage in the back, then felt the X-Trail shift slightly. He looked in the mirror and saw that Eldridge had stood on the lip and was holding on to the raised tailgate like ... like one of those blokes on a stagecoach. 'Let's go!'

'They're all mental,' muttered Barney, putting the car in gear and moving off.

Barney had never driven up Longsleddale before. Some of these dales gave off a creepy vibe that made the hairs on your neck stand up, and this was one of them. Probably to do with the atmospherics. And then the sparks started.

The road ahead, and especially the dry stone wall to the left started giving off sparks, like someone had attached jump leads to them and plugged the landscape into the national grid. He slowed right down and was about to stop when Eldridge shouted, 'Keep going and get ready to turn left.'

The sparks cascaded, the wall shimmered, and then it burst into flames ahead of them. 'Put your foot down and drive through the fire. Clarke's life's at stake! Go!'

'Not my car,' said Barney and did what the madman said. He did close the window first, and when liquid fire lapped over the car he nearly yanked the steering wheel off the dashboard. Only sheer fright kept his foot on the accelerator.

'Stop!'

Barney slammed on the brakes and came to an emergency stop with the front bumper against an old barn. Where the hell had that come from? He leapt out of the car and went to grab the fire extinguisher – if there was one. Because Eldridge must be on fire. Liquid fire.

'Well done, Barney. That took guts.'

Not a hair singed. Nothing. The bloke looked totally unharmed. Unhinged, perhaps, but unharmed. And what was that? It looked like a magic staff...

'This way.'

Eldridge jogged round the corner of the barn and into a stable yard. On the way, they passed a small car park, complete with minibus, top of the range Mercedes 4x4 and a Rolls Royce Phantom. It was only when he got past the gleaming vehicle that his police brain twigged what was wrong. Instead of number plate, the Rolls had a coat of arms. WTF?

Eldridge was making a beeline for a girl on a horse, and Barney followed. Only it wasn't a girl on a horse, it was a unicorn. At that moment, something in Barney's brain bent out of shape, and a pounding headache brought flashing lights to his eyes. Was he having a stroke? He sank to his knees and clutched his face.

Cold hands touched his neck and wrapped themselves round his hot fingers. 'Hey, it's OK. It's all right,' said a girl's voice. 'Just give it a second. The pain will go.'

He was afraid to move. Afraid to find that he couldn't stand or walk or speak properly. The pain had gone, though. Carefully, he lowered his hands and blinked. It was still a unicorn, and that horn looked bloody sharp.

And the girl still had her hand on the back of his neck. He glanced down at a pair of immaculate black boots, barely dusty. 'Welcome to the world of magick,' she said. 'That's magick with a "k". Let me give you a hand. You've had a worse reaction than normal.'

She leaned back and showed a lot of strength for someone that tiny and young. Barney got pulled to his feet and shook his arms and legs. Still working.

A grim-faced Eldridge was still holding his magic ... magick staff. And now Barney knew why there were assessors and Unions and what the hell Conrad Clarke was up to.

'I'm so sorry,' said Eldridge. 'You can blame Inspector Gibson for that. I should have thought about it.'

'Inspector Gibson gave me a stroke?' said Barney. Was Eldridge still talking in English?

'Excuse me.' Eldridge leaned in to Barney and reached unerringly into his coat, like a pickpocket. He extracted Barney's warrant card and waved it at him. Something about the Westmorland crest looked different. 'You've been carrying around a Forgetting Charm. It was triggered when you came across something your mind couldn't process. Bloody amateurs.'

He had to ask. He had to know… 'Is Erin…?'

'Yes, now are you coming with me to see what's happened, or do you want to wait here for Cordelia? It could be very, very dangerous up there.'

Barney looked around the yard. There was something moving in the shadows within one of the roundhouses. Something with wings and way too many teeth. And it looked hungry. 'We take an oath to run towards danger, sir.'

'Good man. I'll fill you in on the way.'

And with that, Eldridge turned and strode off, eating up the ground like a mountain goat. Barney had to run to catch up, and the first thing Barney said made Eldridge stop so suddenly that Barney tripped over. He still wasn't quite right.

What he'd said was this: 'There's that raven again.'

Eldridge scanned the trees that lined the gorge ahead. 'What do you mean, *again*?'

'There was one by Harry. On the branch when I got there. I thought at first it was going to, you know, mutilate him. But it scared off the real carrion birds.'

Eldridge saw something and scowled. 'I wish you'd put that in your report, Barney. Things might have turned out very differently. You're wrong about the raven, or that raven in particular. It's the biggest carrion bird of them all, and it answers to someone who loves nothing more than a pile of corpses.'

'Sir?'

Eldridge made a sweeping movement with his staff, and the raven rose from the bare branches, cawing defiance and climbing into the sky. The assessor started his fast walk again, and his next comment was spoken to the wind. 'And the raven eats from Conrad Clarke's hand.'

## 25 — In for the Kill

The gap in the cliffs was barely wide enough for one horse, and I made Scout stay behind us. For the first thirty metres, I was a total sitting duck for anyone on the rocks above. Or for the rocks themselves if they fancied it. I wouldn't put it past a Fae gorge to have a mind of its own and suddenly decide to become an avalanche of death.

My neck ached from turning to look up, left, right and behind. Nothing. No Sprites lurking over the ridge. No sudden forks to put me into a maze. Perhaps it was my lucky day. The horn sounded again, more urgently, and the defile widened to form a wide, dry river bed. I dug my heels in, and Agrippa responded. I reckon that when we rode out of the gorge, we'd done two of the six furlongs. One third of the way there.

The dry gorge ended with a lip, and only Agrippa's experience helped him keep his footing as he scrabbled to stay upright down a bank of loose stones on to a scrubby plain covered with large rocks and stunted trees, the whole thing bounded by cliffs. To make life really interesting, the sounds of the horn echoed around and bounced off the boulders, making it impossible to get a direction. Impossible for me, anyway.

I reached into my jacket and took out Saïa's bra (lots of scent there). I dropped it and let Scout get a good sniff. 'Find her, boy. Find Saïa!'

Sniff. 'Arff.'

He is not a bloodhound, but he knows a good smell when there's one in the air. He started scouting around, darting between the boulders and stopping to check. And then his ears pricked up and he listened to something I couldn't hear, and when Agrippa's head turned in the same direction, I knew we were on to something.

Scout shot off, and I urged Agrippa to follow. In a few seconds, I heard it myself: the howling of wolves. Faster, got to go faster.

*Shooom.*

An arrow flew through my personal space, barely bending to miss Agrippa's neck, and a stabbing pain gripped me behind the eyes. My Ancile had worked, but only just. Many more arrows like that and my head would explode. I steered Agrippa round a bungalow sized rock and rode straight into a trap.

Someone was lying through their teeth. It seems that Sprites *do* hunt. Four of them, mounted on their little unicorns followed us into a dead end, and behind them was the archer, mounted on a sleek black mare. I wheeled Agrippa round and faced the enemy. I dropped the reins and took out the Hammer.

The Sprites and the archer stopped about twenty metres away. He towered above them, and like Prince Harprigg, he was in the forest form of green jacket, ponytail and pointed ears. He held an arrow notched in his bow but wasn't aiming at me yet. 'This has to stop,' I said.

'We've barely started,' he replied. 'All the fun is yet to come, but I've been ordered to hold you in here.' He bared the extra teeth. 'You can try to escape if you want. I'd like that.'

I touched my Badge, and felt a tiny breeze stir in the gully. The smell of fresh flowers floated for a second on the air and dispersed. 'In Nimue's name, stop the slaughter.' There was no point invoking the Watch to the Fae – he was enjoying himself far too much already. I lifted the Hammer and took the two handed grip. The archer didn't seem bothered.

'This is our realm,' he observed. 'Dwarven magick won't work here.'

I lowered the Hammer for a second. 'I think you're bluffing. Let's find out.' Inge had given me a whip, and I'd hung it off the saddle rather than carry it. I slipped my left wrist through the loop and let it dangle.

I didn't think he was bluffing. I was, though. I was bluffing myself that I could try a Work of magick I'd never succeeded at before. Glamours.

I've seen through enough of them to understand the basic principle: visual intent + Lux = illusion. I started to raise the Hammer and stopped half way, trying desperately to keep going an illusion that I was pointing the gun at his face. I braced myself ready to shoot and dropped the Glamour. I had less than a quarter of a second to aim and fire at his horse's leg, something I never thought I'd do. It gave me no pleasure at all to see the beast rear and collapse, trapping the archer underneath it. I dug my heels into Agrippa and used the whip to reinforce the message.

The Sprites weren't armed; they didn't need to be when they were riding a horse with a sharp horn. The unicorns panicked at the gunshot and the scream from the horse. One unicorn threw its rider and another gouged at one of the Sprites, catching it in on the wings.

Scout knew what to do. Agrippa charged forwards and Scout went for the front fetlock of the one beast who could get in our way. I had to ignore him and keep going, hoping he was as good at jumping back as he was at jumping up.

Agrippa galloped out of the gully and I swung him left, towards where Scout had heard something before. In a few strides I had to choose between an open area and an arch. I closed my eyes and put everything I could into my ears, trying to enhance them with Lux. Nothing. The underlying biology is just knackered. I pulled up Agrippa and opened my eyes as a cloud of black and white dust shot past and through the arch. It looks like Scout had escaped, and it didn't take him long to find the trouble.

Saïa hadn't escaped. The Queen's Hounds had found her and Galleny had bound her hands and tied a rope round her neck before tying the rope to a ring set into a stone. Whoever had been lying about the Sprites had certainly told the truth about stripping her half naked, and around her terrified form, the battle raged.

Magickal conflict tends to be short. Usually, one side will have overwhelming firepower, and the other side either surrenders or is dispatched in short order. Not today. A quick glance round the arena told me that the Fae were all present and correct this time: Galleny, his Gamekeeper and two other Fae on horseback were joined by a human Mage and four of the Queen's Hounds. The human was their Madreb, and she was keeping well out of the way. The wolves had surrounded the rock where Saïa was tied, and that was where the Ripleys were heading, with numbers on their side.

There were six Ripleys altogether, and they'd come prepared. Four of them had reached back in time and taught themselves to use a round shield and long spear, and they'd taught themselves well. They were facing a highly mobile mounted enemy, and they needed to protect the other two members of the Family.

Two of the warriors were female, and one of the men was clearly the leader, a giant in black who was shouting orders as they wheeled round and tried to edge towards the rock. Behind them was another woman, older and armed with a staff, and there was something familiar about her in a much more immediate way than I'd felt with Perci. I dragged my eyes away from her and focused on the sixth human in their party. Standing well back for now was a second Madreb, and the Ripleys had come with their own pack of Mannwolves.

Six of them surrounded their Mage, but it was the others who gave me a bad feeling. The Ripley's Madreb had four cubs next to her, and they were on leashes gripped in her left hand. Mannwolves never submit to the leash. Ever.

There was a huge amount of noise going on, and that's the only reason no one spotted us at first. I looked back at the Ripley Mage with the staff and remembered who she was. On the way to finding Welshfire the Dragon, our path had led to the door of a Mage called Stella Newborn, and I'm guessing that she was Saïa's mother, because Kian had said that she'd gone away and come back. To say that Stella Newborn and I parted on bad terms would be an understatement, and there was certainly no love lost between the Fae and the King's Watch. Right now, I was going to keep a watching brief. If both sides ganged up on me, I'd be dead as soon as they caught me.

The Fae were circling the Ripleys, trying to get at Stella or their Madreb, and being forced back at spearpoint. Every time the Ripleys tried to advance, the Madreb of the Queen's Hounds would do something tricky with the landscape, and that's when I clocked her as the most powerful Mage here.

The arena was huge, dusty and covered with boulders. Boulders that moved and swapped places. In size, I reckon that this was the last two of the six furlongs. My observations can't have taken more than ten seconds, and in that time the rock to which Saïa was tied had moved twice. It didn't trundle, it just relocated about thirty metres away, and the Queen's Hounds relocated with it. And that wasn't the only bit of the arena that had joined in on the side of the Fae.

I watched the Ripleys advance towards an open piece of ground, shifting right to avoid a charge from one of the Whippers-in. At the last moment, Stella screamed for them to halt, just as the ground opened up in front of them. When they moved again, they didn't head for the target rock, they moved crabwise while Stella performed some Work to stabilise the arena.

It was in a moment's lull after she'd finished that the Queen's Hounds smelt something new. Us.

One of the she-wolves howled a warning and faced in our direction. In seconds, the whole field of battle had clocked us, and suddenly their priorities had changed.

'Get him!' shouted Galleny. 'Both of you, take out the Witchfinder.'

It was my turn to give orders. 'Scout! Stay! Lie Down!' And then I drew my sword and urged Agrippa into motion, aiming for the Madreb of the Queen's Hounds. The closest Whipper-in paused while his partner came across the arena, then they both galloped to intercept me.

'NOW!' said the Senior Ripley, and his Madreb ordered their wolves to attack the Queen's Hounds, and while the Whippers-in were coming for me, the rest of the Ripley clan tried to charge.

I had one advantage, and I had to make it count. The Fae were coming from my right, at an angle to intercept me and keep me from the Queen's Madreb. I pulled Agrippa's reins even further right, and he changed his gait to increase the arc. I kept pulling and turning, and put a large rock right in my path. The two Knights tried to change direction, and one of their mounts shied away, barging into the other and making a right shambles. All I had to do was get the timing right. A little faster, use the whip...

...And Agrippa sailed over the rock to a perfect landing. Inge had said not to push him too hard, and I eased off the reins to let him slow down in his own time while I twisted round. I'd thought that the distraction would allow the Ripleys to make it as far as Saïa, but no, all it had done was allow the Fae to spring their trap.

The Ripleys' wolves had loped around to the left, and as soon as they'd passed a line, the Queen's Madreb made one huge effort to raise a ring around the target rock, now fixed in its final position and trapping *all* the wolves inside. Galleny and the Gamekeeper knew what was coming, and they'd galloped ahead so that the ring rose underneath them, leaving them on the flat top. It was a bit like being on top of an earth rampart. Both dismounted and did something to calm their horses.

I started to turn in a slow circle, keeping the new fixture between me and the Whippers-in. The Ripleys now faced a terrible obstacle. If they tried to charge up the slope, they'd be horribly vulnerable to Galleny and his sidekick: Fae blades are long and have the sharpest edge. The Ripleys had clearly practised their shield and spear work against horses, but together? Up a slope? Not yet.

Howls and barks were coming from inside the ring, and to complete the show, the centre rose to make a flat top, and we could all see what was happening. As the ground levelled out, I felt a wave of Lux ripple through the arena and caught a movement to my right. The effort of rearranging the landscape had taken its toll on the Fae's Madreb, and she sank to floor in a faint.

On top of the mound, the six Ripley wolves were in trouble. They were fully grown, yes, but the Queen's Hounds had been working together all their lives, and they had the Gamekeeper's help. It didn't take long for two of them to cut off one of their opponents and rip his throat out.

The Ripley wolves backed away, and I didn't blame them. At that point, their Madreb screamed at them to attack, and to reinforce the message, she cut the leash on one of the cubs, kicking it into the arena. The poor little creature looked bewildered. He or she had probably just watched its father die on the rock, and the overload was too much. With its tail between its legs, it just ran, out of the arena and into the badlands of the Gauntlet.

The Ripley wolves howled in protest until their Madreb showed her knife to another leash, at which point they attacked, and the humans joined in, running up the slope while Stella tried to raise a dust storm to put Prince Galleny off his stroke. In the chaos, I urged Agrippa back to life.

There was a quarter of the arena's circumference between me and the Ripley Madreb, and now I'd committed myself, the Whippers-in had a target to aim at. We all converged on the woman with three wolf cubs, and it was a question of who would get there first.

'To me, to me!' I shouted at her, getting her to run in my direction. Having seen me being attacked by the Fae, she thought that her enemy's enemy was her friend. And that was her second big mistake of the day.

One of the Ripley men had reversed and was heading for the two Fae with his spear, drawing them on to himself at huge risk, and that left me a clear run at their Madreb. She thought I was going to ride past, and I did, but only after I'd switched my blade to my left hand and given it an extra charge of Lux. I leaned right out of the saddle and swung at the leashes holding the cubs.

I cut the leashes and took a chunk out of her hand, too. At the same time, one of the Whippers-in sent the spearman flying and the other slashed deep into his back. The battle was see-sawing in the Prince's direction, and I had to act quickly. I pulled up next to the fallen spearman and leaned down, exposing my chest.

'Give me your spear and I'll save Saïa,' I said. 'I give you my word, as Odin is my witness.'

He hesitated, then turned his spear to offer me the haft. I grabbed it and urged Agrippa to take on the mound. Sweat was bubbling along his flanks, and he didn't have much left in the tank. 'One more go,' I urged. 'Up, up.'

The other Ripleys had fallen back from the mound, having failed to support their wolves, who were now down to four, with another dead at the hand of the Gamekeeper. A spear is not a lance, but it would do. If Agrippa made it up the mound without stumbling, and if the Prince held his ground, I'd skewer him. He stepped aside, ready to fall on any weakness, and Agrippa's front hooves hit the incline.

He slipped and pitched, and nearly collapsed, but the last ounce of power in those back legs pushed him up and he made it. He hadn't even come to a stop, and I was off his left side, away from the Prince. I dropped the spear, put my sword back in my right hand and chucked my dagger at Saïa's feet. Agrippa could smell the blood of wolves across the mound, and he wasted no time clearing off now that he didn't have a mad human on his back, and that left me to face the Fae.

The Whippers-in had dismounted, too, and now the four Fae were closing in on me. As expected, the Prince sent the two junior Knights to soften me up while he and his sidekick tried to get at Saïa. The two Knights were both in hunting garb and were showing their teeth.

'Smell it,' I said. 'Smell the cold-forged iron.'

It was enough to slow them down; I even saw their nostrils contract. It was enough for Saïa to get herself free. She jabbed at the one on my right, who instinctively turned to defend himself and exposed his side. I thrust, I drew back and I parried the second Knight while the first one collapsed screaming on to the mound. Saïa dropped the spear and ran towards her Family.

'Neatly done,' said the Prince. 'Reckon you can take three of us?'

'On my own, no, but I'd watch your back if I were you, Prince.'

The Ripleys were advancing again, and this time the Fae couldn't afford to turn round or I'd be on them, so they ran round the mound, and the Prince summoned his hounds. 'Get the Witchfinder,' he said to them.

'Enough!'

Her voice rang around the arena. A voice centuries old and accustomed to unswerving, total obedience. For the first time in my life, I was in the presence of Fae royalty. The Queen of the Derwent, riding Keraunós, was on top of the rise that contained the archway I'd ridden through. She was at least two hundred metres away, but I could see every detail of her and her mount, projected by magick as if she was on the side of the mound. Now that's what I call making an impression.

She rode Keraunós the only way that a Unicorn can be ridden – with no saddle or bridle, and she was dressed all in white, from her soft leather shoes to the silk lining of the hood on her white cloak. Behind and to her sides was her retinue, all at the right level of detail for such a distance, and the only one who stood out was Hipponax, the other High Unicorn.

The Queen surveyed the field of battle and shook her head, more in sorrow than anger. The three surviving Fae had all bowed respectfully and stood still, their weapons lowered; the Ripleys took advantage of the respite to tend to their wounded and give Saïa a jacket to cover her nakedness. I put my sword away and picked up the discarded spear. It's less insulting. I also whistled for Scout, and he bounded over to join me. The poor little mite was shaking with fear, and I gave him a big hug for being such a good boy and waiting.

Keraunós made the tricky descent look easy when the Queen urged him down the slope and across the arena to make the fourth corner of a diamond with the Ripleys, the Fae and myself as the other three. On the other side of the rock to me, the Queen's Hounds had gone to comfort and protect their Madreb, and the Mannwolves who'd come with the Ripleys had formed a group around their cubs. The rest of the Queen's entourage from the top of the arch took the long way round.

The Queen looked slowly around the arena, noting the two dead wolves and Whipper-in. When her eyes stopped moving, they settled on mine, and believe me, the ice-cold glare of those blue orbs was a lot more terrifying than the tip of Prince Galleny's sword.

Now that she was even closer, I could see just how fine was the silk of her dress and hosiery, and how the unrelieved white was broken up by threads of gold and gold jewellery at her neck and wrists.

'Well met, Lord Dragonslayer,' she said, with a voice like running water. Suddenly my mouth was as dry as the arena's dust, despite the relief at hearing her say *well met*. It was as good as a promise not to hurt me.

I forced myself to swallow sand and bowed as low as my joints would allow me. 'Well met, your grace.'

She looked at the two opposing sides and returned her gaze to me. 'There's no point in asking them what happened. You tell me, Lord Dragonslayer.'

What? Why on earth was she asking *me* about it? Clearly she didn't trust Prince Galleny to give a straight answer. With the Fae, it pays to keep it short and sweet. They have a notoriously low boredom threshold when it comes to mortals.

'Your prince kidnapped Saïa Ripley. He stripped her and tied her to the rock as bait. When her family arrived, he attacked them. I was doing my best to break it up.'

She nodded thoughtfully and pushed her fine white hair behind a shapely ear. Human shaped. 'I hear you have an interest in this matter.'

I inclined my head again. 'Yes, with both parties.'

'Then I shall save you the trouble of dealing with the People of Borrowdale.' She looked behind her, and I nearly heaved up my breakfast. When she turned, her whole upper body rotated like an owl's head. Beyond gross.

Her retinue had appeared and were keeping a respectful distance. One of them had arrived separately, and she waved him over. Prince Harprigg dismounted and walked up to stand at his queen's side. 'How is the huntsman and his mount?' she asked him.

'Only the huntsman's dignity is wounded, your grace, and his mount can be saved.' That would be the archer and the horse I shot. Harprigg looked at Scout with annoyance. 'One of the little mounts has a bite to the fetlock, but it will heal.'

'Way to go, lad,' I murmured.

The Queen nodded and returned her attention to me. 'The huntsman was supposed to keep you away from things, Lord Dragonslayer. That's why Harprigg blanked the minds of our grooms and why he didn't argue when you suggested he leave.'

Well, that explained why Flora and Inge had got it wrong. A point to remember for the future.

She sighed. 'I had hoped this matter could be settled without troubling you and that we could all get on with our lives. Perhaps the gods wanted you here. That thought may save the huntsman's dignity.' She thought that insight was amusing for some reason. 'Tell me, Lord Dragonslayer, is it true that you took the amulet of Lara Dent as Plunder?'

A tiny whisper from my unconscious told me to keep the full truth to myself. 'The late Count of Force Ghyll destroyed it when he tore it off the wearer's neck. According to my expert on these things, it is extinct.' All of that was true, but what I hadn't said was the wearer's true name: Morwenna Mowbray. I didn't want that name sounded out in public.

She turned her attention to Prince Galleny and the Gamekeeper. 'You two. Lay down your arms and approach.' Galleny moved quickly to obey, but his Gamekeeper shot me a venomous look before she complied.

The Queen adjusted the lie of her skirts and pushed her hair back again. 'You have disappointed me and disobeyed me,' she said to her prince and consort. 'I consented to a confrontation with the mortals. I did not consent to a hunt. You have cost the life of one of the People.' When she said that, she

253

pointed to the Whipper-in that I'd killed. That's the Fae for you: their idea of responsibility and justice is somewhat malleable.

She sighed. 'You are to be punished by being stripped of your rank and made vassal to Prince Harprigg. You will become Count of Force Ghyll and confine yourself to training horses. The sídhe of Galleny is forfeit and will be disbursed to pay for your failure.'

Galleny's eyes never left the Unicorn's hooves while his Queen spoke. When she had finished, he bowed and said, 'My queen is merciful.'

'I know. I shall pronounce it.'

No one, human, Gnome or Dwarf, has ever understood the Fae language. The audible parts include words from human Proto-Celtic, but they also speak in frequencies beyond human and canine hearing, and there is definitely a magickal component somewhere. Listening to it was just as beautiful as hearing her speak in English, to which she reverted when she'd finished. 'And now bend the knee.'

Galleny – sorry, *The Count of Force Ghyll* – went to Harprigg and went down on one knee before taking out his sword and laying it at his lord's feet. The next thing shocked everyone, I think, except the Queen. Harprigg picked up the sword and used the flat of the blade to whack his vassal so hard on the face that I could hear the *crack* of bone from here. The Count sprawled in the dirt, and Harprigg tossed his sword on top of him. 'Stay down,' he said.

Was it an illusion, or had the Gamekeeper started to edge away? It didn't matter, because once her queen looked at her, she was rooted to the spot. The Queen's judgement was short and to the point. 'You are not worthy. I pronounce it so.'

'No!' screamed the Gamekeeper.

There is no execution in Fae justice, outside of trial by combat. The worst punishment they have is to be banished from every sídhe in the Queen's empire, and that was what the Queen had pronounced. It wasn't just humiliating: it would soon be fatal unless the Gamekeeper found sanctuary in another queen's lands, and no queen who wanted to be on good terms with the Queen of the Derwent would offer it.

Her grace spoke the words, and the Gamekeeper raged in fury, spitting on the ground and sporting a face that looked like a gargoyle.

'Get rid of her,' said Harprigg to the prostrate count. 'Kill her if you can.'

The former prince staggered to his feet and picked up his sword. He started to move towards his former vassal, but she was on her way, running away from the arch, away from the route home and out into the wilds of Westmorland. The count jogged after her, to make sure that she was really gone.

'I shall leave you to your business,' said the queen to me.

She rode off with her personal entourage in her wake. As she left, the Madreb and the Queen's Hounds approached Prince Harprigg. 'Gather the horses,' he ordered, shooing away the other Whipper-in.

The Madreb didn't bow to Harprigg, but she did lower the hood of her robe and smile a lover's smile. He took her hands and kissed them, and whispered something in her ear. She was older than I'd expected, and had great poise. She ignored the Ripleys, but she looked at me, giving me the full appraisal before inclining her head. 'I shan't forget what you did,' she said, flicking her head towards the distant wolves and their cubs.

I bowed back. 'Ma'am.'

The Fae Knight gave her a horse, and she hitched up her robes to mount, which she did with grace before leaving with her escort of wolves. I'd never seen her before, and I didn't know her name; I'm not sure whether the fact that she was black and had a West Indian accent was the most interesting thing about her or the least.

The other Fae were ready and followed her out, with Harprigg giving me a curt nod on the way. That had gone a lot better than I feared it might, to be honest. And now it was time for the Ripleys.

## 26 — Healing Properties

All of the Ripleys are Mages, of course, and I'm not really any good at telling how good a Mage is unless we lock horns, but I presume that the Senior holds that position because he can walk the walk. The fact that he was six foot two and broad across the shoulders probably helped with his image as well. Now that I could see them properly, there was a clear family resemblance between all seven of them.

As I walked over to where they were gathered, I hefted the spear. I'd noticed that it was very light when I picked it up. This was a very modern spear, with the shaft made of aluminium tubing and the head of steel. Gnomish work, I think, judging by the runes chased into the cutting edges. I briefly extended my Sight, and my guess was proved right: part of the head was cold-forged and backed up by runes to negate Quicksilver magick. No wonder the Fae had been reluctant to close in on their enemy. The Ripleys must have been planning for a violent encounter with the People of Borrowdale for some time.

I stopped about five metres from the Family and tried to activate a subsidiary work in the spear – a little something to help you plant the base in the ground. Even in the rocky arena, it worked, and I left it there. The Ripleys had spread out in a line with the Senior in the centre, Stella to his right and Saïa to his left. The guy whose back had been slashed was at one end, lying on his side, and their Madreb at the other end, sitting on her haunches and cradling her hand with her back to me. Saïa made the first move before I'd finished planting the spear.

She still had my dagger, and she carried it carefully by the blade. She laid it by the spear, away to my right, and said, 'Thank you, Lord Guardian. I owe you a personal debt.'

'Are you okay?' I asked. 'Apart from the obvious.'

She gave a brief smile. 'Yes, thank you.'

'Then your thanks are enough. I did what I did as Deputy Constable of the King's Watch, here at the request of the Particular.'

She looked confused, and backed off. I moved a little, to be closer to the Senior, and he looked suddenly very unhappy. 'What are you saying?' he asked.

'A great wrong was done to your family today, Mr Ripley. A great wrong was also done to the Eldridges and the Zinchenkos. I'm afraid your Union and three others requested that the Watch take over the investigation, and I'm giving you notice that…'

'Arff! Arff!'

I whirled round as she struck, and Scout's warning meant that the Madreb stabbed me in the side, not the back. She added Lux to the blow, and I collapsed from the shock more than the pain.

She released the Silence she'd used to sneak round my back and let me have it verbally. 'How does that feel, eh?' She showed me all that remained of her left hand, now wrapped in a blood-soaked cloth. 'You should have finished the job, Witchfinder, because I'm going to.'

I was on the floor, clutching my side with my left hand. I don't think I could stand if I wanted to. I scrabbled over my shoulder and tried to draw my sword but the angle was wrong and I dropped it.

'Sura, no!' said Saïa.

When she tried to come to my aid, Stella grabbed her arm to stop her.

'I think the leg this time,' said the Sura.

My bad leg wasn't responding very well. I left it and tried for my gun.

And then the Madreb discovered that she wasn't the only one who could make a Silence.

The first wolf leapt from behind and knocked her down. The second one grabbed her right wrist and bit deep. The third one took an ankle in her jaws. The fourth one went for the throat. She howled long and high when she'd finished.

'Help him,' said Saïa, and that was the last thing I remember until I was licked awake by a large wolf and a very worried dog. Of the Ripleys, there was no sign.

The King of the Ripley wolves had died on the mound, and it was the pack Queen who was using magick above and beyond her dual nature on my wound. Scout is just a dog, so he was licking my face, and I don't know who was following the other's lead.

'What a shit place to die,' I told the wolves. I talk to Scout all the time, but these are not wolves, they're Mannwolves, and they understand English perfectly. The terrible burning pain had subsided a little thanks to the pack Queen's ministrations. I haven't mentioned the pain before, because I was trying to ignore it. Sadly, I couldn't ignore the flow of blood, and her magick had done nothing for that yet. I fumbled a handkerchief out of my pocket and pressed it to the wound.

The Queen padded round me, blood fringing her muzzle where she hadn't licked it off. With great delicacy, she picked up the hilt of my sword in her jaws and dragged it to be near my right hand. And then they all lay down in submission.

I somehow found the strength to take the sword. 'Do you want my protection?'

A variety of wolfish sounds signalled their assent. They speak in wolf form, but the vocabulary is pretty limited. I've forced myself to learn the basics now I have my own pack.

'Good. But you have to start at the bottom. Alex and Cara are King and Queen of the Elvenham pack. Understood?' More agreement. 'Then my arm is your shield, and Great Fang is your blade. You have my protection.'

They stood up, and I dropped the sword. The Queen nudged another female closer to my hand and tried to chew at the collar embedded in her sister's neck. Something magick made the Queen yelp and jump back. She used her muzzle to point at the collar, then looked at me. Oh. Right.

I grabbed the collar and let go with a spasm that made me groan and see stars in the vanishing daylight. 'Sorry. Maybe later. Other priorities right now. Here are your orders. One must go and look for your cub. The rest have to go through the arch. Find your way through the Gauntlet to the woods, and then the stables. Someone will be coming for me, and I need you to show them the way. And if they don't get here in time, Eseld Mowbray will be your new Protector. I name her so. Understood? Then what are you waiting for?'

It would have been nice if I'd had a nice rock to lean against rather than the stony ground. There were rocks aplenty in the arena if I had the strength to move. I didn't. I barely had the strength to move my hip off a sharp stone and find a position lying on my right side with my left hand clamped to the wound.

I had to force myself to stay awake. I even tried singing a verse of Jerusalem, but my throat was too dry. There was an outside chance that my phone would get a signal in here – it was still bonded to Vicky's phone in some way, but what could she do? Besides, it was in a really awkward place. What kept me going was Scout.

He'd danced around the wolves and half followed them out of the arena. Like a human, he'd rather be doing something than nothing, and I didn't have the strength to call him back. He soon returned, and stood guard over me in true Border Collie fashion. That is, he stood guard for ten seconds, then he sat down. He moved around. He lay down. He licked my face. He ran back and forth. He peed on a rock. He came back and stood guard again.

And then he heard something, he barked and he was off. He came straight back with a howl, because he's a quick learner. Any man whose face I've smashed in is not a friend, and I was about to find out if Kian Pike was an enemy.

He took his time walking across the arena, frowning at the dead wolves and stopping well short when he saw the gaping wounds on Sura's body. 'What happened here?'

'Payback for the way she treated the Ripley Pack.'

The confusion on his face was genuine. 'What pack?'

'A pack of Dual Natured wolves.'

He saw my knife next to Sura's hand. He saw my wound, and he put two and two together. 'So the mad bitch managed to do some good before she died. Good riddance.'

He came closer, and Scout bared his fangs with a growl. He stared at my wound and the size of the red patch in the dirt. Satisfied, he nodded his head. 'I'm sure you've got the cavalry on the way. Let's just make sure they don't get here in time, shall we?'

He retreated quickly and took out a small stick. I'd taken out my gun earlier. More for comfort than anything. I picked it up, but I couldn't get an aim on him without rolling over, and I didn't have the energy for that.

'We'll just shift this zone a bit further,' he said. The word *bit* came out as *bid* because of his broken nose. Did I regret smashing his face in? Not a bid. If I hadn't, he would have betrayed me on the battlefield by siding with the Ripleys and the gods only know what bloodbath would have ensued.

He focused on his stick and bent down to start drawing a wide circle in the dust. As he passed in front of me, the other side of the arena became blurred behind a wall of magick. I thought about trying to shoot him when the angle was right, but I couldn't hold the gun straight enough with one hand.

Half way round, he paused to wipe his hands. 'Where will you go?' I asked.

'What? I thought you'd fainted. I'll slip out of the back entrance, and if anyone asks I'll say that I must have missed you.'

He'd completed three quarters of the circle when Scout barked, looking at the rough path where the Ripleys had entered. Kian ignored Scout, but he didn't ignore the howl from one of my wolves who stood on the ridge.

'Is that one of Sura's or one of the Queen's?' he said.

'One of mine, actually. If you leave me here, they'll follow you, and if they don't kill you, Mina will.'

'Right. Of course she will. I'll take my chances, thanks.'

'No you won't.' We all turned to see who'd spoken. It was Matthew Eldridge. 'Kian Pike, you are under arrest. Now pack it in and lie down. Barney, put these on him.'

Behind Eldridge was an utterly bamboozled Barney Smith, who was trying to stay as far as possible from the pack's Queen, now in human form. And naked, of course. And looking about sixteen.

Sometimes my eyesight is a curse. If it wasn't so good, I wouldn't have been able to see her scars. All across her young body were welts and marks of damaged tissue. In lines. And that meant they were deliberate. Around her neck was a raw wound where the collar had been.

Eldridge threw the collar on to Sura's body and passed some old fashioned handcuffs to Barney. Kian Pike legged it.

He didn't get far. The three wolves and Matthew saw to that, with a nervous Barney following to finish the job.

The Queen came over to me and squatted to my side. She gently removed my rigid arm from the handkerchief and pressed it herself. I felt more magick as she smiled at me. 'Thank you, Lord Protector.'

'What's your name?'

259

She glanced at Sura's body. 'The Twisted One named me Number Three. May I choose my own name now?'

'You may.'

'I shall take your mother's name. What is it?'

'Mary.'

'Thank you.'

Matthew came back and hooked his thumbs in his belt. 'Right. How the fuck are we going to get you back to the stables without you dying on us?'

'You're not. You're going to take me through the exit here. It comes out on the top of the fell. The air ambulance will have no problem landing there. It'll be even quicker if Barney's got his Airwave radio.'

'Don't worry,' said Mary. 'I'll hold you.'

And that was without doubt the most comforting thing I've heard since my real mother uttered the same words when I fell off a pony aged five.

Tom Morton flicked the switches, and the LEDs flooded the incident room with daylight. He glanced around and found it unchanged since Thursday evening. Apart from the detritus of Barney's time at the computer, that is. By god, he was a messy eater. Crumbs everywhere and an overflowing bin, full of plastic sandwich cartons and God only knows what else. Tom peered suspiciously into the collection of mugs and grunted. At least they were clean.

He went round turning on the heating and stood next to a hot air blower while he waited for the piercing chill of a November evening to thaw. It was bloody cold outside and no warmer in here. He was still standing there, deep in thought, when Matthew Eldridge knocked on the door and stuck his head round.

'Hello, Tom. Can I come in?'

'Of course. I was hoping you'd drop by. Take a pew.' It was warm enough to move away from the heater now, and Tom risked taking off his overcoat.

'Any updates from Preston?' asked Matthew.

Tom checked his phone, even though it hadn't pinged while he was standing there. Nothing. 'No news, so that's good news. It's a wait now to see if he gets an infection.' He smiled. 'You could get a paper out of it.'

'Sorry?'

'My sister's a GP and her husband's a trauma surgeon. Every time he gets a nasty case on his table, he says, "There's a paper in this." You could write a paper on the antibiotic properties of werewolf saliva. So much gunge had leaked from Conrad's punctured kidney that he'll be lucky if he's not on a drip for weeks.'

'Poor sod. That'll cramp his style.'

'You didn't see him when he had pins sticking out of his leg. He's come back from worse. I think it's warm enough to risk venturing to the break room. I'll put the kettle on.'

He was coming back with the kettle when the outside door flew open and a wild looking Cordelia Kennedy burst in. 'Is that Matthew Eldridge's car outside?' she said. 'Is he here?'

Strange. Cordy was Conrad's partner, and her first question was about Eldridge, whom she'd never met. Perhaps she'd been on the phone to Mina before she got here.

'In the incident room.'

She saw the kettle in Tom's hand and closed her eyes. He watched her shoulders visibly relax as she calmed herself down. 'Thanks, Tom. I'd better use the loo now I'm here.'

They weren't expecting anyone else tonight. Mina was at Conrad's bedside, Elaine was coming up in the morning and Lucy was down in Preston, ready to return with Barney and Mary after Barney had finished dealing with the bureaucracy of emergencies. Lucy also had some clothes to replace the Air Ambulance jumpsuit that Mary was currently sporting. Apparently. Tom tried to keep that image out of his head.

While he made the tea, Cordy talked magick stuff to Matthew, and seemed to be focusing on the properties of this Gauntlet place. Again, was that top priority? Perhaps she was waiting for Tom to lead the discussion.

Tea in place, that's exactly what he did.

'Thanks for coming, Matthew. Are the pack okay?'

'They are now. Safely installed in my house, with my apprentice looking after them. And they need a lot of looking after. Especially their unofficial mascot.'

'Who's that?'

'Scout. We couldn't put him in the air ambulance, could we?'

Tom's mind was boggling at the thought of seven wolves and a border collie running round Matthew's bachelor longhouse.

Cordelia had been watching Matthew intently. 'Had they been tampered with?'

Another strange question. Tom was getting used to being excluded from the technical discussions of magick. It was a bit like nuclear engineering in that sense: you didn't need to know about it to arrest the spies. What he had caught on to was the tone, and Cordelia's questions sometimes seemed to have another agenda entirely.

'They've been horribly abused,' said Matthew grimly. 'Sura handled them so badly that she was forced to keep them all in collars and stopped them shifting to human form for days at a time.' He shuddered. 'Most of them have scurvy from lack of vitamin C. It's the one vitamin that doesn't pass between the two forms. It'll be a long road for them.'

Tom's fingers had gone white from clenching them. He forced them to relax and changed the subject. 'I'm leaving everything that's happened today for the King's Watch to sort, Cordelia. As for Kian Pike, he's yours as far as I'm concerned, Matthew. My focus is still on your brother.'

'Good,' said Matthew. 'Is that why you sent me those questions for the pack?'

'Yes. Believe it or not, Barney found most of the evidence this morning, and now that Tracey's run the extra report, I've got confirmation.'

'Who's Tracey?' said Matthew and Cordelia in unison.

'The best Crime Scene Manager north of the English Channel. According to her own estimation. She got Harry's trousers processed for trace evidence, and we'll be able to match any DNA with Sura Ripley in due course. That's not what I'm concerned about. She also found non-human DNA. Specifically, she found wolf DNA when she re-ran the tests, so the pack was there when Harry was captured.'

'That makes sense,' said Matthew. 'Right. Here we go. According to Mary ... I'm sorry, I can't get used to that name.'

'How do you think Conrad feels? How do you think his mother will feel when she finds out? Go on.'

Matthew shook his head. 'According to Mary, five of them were bought as cubs. They'd only just been weaned, and they have no idea where they grew up. They could barely speak English. The late King was brought in recently as an adult, and he came from a pack in Ulster, but has no idea how he ended up here. One day he was running over the Mourne Mountains, the next he was dumped in a forest near a lake and told to teach the others how to hunt properly and use their magick. Two of the cubs are his. Were his. He died.'

Tom grunted. 'Did you show them pictures of Ullswater?'

Matthew slurped his tea. 'Did you know that Ullswater means Wolf Water? Funny that. Yes, they've been living in a compound on the eastern shore, guarding a big hole in the ground. When they smelled Harry, they cornered him and waited for the Twisted One to arrive. Quite a good name for Sura, that. Anyway, she lived in a cottage separated from the pack accommodation by a barrier. They have no idea what happened to Harry after Sura dragged him into the cottage.'

'They never saw him again?'

'No. They didn't help Sura move him to Ulverston or hang him in the tree.'

'Thank you. We'll go there tomorrow. The four of us. Erin Slater will come too, because she's the only other Mage on hand who I trust. Is that okay?'

'Fine by me.'

'Good. The other thing I need is all the names, addresses, aliases and any contact information you have for the Ripley family. Including Sura.'

'You can start with this,' said Matthew, sliding a mobile phone across the table. 'Conrad insisted we take her phone, thumbprint and a DNA sample before we left her to be absorbed by the Gauntlet.'

Tom took the phone and slipped it into an evidence bag. 'We'll make a copper out of Conrad Clarke yet. What time shall we say?'

The door opened, and the two Mages swivelled into defensive postures. Tom tried not to panic when Philippa Grayling and another middle-aged woman came in.

'You don't need to go to Ullswater,' said the unknown visitor. She focused on Tom. 'I'm Stella Ripley, and I've come to make a statement about my daughter, Sura.'

'The Twisted One,' said Matthew.

'As you say,' said Stella. 'I had no idea what she'd truly become until this afternoon.' She tried to square her shoulders, but they were carrying a heavy load. 'The Family will pay Weregild to the Queen of the Derwent.'

'What on earth for?' said Tom.

'Isn't that where the Mannwolves have gone?'

'Oh no,' said Matthew. 'They're in the Elvenham Pack now. You can pay the Deputy Constable.'

Stella barked a laugh. 'The gods are rubbing our noses in it today. Before you say anything, Mr Morton, I will also make a statement acknowledging my involvement in … in what we did to your brother, Matthew. Sura killed him, and for that I am so sorry. When I found out what she'd done, I ordered my nephew to help me try to cover it up.'

Matthew stared at Stella. His lip twitched as if he wanted to say something, and he blinked hard. Whatever it was, he swallowed hard and bottled it up. The words that actually came out were forced through gritted teeth. 'That is a matter for the King's Watch.'

Tom breathed out. He had not been looking forward to getting Matthew out of the room before Stella made her statement, but Matthew wasn't finished.

'I shall be on my way when I've discovered what the Chief Assessor is doing here. I hope she's come to tell me that she's handed in her notice.'

Philippa Grayling flinched back as if she'd been slapped. 'I'm sorry that it has come to this, Matthew. That one of the great Families of the Particular should have fallen so far and that your brother had to pay the price.'

The fury that Matthew had been holding in check when he spoke to Stella was unleashed on his boss. He lifted his finger and pointed to her face. 'You. You have blood on your hands, too. You appointed Kian to assess his own family. If someone else had been assessor for the Eden Valley, they might have caught the Twisted One before she killed Harry. If you had called in the Watch when the gods offered it to you on a plate, two grooms would still be alive. If you hadn't turned a blind eye yesterday, two cubs would still have a father, Clarke wouldn't be fighting for his life and Sura would be facing justice.'

Philippa Grayling took it all on the chin, staring at a point over Matthew's shoulder. When he'd finished, she looked him in the eye. 'I'm so sorry for what happened to Harry. That he should have been reduced to a disposable toy is the true tragedy.'

It was Tom's turn to feel utter fury. Blaming the victim was the lowest form of police action. 'Is there a complaints procedure, Matthew?'

'Yes. It has to come from the Union chairs.'

'Then I suggest you go and talk to yours. And the other three who called in the Watch.'

'A good idea.'

'But first, why did you leave Conrad to bleed to death?'

It was the question that had been burning through Tom since he'd first heard the headlines of what had happened, and he wanted Matthew there to hear Stella's answer. Or non-answer.

'We tried,' she said. 'Saïa was most insistent. We simply couldn't get close to him for the wolves. We told them to go and get help, and we assumed they'd summon the Fae. After watching the Queen of the Derwent make her dispositions, we assumed she wouldn't leave him to die.'

'Matthew? What did the pack say?'

'Mmm,' said Eldridge. 'That was the one question I couldn't get a straight answer on. I think they'd gone a bit feral after killing Sura and didn't come down until Conrad woke up. It can happen.'

Tom had been scrawling a quick note while this went on. He tore off the paper and passed it to Matthew.

*Send me those names and numbers. Rendezvous at Pooley Bridge 1400 tomorrow.*

Matthew read it and nodded.

'Thank you for your help today, Matthew,' said Tom. 'It's a shame it came to this.'

The two women stood aside as Matthew made his way outside. During the confrontation, Cordelia had made herself as still as possible, and the first person to acknowledge her had been Matthew when he said goodbye. Now that he was gone, she sat up straight again and adjusted her braid, moving it from one shoulder to another.

The women took a step further into the room, but Tom didn't offer them a seat. Still furious, he said, 'What *are* you doing here, Ms Grayling?'

'Acting as a friend to Stella. When dealing with Witchfinders, it's better safe than sorry.'

Tom leaned back on his chair and folded his arms. 'I'm only an assistant here. Technically this is a Watch enquiry. Tell me, Officer Kennedy, what would the Deputy Constable say?'

Cordelia kept a straight face. 'I think he would tell Ms Grayling to fuck off and that suspects have no right to legal representation under the Orders of the Council. I'd be more polite.'

Tom slammed the legs of his chair down and thumped his arms on to the desk. 'I'm with the Deputy Constable on this one, Ms Grayling.'

Philippa Grayling pretended not to have heard. 'I said this was a mistake, Stella. Let's go. You can submit your statement to me and I'll pass it on through channels.'

Cordelia stood up and reached her hand into her rollneck sweater. She took out a beautiful piece of enamelled fretwork jewellery on a gold chain. She held it for a second, and Tom recognised the piece as being a raven. The workmanship was exquisite and conveyed the bird in sweeping lines and glittering feathers. The fretwork made it light, but it was still large. Cordy laid it on her chest and revealed that the raven's eye was the badge-thingy that Conrad had on his gun: the mark of Caledfwlch.

'Shall I?' said Cordelia.

'No,' said Stella hurriedly. 'I'm here of my own choice.' She turned and put her hand on the Chief Assessor's shoulder. 'Thank you, Philippa. It was enough that you came here with me. I can face the music on my own.'

'That's not the point,' said Philippa.

'Yes it is. This is a test I must face alone.' She tried to chivvy the Chief Assessor with a smile. 'What's the alternative, eh?'

The alternative was presumably to kill Cordelia. Probably Tom, too. Unlike Conrad, Tom did not draw any comfort from the thought that he would be avenged.

Stella Ripley patted her companion on the shoulder and came into the room. She chose a place opposite Tom and pointed to a chair. 'May I?'

'Please,' said Tom. 'I won't be long.' He grabbed the kettle and walked towards the door, deliberately putting Philippa Grayling in his path. 'If you'll excuse us, ma'am.'

Philippa's shoulders visibly slumped and her head tipped forwards. Without another word, she turned on her heel and walked out of the incident room.

Out in the corridor, Tom watched her leave the building, and then leaned his head on the cold wall until his breathing had returned to normal.

265

## 27 — Unfinished Business

Now that half term was over, the little village of Pooley Bridge looked as if it were going into hibernation, and there was plenty of room in the central car park. There was only a couple of hours of daylight left, if that, and there was definitely rain on the way.

'It was a struggle to get her to wear anything,' said a bemused Matthew Eldridge. He was standing back from his car, surveying the sartorial choices of Princess Mary Elvenham. Well, she wasn't really a Queen any longer, was she?

'Where did you get a Snow White costume from, Matt? It is Snow White, isn't it?'

'She wanted Elsa, but the charity shop only had Snow White. She said that if she had to wear clothes, she was going to wear princess clothes. You wouldn't think she had a small child, would you? Poor kid. Poor kids.'

Mary was playing a game with Scout while they waited for the others, and she was *Mary Elvenham* now. She'd insisted on having two names because she could, and Matthew had put his foot down, saying that the original Mary Clarke might be unhappy with an impostor, so Mary Elvenham it was. The border collie had bonded with Mary, and had howled the place down when she tried to leave him behind to come here.

'There they are,' said Tom.

Erin parked her Mini rather badly and got out with a big smile on her face; Cordy looked a lot more uncomfortable, probably because Mina had handed over her Army combat uniform, and it really didn't suit her. Erin locked the doors and came over. She looked from Mary's costume to Cordy's uniform to Matthew's Day-Glo jacket and snorted with laughter.

'Looks like you and I didn't get the fancy dress memo, Tom.'

He ignored her, for Cordy's sake, and said, 'Did the move go alright?'

'Yeah, thanks. Part One anyway. Sprint House is gorgeous, you know. I almost feel like a princess living there. Maybe I should ask Snow White for some fashion advice.'

'Ha ha.'

Erin lowered her voice. 'What's her real name?'

'Mary.'

'Noooo! That's gonna be so awkward. We'd better go, hadn't we? Point of order, Chief Inspector, I am going in the front or not at all.'

Tom held up his hands. 'If Matt can cope with you in the front, then fine.'

Scout came running down the street and gave Erin an enthusiastic greeting. 'Get off my leg, you oversexed brute,' she said, holding out her hand. 'You must be Mary.'

When the Mannwolf came closer, the grin on Erin's face turned to shock, then anger. Mary didn't shake hands. She took Erin's fingers and kissed them with a curtsy. Tom wondered if she even knew what shaking hands was. The whole princess thing was apparently because Stella had given them an old TV and DVD player a couple of years ago. There was no TV reception in their compound, so all they'd watched was a random assortment of children's films that the Twisted One had picked up, possibly from the same charity shop that had supplied Mary's outfit. At least Matt had persuaded her to wear thermal base layers, and his apprentice had given the girl an old pair of running shoes.

Erin took Mary's hand and pulled her in for a hug. The Mannwolf flinched and nearly struck out until she felt the love. Had anyone – any human – ever given her a hug in her entire life? Tom shook his head and got the file from his car.

They were travelling in Matt's vehicle because it was big enough to fit them all (including Scout), and because the road down the eastern side of Ullswater rapidly turns very narrow, then very steep, and finally into a dirt track which leads to the Occulted property where Sura had kept the pack and where Harry had been murdered. Stella Ripley was waiting for them at the gate.

Tom had wanted to bring Tracey Kenyon down and tear Sura's cottage apart looking for forensics, until Matthew told him that there was actually a book called *CSI for Mages – how to Leave No Trace*. With this much warning, the Ripleys would have the site of Harry's death cleaner than an operating theatre.

When they got out of the car, Erin grabbed his arm. 'Do you really need me for the other stuff? I'd rather help Mary.'

'Of course.'

Mary had come to recover the few possessions her pack had been allowed by the Twisted One. It wouldn't be easy. Tom had checked to see if Mary had any personal grudge against Stella before agreeing to the visit, and apparently the pack knew Sura's mother as the Nice One.

Stella had already dismantled the Wards and barriers around the pack's former home, and half of the party went through. With stiff reluctance, Stella led the rest of them through the woods, up a hill and to an unfenced site of ecological vandalism.

She had a set of keys and offered them to Tom. 'I shall leave you to it, Mr Morton. If you take anything from the cottage, I'm sure you'll let me know. You know where to find me when you've finished with the keys.'

Tom hoped he never had to see the woman again, and indulged himself a little. 'Perhaps Watch Officer Kennedy can hand them over at your trial.'

Stella zipped up her coat and walked off without replying. Late last night, Hannah Rothman had said she'd press her other deputy to charge Stella and Stella's nephew with something that would have a custodial sentence. Good.

He turned to the wasteland in front of them, complete with abandoned mini-digger.

A flattish section of the hill had been torn up completely, trees, bushes, peat and all. Rain had already washed a lot of it away, exposing bare, dead rock that Mother Nature had spent thousands of years trying to cover with life. All gone.

'The Lattice Ward is still here,' said Matthew. 'I didn't think Harry had it in him to get through.'

'Why?' said Tom. 'What is all this for? Even the Gnomes are careful when they dig these days.'

'This wasn't a mine,' said Cordelia. 'It was an excavation. They were digging up something that was buried. I can feel the bend in the Echo here. Until the Ripleys wrecked it, this was a place of great hidden power.'

'Any clues as to what they found?'

'Stripped bare,' said Matthew. 'It was valuable enough for the Ripleys to pour huge amounts of magick into hiding their work, and valuable enough for Prince Galleny to send Harry to steal it.'

They stood there for a while. 'I don't like loose ends,' said Tom eventually. 'I don't like them, but I can live with them. The crime here was Harry's murder, and this place tells us nothing. Unlike the phone and data records.'

'Oh?'

Tom opened the folder and passed copies to Cordy and Matt. 'Sura made several calls to her mother and the Family Senior after the time that Harry was captured, as Stella said in her statement.'

Stella's statement had gone on to say that they told Sura to question Harry, not to torture him.

'There is no evidence that any of them moved away from the Eden Valley until Sura called to say that Harry was dead. And that is that as far as I'm concerned. I spoke to Conrad before we came out, and he agrees.'

He turned and started walking down the hill. He could barely see the lake in the gloom, and it was starting to spit with rain.

'How is he?' asked Matthew.

'Stable. They're hoping to move him out of critical care today. According to Mina.'

Matthew didn't do social interaction very easily. 'Give him my best wishes, Tom, if you're in touch. Or you Cordelia. I hope I can meet him and his fiancée under better circumstances.'

'Thanks. We'll let him know.'

'What about the Fae formerly known as Prince Galleny?' asked Cordelia as they walked.

'His relationship with Harry was entirely legal, if very exploitative. I think Conrad has unfinished business with him, but you'll have to talk to him about that.'

'Lara Dent,' said Matthew bluntly. 'Or should that be the Mowbray formerly known as Lara Dent?'

'It's beyond me, that,' said Tom. 'I have trouble accepting the existence of Spirits at all, never mind that they can be captured in horseshoe charms. Strictly your department, Cordy. You can sort it out with Matt and Conrad. When he's recovered.'

Erin, Mary and Scout were waiting for them by the car with several bags of stuff. Mary was clutching a DVD of Frozen as if it were the most valuable thing in the world, which it might well be. To her.

'I've had an idea,' said Erin. 'A mad one but a good one.'

'Let's get out of the rain and you can tell me,' said Tom.

'There is a big problem here, Mr Clarke,' said the consultant.

This is not what you want to hear when you're in hospital. The only straw I clung to was that a smile was twitching round his lips. I said nothing and waited.

He flicked through my notes again and nodded. 'The problem is that you could be discharged right now and make a full recovery. Or you could be discharged and develop a serious infection or worse. It is difficult to know.' He paused, weighing up the demand for beds against the chance of relapse. I kept my fingers crossed. 'I think we should keep you in until Friday and monitor you.'

For once, I was grateful. The thought of being out in the countryside at Clerkswell or Middlebarrow Haven with daily trips to outpatients was too much to bear. 'Thank you, doctor.'

He dictated a series of tests to be ordered and drugs to be administered and then moved off with a nod. I risked rolling back and looked at my watch. Only five hours until visiting. Mina had been allowed to stay with me while I was in critical care through yesterday, but they'd moved me to a renal ward at five o'clock last night and she'd been persuaded to go home.

When they wheeled me into the six-bed renal ward, the senior nurse had given me that gallows smile that seasoned medical staff develop as part of their coping mechanism. 'Welcome, Mr Clarke,' she'd said. 'Thanks to you, the average number of kidneys per patient on this ward has gone up from zero to one-third. Make sure you look after both of yours.'

'Or what?' I'd asked. 'Will someone try to steal them?'

'Only if you try to go outside for a cigarette. If you do, I'll remove both of them myself.'

'Noted. I'll be a good boy.'

And I had been. I went to sleep straight after being fed.

I reached for my phone to text Mina the news from the consultant. Judge Marcia had been very understanding yesterday, but according to Mina, she'd been rather pointed in saying that they were hoping to re-start the hearings on Wednesday. Now that I was going to be stuck in Preston, Mina could go to London tonight.

She messaged back, *Out shopping. Will go home then come back for visiting.* When she said *home*, it wasn't her home, it was the home of the surgeon who'd operated on me on Sunday. Mina had declared it fate that a distant cousin of Mr Joshi would be on duty, so that Ganesh could look after me, and it was this surgeon's daughter who had bought makeup for Mina while she was in prison. It's a long story.

I tried to get comfortable and wondered what time a cup of tea would appear and whether Mina's shopping would include any books for me to read over the next few days. Being on a renal ward, water was in short supply, and I was strictly rationed. I was contemplating going to sleep when two illegal visitors appeared. Well, not strictly illegal, and they hadn't had to breach security to get in because they were already in the hospital. Not that security would have been a problem for Eseld.

She wheeled her sister through the ward and stopped the wheelchair by my bed. Morwenna had been holding the drip stand to which she was attached, and Eseld moved it to a safer place. Satisfied, she came over and put her finger on my lips. 'I promised Mina that I'd leave you alone, so I will. Morwenna made no such promise. Text me when you're done.'

She leaned down and kissed my bald patch. Oh, cruel woman.

Mina had said that it was Eseld who offered to stay away. 'She thinks that I am jealous of her, but she is wrong. I am not jealous of Rachael or Sofía, so why should I be jealous of her?'

And me? I think that Mina was right, but for the wrong reasons. Eseld is not like a sister to me, she's like an ex who you've stayed on good terms with for the sake of the kids. Only we'd never been an item and we didn't have kids. Relationships are complicated, aren't they?

I waved to Eseld's back and took a good look at Morwenna for the first time since I'd seen her disappear into A&E at the helipad. Poor kid.

Her hair was still long and lustrously red, but it was tied back so severely you couldn't see it, and the reason for that was that her face looked like she was auditioning for the Mummy Returns. Only her eyes and her lower right cheek were visible, and more bandages covered her whole throat, forcing her to hold her head right up. To complete the torture, she was on two drips:

hydration and antibiotics. She'd nearly developed full-blown sepsis on Saturday.

Her blue eyes bored into me, trying to get over a message. I held out my hand. She grabbed it fiercely, and the jolt of Lux between us nearly pulled our hands apart. She slumped a little, then sat back up when the pain of bending her head kicked in. When she let go of my hand, she looked a little better.

I hadn't felt the intimate connection we'd had at Sprint Stables, but some of her raw emotion had come across. And something else. 'I'm thrilled for you, Morwenna. I'm so glad the twins are safe.'

She patted my hand. No sparks. Then she reached down between her thin hips and the side of her wheelchair. She pulled out an iPad and an iPhone. She passed the iPad to me and pointed to the home button. I pressed it and saw a note-sharing app was open and already had a message in it.

*You talk, I type.*

*Can't be here long. Nurse will find me sooner or later. Not supposed to leave isolation but had to see you.*

*Can never thank you enough. Ever. Just let me be your bitch.* ☺ *Ha ha. I hear you've got enough of those already. I know you want to ask me loads. You can, but not yet. Please. I'm not going to run away again. Home for good now. If they let me out.*

*Please.*

*And will you be godfather?????????????*

'Yes, I'll leave you in peace, Morwenna,' I said. 'I'm not in a position to do anything about it.'

*How are you?*

I told her the latest, and she gave me a double thumbs-up.

I reached for her hand again. 'I'll be second godfather, if you want, Morwenna, but you have to offer pole position to Matt Eldridge. I know you'll never forget Harry, and tell them all about him, but they should have their Uncle Matt, too.'

*Fair enough. Will you be my godfather then? Hang on. Read this.*

She tapped another area of her screen and another pre-prepared message appeared.

*Don't go gunning for Queen of the Derwent. She didn't make me a Vessel and she didn't murder Lara Dent. It's complicated. I'll tell you soon.*

I was about to say something when a nurse and porter appeared. 'What the hell are you doing here, Morwenna? If this happens again, we'll have no option but to turf you out of the infection control room, no matter how much money your family is paying.' She looked at me. 'And who are you?'

'Her Uncle Conrad. She was worried about me.' I looked into Morwenna's eyes. 'Do as you're told. I'll see you when you're better, and not before. Here.'

I passed back the iPad, and she left.

Lunch was awful – low in sodium and low in hydration. Not what I needed. You should always be careful what you wish for, and I was discovering that an extra four days in hospital wasn't going to be a rest cure. At least Mina was on time.

There was something different about her today, and it wasn't just the new red kurti. She came round to my right and gave me a long kiss. Aah. That was it. She looked more relaxed. I told her so.

'Seeing the man you love in hospital is not a relaxing experience, Conrad, and this is the second time since the summer. I hope that the Allfather reveals his true purpose for you soon or I will have to think about trading you in for a younger, more boring model.'

'Any candidates?'

'Bhatta-ji's son is a possibility,' she said with far too much seriousness. Mr Bhatta is the surgeon.

'Oh really?'

'But I think he is *too* young. He would be easy to seduce, but I doubt he'd marry second hand goods like me.'

She used to do it all the time – the barbed self-laceration comes from all sorts of guilt. I think. I try not to respond directly. 'Perhaps that's a good idea,' I suggested. 'Until I'm well enough, he could be my substitute fielder.'

I love Mina's hands and her delicate fingers. She used one of them to jab towards my wound, saying, 'For that, I just might.'

And then she saw the look on my face when I automatically flinched away. Boy did that hurt.

She put her hand to her mouth. 'I'm so sorry, Conrad. Have you pulled the stitches?'

'Aagh. Shit. I don't think so.' I reached to grab her hand. 'Don't cry, love. You'll ruin your makeup. Tell me what it was really like last night. Did you have a good time?'

She kissed my fingers. 'Yes, I did. It made me so happy and so sad at the same time. Happy to be in a house where the dominant colour is not aged oak, for one thing. Happy to be in a house where two wedding ceremonies is the *minimum*, and why not have one in London, too? Happy to be in a house where everyone talks at once and they take the mickey out of your Gujarati accent. And sad that I wasn't given the choice to accept or reject that life.'

I said nothing, and we held hands for a while.

'I know the truth, you know,' she whispered. 'I know that after papa-ji died, my only choice was to be my mother's carer or to be married off to a widower with children. I could have chosen that, but I didn't. I chose Miles. And I chose you.'

She left it a while longer before sighing and letting go of my hand. 'I have been in negotiations this morning. One of them was with Erin. She said she had to see you today, and I can see why.'

I frowned. 'What's up?'

'She can tell you herself. She's waiting outside, as is my lift to the station. I'm taking an early train and I'm having dinner with Hannah tonight at some restaurant in Golders Green. Do you think this Kurti goes with the boots or not? Why am I even asking you? Give me a kiss.'

I did. 'What's up with the Boss?'

'I don't know whether she wants to talk politics or weddings. Both probably. Now, about those negotiations. There was another one.'

She stood up and I drank in the sight of her to keep me going until the weekend. She picked up my phone and shoved it in her bag. WTF?

She'd come in with a carrier bag that she'd dumped under the bed. She reached down and took it out. 'I bought you an iPhone, Conrad. You can sort out the privacy issues and live with it. I am fed up of not being able to Facetime you or send you pictures, or receive pictures. It's time you joined the twenty-first century.'

'My contacts!'

'I am in there, and so are your parents. You don't need anyone else until the weekend. If you're good, I might send the new number to your sisters. Now I must go.'

We kissed goodbye, and I ran my fingers up her spine, feeling the vertebrae slide under my fingers.

'Mmm. Stop it, Conrad. I have to catch the train.'

I still had a silly grin on my face when my next visitors came in. The grin stayed, but my eyes bulged when I saw who was with Erin. I wasn't the only one – all the other patients and a good dozen relatives stopped talking, too. Well, it's not every day you get a visit from Elsa, is it?

'Don't touch the hair. It's a Glamour,' said Erin, pointing to Elsa's hair. I mean Mary's.

Mary looked both happy and terrified. She dropped an elegant curtsy then held out her hand like royalty for me to shake. 'Lord Protector, I'm so glad to see you better. When can you get out of here?' At least she had the gumption to whisper. It was going to be hard enough to explain this to my ward-mates and the nurses without having to explain why a teenage girl called me *Lord Protector*.

'How are you, Mary? How is the pack.'

She nodded her head enthusiastically, and the long white braid nodded with her. Good job. 'Happy for the first time in our lives. And Scout sends his love, I'm sure.'

Erin had already sat down and made herself comfortable. She moved Mary out of the way and told her to sit on the bed. 'I brought grapes but they took them off me. You'll get them rationed, apparently. Anyway, how are you?'

She really wanted to know. There was clearly a lot she needed to tell me, but that's Erin for you. Until she was satisfied that I had the mental and physical capacity to cope, she kept it in. When she'd digested my prognosis, she looked at Mary, who had completely ignored what I'd been saying because it meant nothing to her. With a shrug, Erin raised a Silence that excluded Mary.

'As you can see, Mary has issues,' said Erin. 'I'm hoping she'll understand now. She nearly changed form in the car on the way down. The reality of urban life is sadly short of her expectations, and her sense of smell can't cope with a hospital. She's blocking it. Sura was truly evil, Conrad.'

'Was she?'

'You don't know the half of it. She…'

I held up my hand. 'How good a Mage was she?'

'Not very. Barely at all. She…'

'She couldn't cope, Erin, and she took it out on the pack because that was the way her family had treated her. It doesn't excuse what she did, and I'd have ripped her throat out myself if I had the jaws for it. Did Mary say that Sura enjoyed it?'

Erin sighed. 'No. From what I can tell, she hated herself for what she did. We still have to deal with the consequences, though.'

'We do. Thanks for taking an interest, Erin. I'm grateful.'

'Yeah, well. How could I say no? Look, Conrad, I'll cut to the chase. I want to be their Madreb, only I don't like being called *Auntie*. Can I be their Guardian?' I was already frowning, and it was her turn to hold up her hand. 'Let me finish. The Ripleys owe a huge debt to you for the way that Sura treated the pack. I think you should take their land by Ullswater and move the whole pack there. And change the name to the Birkfell Pack. There. I've said it.'

I sat back as best I could. I spend a lot of time lying on my right side to keep the pressure off my dressings. It was a brilliant idea and a mad one at the same time. The patience of the Northumbrian Shield Wall (who were sheltering the rest of the pack) wouldn't last forever. It would give me a foothold in the Particular. I had many problems with the idea, not least that Erin would flake out sooner or later. The biggest problem, however…

'Won't they hate it?' I asked. 'Going back there?'

Erin cancelled the Silence and tapped Mary's knee. 'Oy, Princess.'

'Yes my lady?'

Mary had been shamelessly eavesdropping on the rest of the ward. I could tell.

'Tell your Protector how you feel about Birk Fell.'

Mary moved her arms, like she had a predisposition to shrug but couldn't find the right muscles. 'It's our home. It has woods and lots of deer. And the lake. Now that the Twisted One is gone, it's perfect.'

'See?' said Erin. 'I'm not just a pretty face.'

'You're not pretty,' said Mary matter of factly. 'More sexy than pretty.'

'Shhhh!'

'You're not wrong,' said the man in the next bed to Mary. 'That's a bonny costume you've got there, love.'

Erin fixed Roger with a glare, and Roger's wife started talking loudly about their son's barbecue. When Roger had looked away, Erin put her head close to mine and whispered, 'Well?'

'It's a brilliant idea. But only if the King and Queen agree. Take the new pack to Northumberland tomorrow. Or get Matthew to take them. Alex and Cara are in charge, Erin, and you haven't even met them. From then on, the pack stays together, and if the *whole* pack likes the look of Birk Fell, then go for it. But before you bring the pack back to have a look at Birk Fell, I want you to contact Prince Harprigg's Madreb. I think she'll say yes, but we're not planting a big flag in the Particular if the Fae object. It would be suicidal.'

She sat back with a smile on her face. 'And that's why you're Lord Protector. You see the big picture. I wonder if I'll see it when I get to your advanced age. Talking of age, where are you going to be for your birthday? It's in a fortnight, isn't it?'

'A week on Sunday, yes. So long as I'm not in hospital, I don't really care.'

She tilted her head to one side. 'You're looking tired. We'll go. I don't want Mina on my case.'

'What about Barney?'

'What about him? We're going on a date tonight. Not that it's any of your business.'

'Of course it's my business. I have full control of the love life of my pack's Guardian. It's in the rules.'

'You wish.'

'However, in this case I approve.'

'So do I,' added Mary. 'Barney is a big man.'

I was enjoying this. Mary had even less filter than Erin, though she did have the sense to lean down and whisper the next bit.

'How far is it to Tenerife? It sounds very exotic. Like the desert lands.'

'You could say that,' said Erin. 'What are you on about?'

'Over there. The sick man thinks Tenerife is too far and too hot. He wants to go to Benidorm. Is Benidorm like Kendal?'

'We're off,' said Erin, rising to her feet. 'I'll explain in the car.'

'Can't we walk back to Blackburn Cottage? It doesn't seem far.'

'I'll explain that, too. Bye, Conrad.'

'One last thing. Write your number down on my pad.'

'My number?'

'Your phone number. Long story.'

'Whatever.'

Mission accomplished, Erin kissed my cheek and Mary shook hands again. This time, she kissed my fingers, too. Sort of. What she actually did was lick them.

Erin was right. There was a long way to go. They need her, and I think she needs them. In the gap between their departure and the arrival of the afternoon doctor, I meditated on the nature of evil. I've come across a fair bit of it in my time. I've done some things that other people might consider evil, too.

Erin was right that beating the pack and putting them in restrictive collars was evil. Can't argue with that. But Sura? I know I chopped her hand off, but when she came at me with the knife, she looked more beaten and whipped than Mary did when she changed to human form. I could see Sura starting to torture Harry Eldridge for information. I could definitely see that. I could see her threatening him with the Blood Eagle.

But could I see her carrying it out? I'm not sure I could. Tom Morton was satisfied beyond reasonable doubt that none of the Ripleys were at Birk Fell. If so, could I see someone else with Sura when she got out the bolt cutters? Yes, I could. I'm not going to forget that, but I hope you'll understand if I say that it won't be my top priority for the foreseeable future.

When the afternoon doctor had pronounced himself happy with my progress, I got to grips with my new phone. It already had a screensaver – a picture of Mina in a red sari, taken by Miss Bhatta. A very good picture, too. That would do nicely.

I sent Mina a message, in which I told her I loved her, updated her on Erin's suggestion and finished with this observation:

*Ankle boots don't suit you. Go for long boots or flat shoes. Hannah may ask you back to her place and insist on walking.*

To which Mina replied:

*I cried all the way to the station. I cried on the train. I only stopped crying because the man next to me started talking loudly about finance for a new office building, and I realised that I am very lucky to have you. I would not swap you for Salman Khan if Ganesh himself offered it to me.*

To which there was only one possible reply:

*But not as lucky as I am to have you.*

# *Epilogue*

## Scene by the Lake
## Thursday 12 November

It was funny how Gnomes could make the most magickal thing seem so mundane. The industrious workers of Clan Skelwith had put red mesh fencing right around the dock at Waterhead Academy and even laid mats across the path to stop their low-loader churning up the school's precious lawns. Convenient, though.

Cordelia had a strong distaste for Gnomes. It was nothing like her visceral hatred of the Fae, but it tended to sour things somewhat. She had no idea how Conrad had managed to break bread with Princess Birkdale, let alone how he called Lloyd Flint a friend. Then again, she hadn't met either of them, so it was wrong of her to pre-judge them. Raven would never have done that. Raven would have welcomed them and pumped them for knowledge and laughed at all their jokes, because that's who she is.

Not was. Is.

For the hundredth time that day, for the millionth time since the accident, she reminded herself that Raven was waiting out there somewhere. Waiting for her. And to find her, Cordelia would take advantage of whatever help the Goddess offered. Tonight, that help came in the form of the Gnomes. Not that they knew anything about it.

The Gnomes needed two lifts – one on the lake to raise the *Thunderer* from its watery grave and another on dry land to get it on to a trailer. Whether the boat went to dry dock or to the scrapheap would depend on how damaged it was and how sentimental Matthew Eldridge was feeling. A job like that needed a lot of prep, and the safety fence around the site was working perfectly to keep the students at bay. The precautions and the foul weather meant that Cordelia had the place to herself.

One thing Conrad had already taught her was that the British Army combat uniform is not to be looked down on. He'd worn it to face down a Queen, her retinue, a powerful Family and two packs of Mannwolves. On his own. And then sent the blood-stained camouflage to be dry-cleaned and mended. If it was good enough for him…

Reluctantly, she uncovered her head and felt the full force of the rain. The one thing she couldn't wear to perform the Rite was a hat. She wiped her face and took off her backpack.

She carefully unwrapped the candlesticks and placed them down. The three Artefacts were one of the two things that linked her to her soulmate, and she carefully removed the package containing the other.

She put candles in the holders and made a triangle with sides of exactly five yards, then she placed the package in the centre and bent down. She opened the flap a fraction and kissed the shawl inside before re-sealing it. No need to get it wet: the magick would shine out clearly through plastic. She stepped back and began with the North candle.

She lit it with magick, and used more magick to deflect the rain, then repeated the manoeuvre with East and West. When they were all burning brightly, she stood at the South side and began the Rite.

'Mother Goddess, Lady Moon, hear my prayers and bring forth the Spirit of Raven.'

The rest was formula and action. She moved through it, using the Charms in the candles to amplify the signature of Raven's essence contained in the shawl. It was a risk, but one she had to take. If any of the students were working on the Spirit Plane tonight, they'd know something was up. Whether they'd come out in the rain to see was another matter.

When the signal was at its loudest, Cordelia dropped into meditation to keep it going. This wasn't the first time she'd tried, nor the tenth. It was the thirteenth. Raven was out there, and if she wasn't in Somerset, she could well be here, near to where she was born, because Cordelia was convinced that Raven had been born at one of the Fae Queen's sídhe here in Lakeland.

'Well met Cordelia,' said a rough man's voice. She opened her eyes slowly to make sure she had sight in both worlds.

The Spirit had taken the form of a man in old riding gear, and he was flanked by two spheres of light – other Spirits who were hiding their nature. Cordelia was not a novice at this. She studied the colours and flashes in the orbs and saw the twists of light that meant *human* and *woman*. Interesting.

'Well met, sir,' she said. 'Whom do I have the pleasure of addressing?'

The man was rough but handsome. Powerful in life, physically and magickally, judging by the size of his shoulders and the sharp lines he'd created in his manifestation. He gave an easy smile and bowed to her.

'Lucas of Innerdale. We've met before, when I was part of the Dragonslayer's Familiar. How is he?'

A shiver ran down her back that had nothing to do with the rain seeping down her collar. *Lucas of Innerdale.* Vicious bigot and murderer. And sometime border collie. Why was he here, and who was with him?

'He is doing well. Have you heard of his trouble?'

'You saw us when you first went to the other world, and we were there again to help him cross over. We saw him carried off with a wolf at his side. We wish we could have done more to help.'

Now that she'd got a feel for the Spirit orbs, Cordelia noticed that one of them had a tiny line of location running from it that stretched across the grass to the Academy. An anchor? She couldn't look too closely, so she turned her attention back to Lucas.

'You were there. You were there when Raven had her accident. Did you see where her Spirit went? Have you seen her since?'

He shook his head sadly. 'No lass, as the gods are my witness, I was thrown so far away by the trauma of separation that I saw nothing. I was nearly gone altogether. I have not seen or heard of Raven since then, but I will look out for her. And I think we have something in common.'

'I am not you, Lucas. I do not hate for the sake of it.'

'The Pale Horsemen were an excuse, lass. An excuse to target the demon of Derwent. You hate her as much as I do, I think. Tell me I'm wrong.'

She couldn't, because it was true. Spirits can lie just the same as anyone, but lies are easier to spot in the Spirit Realm. Lucas was telling the truth, and it lit him up with fire.

'How did you know?' she asked. 'How did you know I hate her?'

'I heard your prayers. I heard you pray for vengeance on the Fae who created Raven. I think we have a common cause.'

'Why? What is your grievance?'

'Not here, Cordelia. Not now. Not until the dust has settled. You'll be leaving soon, won't you?'

'Tomorrow. I'm taking Conrad to Middlebarrow to continue his convalescence.'

'But you'll be back?'

'He will. He may move his pack to Birk Fell soon.'

Lucas nodded. 'It fits. It will give him a foot in the Lakes. A beachhead, I think they call it in his world.'

She considered the Spirit's words. 'He doesn't know, does he? He has no idea you're following him?'

'We're not following him. We're waiting here. Waiting for the right moment. And no, he doesn't know about us. I'd rather he didn't. His aims are not my aims.' He paused, staring at Cordelia but not looking at her face. He appeared to be concentrating on her rucksack. 'What are you going to do with the amulet of Lara Dent?'

'Study it. It is extinct as vital force.'

'Are you sure? Tread carefully, young Witch.'

One of the orbs flashed red, and a refined voice trilled out of the air. 'He's coming.'

Lucas looked over his shoulder in panic. 'Until we meet again. You know how to call me. Go well, Cordelia.'

He collapsed into a sphere, and all three of them flitted away, across the lake. The silver thread became so fine that Cordelia couldn't see whether it was still there or whether it had been broken. From the woods to the west, another Spirit approached, and Cordelia was very afraid.

This one could have been male, female, both or neither. Human or divine. It flashed in rainbow colours, a constant swirl that hid its nature. It moved to the place where Lucas had appeared and paused, then it went to one of the candles.

Cordelia's nails dug into her fingers. What was it going to do?

With another swirl, the rainbow twisted the magick she'd created, then moved to the other candles. Cordelia held her breath. In seconds it was done. Done and gone, away to where it had come from. She checked the candles — her weather protection was dissolving. She calmed her breathing and rolled back the bigger Charm safely before blowing out the candles.

It had been the gentlest of warnings. The Spirit could have burst the triangle and damaged her. It didn't. It called time on her Charms and left her in peace. Whoever it was, Lucas and his women knew about it and feared it.

She rubbed her forehead and flicked water off. By the Goddess she was exhausted. She was also excited.

Conrad Clarke, Dragonslayer and Lord Guardian of the North, Deputy Constable and Protector of the Birkfell Pack would return here in his own sweet time, and Lucas would be waiting. All Cordelia had to do was make sure that she was by his side when he came.

She laughed into the rain. Staying next to Conrad might be the most difficult challenge she'd ever faced.

*Conrad will be back in his next full adventure - Five Leaf Clover.*

*And...*

*Vicky will be along before then to tell the story of the Fire Games.*

280

## *Fire Games— A King's Watch Story*

The Fifth King's Watch eBook novella will be available to pre-order from Paw Press on Amazon in Winter 2020/21.

*When you play with fire, watch you don't get burned...*

**Just because he's saved your life, it doesn't mean that Conrad isn't the most annoying uncle ever.**

**Instead of sending him a card, Vicky has to trek up to Clerkswell to wish him a happy birthday, sympathise about his latest near-death experience and be part of the test audience for his little sister's new side hustle.**

**Sofía is going to be combing magic and magick to put on a special entertainment, and Fire is the at the heart of this show. Before she knows what she's doing, Vicky has been talked into some very dangerous games indeed.**

**Discover how she gets dragged into the orbit of the magickal elite and find out if she gets burned on re-entry.**

**PAW PRESS**

## *Five Leaf Clover*
### The Ninth Book of the King's Watch
### by
### Mark Hayden

*When all roads lead across the water…*

**Conrad has a lot on his plate, and recovering from a punctured kidney is only the start.**

**As well as the Warden hustings, he needs to talk to Morwenna, he needs to see what Tom Morton has come up with and he needs to get his pack of W\*r\*w\*lv\*s settled into their new home. If the Fae Queen lets him…**

**And when he starts ticking off his to-do list, it's clear that he's going to have to cross the water.**

**To Ireland. Where he has no jurisdiction whatsoever.**

**This time the hardest decision is not who to take, but who to leave behind when he goes searching for answers to questions that stretch back hundreds of years. All the way to the Black Death.**

*Available Spring 2021 from Paw Press.*

And why not join Conrad's elite group of supporters:

*The Merlyn's Tower Irregulars*

Visit the Paw Press website and sign up for the Irregulars to receive news of new books, or visit the Facebook page for Mark Hayden Author and Like it.

# Author's Note

This book was started during lockdown in 2020, just before we were allowed to see the family again after months apart. Ha. That didn't last long.

The rest was written during the grey period which followed total lockdown and is still going on now that the book is being published. I was very lucky: no one I know got the virus. We had the beautiful Westmorland countryside to roam around (when not raining), and from the third week in February, I have had the Virtual Inkwell to look forward to - my weekly Skype drinking session with Chris Tyler, to whom this book is dedicated. We all find our own ways of getting through.

Shakespeare said that A good wine deserves a good bush. In other words, a good book deserves a good cover. I'll never be able to prove it, but I strongly believe that The King's Watch would not have been the same without the beautiful covers designed by the Awesome Rachel Lawston.

An addtional note of thanks is due to Ian Forsdyke MBE for casting his eye over the final draft. Any remaining typos/errors are all mine.

The King's Watch books are a radical departure from my previous five novels, all of which are crime or thrillers, though very much set in the same universe, including the Operation Jigsaw Trilogy. Conrad himself refers to it as being part of his history.

You might like to go back the Jigsaw trilogy and discover how he came to the Allfather's attention. As I was writing those books, I knew that one day Conrad would have special adventures of his own, and that's why the Phantom makes a couple of guest appearances.

Other than that, it only remains to be said that all the characters in this book are fictional, as are some of the places, but Merlyn's Tower, Sprint Stables and Blackburn Cottage are, of course, all real places, it's just that you can only see them if you have the Gift...

This book could it have been written without love, support, encouragement and sacrifices from my wife, Anne. It just goes to show how much she loves me that she let me write the first Conrad book even though she hates fantasy novels. She says she now likes them.

Thanks,
Mark Hayden.

Printed in Great Britain
by Amazon

61367669R00173